THE
PRINCESS
KNIGHT

THE
PRINCESS
KNIGHT

G.A. AIKEN

KENSINGTON BOOKS
www.kensingtonbooks.com

KENSINGTON BOOKS are published by

Kensington Publishing Corp.
119 West 40th Street
New York, NY 10018

All Kensington titles, imprints, and distributed lines are available at special quantity discounts for bulk purchases for sales promotion, premiums, fundraising, educational, or institutional use.

Special book excerpts or customized printings can also be created to fit specific needs. For details, write or phone the office of the Kensington Sales Manager: Kensington Publishing Corp., 119 West 40th Street, New York, NY 10018. Attn. Sales Department. Phone: 1-800-221-2647.

Kensington and the K logo Reg. U.S. Pat. & TM Off.

ISBN-13: 978-1-4967-2127-3 (ebook)
ISBN-10: 1-4967-2127-6 (ebook)

ISBN-13: 978-1-4967-2125-9
ISBN-10: 1-4967-2125-X

First Kensington Trade Paperback Printing: December 2020

10 9 8 7 6 5 4 3 2 1

Printed in the United States of America

PART 1

PROLOGUE

As soon as Brother Gemma led her platoon of monk-knights into the monastery courtyard of the Order of Righteous Valor, she knew she was in for some horseshit.

Not hard to figure out. When one was part of a brotherhood of vicious, violent, and war god–loving warriors, one learned to sense when the winds of change had shifted.

She stopped her horse in the middle of the courtyard and examined the area. Her squire, Samuel, stopped next to her.

"Everything all right?" he asked.

"No."

"Is there something I should be panicking about? I'm very good at panicking."

She already realized that, but at least the boy knew himself well.

"I don't think there's a reason to panic." At least not yet.

She dismounted from her horse and handed the reins to Samuel.

"Dagger did well, didn't he?" the boy asked, petting her horse's muzzle.

Gemma had been forced to replace her beloved mare just two months back. She still missed Kriegszorn, but Dagger had proven his worth in battle.

"Dagger has done very well. Your suggestion was a good one."

"Thank you, Brother."

The small, tentative smile on Samuel's face suddenly faded and Gemma knew that, yes, those winds of change had definitely shifted.

She turned and saw Master Sergeant Alesandro walking up to her.

"Brother Gemma."

"Brother Alesandro."

"Your presence has been requested in the Chamber of Valor."

"Why?"

It amused her to see Alesandro's left eye twitch simply because she insisted on asking "why." That's why she asked "why." Just to watch that left eye twitch.

"Because it's an order," he told her.

"But you said request. A request is not an order. An order is an order. A request is more of an option, so I ask why to find out if it's something I really want to do. And quite honestly it's—"

"*Brother Gemma!*"

Gemma blinked. Twice. "Yes, sir?"

He pointed at the monastery.

"So it *is* an order? Fair enough."

She faced Samuel. "Bed down Dagger for the night, would you, Samuel?"

"Of course, Brother."

She gave him a wink so he wouldn't worry—even though she knew he would anyway—and headed toward the monastery.

Alesandro followed right behind, which didn't concern her. He always acted as if she was about to make a wild run for it. He seemed to continually expect the worst from her. She wasn't quite sure why, other than he simply didn't like her. But that was his choice. She knew that not everyone was going to like her. She was fine with that. She was a war monk. She rode into battle and cut down her enemies without a thought. She and the platoon she led had just cut down an entire band of thieves that had been attacking undefended villages. She still had blood on her face and hands. With that going on in the world, why would she care if the master sergeant of her monastery liked her or not? She was more concerned about whether she'd managed to keep her knights alive.

She had. What else mattered?

They arrived at the Chamber of Valor, one of their most important rooms in the monastery, and Gemma walked in. She immediately assessed what she saw before her.

Grand elders were in attendance. Monks who worked directly with the grand master of their order on important decisions. Also waiting were her three battle-cohorts, Katla, Kir, and Shona. Bound together from day one, the four of them had trained together since they were novitiates, had experienced their first battles together, had risen through the ranks together, and to this day were as close as four people could be after washing pieces of their enemy's brains out of one another's hair.

Last of those awaiting Gemma's arrival were several generals, including the dreaded Lady Ragna. The monk-knights called her "Lady" Ragna because she was not a lady and they all hated her. Not exactly a joke that played well but few cared. Whenever the woman walked by, the area cleared like rats running from a burning forest. The only ones who didn't run were the monk-knights chosen for Ragna's army. She had her own legion, used only when called upon by the grand master and elders.

And then there was Brother Sprenger and a few of his minions. Sprenger hated Gemma, so she was surprised to see him here. Unless he had another complaint to lodge against her. Over the years, he'd had quite a few of those. So many she barely noticed them anymore. They came in scrolls and she had to listen while a general informed her of what she'd done wrong. When it was over, she'd put the scroll in a box. One day she planned to piss on that box, but not yet. She wanted something substantial to piss on. A real tower of piss-scrolls.

Gemma took her place beside her battle-cohorts, bracing her legs apart, clasping her hands behind her back. She waited while one of the generals began to drone on about . . . something. She honestly wasn't paying attention. Life was too short to be this bored.

Finally, after a good thirty minutes—she hadn't even had a bath yet! Did they not see she'd just come back from another hard-won battle? Couldn't all this have waited until she had gotten the blood of her enemies out of her hair? It was so damn sticky! She wanted nothing more than to scratch her scalp with both hands!—the general got to the point.

"On this day, we brothers are here to advance you cohorts from lieutenants to majors and to grant upon you all the benefits that accompany said advancement."

Huh. Look at that. She was getting a promotion. That was nice.

"Please, Brother Shona, Brother Kir, Brother Gemma, and Brother Katla, repeat after me—"

"Wait!" a voice rang out.

Brother Thomassin, an elder, looked up from the important missives he'd been reading during this whole boring ordeal. "Brother Sprenger?"

Sprenger walked into the center of the chamber and stood there a moment for maximum effect before announcing, "I refuse to sanction this advancement for Brother Gemma."

Thomassin stood so fast, his chair skidded back, nearly knocking out his poor assistant, which was actually kind of funny because the man was six-five and nearly three hundred pounds. He'd fought in more wars than Gemma could count. But then so had Thomassin.

Gemma's battle-cohorts didn't hide their annoyance either. They dropped their proper "listening to their superiors" poses and stood ready to argue with anyone and everyone.

The only one who didn't react much was Ragna. Although she did smirk. The bitch.

"She is *not* ready for such an advancement and if you insist on this course," Sprenger continued, "I will be forced to take this to the grand master."

"Excellent," Thomassin shot back. "Why don't we all take it to the grand master this very minute? I'm sure he'd love to hear your reasons as to why—"

"It's okay."

The brothers stopped arguing and everyone focused on her.

"What was that, Brother Gemma?" Thomassin asked.

"I said it's okay, Brother Thomassin." She shrugged. "I'll wait until next time."

"No," Katla pushed. "You will *not* wait until next time. We all go now or we all wait—"

"Do not get hysterical."

"I am *not* hysterical. I'm pissed."

"If you don't get the rank now," Shona reminded her, "you'll have to wait another five years before you'll be eligible again."

Gemma shrugged. "Those are the rules."

"How are you okay with this?" Kir asked. "I'm not okay with this."

"But I am okay with it." And she really was. Of course, the reason she was okay with it was because—

"How is that possible?" Sprenger asked, now standing right in front of her, leaning in close to ask her the question. "Are you plotting something?"

That was such a weird, insane question. "Plotting what? What is there to plot?"

"Your battle-cohorts will be advancing. You will not."

"And yet . . . life goes on. Amazing, isn't it? For example, we had this pig—"

"Pig?"

"Yes. And Daddy loved that pig. He didn't think he'd ever get over the death of it. But the pig had piglets. And soon, he had to go on. Because there were piglets to take care of. You see?"

Gemma let her smile fade and she began to frown, focusing her gaze on his jaw.

"Brother Sprenger . . . is that a rash?"

"What?" he asked, leaning away from her.

"Yes. Right . . ." She took her middle finger and forefinger and slid them along her own jawline. "Here."

He instinctively slapped his hand over the old wound, his glare for her and her alone. When her smile returned, wider and—she was sure—brighter than before, he took that same hand and pulled it back as if to backhand her.

"Brother Sprenger!" Thomassin barked, stopping Sprenger before he did something he could not come back from.

"I was just going to suggest a good healer in town who can help with that sort of rash, Brother," Gemma lied. She shrugged and looked to Brother Thomassin and the other elders. "Since I am no longer needed here . . . ?"

Angry and frustrated for Gemma but not wanting to turn the situation into a bigger dilemma than it already was, Thomassin dismissed her with a wave of his hand.

Gemma gave her cohorts a wink and, with a miming action of her hands, a promise of celebratory drinks of ale later that night, she removed herself from the Chamber of Valor.

But before she'd taken three steps toward higher floors and the sleeping cells of the brothers, she was picked up by one of the grand master's assistants and carried to his private study like a sack of rye.

"Is this necessary?" she asked the man. "I could have walked."

The assistant knocked once on the door to the study and brought her inside, placing her in front of the grand master's desk. He then quickly walked out, closing the door behind him.

"I'm assuming you wanted to see me?"

Busy writing on a parchment, he told her to wait by gesturing with a flick of his hand. Gemma went across the room to the small statues standing on one of the many bookshelves and picked up a representation of the war god Morthwyl that one of the monks had created out of stone. Although they respected and called to many war gods in their prayers, it was Morthwyl who was their main deity. It was his name they called when they rode into battle. It was his table they hoped to feast at when they died a death of honor and blood.

"Stop playing with that."

Gemma put the war god she'd been using to attack another war god back in its place on the shelf. "Sorry."

"I saw the seer today."

"The pretty blond one? Or the old hag? Or the one with the twelve kids? Or the one who said she ate her twin while still in her mother's womb? Or the one who controls fire?"

"No. Gary the sorcerer."

"Ohhh. Yes, of course."

"He has some terrifying information about the future of our brotherhood. Some of which, not surprisingly, involves Brother Sprenger."

"But Sprenger started it."

The grand master stopped writing and looked up from his parchment. "Sprenger started what?"

Gemma blinked. "Nothing."

"Gemma."

"Joshua."

In this room, when they were alone . . . she could call the grand master "Joshua." He'd been her mentor since the beginning. Before he'd become grand master. The one who'd guided her through all the tough times, had been there when she wasn't sure she could make it through. But mentor and mentee didn't really describe their relationship; it was deeper even than that. Did that mean she took Joshua for granted? No. She would not ask him for anything she didn't think she deserved. Nor would she ask him to fight for her over something as ridiculous as rank. They didn't waste their relationship on horseshit. It was too important to both of them.

"So what did the seer want to tell you?"

He motioned to the chair across from his desk and Gemma dropped into it.

"The Old King will die soon."

"Good."

"Yes."

"But I guess that means one of his idiot sons will replace him?"

That's when Joshua stared at her for a long moment.

"What?" she asked when he didn't reply.

"The seer actually sees a different ruler."

"Oooh. Interesting. Someone we can fight for? Or someone we're going to have to kill? I'll be honest . . . I'm not sure which I hope for. Both sound intriguing."

"I honestly don't know the answer to that question. Because the ruler he sees, Gemma . . . is your sister."

Truly confused, she could only ask, "Sister? Which sister? I have a lot of sisters. And brothers and cousins and aunts, uncles—"

"Beatrix."

She gazed at her mentor for longer than she meant to. She gazed and gazed until it happened all at once. The laughter exploded out of her so hard that she ended up on the floor, rolling around in her blood-covered tunic and chainmail, barely able to stop herself from pissing on it as well. It went on for ages, Gemma unable to stop herself, even as tears streamed down her face and her laughter turned into desperate coughs and struggling for air.

But, eventually, she noticed that Joshua did not join in with her laughter. Unlike most of the brotherhood, Joshua did enjoy a good laugh from time to time. So when he didn't this time, she forced herself back into the chair and asked while she wiped her tears and gave a few remaining chuckles, "You are kidding, aren't you?"

When he did not reply with a very strong, "Of course I am!" Gemma's laughter died in her throat, along with a bit of her soul.

"Beatrix can't be queen," she argued. "She's a child."

"To be queen or king, she just has to be out of the womb."

"She has no training."

"To be a royal? She could be a head in a jar and still be an effective royal."

"But I hate her."

"Unfortunately, I don't think that fact will come into play."

"It should. It should be the most important thing in the universe."

"You know we're monks, yes? Humility and all that."

"We're not just monks," she reminded him. "We're *war* monks. There's no humility. There's swords and blood and, if we're lucky, very good ale. So what do you want me to do about my sister? Have my parents send her to a nunnery, which I have been suggesting since shortly after her birth?"

Once more, Joshua simply gazed at her without speaking.

"What is that look on your face? Why do you just keep staring at me like that? What aren't you telling me?"

"This isn't about your sister being inadequate to lead, Gemma. In fact, the seer seems to think Beatrix will be more than ready to lead as queen."

"Oh." She shrugged. "Fine. Then what's the problem?"

"There is concern about what your sister will do once she's in power."

"Because she's a woman?" There had never been a woman who'd led these lands as queen. Only kings born into certain bloodlines or men willing to take the crown.

"No. Because she might be missing a soul."

Gemma frowned. "Literally . . . or figuratively?"

"Either or both. It's unclear at this point. But the brotherhood is not willing to take the risk."

Sitting up straight in her chair, Gemma asked, "Exactly what does that mean?"

He rested his arms on his desk. "Plans are already in motion."

"Plans? What plans?"

"To kill your sister."

"You're going to kill my sister?"

"It's not my preferred choice, but I don't make these kinds of decisions alone. And you know that."

"The elders. They've decided to kill a child."

"She's of age, Gemma. And it's what we do."

"You don't know my family. They won't let this happen."

"That's why you need to leave. Now. Go home. Save your family."

"But Thomassin? Bartholemew? Brín? They all agreed to this as well?"

"It was decided it would be easier to send you home on your own to get to your sister than to try to stop the rest of the elders here. They would just go around us. At least this way, with your help, your sister will have a chance of being saved."

"But the elders were just trying to—"

"Advance your rank?"

"Yes." She lifted her hands but quickly dropped them. Sighed. "But Sprenger stopped them."

Joshua laughed. "He's such an idiot. If he knew why they were advancing your rank, he would have let it go through. The plan was for you to be sent out on a mission with your fancy new rank. And while you were gone—"

"A separate unit would go kill my sister."

"Unfortunate but accurate. But I'm not going to let that happen. Any of it. Go save your sister. Put her in hiding. When it all blows over, she can either be queen or go back to her normal boring life with both of you hating each other."

"But if I do this . . . won't I be betraying the brotherhood?"

"You'll be leaving on my orders. They'll know that . . . eventually."

"Oh, that makes me feel so much better."

Joshua chuckled. "What have I always told you, spoiled child?"

"We have to play this smart," she said in a high-pitched voice that always made him laugh.

"Now go. Your squire is waiting with your horses by the hidden tunnel in the stables. You can get out that way."

"Samuel can't come. That isn't fair to him."

"Gemma, he hates it here. He'd rather risk his life with you than stay here in safety."

"I'm going back to the family farm, Joshua," she said, standing. "I doubt there will be much danger as long as my dad's pigs don't get out of the sty again and chase the children."

CHAPTER 1

Two years later . . .

Gemma Smythe raised her shield against the sword battering against it, again and again. When the blows weakened, she swung the shield wide. The soldier attacking her was thrown off, and Gemma moved in, slamming her sword into his side. She yanked it out, and thrust again, this time into his bowels. She tore him open and let his insides spill out before kicking him in the chest to send him spinning away.

Another attacking soldier slipped in his friend's entrails and went down. Gemma finished him off quickly, removing his head. Then she used that head to distract the soldier behind him by kicking it into his face. She turned away once her own men swarmed the soldier and took him down.

Gemma wiped blood from her eyes and evaluated the battle going on around her.

Annoyed when she didn't see what she wanted, Gemma bellowed, "Find the duke and his wife! If they're here, get them!"

The soldiers she led ran off to do her bidding but the Amichai, now loyal to Keeley, suddenly surrounded her, their war kilts, weapons, and themselves covered in the blood and gore of the enemy.

She studied the group surrounding her before calmly asking the one standing right next to her, "What the fuck are you doing?"

That smile. That smile she loathed with such venom flashed. "Protecting *you*, my princess."

"Call me that one more time..." she warned through gritted teeth, causing his smile to grow. She forced herself to calm down. "You should be protecting Keeley. Not me."

"But she sent us to you, my lady. She's quite concerned with your safety and we are here to serve and protect. We wouldn't want her sister struck down at such a young age, now would we?"

Gemma faced the one being she could barely tolerate. "Why?" she asked him. "Why do you go out of your way to irritate me?"

"I'm following orders. Isn't that what you told me to do? Follow orders? To the letter, I believe, was your command."

He was playing *that* game, was he? A game she'd played herself a few times when a monk from another monastery tried to take over her own. But those monks always thought they knew better, that their orders were more important than those of her grand master. It had been Gemma's pleasure to take them down simply by following their orders ... maliciously.

The Amichai was being unfair, though. She wasn't some grabby monk in search of power. She was simply attempting to protect her eldest sister, Keeley. The gods-damn queen. At least one of the queens.

For a land that had never had a queen leading it, there were now two. Queen Beatrix, who led beside her husband, King Marius, and Queen Keeley, who led beside no one.

It seemed as if Gary the seer had been right about Beatrix. She was a soulless bitch who would do anything to be queen, even if that meant wiping out her entire family to make it happen. Luckily for the family and for the people, Keeley wasn't about to let that happen.

At the moment, their world was split into east and west. Keeley was queen of the western lands, including the Hill Lands. King Marius, ruler of the east.

Many believed that Beatrix was merely a royal womb for Marius to plant his seed in, but Gemma and Keeley knew better. Their sister hadn't done all this *not* to have the true power of the crown. She would simply have to find a way to manipulate her husband as she manipulated everyone else in her life.

Gemma didn't doubt for a second her younger sister had already found a way to make that happen. But she couldn't worry about Beatrix right now. Not in the middle of a battle with an idiot grinning at her.

"*No*," Gemma finally stated, pointing across the battlefield to the only queen she cared about at the moment. The one who refused to listen to reason and stay on royal lands as Gemma had strongly suggested. The one who was busy wielding her ridiculous hammer as soldier after soldier attacked her, all of them hoping to be the one to take the queen down and win the rewards promised to them by the remaining sons of the Old King. "Do you not see that the queen is in peril?"

"She has my brother and my sister fighting at her side. What more could she need? Besides, her orders were quite clear, Princess. She wanted me to protect *you*. You poor, weak thing."

If her fingers weren't holding her sword, she'd curl them into a fist and throttle him. Instead, though, she used her annoyance to cut her way through the ongoing battle, making a path straight to her sister, Queen Keeley of the Hill Lands.

"Oy!" she barked at her royal majesty. "Did you send him to me?"

Keeley Smythe, Gemma's eldest sister and, at one time, the ruler of all eleven of their parents' offspring, was busy battering at the enemy commander with her favorite hammer.

"*Keeley!*"

Keeley's big shoulders jerked in surprise and she yanked up her weapon, sending an arc of fresh blood Gemma's way. But she was quick and moved to the side so that it hit the Amichai right in the face. His glare was worth *everything*.

"What?" Keeley demanded, stepping away from her opponent's caved-in chest. "What you yelling at me for?"

Gemma waved her sword at Quinn of the Scarred Earth Clan, enjoying the way his head jerked back when the blade got a little too close to that pretty but blood-soaked face.

"I said, did you send him to me?"

"You were all alone."

"And you thought *he* could help?"

"I'm helpful," the Amichai argued.

The sisters looked at him, then looked back at each other.

"What's really going on?" Gemma asked Keeley.

"What are you talking about?"

"You send this idiot to me—"

"That's a little mean," he muttered.

"You didn't even tell me about today's battle—"

"Well—"

"And where's my battalion?"

"Now you ask?"

"What does that mean?"

"You seem tense," her sister said. She took a step back, looked Gemma over. "Your shoulders are tense. Your neck tight. You're doing that thing again with your posture. Want me to fix that for you?"

Gemma would never understand her sister.

"I'm not a horse!" she snapped.

Keeley frowned. "Uh . . . I know. Wait . . . *are you*? Is that what you're saying?"

The Amichai snorted, quickly turning away so Keeley wouldn't see him laugh. Gemma could only gawk at her.

"What?"

"It's possible. I was too young to remember your birth. Maybe Mum just snuck you in."

"I'm saying you can't just fix me because I'm *not* one of your bloody horses!"

"Oh! That's what you mean."

"What did you think I meant?"

"I really didn't know. Things with you have been . . . difficult. Since . . . well . . ." She gestured at Gemma and Gemma looked down at the chainmail and bits of armor that her mother had made for her many months ago.

She lifted her gaze to her sister's. "Since . . . when?" she asked.

"Uh . . ." Keeley looked at Quinn but he quickly turned away again.

"I'm not part of this conversation," he explained to them. "Instead, I'm looking meaningfully off"—he motioned with his entire left arm, gesturing out, his four fingers pointing, the thumb tucked in against his hand—"that way."

"Since when?" Gemma pushed, now ignoring the battle going on around them.

"Since / . ." Again, Keeley gestured at Gemma's entire body. "This."

She wanted her sister to say it. Out loud. For everyone to hear it.

"This? What's this?"

"You know."

"No. I'm unclear."

"Uh . . ."

Keeley suddenly reached behind her and when she swung her arm back, she held their cousin Keran. She was more than a decade older than the two of them and a bit of a black sheep because she wasn't a blacksmith like the rest of their mother's side of the family, but had belonged to a fighting guild. She wore the scars of those years quite proudly—since she was still alive. She'd even managed to retire while still able to stand and walk on her own. That was mostly unheard of when it came to the fighting guilds.

"Ale time?" Keran asked when she stood in front of her cousins.

"No," Gemma snapped, disgusted. "We're not done yet."

"Oh. Then what do you want? I was in the middle of killing."

"Keeley needs you to say what she's too afraid to say."

"Keeley's never afraid to say anything. Just this morning she asked her mum if she's pregnant again or if her ass is just getting wide. I don't know anyone else brave enough to ask *your* mother if her ass is just getting wide."

Gemma leaned around Keran to view her sister. "Tell me that woman is not pregnant again."

"I think her ass is just getting wide."

Relieved, Gemma leaned back and said to Keran, "Well, she's afraid to tell me something."

"About the snarling? The snapping? The way no one can talk to you anymore?"

"That's quite a list, Cousin."

"Or are we talking about the drinking?"

"*The drinking?*"

Considering there were nightly bets among the troops on how fast the queen's cousin could down a pint of ale, Gemma was a little insulted that anyone was questioning her occasional drink. Especially if that questioning was coming from gods-damn Keran of all people!

"All right then!" Keeley cheered.

"Oh, wait," Keran went on, "or is this about—"

"Thank you, Keran!" Keeley said, casually tossing their cousin back into the ongoing battle.

Their cousin wasn't a small woman but she flew like a leaf on the wind, landed on her feet, and immediately began hacking away with her axe at the closest enemy soldier without even missing a step.

Gemma moved up to her sister, raising her chin so she could at least attempt to look Keeley in the eyes. "My drinking? What drinking?"

"You know what I need you to do, luv?" Keeley asked with her big smile and adorable charm. She pointed at the duke's castle. "Look in there. See if the duke and duchess have left us anything."

"You're just trying to get rid of me."

"Would I do that to you?"

"As a matter of fact—"

The queen didn't even let her finish. She just spun her around and shoved, sending Gemma off in the direction of the castle.

It was humiliating.

"Why are you back here?" Quinn's brother, Caid, asked.

"I was keeping an eye on Princess Bitchy Leggings as the queen asked me to do. But she is in a mood. I'd be better in a fighting pit, unarmed and naked."

"I didn't think she was coming today."

"Apparently that plan changed and the enemy has been paying for it ever since. She's just been lopping off heads all day. I shouldn't mind but it seems so senseless."

Caid shrugged. "At least she's on our side."

"I'm sorry to interrupt you two," said their sister, Laila, as she used a spear to fight off their enemies. "But do you two mind assisting in keeping the queen alive? She's all alone over there!"

Quinn and his brother looked over at Keeley Smythe, Queen of the Hill Lands.

She was swinging her hammer wide, knocking down three attacking soldiers. She then lifted her hammer up and over, massive, sweat-covered muscles rippling as she brought the weapon down, crushing the soldier into the ground. When she buried the head of her hammer into another soldier's chest—crumpling the steel armor that had been protecting it—the brothers looked back at their sister.

"Are we worried about her?" Quinn asked his sister. "Really?"

Impaling a soldier through his helmet, Laila snapped, "All right, listen up. You two seem to forget who you actually report to since you"—she pointed at Caid with her blood-soaked steel spear—"are lucky enough to fuck the queen. And you"—she pointed at Quinn—"have been lucky enough not to be executed by the queen. So I'll make it very clear. The only one either of you takes orders from . . . is *me*."

"Because you're Mother's direct heir? Or Father's favorite?"

"Both, which is why I rule you two *like a god*."

"She'll be a tyrant one day," Quinn muttered to Caid.

"Now Caid, go to Keeley. You lot with him," she ordered, motioning to the other Amichais fighting nearby. "And Quinn—"

"Please don't send me after—"

"You go with Gemma."

He dropped his head forward. "She hates me. I don't mean that lightly. I mean she really hates me."

"You love it when others hate you."

He shrugged. "True."

"Then go. And watch your back. We're not done here yet." His sister looked around, her gaze narrow. "Something feels off."

His sister was never wrong about that sort of thing. She was a centaur, and like any true herd animal, she had the strong senses that kept them safe and alive. Because she could smell danger on the wind and sense trouble through her hooves.

So Quinn stopped questioning her and simply followed the terse princess who was abusing their enemies so brutally. He was truly concerned she might one day be convicted of war crimes by her own sister.

Gemma battered her way through the ongoing battle to the open gates of the duke's castle. They weren't under a royal siege because he and his wife had sided with Queen Beatrix and her idiot husband, but because they'd raised an army to assist in the oncoming war between the two queendoms. That was something even Keeley wouldn't overlook.

What Gemma hadn't expected, though, was that Keeley would attack Duke Reinhold preemptively, rather than waiting for his power to grow. Keeley usually preferred diplomacy to war. Maybe their mother had said something to her, because Gemma had woken up this morning to find her sister and her army already moving out.

Why Keeley hadn't alerted Gemma to her decision earlier, Gemma still didn't know, and their earlier conversation with Keran hadn't helped matters. The battalion that reported to Gemma was still at the homestead with the family. Gemma, however, would prefer they were here. She'd been training them for this sort of fighting. To attack fast and hard, under the cover of darkness, giving their enemies no time to put up a proper defense or offense. It was a brutal, unfair tactic, but if they were going to win against Beatrix and the son of the Old King, they'd have to stop thinking like fairminded individuals and start thinking like men.

A hysterical soldier ran toward her screaming and Gemma turned, brought her sword up and across, splitting the man open from just below his left shoulder, through part of his chest, to the other side of his neck, sending the man's head—and a large chunk of his upper body—flipping up and away as the rest of his body dropped before it reached her.

Gemma drove her sword into another oncoming soldier, then pushed him out of her way. She kept moving, entering the castle walls without any of the other enemy soldiers following her. She had expected to find a battle inside. Men defending the duke and his family. But she soon realized that the royals had made a quick exit from their old home, probably heading toward Beatrix's lands.

Although Gemma would have preferred to get her hands on the duke, this situation was tolerable. Keeley's army was decimating the duke's army and without any of his soldiers, he would be of little use to Beatrix and her husband. That worked just as well as taking the duke captive.

Keeping her sword at the ready, Gemma moved among the remains of the duke's home. She had no use for the things he'd left behind. A few objects of actual gold and steel and silver would be taken and given to their mother to be made into weapons by the blacksmith. But Gemma was looking for more. She was looking for information. Anything that could help them in their ongoing battle with Beatrix.

Far in the back of the castle, she found a room with several large tables. On them were maps and communications on parchment between the duke and King Marius, also known as Marius, the Wielder of Hate. Without meaning to, Gemma again found herself grudgingly worried about Beatrix being the wife of a man infamous for his brutality and heartless nature. It irritated her that she cared at all. Clearly Beatrix hadn't cared about family when she'd buried her blade in Keeley's gut. Her own sister. And for what? A chance at being queen? Keeley had spent her entire life caring for Beatrix. Taking care of her, giving her money, making sure she had all the books she could possibly want and, most importantly, ignoring the obvious fact that Beatrix was an evil bitch who should have been put down at birth the same way they put down diseased pigs on their farm.

Yet despite knowing all that, Gemma still found herself worrying about Beatrix. Worrying about the life she was living with someone like Marius. And she hated herself a little for giving a horse's shit one way or the other. Beatrix didn't deserve Gemma's worry. She didn't deserve anything except a blade to the neck. Not that Keeley would ever let that happen.

"We should burn this place to the ground," a voice said from behind her, "so they can never return."

Gemma gripped her blade tighter but did not turn around.

"I wish you would stop sneaking up on me."

"I didn't sneak up on you. It's my legs."

Confused by that statement, she finally turned to face Quinn.

"What?"

"It's my legs." He looked down at the long, muscular legs that stretched from under the leather kilt that every battle-ready Amichai wore. There were small scars over the length of each leg but on his left one was a very long, very jagged scar that reached from behind his knee around to the front of the thigh and up, until it disappeared under his kilt. "When I only have two, I seem to move very lightly. I barely make any sound at all." He gazed at her a long moment before continuing. "But when I add the other two—and hooves, of course—then suddenly I end up making much more noise than I mean to. Unless I wrap my hooves in cloth. Then my stride is less noisy."

He stopped again . . . and gazed at her before finally finishing with, "I'm always surprised you humans aren't quieter when you move. You only have two legs. How hard is it?"

It was still strange for her. Even now. To have these discussions with the Amichais. To say out loud that no, they weren't human. They were centaurs who merely took on human form when they wished. Sometimes Gemma walked into her sister's bedchamber and found Caid of the Scarred Earth Clan complaining about something minor while his long black tail swatted at one of the stray cats that roamed the castle walls and liked to hang from the Amichais' tails. He didn't even seem to notice he was doing it. Nor did he notice the kittens climbing his horse legs. And Keeley, who sat on the bed, listening to his complaints and petting a baby goat, didn't seem to notice or care either. That's when Gemma knew life among the Smythe clan had well and truly changed.

"Are you still following me?" she asked Quinn, whose white-blond hair often made her think the gods had gone out of their way to make him the exact opposite of his black-haired brother, Caid.

"I'm only here because I was ord—"

"If you say 'ordered' one . . . more . . . *time* . . ."

"So I can't say 'ordered' or 'princess'? And yet you are a princess who I was ordered to follow."

Gemma stepped around him. "Fuck off, Amichai. I have no time for you or . . ."

Gemma's complaint faded when the Amichai moved past her and stopped, his head tilting one way, then the other. He heard something. Was trying to follow the sound.

"This way," he barked before setting off.

Gemma immediately followed. Together, they made their way deep into the empty castle, cutting through the kitchens and out an exit into the open fields. A dangerous way to live, with no protection at one's back like a small courtyard.

She stood next to Quinn, sweeping her gaze across the grassy, open area until she saw him. His bright yellow robes flapped as he desperately ran toward the castle while a man on horseback charged after him, his big axe ready to remove the runner's head.

"Do you know either?" Quinn asked her.

"The one in robes is a monk. A pacifist order that does no harm to any. I don't recognize the armor of the other."

"Good enough," Quinn said as he unslung the longbow strapped across his chest and pulled an arrow from the leather quiver hanging from his sword belt. He nocked the arrow, aimed, and released.

The hit was direct, in the chest, taking the rider right off his horse.

As much as Quinn annoyed her, Gemma couldn't ignore the Amichai's skill with a longbow, only rivaled by his sister, who used a composite bow as if it were an extension of her arm.

Still, Gemma wasn't about to tell Quinn any of that. He was arrogant enough already.

Gemma brought two fingers to her mouth and whistled. Quickly, as if he'd just been waiting for her call, Gemma's horse trotted through the castle and into the field, stopping right beside her.

Dagger tossed his black mane, which had been braided into four thick plaits so it didn't get in his way during battle, and pounded his front hoof against the ground. She mounted him with ease and clucked her tongue against the top of her mouth once. Dagger galloped toward the hysterical man still running toward them. As they neared, Quinn heard his screams for help as the monk stumbled, fell, then got back to his feet again.

Gemma reached him first and when she stopped, the man dropped to his knees beside her.

"Please! Don't hurt me! Please! I am a pacifist monk! I am a pacifist monk!" he screamed. Begging.

Gemma stared down at him.

"I know what you are, Brother. I won't hurt you. No soldier should be hurting you. They should only come to your monastery for healing and care. As a sanctuary."

Still on his knees, the monk shook his head.

"They've killed them all!" he screeched. "All of them! They've killed every one!"

Gemma glanced off, her brows pulled low, her blue eyes dark, her expression unreadable. Quinn watched her closely, curious to see what she would do. When monks from different orders passed through their town, Gemma wasn't exactly welcoming. At best, she simply ignored them. At worst, there were nasty fights in the nearby taverns that ended with her getting sewn up the next day and refusing to discuss the cause of the brawl.

But this felt different.

After a moment, Gemma looked over her shoulder and pointed at a unit of Keeley's soldiers.

"You lot!" she called out. "With us!" Gemma held out her hand and the monk grabbed it. She hauled him onto Dagger's back and set the horse racing forward. Quinn followed.

When they reached the nearby monastery, the monk immediately slipped off Dagger. He walked to the open front doors, dropped to his knees in his gratingly cheery bright yellow robes, clenched his hands together, focused his eyes on the brilliant sky above, and unleashed prayers that were no more than sobbing cries to his god.

Not knowing how to respond, Quinn passed him without a word and entered the monastery.

Gemma had already beat him inside and was now in the main hall. She was already down on one knee, the tip of her blade pressed against the stone floor, her right hand gripping the pommel; her head bowed in prayer.

He understood why. It was a normal reaction for anyone who'd given their life over to the gods, which she had. Although in the last fourteen months, few could tell. He clearly remembered that morning when he'd walked by her bedroom to see her packing away her monk's robes and chainmail and weapons in a trunk at the end of her bed. Her mother had then outfitted her in all new gear, made just for her by the renowned blacksmith, but it wasn't the same, was it? Seeing her in mere warrior's garb. Not to Quinn anyway. He was used to seeing the queen's sister striding around in her black tunic with the blood-red rune emblazoned on the front and back, and the exquisitely made black chainmail that proclaimed she was the warrior of a god.

Quinn didn't know what had happened. What had made her

take off her robes and stop answering to the title Brother Gemma, and he didn't ask. Although he loved tormenting her, it had never felt right to play with her about something like that. Gods were a personal thing.

But seeing her on one knee, her sword held tight in her hand, and her head bowed . . . With or without her robes, Quinn knew that she had not truly left her gods behind. How could she when faced with something like this?

Because they were all dead. All of them. Every monk who'd been in the monastery was dead; their broken and bleeding bodies piled high in the middle of the hall. Some tied to pillars and riddled with crossbow bolts. Most of the bodies bore signs of torture before death.

There was so much blood. He'd only seen this much blood on battlefields.

Gemma finished her prayer and stood, turning to face him.

"These monks," she said softly, keeping her voice low in deference to the dead, "like the one outside, were not war monks. They were pacifist monks. They were here to help the weak and suffering. This place was a sanctuary for any who came here for help. Even the Old King never crossed that line. And he was known to cross almost every line."

"Why would your kind do this?"

She shook her head. "I can't speak for the ways of men, Amichai."

He frowned at her response. "I'm not speaking philosophically, woman. I mean *why* did they do this? Now?"

"Oh!" Gemma took a look around. "Oh, I don't know. Maybe because they could. With the battle for power going on, the attackers figured they could take whatever gold and silver they could find."

"You think thieves did this?"

"You don't?"

"Thieves usually just come in, take, then go. This . . . seems excessively cruel. Even for your kind. Don't you think?"

"I guess."

Quinn studied her. "You guess?"

"What do you want me to say, Amichai?"

He wanted her to say that she cared. He wanted her to say that she would stop at nothing until she found out what had happened here. He wanted her to say she would track down the bastards who'd killed these defenseless monks, skin them alive, and place them assholes first on standing pikes. *That's* what he wanted to hear her say. Because that's what Brother Gemma would have said when he'd met her. But since she'd packed away her robes . . .

"I'm going to get your sister."

"For what?" Gemma asked. "It's disgusting thieves with no sense of honor. We'll bury the dead and be on our way."

"Och!"

Gemma blinked. "Did you just 'och' me?"

"I did. And I'll do it again." He leaned down, close to her face. "Och!"

"Oy! You spit in me eye!"

"Deserved. I'm getting your sister."

"She won't say anything different!" Gemma called after him. "You're being overly dramatic about *all* of this!"

Keeley took one turn around the room before she faced Gemma, spread her arms wide, and announced, "Thieves didn't do this."

Behind Keeley's back, Quinn mouthed, *Told you.*

If Gemma had long enough arms to slap him where he stood . . .

"This is the work of soldiers."

"We don't know that."

"Are you blind?" Keeley took another turn around the main hall, shaking her head and making distinct sounds of disgust; her brow furrowed. "This is so disturbing. Do you not find this disturbing?" Keeley asked. And, before Gemma could answer, "*How do you not find this disturbing?*" she bellowed.

"*I didn't say I don't find this disturbing!*"

"Where's the monk?" Keeley asked Quinn. Because suddenly they were friends.

"This way, Your Highness," Quinn said with a sweeping gesture of his arm.

Keeley walked past Gemma, not even looking at her. When Quinn followed, Gemma pulled back her arm to punch him on the side of the head but Caid caught hold and pulled her in the opposite direction. They went into a small hallway, where he released her.

"What's going on?"

"Your brother—"

"Other than that. What's going on *here*?"

Gemma let out a sigh. "I don't know. It looks like thieves to me."

"Does it really? Usually you're more paranoid than that."

"I'm not paranoid."

"Gemma, you're the most paranoid person I know. And I know my father. And your uncle."

Gemma briefly rubbed her forehead. "All right. Maybe I was a little dismissive. Normally I'd be a little more . . ."

"Questioning?"

"Yes."

"So be questioning now. If my brother is asking questions . . . my *brother* . . . there must be something. Look around. Be the old you."

"The old me?"

"You've been different lately."

"How?"

"I don't know." He shrugged. "To be honest, you remind me of your cousin."

"*Keran?*" she exploded. "I remind you of Keran?"

"Don't know why you're yelling. I like Keran."

"That's hardly the point." Gemma looked away from the Amichai, dismissing him with a wave. "I . . . I . . . I'll look around. See what I can find."

"Great," Caid said flatly. "Thanks." He studied her for a moment. "Are you all right?"

"I'm fine. Just . . . go."

"Do you want me to find you some ale?"

Gemma glared up at him. "*No.* I do not want you to find me any ale. I do not *need* any ale."

"No, no. Of course you don't."

Insulted by his tone, Gemma opened her mouth to reply but he'd already walked away. If he'd been in his natural form, she'd have kicked him in his horse rump.

No, she wouldn't do any of that. She needed to calm down. She needed to be rational.

If Caid thought something was strange about all this, he was probably right. Unlike his ridiculous brother, Caid was a thoughtful centaur. A good match for her sister, who thought this harsh world was filled with nothing but do-gooders wanting only the best for others.

She'd started to head down to the sleeping chambers, away from the main hall, when Laila came toward her. She was sliding her weapon back into its sheath when she stopped by Gemma's side.

"No one left alive. Only the monk. He's very lucky." She shook her head. "What happened here?"

"I have no idea. Caid wants me to take a look around."

"Good idea. Your sister is talking to the monk. And the troops are preparing burial pyres."

"Don't. The pacifists bury their dead. Tell the soldiers to dig graves."

"Why would anyone bury their dead?"

"It's something they do."

She scrunched up her face. "Ew."

"Try not to be so judgmental in front of the monk, please."

"Make sure I'm burned," Laila insisted. "I don't want to spend my afterlife rotting away in the dirt. With the bugs. Or if I can't be burned, leave me out for the elements. So I'm eaten by predators."

"Must we really have this conversation now?"

"Just making sure it's clear. You humans are . . . strange." She looked Gemma over. "You all right?"

"I'm fine."

"You want some ale? I'm sure there's ale somewhere around here."

Gemma gritted her teeth. "I do not need ale. And the pacifist monks abstain."

"Seriously?"

"From ale and sex and violence. They avoid anything that might make one's cock hard."

"Ah. I see. Well . . . we'll be home soon enough." She patted Gemma on the shoulder and walked off.

Gemma briefly thought about screaming and tearing the walls of this pacifist house down around her ears but she would never disrespect another god's house of worship, whether she worshipped that god or not. Instead, she went on her search.

She searched and she searched. For nearly an hour. But she found nothing that seemed out of the ordinary. From what she could tell, the intruders had taken all the gold, all the silver, anything that might be worth something as any good thief or thieves would.

"I knew this was a waste of time."

She started toward the closest exit but stopped abruptly.

Gemma went over everything in her head one more time. Everything she'd seen or not seen during the time she'd been inside the monastery. That's when she knew what she'd missed. How blind she'd been.

"Fuck," she barked before she took off running. "Fuck!"

The graves had been dug and the troops were carefully laying the bodies of the brutalized brothers into the dirt while Keeley, Quinn, the Amichais, and the last remaining monk looked on.

That's when Gemma appeared out of nowhere, jumping in front of the easily startled monk.

"I need to talk to you," she said, grabbing him by the sleeve of his bright yellow robes and beginning to lead him off until Keeley pulled him away.

"What are you doing?" Keeley demanded.

"I need to talk to him."

Keeley, taller than her sister, leaned down a bit. "Can't this wait? We're burying his dead."

"This is important," Gemma replied.

"So's this."

"Back off."

"You back off!"

"What is going on?" Laila barked.

"I need to speak—"

"And I said it can wait."

"You can just ask," the monk said softly.

And Keeley actually looked as if she wanted to wring her younger sister's neck.

"The artifacts of the monastery," Gemma asked, "where are they?"

Staring at Gemma, the monk blinked. Once, twice. "We . . . we have no artifacts, my lady." And they all knew the monk was lying.

Gemma had no patience these days for poorly told lies, and she rolled her eyes in exasperation. Keeley, however, tried her ridiculous honesty.

"Brother, you can tell my sister anything."

"Keeley, stop."

"She's one of you," Keeley explained.

"One of us?" the monk asked.

"Keeley, stop talking."

"Aye! She's a monk from the Order of Righteous Valor."

The monk began to blink more. Actually, he blinked ten or twelve times in a row before he stumbled back, slamming into Caid.

"You . . . you're a . . . a . . . war monk?"

"Brother, please . . ." Gemma raised her hands, palms out. "Before you panic—"

"*War Monk!*" he screamed hysterically before running away.

Gemma briefly closed her eyes before turning on her sister. "Why did you say anything?"

"Why do you belong to an organization that terrifies people?"

Fair question.

A fair question that Gemma didn't bother to answer. Instead, she ran after the monk.

"Well, don't chase after—"

When her sister ignored her, Keeley threw up her hands and charged after Gemma.

The Amichais looked at each other. Keeley was queen. Gemma was eldest sister to the queen. A princess. There were at least three units of soldiers burying bodies that could chase the monk from here all the way back to the Amichais' mountain home. And yet . . .

Laila and Caid focused on Quinn.

"Oh, come on!" he argued. "Why do I have to do it?"

"I don't feel like running," Laila replied.

"I don't want to," Caid growled.

"And you know what will happen once they catch up to each other. And that poor monk will die of a heart attack once he sees what those two can do to each other. We'll never find out the answer to Gemma's questions. So go," Laila ordered, gesturing with both hands.

"Fuck." He shifted to his natural form and took off after the sisters.

It wasn't hard to find them. The monk's yellow robes were as bright as the two suns. Gemma was nearly on him when Keeley tackled her from behind, the pair going down hard.

Quinn kept going, reaching the hysterical monk and grabbing him from behind. By the time he had the man under control, he was back to two legs so that when they were facing each other, the monk wouldn't be any more frightened.

"Breathe," he ordered the poor man. "Just breathe."

"She's a—"

"Yes. She is. But she won't hurt you. I promise. On my life and the life of my people. Understand?"

The monk gawked at him for a long moment, but finally nodded.

"Now, she's going to ask you questions, you'll answer them . . . yes? You'll help?"

"I will."

"Good. Now . . ." Quinn looked over his shoulder; shook his head. "Give me a moment."

He released the monk and returned to the sisters, grabbing them by the collars of their blood-encrusted chainmail shirts and pulling them to their feet. He yanked them apart and shook them for good measure.

"Stop it! You're scaring the feeble monk!"

"I told you not to say anything!" Gemma felt the need to remind her sister, yet again.

"I still don't understand why you're part of a group that sends terror into anyone who even hears the words 'war monk.' As soon as they're said, people piss themselves and run. Does that not concern you?"

"No! It does not concern me. Because our reputation was earned—"

"On the backs of dead babies?"

The slap across the queen's face rang out through the land like the warning of a town bell; Quinn could actually feel it in his back teeth.

The women were at each other once more and he wasn't even sure he wanted to attempt to separate them again. He didn't want to risk important parts of his body. It was the monk who decided to intervene. Not with words or pleas, but a burst of bright energy that sent both females spiraling in opposite directions until they landed facedown in the dirt, gasping for breath, eyes wide in startled panic.

"My brothers are dead!" the monk nearly screamed. "And you two royals attack each other like feckless harpies!" Tears began to stream down his face but they seemed more from despair and frustration than fear. "Both of you, stop it!"

He looked away and wiped his tears with the sleeve of his yellow robe. "Now ask me your question, War Monk."

Panting hard, but not from her fight with her sister, Gemma got to her feet. She brushed off her knees and asked, "Where did your order keep your artifacts? Your *true* artifacts."

The pacifist monk studied her hard before replying, "There are several locations in the monastery—"

"I could be wrong, Brother, but I'm almost positive they're not there anymore."

"What?"

When Gemma took a step forward, the monk took a step back, so she stopped.

"I think whoever attacked your monastery tortured your elders because they wanted your artifacts. Not your gold. Not your silver. They wanted your power."

"How powerful could pacifist monks be?" Quinn asked.

"Well," Gemma grudgingly admitted, glancing down at the dirt and scrapes she'd gotten from her tumble across the ground, "consider the power we just experienced from this monk, who I'm guessing worked in the"—her gaze locked on him and the monk quickly looked away—"stables? He probably managed to survive by hiding in the tunnels that are built under all monastery stables, and he does smell of horse and sheep shit. So he's not an elder. Nor is he important enough or powerful enough to work in the library. But he was still able to toss us across this field like kittens." She nodded. "We need to get back to the monastery and find out if the artifacts are still there."

"And if they are?" the monk asked.

"They're yours," Keeley said, also standing now. "We're not going to take what belongs to your monastery, Brother. We're just trying to help."

He nodded and began walking back toward his monastery and the others. The sisters followed and Quinn brought up the rear. As they walked, he noticed the sisters begin to jostle each other. Then the slapping began. When they took hold of each other, he leaned down and reminded them, "Don't think for a moment that I won't drag both of you back there, by your ankles, in front of your entire army. Because if you're wondering . . . yes, I *am* that big a dick."

"We are aware," Gemma muttered.

"Great!" he cheered, slapping them both on the backs. "I was worried you didn't know what my father truly loves about me!"

CHAPTER 2

The bodies were buried while the suns were still in the sky, but the monk was not there. He was inside the monastery with Keeley, whom he seemed to trust, and Gemma, whom he didn't trust at all.

While they watched, he went to every space within the walls that had, at one time, held the order's artifacts. None of them remained. Not one.

Unable to bear the weight of such loss, he sat down on the first bench he came to in the kitchens and didn't move. Gemma didn't sit beside him. She knew he wouldn't like that. So Keeley did.

"I'm so sorry, Brother," she said in that way she had. The way that told you she meant it more than anyone else in the world could ever mean it. Because she did. She felt others' pain in a way no one else did.

"I have nothing."

"There are other pacifist monks you can go to in the Chessly Hills," Gemma reminded him. "I'm sure they will take you in."

"Or you can come with us," Keeley offered.

"What?" Gemma asked, trying not to sound as annoyed as she felt.

Keeley glared at her sister. "We can't just send him off to people he doesn't know."

"He doesn't know us."

"He knows us now."

"He hates me."

"He doesn't hate anyone."

"How do you know?"

"I know!"

"Can I speak to you in private for a moment?"

"*No.*" She smiled at the monk. "Please. You can stay with us until you decide what you want to do and where you want to go. It will also give my sister more time to look into what happened to your order's artifacts."

"They've probably been destroyed."

As soon as the words were out of her mouth, Gemma knew she should have waited to say that to Keeley in private. Especially when both of them looked up at her in horror, the monk's eyes filling with tears and her sister's eyes filling with rage.

"Excuse us a moment, Brother," Keeley said before standing, grabbing Gemma's arm, and yanking her from the kitchens.

"What is *wrong* with you? Do you need some ale?"

Gemma yanked her arm away. "What's *that* supposed to mean?"

"Isn't it time for you to meet Keran at the pub? Are you angry because we're holding you back from a good drinking session? Is that why you said something so ridiculously cruel to that poor man?"

"I do *not* need a drink," she bit out.

"Since when?"

"Since ever! I am not a drinker!"

"Oh . . . Gemma."

Gemma scrubbed her hands across her face. She decided not to have this discussion with her sister in a monastery. She simply wouldn't.

"Can we just go?"

"So you can drink?"

"*No.*" She barely stopped herself from slapping her sister . . . again. "Because there is much we need to discuss."

"Fine. But he's coming with us."

"I don't care. But you'll need to find a place where he can greet the suns every morning."

"And where you won't terrify him every day?"

Gemma shrugged. "Yes."

* * *

By the time they'd returned to what the locals liked to call "Forgetown," the horses and equipment had been unloaded, hunger and thirst sated, and the majority of blood and gore removed, it was late into the night. The small core of Keeley's "advisors," as she liked to call them, found themselves at the hall table discussing the sobbing monk and his dead brothers.

"I don't understand what the problem is," Laila admitted after Gemma gave a very short and not very helpful explanation about the monastery's artifacts. "Thieves stole their artifacts. Perhaps they stole them on order."

"Why would anyone do that?" Gemma flatly asked.

"I don't know. Why would anyone keep the bottom jaw of a dead man?" Laila asked, referring to one of the artifacts the monk had described.

"A dead monk."

"You say that as if it's supposed to mean something to me."

"There's power in religious artifacts."

"Including a jawbone?"

"Yes."

Quinn rested his elbow on the table and his chin on his raised fist before asking Gemma, "What artifacts does your order have?"

"None of your business."

"Jawbones?"

"We believe in the power of steel. Not in the power of a dead man's teeth."

"Oooh," Quinn teased, "such a tone about other religious orders. Such a snob."

"Shut up, Amichai."

"Don't get snippy with him because you haven't had your nightly drink yet," Keeley snarled.

Gemma slammed her fists on the table, and the power of the blow vibrated up through Quinn's elbows, up his arms, through his fingers, and into his head. It was one of the most intense things he'd felt in ages. There was so much strength behind the motion.

"I am *not* drinking!"

Laila and Caid simply blew out breaths but Keeley rolled her eyes in disbelief.

"Oh, come on!" the queen cried out. "No one believes that for a moment! You're at the pub every night with Keran!"

"I go there to think."

"At the pub?"

"I like the noise."

"And the drink."

"I get a pint. I nurse it."

"Then why have you been acting so strangely?"

"I have a lot on my mind."

"Like what?"

"Everything!"

"Think you can be more specific?"

"Can we get back to the artifacts?" Laila cut in before the sisters began rolling around on the ground again. "I really just need to go to bed and I am not in the mood to figure out if Gemma's in denial about her drinking problem."

"I do not have a drink—" Gemma cut herself off, shook her head. "I'm not doing this with you lot. I'm not." She took in a breath. Let it out. "Every religious order has artifacts of its own. They all have their own power. Some more than others. Some can barely heal a spider bite. Others can destroy the countryside between here and the Baleful Forests."

"What could the pacifist monks' artifacts do?"

"I don't know. They've never been very friendly with the orders of the war monks."

"How shocking," Keeley said with great sarcasm. "Considering how that brother ran from you screaming."

Gemma raised her forefinger toward her sister. Telling her with that one finger to stop talking.

That's when Quinn chuckled a little.

Fed up with everyone, it seemed, Gemma turned her glare on him.

"What's so funny?" she practically snarled.

"Well . . . it's not funny as in funny. But funny as in terrifying."

"What's that?" Laila asked.

"The thought of Beatrix getting her hands on something that powerful."

He'd spoken without much thought but it was as if he was in his horse form and had lifted his tail and dropped a load of shit into the middle of the dining table.

Laila leaned forward, her gaze locking on Gemma. "Beatrix . . . She wouldn't toy with the gods like that, would she? Going after their people?"

Gemma and Keeley, no longer bothering to be angry at each other, exchanged glances.

"Well," Gemma began, "Beatrix was never one for religion."

"What does that mean?" Caid asked.

Keeley shrugged. "She never involved herself in the harvest rituals or the festivals."

"Does she believe in the gods?" Quinn asked.

"She believes," Keeley said.

"But," Gemma quickly added, "she doesn't really worship any god."

"At all?"

"Not really."

"She went through a research phase," Keeley explained. "Read lots of books on many gods, but when she was about fourteen, I think, she finally said she didn't find any that she agreed with. Or liked, for that matter, and she wasn't about to cut a bull's throat because all that blood was just messy."

"Do you have to sacrifice a bull to all your human gods?"

Gemma shook her head, clearly annoyed. "No. That was such a horseshit answer."

"So this attack could have been Beatrix."

"This could have been something Beatrix *ordered*," Gemma clarified. "But why that particular religious sect . . . ? It's not like they're well known for their power."

Quinn shrugged and again, without much thought, simply suggested, "Maybe there are others."

"Maybe what?"

"Other sects. Other orders. That she wants artifacts from."

And again, it was that "he'd-just-shat-on-the-dinner-table" look.

Gemma focused on the table for several long seconds before she said to her sister, "I'll get a list together."

"I'll get the horses. You three meet us out front in five minutes."

Laila let them get about ten feet from the table before she called out, "Oy. What are you two royal idiots doing?"

When it was just the five of them alone, she never bothered with the niceties of court. Not anymore. These days they often didn't have the time.

"We're going to—"

"You two aren't going to do anything," Laila said. "Do you know why?"

"Because we're tired after a day of butchery?" Keeley asked.

"No, my luv. Because you're queen. And you," she said, pointing at Gemma, her eyes rolling before her sister could even finish, "are the princess and a very valuable general. The two of you need to be"—and both Quinn and Caid leaned away because they knew what was coming—"*here!*" she bellowed, most likely waking up the entire household.

And with that, she stood. The chair she'd been sitting in flew back and hit the floor hard.

"We continue to go through this every few weeks! You two think you can just saunter in and out of the queendom that you *rule*! Do you see my mum roaming around here? Hanging out with the children she adores? No! Do you know why? Because this is not where she rules! She stays with her people! So, no, my dearest human friends! You can't go traipsing off in the middle of the night to check on some random list of religious orders to see if your sister has attacked them too! Because your work is *here*! Is there a chance, possibly, that you—*finally!*—understand what I am *telling you?*"

The two royals looked at each other and, slowly, made their way back to the table.

After a moment, Gemma said to Keeley, "I need your five fastest riders."

Keeley nodded. "Done." She walked out and Gemma exited in the opposite direction.

"Feel better?" Caid asked their sister.

"I don't know why I have to keep saying it."

"Because they weren't born to be royals like you. Keeley thought she'd spend her entire life making warriors' armor and on slow days her neighbors' cookware."

"It's been two years."

"Have you known anyone more a blacksmith than Keeley Smythe?"

With a long sigh, Laila's head dropped and Quinn picked up her chair so she could sit down.

A few minutes later, the sisters returned, Keeley with five soldiers who had not gone with them into battle that day. Three women and two males, thinner than the brutes who charged head-first into combat. Quinn guessed these five were messengers. The ones who brought messages back and forth from the front to the commanders in other parts of the battle. They wore the scars of survivors, so none of them were dilettantes.

Gemma gave them scrolls and directions and off the five went.

"Where are they going?" Caid asked once it was just their small group again.

"There are five different sects within a half day's riding distance from here. Two monasteries, a church, a convent, and a coven. We'll see if any of them have heard anything or have had any problems. I've also offered them the protection of the crown."

"Oh, that was nice," Keeley said, smiling.

And Quinn realized that Keeley wasn't speaking with sarcasm or malice. She truly meant it. Usually only the queen herself could offer such a thing, but Keeley wasn't one to stand on ceremony.

"And until the riders get back?"

Gemma shrugged at Laila's question. "Get some rest?"

"While you get a drink?" Keeley asked. And there was that sarcasm!

Mouth dropping open, Gemma gawked at her sister a moment before storming off.

"Pub's that way," Keeley said, pointing toward the front doors.

They heard Gemma growl before she disappeared up the stairs to the bedrooms on the other floors added on to the rambling building by the sisters' insane but brilliant uncle.

Quinn and his siblings stared at the human queen until Quinn finally asked her, "Now you're just ruthlessly fucking with her, aren't you?"

She snorted a laugh before bending over at the waist. "I am!" she squealed in between laughs.

"What is wrong with you two?" Laila demanded in disgust before walking away. "Both of you . . . just so strange!"

"Don't listen to her," Quinn assured Keeley. "Because I'm having the time of my life."

CHAPTER 3

As the two suns rose several days later, Gemma grudgingly rolled out of bed. She dragged on leggings, bound her breasts, and pulled on a loose shirt. She didn't bother with boots but instead wrapped protective linens around the balls of her feet and the heels. Before walking out the door, she put on her sword belt and added all her weapons. Her swords, her knives, her axe, and as a final touch a sack of heavy rocks.

She groaned in misery at the last bit but she believed it was necessary to her training. If she could move with all this crap, she could move carrying anything during a battle.

With a last heavy sigh, she opened the bedroom door but quickly stopped. Her sister Ainsley was standing there with her bow hanging from her shoulder, a quiver of arrows hanging from the belt around her waist.

"Learning the bow, are we?" Gemma asked her sister with a small smile. "How adorable."

"Yes, very adorable. Of course, I've been learning since I was three and now I'm nineteen so I've advanced a bit since those *adorable* days."

"You're nineteen now? When did that happen?"

"*Anyway*," her sister went on, "you need to talk to Archie."

Gemma walked past Ainsley and started toward the stairs, tossing over her shoulder, "Talk to him about what?"

"He's been telling the older kids they'll have to cut the younger kids' throats should we be invaded."

Gemma stopped and faced her younger sister. "He said . . . what?"

"What part of that statement was not clear? Because I feel I was quite clear."

"Why are you telling *me*? Tell Mum and Da."

"Tell Da, he'll stab his brother in the face. Tell Mum . . . she'll make Da stab his brother in the face. Keeley will start screaming. I tried talking to Archie myself but I don't think he takes me seriously."

"Why not?"

"I have no idea. I mean, some days I'm not sure anyone even notices I'm in the room, much less that I'm part of—"

"Forget it, I'll talk to him myself."

"—the family."

"What did you say?" Gemma asked as she again moved toward the stairs.

"Nothing. Nice rocks by the way."

"Always the smartass."

Gemma headed down the three flights to the main hall.

Why was Uncle Archie the way he was? It was as if he went out of his way to test the gods themselves. Although even she had to admit, she'd underestimated Uncle Archie. When they'd first arrived here, this was nothing but an abandoned longhouse briefly taken over by the bastards who had invaded the town. When Keeley had taken over she'd tasked Archie with reinforcing it and the surrounding territory against any attacks. It was really just something to keep their father's insane brother busy while the rest of Keeley's inner circle made bigger, more important plans.

Then, one day, dwarven stone masons had arrived. Apparently their uncle had great connections with them. They'd met for several weeks in one of the nearby houses. Anytime Gemma walked by, she could hear arguing. Angry arguing that involved cursing and threats.

But when the work began, it was a sight to behold. It was like nothing she'd seen before. There had been no simple reinforcing of gates or adding to battlements. Oh, no. One morning, they all left the longhouse for their daily routines, and when they returned later . . . they suddenly had a three-story tower sturdy enough to withstand boulders hurled at it with great speed. The simple wood gates were turned into massive steel walls that surrounded so much of the nearby territory that the small town became a city that needed a home. Some changes took weeks and months but others took mere days or even *a* day. The dwarf masons had tools that allowed them to build certain things in a matter of hours. At first, Gemma assumed those sorts of things would be . . . weak. Merely placeholders until something more permanent could be built. She quickly learned how wrong she was.

She also learned that the stonemason dwarves weren't any friendlier to the centaurs than the blacksmith dwarves. And that the centaurs enjoyed kicking the dwarves with their back legs as if it was an accident while the stonemason dwarves enjoyed dropping their big, short-handled hammers on the centaurs' hooved feet.

"Sorry!" they'd each toss out as those "accidents" happened.

Keeley, Gemma, and their father eventually had to stop more fights between the two species than they'd ever had to break up between rabid pit dogs and wild hogs from the hills.

Of course, Gemma now understood that her uncle wasn't merely insane. He was also an engineering genius. He'd accomplished in two years with twenty dwarves what most humans would be lucky to do with one hundred men in fifty years.

When Gemma arrived in the main hall, her parents were already awake. Her siblings were at the dining table, most of them complaining about the early hour. Except those who had a future in farming; they were eating their food quickly so they could join their father in the fields and help him feed the pigs.

Her mother stopped her. She kissed her on both cheeks before adding two more rocks to her sack.

"Do you hate me so?" Gemma demanded.

"Don't be weak. I used to carry more when I was your age."

"You carry more now. And you used to carry the same when you were eight."

"Your grandmother was very demanding," Emma Smythe reminded Gemma, carefully tucking the stones into her sack and tying it shut. "I'm much nicer than her or my sisters. They think I'm not tough enough on you and your siblings."

Gemma couldn't help but smile despite the extra weight. "But they don't have Keeley."

"Exactly." Her mother stood in front of her now, her grin just as wide. "They don't have Keeley." And Emma Smythe wasn't talking about Keeley the queen. Although proud of what Keeley was doing at the moment, her parents were much prouder of her work as a blacksmith. Before all this queenly shit, Keeley's reputation as a blacksmith had begun to grow far outside their little town. Swords for hire had started to come from all around to get weapons from her and her alone. For a Smythe, that was a high honor.

"I'll see you in a couple of hours," Gemma said, leaning over her father so she could kiss him on the forehead before running out the door.

She turned left as soon as she was outside and ran past the local tradespeople setting up their tents and tables. Some soldiers nodded in her direction. Those who reported directly to her saluted and she acknowledged them with a nod but kept moving. Once she was free of town, she moved through the trees and headed toward the hills. She charged up and down the slopes, through the smaller forests and streams. She didn't stop until she hit the Green Mountains. It was a smallish mountain range some distance from town, which Archie liked—"Makes it harder for them to attack us from behind . . . so we won't have to kill the children," he'd muttered, walking by her one day. At the time she really hadn't thought too much about what he'd said, but now she was really starting to worry that his concern for his nieces and nephews was becoming an unhealthy obsession.

Gemma ran halfway up the middle mountain and stopped. She took a moment to catch her breath before pulling out her sword and axe and dropping to one knee. Burying the head of the axe and the tip of the sword into the ground, she sent out her prayers to the main god of her order, Morthwyl. But, as usual, her plea felt hollow and empty.

Before the past year, it always felt as if she were talking directly to her god. It felt as if he stood before her listening to her words. She could almost feel his hand on her head or her shoulder.

Then . . . nothing. She hadn't lost faith. That was different. She knew her god existed. She knew he still had a hand in the workings of this world and others. Instead, it was as if he'd turned his back on her and walked away. Yet she continued to pray to him every day. Each kill she made during a battle, she offered to him. Each waning moon, she fasted in his honor. And, most importantly, when she managed to raise a body to do her bidding, she knew it was through the power of his spells.

So why did she feel he had deserted her? What had she done to disappoint him? Was it leaving her order to protect her family? The monks of her order would probably say yes, but she knew what she had done was the right thing. Letting her order murder her family—which was what they would have had to do if they'd come for Beatrix—would have gone against everything she believed as a Smythe and as a war monk. She'd followed her gut, because she had to. It was her only option.

And, two years later, here she was . . . praying to a god who no longer heard her.

With a sigh, Gemma got to her feet and went through her daily drills. She'd been doing them since she'd started with her order, working to perfect them each and every day. At first, she'd thought she'd get bored by them. The first year, she *did* get bored. But now, all these years later, she found them comforting. The one thing she could rely on.

After finishing her drills, she returned her weapons to her belts and started running up the mountain paths again. She decided to go higher than usual. Which was especially hard, now that she was carrying the extra weight. But she was in the mood. It was a beautiful, cool day and she needed the extra push.

She wasn't trying for the very top—the air was simply too thin—but the mid slopes would do nicely and would provide the added benefit of revealing where their security was weakest down below.

When she reached the point she wanted, Gemma placed her hands on her hips and gasped desperately for breath. She looked out over the town but her legs began to cramp from the climb, so she turned in a circle, her breath still coming out in harsh—

It came at her from a mountainside burrow she hadn't seen, the size nearly double that of any male. Giant fangs snapped in her face, the creature's growls and barks startling her, making her swing her arms out, hands raised to protect her face. Those damn blazing eyes of fire forced her back and back . . . right off the edge of the mountain.

Keeley was bathing with the centaurs in the Eagle River when something crashed into the water from above. She brought her arms up to protect her face from the deluge, assuming it was some poor animal dropped by an eagle or owl that had lost its prey. It was called Eagle River for a reason.

Until Quinn sauntered forward, his tail splashing water on his rump as he stared at the spot where the water had been disturbed.

"What's wrong?" Laila asked her brother.

Frowning, he glanced at Keeley. "I think that was your sister."

"*What?*"

He abruptly shifted to his human form and dove into the water. It took him a bit, but when he returned to the surface, he dragged a sputtering Gemma with him.

"Gods!" Keeley cried out, swimming over to the pair and helping Quinn drag her sister to the river's edge.

Once they got her on the dirt, Keeley first ripped off that stupid bag of rocks before placing Gemma down onto her stomach so her sister could bring up any water trapped in her lungs. Which turned out to be quite a bit.

"Are you all right?" Keeley finally managed to ask.

"*Those fucking beasts!*" Gemma screamed.

"She seems fine," Quinn drily remarked before sitting on the ground.

Keeley immediately looked up at the sky. Ever since she'd discovered the existence of actual dragons in the world, she'd been terrified they'd attack her lands. She still had nightmares. The one she'd met had been huge! And spit lava! And could talk! Of course, why would a dragon drop Gemma when it could have just gobbled her up in one bite? Like a snack.

"What kind of beast?" Keeley asked her sister. "A dragon? Did you see a dragon?"

"Not a dragon!" Gemma gasped out. "Your damn dogs!"

"Wolves," Quinn corrected.

Slowly, Keeley refocused on her sister. "The wolves? The wolves aren't around. Unless you've been bothering that nice new pack about six leagues away. But they're just normal wolves. You should leave them alone."

"*Your* wolves," her sister insisted.

"My wolves aren't here."

"They're up in the mountains."

Keeley blinked. "How did you know that?"

"*Because one of them attacked me!*" Gemma screamed hysterically.

"*Well, what were you doing up there anyway?*" Keeley screamed back.

The siblings glared at each other until they heard Quinn's raucous laughter.

When they focused their glares on him, he barely managed to get out to Gemma, "I . . . I love how you . . . you thought . . . she was going to be on your side about . . . about . . . this."

Then he fell back on the ground and continued to laugh.

Gemma hated to admit it, but the bastard was right. Her sister was *never* on her side when it came to those fucking demon wolves.

She'd already been in training at the monastery when Keeley had discovered the first one alone in the woods near the family farm. A pup being tormented by priests trying to destroy the demon. Gemma was sure those priests could have made it a quick, clean kill but had probably delayed it, hoping to bring themselves closer to their chosen god. A mistake her sister would never understand or forgive. Gemma could imagine the whole thing and knew her sister well enough to know she'd thought she was saving an innocent soul, not rescuing the offspring of a pit demon.

From what her siblings told her, Keeley brought the pup home until its wounds had healed but returned daily to where she'd found it until the mother came back looking for its young. Smiling at the fierce-looking mother that stood as tall as Keeley despite being on all fours, Keeley had handed the pup off to its imposing mother, expecting never to see the creature again. But the pup did not stay away. He returned to her again and again, and soon began to bring friends. All of them with fire for eyes and blood for drool.

Yet she treated them as she would any friendly wolf or bear or deer. It was Keeley's way.

Gemma's mother wasn't really a fan of those wolves lurking in the forests around their home but her father took to them immediately. Although he wouldn't let them near his pigs. Apparently that was a problem until Keeley told them to leave her father's pigs alone . . . and they did. Her father was quite pleased, but Gemma didn't understand why no one saw a problem with wolves understanding the meaning of human words.

These same demons had followed Keeley and her family to their new lands. They watched over the territory and the queen, so it was strange when the whole group of them seemed to vanish one day without warning. Even stranger that Keeley didn't say a word about it.

It made sense, though—now—that Keeley had known exactly what had happened to the wolves that were as close to her as their father and her centaur.

"Why are they up in the mountains, Keeley?" Gemma asked her sister.

She shrugged. "The pack has a new litter. They were born about eight weeks ago. They went up there to keep the pups safe until they were old enough to care for themselves."

Appalled, Gemma demanded, "You're letting them breed?"

"Letting them? It's their right. Just like it's our right."

"In one of the hells. They can breed in one of their hells, but not here."

"That is the most ridiculous thing I've ever heard from you, and I've heard many ridiculous things!"

Gemma tried to get up but she'd hit the river hard and her body wasn't exactly cooperating. An arm appeared in front of her. She grabbed it, using the support—and Quinn—to get herself to her feet.

"Do you think I'm just a horrible person?" Gemma asked her sister.

"Yes."

"*Keeley*." To Gemma's surprise, this came from Quinn himself.

"You don't mean to be," Keeley clarified. "And you never were before. The old Gemma would have found wolves with eyes of fire interesting and strange. Something to explore. But then you became a monk and everything now is pure evil or not evil. There's no in between for you anymore. And the world we live in is all about the in between."

"You think the denizens of the hells are in between?"

"I think all animals are in between. The she-bear that mauled Old Matheson wasn't evil. She just thought he was a threat to her cubs. The wild boar that kept eating Da's piglets wasn't evil, it was just hungry. Remember? That was the bad year we had the drought. Or the time Da chopped that bear's head off and roasted it on a spit, he was just pissed it kept eating the piglets. Da wasn't evil then either. So do I think the wolf female chased you off the mountain because you were too close to her pups and she saw you as a threat? Yes. I do. I'd see you as a threat, too, if I was her. It's the in between, Sister. You used to understand that."

Keeley shrugged and walked off, while one of the centaurs handed her a long piece of linen to dry her wet body.

"Why's my sister naked around a bunch of bathing centaurs?" Gemma asked Quinn.

"I told her centaurs don't care about the naked human body."

"Did you say that just because you wanted to see her naked?"

"I had to. The size of her shoulders and thighs absolutely fascinated me. Then it just became a regular thing."

"Caid doesn't mind?"

"Not so far."

"I'll make sure to point it out to him."

"Why do you hate me so much?"

She started back toward the mountain so she could return to her training. "You make it so easy."

"Hey!" he called out and she faced him. "How far up were you?"

Gemma lifted her face to the sky, squinting against the two bright suns. She found the spot and pointed. Quinn's gaze followed and he snorted.

"The gods really do protect you monks, don't they?"

"What do you mean?"

"Woman, you never should have survived that fall. At least not without a broken back. And yet you walk away."

Gemma stared at the spot she'd fallen from and realized that the centaur had a point. Whether she'd fallen in the river or a giant pile of pillows, she should have been injured if not outright killed. And yet . . . she felt relatively fine. No broken bones. No internal damage, from what she could tell. Her brain seemed relatively intact since she'd had an entire philosophical debate with her sister on evil.

Did her god still protect her?

"Oh . . . and, Brother Gemma," Quinn called out to her, his centaur body returning to the river, "feel free to join us at your leisure whenever we are bathing."

Rolling her eyes, Gemma snorted and once again returned to her training.

Quinn was walking past one of the buildings under construction when he heard Gemma's uncle talking. He glanced in and saw the stonemason dwarves working hard and the Smythe siblings listening to their uncle. But instead of their uncle explaining how the dwarves could work so fast and so well, he was demonstrating on one of the younger boys how to expertly cut a throat.

It took a second to sink in, so Quinn had passed the building before he realized what he'd just seen. But he stopped and spun back around.

"Archie!" he barked when he stood in the doorway.

"What?" the man asked, with his nephew's chin lifted up and a wooden dagger used for training pressed against the boy's throat.

"What are you doing?"

"Doing about what?" he asked, confused.

Quinn gestured at Archie with both hands.

"Oh, this."

"Yes. That."

"In case we're invaded. Figured the children should know how to die with honor."

"Okay." Quinn quickly pointed at a dwarf who was standing near him and warned, "If you drop that hammer on my foot, I will stomp you to death with my hooves. Understand?"

The dwarf moved away and Quinn walked outside into the bustling town. Every day more shops and stands opened up and more tradespeople moved in with new wares to offer. Quinn loved it. It reminded him of home.

Focusing intently, he finally heard what he was listening for and followed the sound until he reached the stall. An exhausted Gemma stood there buying a cooked chicken and bread. Her meal after training. She could get the same thing from the castle cook but she liked to buy her dinner from the townspeople sometimes.

"We have a problem," he told her.

"What now?"

"Archie."

Her eyes crossed but she followed him back to the construction site. At this point, Archie was letting the children take turns slicing each other's throats with the wooden dagger. Horrified, Gemma shoved the paper-wrapped food into Quinn's arms, not warning him it was still hot, and rushed into the room.

She grabbed the mock blade from her youngest sister.

"What the unholy hells are you doing?"

"Teaching the children how to—"

"No!" she told her uncle. "Just no. You are not teaching them that."

"They have to learn. What if we are invaded?"

"Make sure they can't get through our castle walls, old man. Do something other than teach our children to accept death?"

Archie placidly gazed at Gemma, then the children.

After a full minute, he said, "It's smarter for them to accept death."

The dwarves laughed, so Quinn flashed the fangs all battle centaurs possessed and they disappeared into the walls. Unlike the blacksmith dwarves, they weren't ready to jump into a fight unless absolutely necessary. For blacksmith dwarves, it was always necessary.

Gemma turned to the oldest among the children at the moment. "Isadora, take the children home, please."

Isadora did as ordered and Gemma waited until her siblings were out of hearing range. When she felt confident they were mostly alone, she faced her uncle and punched him in the throat.

As he grabbed his neck with both hands, trying hard to breathe, she stepped in close and said, "I'm doing my best to save you from the wrath of my mother and Keeley. But if you do this again or you even mention an honorable death or a death of any kind around the children, I will personally disembowel you. A skill that is taught to every war monk novitiate. So do not fuck with me, Uncle. Have I made myself clear?"

Archie didn't answer. He was too busy bending over, coughing, still attempting to breathe.

Gemma grabbed him by his hair, right at the base of his neck, and yanked his head back. "Have I made myself clear?"

He nodded since he could not speak.

"Excellent."

Gemma returned to Quinn's side, scooping her food out of his arms.

"That could have been handled . . . nicer," he suggested.

"Then next time you may want to tell someone who *didn't* spend ten years of her life with war monks."

She did have a point.

He watched Gemma disappear among the townsfolk outside. When he turned back around, Archie was glaring at him, but all he could do was shrug and mutter, "Yeah, sorry. Didn't know it was going to go like that. Guess she has a lot on her mind right now. But, you know. Maybe not so much death with the children. Just a thought." Archie's eyes narrowed.

"All right . . . well. See ya!"

Quinn walked out, briefly stopping when a dwarven stone hammer dropped from the scaffolding right above his head, barely missing him.

Those dwarf bastards.

Keeley wasn't sure her sister would want anything to do with her after their morning argument but once she'd completed her training, Gemma didn't seem to have any problem joining her in the study to go over the latest reports sent to them concerning King Marius and their sister Beatrix. He was building armies in the south with mercenaries and terrifying the locals at the border between their territories.

At the moment, Marius had the much-richer lands of the east, with their thousands upon thousands of acres of grain fields owned by wealthy royals. Meanwhile, Keeley had the more treacherous hill territories filled with wild game and dangerous tribes. But she'd already begun to build alliances with many of those tribes. Although even she knew some of those were tenuous at best. She had to tread carefully but she found the challenge a little thrilling, not that she'd mention that to anyone but Caid. Gemma already thought she was "too reckless" and Laila insisted on seeing her as "unrealistic" and "naïve." Honestly, the only one who seemed to have any faith in her outside of her doting parents was Quinn, which seemed just . . . wrong.

Keeley discreetly glanced up from her papers at Gemma. These days her younger sister seemed nothing but angry. Angry at Beatrix? Definitely. Angry at her precious gods? Perhaps. Angry at Keeley? When wasn't she? But there was more to it, Keeley just hadn't figured out what was at the heart of it all. It had started months ago. They could all feel it. But then the day came when Gemma had walked downstairs in brown leather leggings, with a brown fur cape. It was the drabbest thing Keeley had ever seen anyone in her family wear and, except for Beatrix, no one in her family gave a damn about fashion at all.

Eventually their mother outfitted Gemma in proper chainmail but she hadn't put her monk gear back on in more than a year. Keeley never thought she'd miss any of that shit, but she found she did miss the way it had made her sister glow a bit. Now her sister was always sad or angry or sad and angry. It had gotten to the point that Keeley almost hated being around her. If she had to hear her sigh dramatically one more time . . .

"So, what do you both think?"

Keeley frowned, exchanging confused glances with Gemma before they both looked across the room. Ainsley leaned against a bookcase. She'd grown into a beautiful girl with all that long red-blond hair and bright green eyes, but she was a strange one. Always sort of lurking around. She hung out in trees a lot.

"How long have you been standing there?" Keeley asked.

"Twenty minutes. Talking . . . to *you*."

"You were talking?" Gemma blinked. "About what?"

Ainsley briefly closed her eyes. Took in a breath, let it out.

When she opened her eyes, she said, "All right. Let's try this again, shall we?"

"There's that tone," Gemma muttered.

"I was thinking perhaps I could train with some of the new army recruits. Perhaps learn how to handle a sword. I'm proficient at the bow, but useless with a sword."

Keeley and Gemma stared at Ainsley for a bit, then at each other.

After a few moments, they couldn't help themselves . . . they burst out laughing.

"You're a baby!" Keeley yelped.

"We're not giving you a sword!" Gemma added.

"You don't give babies swords!" Keeley agreed.

"Both of you were using swords before you were nineteen."

"And when you're nineteen—"

"*I am nineteen*," Ainsley snapped.

Keeley frowned, looked at Gemma. "When did she turn nineteen?"

"I don't know. We should ask Mum."

Clearing her throat, Keeley suggested, "Perhaps once you get good with the bow."

"I am good with the bow."

"No. Seriously *good* with the bow. Not just Da telling you you're good with the bow."

Without taking a step away from Keeley and Gemma, Ainsley brought her bow off her shoulder, pulled an arrow from her quiver, aimed out the window near the table her sisters sat at, and let the arrow fly.

Keeley snorted. "What the fuck is that supposed to—"

"Thanks, luv!" their father called from outside.

"Welcome, Da!" Ainsley called back without moving . . . or blinking. That's when Keeley realized her sister never raised her voice. She rarely showed anger. Or happiness. Or anything. Unlike the rest of the Smythe children, she didn't really react to much.

Gemma pushed her chair back and went to the window. She leaned out and when she came back in, her eyes were wide.

"She hit a falcon."

"I actually nicked his wing," Ainsley explained. "Da wants a falcon. Now he has one once he helps this bird to heal."

Again, Keeley cleared her throat. "That's just—"

"Luck? You think that was luck? Fine."

With an arrow already nocked, she aimed it at a spot in the room and unleashed it. It went through a small hole in the wall.

The intense cursing coming from inside the wall shocked them all and Keeley jumped up and went to the spot with her hammer. She hit the stone a few times until she and Gemma could remove chunks of it with their hands, revealing one of the dwarven stonemasons.

Coughing from the rock dust while trying to pull the arrow from his leg, he forced a smile at the queen.

"Your Majesty."

"That one has been spying on you for a month," Ainsley pointed out. "Although they've all been spying on you a bit, Keeley. They like watching you. You and your hammer."

Keeley reacted automatically. "Ewwwww."

"My queen," a servant said as he entered the room, stopping when he saw the partially destroyed wall and the wounded stonemason dwarf. "Uhhh."

"What is it, Carl?"

"Uh, Lady Laila asks that you come to the main hall. The riders you sent out the other day have returned."

Grateful to have something else—*anything* else—to deal with at this moment, Keeley and Gemma rushed for the door, causing the servant to practically fall to the ground in an attempt to get out of their way. Keeley caught him and put him back on his feet before she caught up to Gemma. They strode down the passages together until they reached the main hall. But they both stopped short when they saw their mother and father sitting at the dining table; Caid, Quinn, and Laila stood next to the table along with three of the riders. It wasn't the missing riders that concerned them. It was everyone's expression.

"What?" Keeley asked. "What's wrong?"

Laila motioned to the riders and they each dropped a large burlap bag to the ground.

"What's that?" Gemma asked.

"What's left."

"What's left of what?"

"The monks. The priests."

Keeley took a step back but Gemma's body jerked forward. "What? *What?*"

"These are skulls," Laila stated, pointing at one bag. "These are some bones," she said, gesturing to another. "And these are just some bits. Some ash."

"No. That's not possi—No."

"Are any left?" Keeley asked, horrified by what she was being told.

"The witches survived," Quinn said. "The reason the rider who went to them isn't here is because he had to go to the healers in the village."

Gemma let out a long sigh. "What did the witches do to him?"

Quinn fought hard not to smile. "They gave him a tail."

"A what?"

"A rat tail. It moves on its own and everything."

Keeley's lip curled. "Ew! What is wrong with everyone?"

"Apparently those witches were not friendly."

"That poor man!"

Unconcerned about the man and his rat tail, it seemed, Gemma cut in, "What are the witches doing now?"

"Going underground," Laila stated. "Literally, I believe. Traveling through tunnels and moving to safer territory."

"And all the artifacts of the monks and priests . . . ?"

"Gone. Most of the walls of the churches and temples were not even left standing. They were destroyed down to the last stone."

"There's no doubt then. These religious orders are being specifically targeted."

"Just as you said, Gemma. This isn't about gold or silver. This is about power."

"No, it isn't just about power," a soft voice said from behind them and they turned to see the pacifist monk coming from the passage that led to the kitchens. "This is also about desecration."

"But why?" Keeley's mother asked. "Why would anyone do that?"

"To destroy our beliefs and the beliefs of the populace," he said, walking toward them. "To make room for another. Someone else's chosen god."

"What's one more god?" Keeley asked. "There's room for as many gods as we could possibly want."

"Not for a god that wants to rule all."

Keeley began to pace. She knew the monk was right. A power-hungry man was dangerous enough. But a power-hungry god . . . that was a nightmare. Put the two together? She had to do something, and she had to do it now.

"We need to send out battle units immediately. Any sect or order that wants our protection will have it. They can stay here. Now, Brother—" It suddenly occurred to her she didn't know the monk's name.

Shocked that she was actually looking to him for something, he said, "Emmanuel."

"Brother Emmanuel. As a pacifist monk, you can be the man in the middle, so to speak. When these groups come in, I will need your help keeping those who aren't friends away from each other. Those who are able to get along can room together. You can also work with my uncle to arrange for sleeping quarters. Do you mind doing that?"

It was the first smile they'd seen from the man since the day they'd all met him. "That would bring great joy to my life, Your Highness. To help you with this."

"Or you could call me Keeley. Since we'll be working together a lot. Anyway, just do your best." She motioned to several nearby soldiers. "Get my generals."

She faced Gemma. "Beatrix?"

Gemma thought deep on that, but it was their father who actually answered for them, shocking them all. Because he hadn't spoken of the wayward Smythe in some time.

"The only way this is Beatrix is if there's some deal involved."

And they knew he was right. Of course, then the question became . . . what deal?

CHAPTER 4

"Do you know what I find disappointing?"

Agathon, the Follower of Her Word, lifted his head from the work before him. He thought his expression was flat. He'd always thought he'd taught himself to have no expression at all. But maybe he had lost that skill after two years with Queen Beatrix. Or maybe she could see right through him as no other royal ever had before. She did seem to have that skill.

"I don't mean *you*," she said after a long sigh. "So you can stop looking so panicked. It's everyone else. Everyone *else* disappoints me."

"How is that, my lady?" he bravely asked. Bravely because he rarely questioned anyone. But the queen seemed to appreciate his questions. Or maybe she was just lonely and desperate for someone to show interest in her words.

Then again . . . he didn't think she was capable of being lonely. She seemed to have no real desire or need for another soul.

"Because," she replied while staring out the window, "all they need to do is play their roles and yet they do not cooperate. Forcing me to do things I find rather distasteful . . . but necessary."

He was surprised. He didn't think she found anything distasteful. Except clutter. She didn't like clutter.

Agathon opened his mouth to ask more questions but the study door slammed open and the king stormed in.

Dropping his head low, Agathon started toward the door, keeping his back to the walls and slinking along, desperate to leave as quickly as he could manage, but Beatrix stopped him with two words.

"No. Stay." Slowly the queen turned and looked at her husband of two years. It was, perhaps, the strangest relationship Agathon had ever seen and he'd been the Keeper of His Word for the Old King himself. A man with many wives and concubines and offspring. Most dead since the day of his final breath.

King Marius, the Wielder of Hate, towered over his tiny wife, his face full of rage. It was rumored that their first night together had been a nightmare for the queen but Agathon truly doubted that story. He wasn't even sure the queen had ever had carnal knowledge of any man or woman. The queen seemed to have no interest. And although that had never stopped the Old King or any of his sons before, King Marius seemed . . . wary of his bride. Not that Agathon blamed the man. Agathon greatly doubted the king would risk the cock he so greatly loved just so he could say he'd thrust it between his wife's thighs.

Of course, wary was the safest stance for anyone when dealing with Queen Beatrix.

"Yes, my king?" she replied with no hint of emotion. No fear. No panic. No interest. No anything. Nothing more than . . . politeness?

"What have you done?" he demanded. "*What have you done?*"

The bellow would have any other member of the kingdom running for their life. Not that it would do any good. When the king bellowed like that, his blade always followed, tearing through a gut or lopping off a head.

But with Beatrix, the king simply bellowed and waited, his hands balled into tight, angry fists.

And yet, even though her hair blew back a bit from his explosion, the queen did not flinch. She never flinched. Agathon was beginning to believe she was incapable of flinching.

"First," she said calmly, "I'd ask that you explain to me what you're talking about."

The king began to pace around the bedroom while Agathon pushed himself into a corner to avoid the king's wrath.

"You're having monks killed? Nuns? Mages? *Witches?*" the

king finally demanded. "Monasteries and churches burned? Their treasures stolen?"

Agathon couldn't help but gawk at the queen. Could she have been so reckless? So crazed? She was bold, it was true. Especially when it came to waging war. And the king, out of fear, gave her more leeway than any king had ever given his queen. But to toy with the gods in such a manner? To kill their earthly representatives?

Beatrix said nothing until the king again faced her and yelled, "Well? *Answer me!*"

The queen studied her husband for several long moments, but it wasn't to craft an answer. She never did that. She was boldly direct. To the point of recklessness, in Agathon's opinion.

No. Beatrix was analyzing.

"I never did any of that," she finally informed the king.

His eyebrows went up in surprise. "You didn't?"

"No. Would it have benefited us, if I had?"

"No!"

"Just checking."

The king began to pace again. "If not you then . . . your sister?"

The queen suddenly laughed. It was such a surprising sound, coming from her, of all beings, that both Agathon and the king froze and looked at her. Almost as if they were wary deer that had just heard a branch crack in the forest.

"*My* sister?" the queen said, still laughing. She waved her hand. "That's a good one." Her laughter died away. "No. Not Keeley. Never Keeley. If she knows about any of this, I'm sure she's running around attempting to fix it."

"Disgusted by such an affront to the gods?" the king asked.

"More like appalled by the harm to all the innocent people," she said with an eye roll of annoyance. "My sister, always attempting to save the world.

"Of course," the queen continued, "if it wasn't us and it wasn't Keeley . . . who was it?"

The angry redness that had covered the king's face drained, leaving him looking pale and afraid.

"Oh, gods," he groaned.

"What?" She looked back and forth between the king and Agathon. "The twins?" she suggested. "They must need gold and silver for their pathetic little army. I heard they're losing men every day."

When her gaze rested on Agathon, he could only shake his head.

"Then who?"

"Cyrus," the king replied before he dropped into a chair, resting his elbows on his knees and his head in his hands.

"Cyrus the Honored? The one who didn't kill any of the Old King's wives? Or any of his half brothers? The one that half your father's army left with as soon as the old bastard died? *He's* killing your precious monks and priests? Destroying their temples?"

The king leaned back in the chair until his head could rest on the wall behind him.

"My precious brother earned his name because he followed a strict code of honor. He never wavered from it. Everything he did was in the name of his one god. Or, as he called it, his one *true* god."

"Who only worships one god?"

"My brother. Some cult his mother belonged to. She infected him with that stupidity. But her son took the teachings many steps further. He has a strong code, but living under that code, he made my father look like a soft, fluffy bunny."

The queen glanced at Agathon and he gave a small nod, letting her know that her husband's words were true. Agathon had attempted to flee with Cyrus's army when the Old King died but he'd been unable to get out of the castle. He believed he could pretend to worship any god Cyrus wanted him to, and Cyrus wasn't actively attempting to kill the Old King's direct bloodline . . . unlike Marius. Besides, Agathon had had no other choices. The twins were as volatile as Marius, and traveling on his own would only make Agathon a ready victim for any thieves on the road.

But now that the restraint of the Old King had been lifted from Cyrus, Agathon wondered if something truly terrible had been unleashed in Marius's half brother.

"All this time," the king continued, "when we didn't hear much from my brother, I thought maybe he'd found another territory to focus on. Now I think maybe he's preparing to come after the crown. We're going to have to worry about him *and* your sister."

Instead of appearing worried, though, the queen smiled. And, gods love him, the king looked as Agathon felt. Panicked.

Because of that smile.

It wasn't something she did. She had a fake smile she used on the royals who visited but it was only to placate those who provided soldiers and gold. Her true smile, she kept to herself. But on those very rare occasions when she did unleash it, the recipient was unsettled.

And both Agathon and the king . . . they were unsettled.

They both leaned away from her as she raised her forefinger and waved it with that smile on her face.

"This is perfect."

"How?" the king asked. "How is this perfect?"

"First, we send out troops under your seal, inviting all monks, priests, nuns, witches, whatever, to our castle and grounds for their protection."

"Uhhhh, my lady . . ." Agathon regretfully interrupted.

But Beatrix only had to look at him once and roll her eyes, before she amended, "Fine. Send it under *my* seal if it will make them feel safer."

"You have a seal?" the king asked.

"Of course I have a seal."

"I never gave you a seal."

"Can I finish?" She didn't wait for him to answer. "We bring them here, we give them all sanctuary. Now, my sister has probably already started this process because I'm sure she's just soooo upset about the killings."

The king frowned at her flippant tone.

"Is . . . is she going to slaughter them all once she has them in her clutches or something?"

"Oh, no! She'll absolutely give them protection. Trust me, I know my sister. She is *very* upset about all this."

"But you don't care."

"I don't care at all."

"Then why are we doing it?"

"Because this puts religious orders and their gods in our debt. Make sure you get as many war monk orders as you can, Agathon."

"Yes, Your Majesty."

"You know what else?" she asked the king.

"Other than that you're incredibly disturbing?"

"Yes, other than that."

"What?"

"My sister, warrior for good that she is, can't stay away from a fight. If Cyrus is killing innocents, Keeley won't stop until she destroys him."

"Cyrus will destroy her first."

"It doesn't matter," Beatrix said with a laugh. "That's the beauty. It doesn't matter if she kills him, he kills her, or they kill each other. When it's all over . . ." She shrugged. "We destroy what's left and take the crown. We take it all."

"You mean *I* destroy what's left and take the crown. *I* take it all. Right?"

There was that smile again. And it spread across her face like leprosy across an infected body.

"Absolutely."

The queen turned away from them and walked to the window she'd been staring out when the king first stormed in.

"Get to work, Agathon," Beatrix tossed over her shoulder, her gaze once again focused outside; her mind furiously working on her future plans. "There's much to be done and so little time. Dear Cyrus the Honored seems to have a calling from his god."

CHAPTER 5

Her head was dragged up from the ground while blood poured onto the cobblestones. She was grabbed by both arms and lifted to her knees. She was too weak to fight. Too weak to speak. Too weak even to cry. Carried to the stake to join her already burning brothers. Flames surrounded her; her screams joined the others. And her loyal gods were no longer by her side. Her betrayal too great. They would never forgive her; never accept her into their halls.

Forever she would be known as the Great Betrayer and there was nothing she would be able to do about it. Except scream while she burned . . .

But one of the soldiers grabbed her, pulled her from the flames. He shook her.

"Gemma!" he screamed at her. "Gemma!" She punched at him. She would burn with her brothers. She would not be a slave to those who would kill those loyal to their gods.

"Gemma!" he called again, continuing to shake her.

She decided to fight him, even though she was covered in flames and blood and stank of betrayal.

Gemma wrapped her right arm around his throat and swung her body onto his back. She wrapped her legs around his waist and placed her left arm against her right so he couldn't break her hold. Then she tightened her grip. If she took only one more enemy with her, it would be this one. She would take this one to honor the god she had deserted. He would be her sacrifice. It might not get her into Morthwyl's hallowed halls but at least she could wander the valleys of his hells with her head held high.

The soldier no longer called her name, too busy gasping for air and desperately attempting to drag her arms off his neck.

But then Gemma was growing, expanding.

Gods! Morthwyl was making her a giant! She grew and grew, reaching amazing heights! Standing tall!

Then she saw . . . antlers? Why did she see antlers? Did she have antlers? Did she have antlers instead of a face? Would Morthwyl have done something so cruel?

No! No! She didn't want antlers for a face!

She immediately slapped her hands to her face, rubbing her fingers over the flesh, ready to rip off any antlers she might feel where skin should be. But she felt nothing but human flesh. As she continued her examination, the world beneath her shook and jerked and Gemma went flying. Away from the flames. Away from the persecution. Away from the evil soldiers and her burning brothers and into a wall that didn't move.

Gemma awoke and instantly knew she lay slumped on the battlements of her sister's castle.

Shocked and still reeling from the dream that was beginning to feel like a premonition, she looked around and saw Quinn standing a few feet away from her in his natural form. Not just as a centaur but a centaur ready to defend his kind to the death. She could see fangs, claws on his hands, and a rack of antlers that crowned the top of his head.

She could also see marks on his throat where she'd attempted to kill him.

Shifting and shaking her off had been his only option.

He moved closer to her, hooves clomping against stone.

"Rough night?" he asked.

Gemma let out a breath, and that's when she realized that a tear was slowly streaking down her cheek. She wiped it with a finger and replied, "You could say."

He jerked the head that carried an antler rack as easily as she wore a helmet. "Come on. Let's talk."

* * *

Quinn shifted back to his human form and opened the battlement door, waiting for Gemma to get off the ground and walk through. He didn't help her. Not because he was angry at her. He wasn't. But because he didn't think touching her was what she needed at the moment. He'd known her about two years now and she had never liked being coddled. By anyone. Not her siblings. Not her parents. Not the many pets that ran free around the castle.

Gemma Smythe had her own space and she let you know when you could enter it and when you couldn't. Right now, she didn't seem to want anyone too close.

She passed him silently and he followed her down the narrow staircase to the fourth floor. From there they cut through the hall to the regular staircase, which led them down to the first floor and deep into the castle to the kitchens. She sat at the big wooden table where the head cook did all the butchering and baking and yelling. The woman was feared by many because, when annoyed, she tended to throw her cleaver. She hadn't hit anyone yet, though, so Quinn didn't understand why everyone was so testy about it all.

He motioned for Gemma to sit down at the table and then got out the wine and meat pies the head cook kept hidden for him.

Quinn placed them on the table and sat on the bench beside Gemma. He didn't sit too close but he didn't sit on the other side since the table was wide and he didn't want to yell across the room.

"I'm sorry," Gemma said softly. She had her eyes shut tight and began to rub her forehead with her hands. "I don't know if that was a dream or a premonition."

"A premonition?"

"I was being burned at the stake." She dropped her hands, opened her eyes wide. "Me and my entire order. And do you know whose fault it was?"

"Whoever is killing all the monks?"

"My fault."

"Gemma, that's insane."

"Is it?"

Quinn took a bite out of one of the meat pies. That was to stifle his desire to call her an idiot.

When he was done chewing, he instead said, "You and your sister both do this, you know?"

"Do what?"

"Take responsibility that's not yours. When Marius wiped out your entire town, even though it was no fault of hers, Keeley still felt it was her responsibility to fix the situation. When you broke my nose, you didn't take responsibility for that. But the destruction of your order—which may or may not have actually happened—that responsibility you line up for."

"I had a premonition."

"A premonition or a dream?"

"Could be either."

"But probably only one."

"Why are you arguing with me about this?" She dismissed him with a wave and grabbed a pie. "You don't even believe in anything magickal."

"I have hooves, woman. I am magick." He pointed at her uneaten pies. "You going to eat those?"

"I am."

"All of them?"

Gemma pushed one over to him.

"I wouldn't worry," Quinn told her between bites and sips of wine. "Your sister is moving on this like all these people are loyal only to her."

"I know. I know."

"She's offering them all sanctuary. They'll be protected here."

"I *know*."

"And your sister would never let you burn."

She glanced up at him, her frown deep, juice and crumbs from the pies around her mouth. He realized it was an expression of confusion. And Quinn suddenly understood her confusion. She didn't understand why he thought she was concerned about being burned at the stake. Because she wasn't concerned. She'd burn for her brothers. Just as she'd burn for her family. Her concern was that she wouldn't burn with them.

Quinn was desperately trying to grasp her logic but he couldn't. He didn't have that kind of loyalty to . . . anyone. Maybe his sister. He could imagine dying to protect her. And their mother. But that was about it. Of course, he had never committed his sword or soul to a god. Any god.

"I need to get some sleep," Gemma said, pushing the last pie over to him and standing.

"It was just a dream," he felt the need to insist. "All this is just upsetting you right now."

"I'm sure you're right." She stepped away from the table but abruptly stopped and faced him again. "Did you follow me up there?"

"Don't flatter yourself," Quinn immediately shot back. "I was already on the battlements."

"Why?"

He continued to eat. "Eh. I'm not a big sleeper."

"What does that mean?"

Quinn shrugged. What did she think it meant?

"So you were just up there . . . doing what?"

"Just be glad I was there. You were about to go over the side."

"I was?"

"That's the only reason I grabbed you. Because this time there was no river for you to fall into."

"Well . . ."

Quinn couldn't help but smirk a little. "It's all right, you can say it. I won't tell."

"Promise?"

"On my honor."

"You have no honor."

"You should tell me anyway."

"Fine." She blew out a breath, as if this would be the hardest thing she'd ever had to do, and she'd once faced down a volcano dragon along with her sister. "Thank you for saving my life tonight."

"See? Now that wasn't so ha—"

"Shut up," she snapped before stalking out.

"Why do you toy with her so?" the head cook asked, coming into the kitchens from the back room she slept in.

"I can't help it. I know it irritates her."

"Just like me son," she said, before kissing him on the forehead. "He's irritating too."

She picked up the empty platter. "Did you get any sleep tonight?"

"Not much. But I don't need much."

Pausing, she jerked her head at where Gemma had left. "You do know—"

"I know, I know," Quinn sighed, already disgusted with himself.

"You know what?" Laila asked, walking in from another entrance. Behind her was Ainsley with an enormous deer carcass over her shoulders.

When Quinn only stared at his sister, the cook laughed. "You might as well tell her. You're going to have to eventually."

"She's right," Laila agreed. "We both know I'm only going to beat the truth out of you."

"You'll try, maybe."

The cook returned to Quinn's side, gripped his cheeks with both hands, and kissed his forehead again.

"Dumb like me son too!" she laughed.

Gemma secured her weapons and pack, then eased open her bedroom door. She checked the corridor, listened for anyone other than guards. When she didn't hear anything, she moved. Down the stairs and out through the back hallways. She nodded at the guards she passed, who barely paid attention to her. As was their way. Once outside, she again checked for signs of her family. Mostly her father. He'd be the only one up *this* early. But it was a very cold morning and he liked to snuggle up to her mum on mornings like this.

Still, it didn't hurt to be too careful.

Once comfortable all was clear, she ran to the royal stables, where her horses were kept. She went right to Dagger. But he was already saddled and out of his stall. Samuel stood beside him; he was dressed and ready as well.

Gemma shook her head and whispered, "Not this time—"

"I'm coming."

"You don't have to come, Samuel. Keeley already told you. You'll always have a place here. And she's made you head of the royal stables. She loves the way you treat the horses. She doesn't trust just anyone with that job. You'd be a fool to walk away from such a position."

"Say what you want—I'm going with you."

"You can't." She let out a breath and admitted the truth. "They may kill me, Samuel. When I return. I have no idea what awaits me when I go back."

"I know. I knew that when we left. But if you go back, I go back."

"How did you even know I was going?"

"I thought you were going back days ago. I've been waiting here the last three nights with Dagger, both of us ready to move out."

"Are you *really* sure you want to do—"

"Are we still discussing this?"

"Shhhh!" she begged, her hands raised to calm him. "You'll wake up me da. And once he's up, everyone's up. Including Keeley."

"Then I guess we'd better go."

Knowing how stubborn he could be, she grabbed Dagger's reins and led the horse out of the stables.

"Your second horse?" Samuel asked.

"Leave her." She wasn't going into battle. Just to inform her order of what was coming . . . and possibly to face her death. She only needed one horse for that.

They walked their horses through the town until they reached the inner gates. Then they mounted, rode over the bridge, and turned east. But they'd only gotten a few leagues before they were forced to stop.

"You *must* be kidding me!" Gemma exploded, glaring at the centaur standing across from her. He was in his natural form but without antlers or fangs. Just his ol' horsey self. Annoying her!

"Did you think I was going to let you ride into this danger alone?" he asked. He was doing that thing with his eyes when he attempted to look sincere. But they both knew he was *never* sincere.

Samuel raised his hand. "I'm here."

Quinn glanced at her onetime squire before refocusing on Gemma.

"You and I have grown so close over the years."

"It's been two years and, no, we haven't. And is all *this* necessary?" she asked, gesturing to the others.

Quinn looked at his sister, her cousin Keran, Cadell, Farlan, and—to Gemma's horror—Ainsley.

"They insisted."

"No, we didn't," Cadell corrected. "But you threw us out of bed—"

"And told us to move our asses," Farlan finished. "It was rude."

Keran shrugged. "I had nothing better to do."

"I did insist," Ainsley said. "Told them if they tried to leave without me, I would scream the bloody house down until Keeley was wide awake."

"I didn't insist," Laila added. "It was simply understood."

"Nothing I can do to get rid of any of you . . . is there?" Gemma asked.

The small group looked at Ainsley. She didn't bother to smirk. "Just keep in mind that Da has always praised my ability to call the hogs. The loudest hog caller in all the valleys, he used to say. Like to test me, Sister?"

CHAPTER 6

They didn't take a break until the suns came up, when they paused by a stream to water the horses.

While everyone was busy stretching and eating their first meal, Gemma grabbed Quinn by his ear and yanked him a few feet away.

"Ow! Ow! Ow! Release me, evil woman!"

"Why are you really here?" she demanded once he'd slapped her hand away.

"I thought you wouldn't want to face death alone."

"I'd prefer none of my friends to face death."

"Awwww. Are we friends?"

"No. I didn't mean you."

"Oh."

Gemma began to pace. "None of you should be here."

"I'm not sure why *you're* here. You seem pretty convinced they're going to kill you."

"I never said such a thing."

"You didn't have to, Gemma. I know the price you paid to side against them two years ago."

"They're still my brothers. And I will protect them as I would my own family."

"They're all war monks. How much protection could they need?"

"All the monks and priests I sent those messengers to were powerful in their own right and they were destroyed. Everyone has weaknesses, if one is willing to exploit them. I won't risk my brothers. I will make them the same offer that every other religious sect is getting from my sister."

"And will they accept?"

She could only shrug. "I really don't know."

"So they may accept . . . or they may draw and quarter you."

"Pretty much. Which is something I'd prefer my baby sister not to see."

"Ainsley . . . I'm honestly not sure it would bother her one way or the other."

They turned and watched Ainsley pet her horse, pressing her forehead against his snout.

"Does Beatrix like animals?" Quinn asked.

"Not at all."

"Then that makes me feel better. Horses are a very good judge of character." Quinn looked down at Gemma. "Speaking of your sisters . . . how do you think Keeley will handle all this?"

And all Gemma could do was let out a rough, "Heh," in reply.

The large wood table the family ate from every day in the main hall hit the wall and shattered into pieces. The guards looked at the parents for guidance on how they should deal with the situation but they both shook their heads. And when the uncle started to go toward his niece, the father quickly grabbed him by his long hair and yanked him back. The younger siblings watched from the safety of the second-floor stairs.

Mary's family had been surprised when she'd come home one day and said she was going to take a job as head cook with the new queen. They thought, at first, she meant with Queen Beatrix. The money was good among those royals, but Mary didn't want to get anywhere near *that* family. She'd worked for royals all her life and they were a sad group of fucks. But when the butcher had told her about this job, she couldn't resist. A blacksmith who'd become a queen . . . if nothing else, it would be interesting. And gods love the light! She'd been right.

Just watching that beast of a woman standing there, raging about her missing sister, big shoulders heaving, big thighs trembling. Queen Keeley wanted to tear the whole place apart. But Mary didn't worry. Unlike those born royal, this one wouldn't take it out on the human beings that surrounded her. She wouldn't slap a serving girl or kill a coachman simply because she could. She wouldn't beat her horse or kick a dog. Gods, the last thing she'd do was kick a dog. Instead . . . she broke a table. Then, when she realized that wasn't enough to vent her rage, she turned to her mother and said, "Mum?"

"Forge is hot and ready. Go . . . just go."

And off the queen went. To the forge that the queen's mother ran. It was the queen's mother who manufactured all the armor and weapons that the soldiers got. And Mary heard nothing but compliments from mean, hardened men who thought women were good for nothing but fucking and cleaning. Word was . . . the queen was even better than her mum at controlling fire and steel.

The uncle started to follow but the queen's mother stepped in front of him and said, "If you mention that goddamn axe, Archie—"

"She owes me an axe. And since she's going to the forge anyway . . ."

"Not a word."

"But—"

"Not. A. *Word*."

"I better get me axe out of all this drama."

"Do *not* ask my daughter for that bloody axe, old man, if you want to keep your hair. Because I'll rip it from your head."

The big uncle grinned at her. "You sexy minx, Emma-luv. You always know how to—"

"*Archie!*" bellowed Angus, his brother—and the woman's husband.

See? Entertaining as fuck.

They rode hard for three days. Only taking short breaks during the day to eat and let their horses rest, and to sleep a few hours at night before moving on.

When they were about a league away from the monastery, Quinn and the other Amichais shifted to human and mounted their horses. His large war horse grunted at his weight and he patted the stallion on the neck. "Sorry, my friend. This shouldn't be for too long, though."

Once they were about a mile away, riding along a tree-covered path, Quinn noticed that Ainsley and her horse were no longer with them. He was about to say something to Gemma when arrows rained down from the skies. None hit them directly but, instead, encircled them on all sides.

The horses reared up yet didn't panic, holding their positions. But all the long arrows surrounding them forced them into a tight circle that would make wiping them out quite easy.

"Hold, good Brothers!" Gemma called out to the trees. "I come with important news from Queen Keeley of the Hill Lands!"

"Brother Gemma?" a voice asked.

"Aye, brothers. It is I. Gemma."

They suddenly appeared, as if the trees themselves had moved out of their way.

"Traitor!" one snarled, pointing a damning finger. But another monk quickly pushed down his arm.

"Have you lost your wits, Brother?" the monk asked. "This is good Brother Gemma."

"She has betrayed us all!"

"She is still a brother and until the grand master makes such an accusation, you will treat her with the same respect we all deserve."

The angry monk sneered at Gemma in contempt, but said nothing more.

"Thank you, Brother Richard," Gemma said with a slight bow of her head.

Brother Richard winked in return and smiled before motioning to the other monks. They moved forward, pulling arrows from the ground. Gemma dismounted from her horse and the rest of them followed her lead.

"Amichais?" the monk questioned, staring specifically up at Quinn. He didn't know why. Quinn hadn't said anything. And he always felt that he was pleasant looking. Unlike his brother. Or even Cadell and Farlan.

"They are part of the queen's council," Gemma replied.

"The Amichais are part of your queen's council?"

"*My* queen's council? She is the queen of us all, Brother Richard. And she has many on her council to offer her wise guidance. Is that an issue for you?"

"It's not for me to say. But if there is a problem, I'm sure we'll all hear of it."

"We should proceed, Brother Richard," another monk called out.

The monks surrounded them, and they walked the rest of the way to the monastery.

Unlike the pacifists' monastery, the home of the Order of Righteous Valor was not what Quinn would call . . . welcoming. It wasn't a house of worship. It wasn't a place of sanctuary for those in need. If anything . . . it was a fortress.

A closed fortress. The gates locked tight. There were armed monks on the ramparts. And armed monks on horseback patrolling the surrounding forest.

The drawbridge was lowered and the gates behind it opened. They crossed over the moat. Quinn glanced down. Something was in the water below but he couldn't see what. And he honestly didn't want to know.

Once they were inside the fortress, all activity stopped and every eye focused directly on them.

A young squire was sent running to get someone in charge while the one called Brother Richard ordered, "Weapons."

"What about them?" Farlan asked.

"Hand them over."

"Over my dead carcass."

Gemma put her hand on Farlan's shoulder. "It's all right, dear friend. Give them your weapons."

"Gemma—"

"They won't harm you. Those who willingly shed their weapons upon entering our monastery are under our protection. Is that not right, Brother Richard?"

"Absolutely correct, Brother Gemma. We live and die by that commitment, friends of Brother Gemma."

Farlan growled unhappily but pulled out his swords, his axes, his daggers, his spear, his small war hammer, his large war hammer, his shield and, finally, his flail. His bow and arrows were on his saddle. The monks looked at the pile at his feet and then back at Farlan. Soon Cadell had a similar pile except he had several morning stars instead of a flail. And a crossbow instead of a bow.

The Amichais were firm believers in being ready for anything.

Quinn and his sister divested themselves of less equipment but that didn't seem to ease the monks' caution any. Then there was Keran. Who had considerably fewer weapons, probably so she could stash an incredibly large number of flasks. So many flasks that everyone gazed at her in wonder. And she only pulled those from her clothes and travel bag because one of the monks kept asking, "What's that metal thing? Is it a weapon?"

"What?" Keran asked when she finally threw down the last one. "I knew it would be a long trip."

"Really?" Gemma softly asked Quinn. "*This* is who all of you were comparing me to?"

When poor Samuel only threw down his one, barely used sword and one eating knife, one of the older monks sneered and said, "Ech. *You.* I don't know why she bothered bringing you anywhere."

Quinn grabbed Gemma's arm before she could start a good throttling. But thankfully, someone who seemed to be in charge had finally shown up. Unlike the rest of the monks in their black tunics with the bright red rune on the front, this one had on a white tunic with a red rune. He gazed at Gemma in a way that Quinn could not immediately read. Was that anger? Disappointment? Fear? Concern? Contempt? None of those? He really didn't know. But he sensed it probably wasn't good.

"Master Sergeant Alesandro," Gemma greeted him. "I bring important—"

"Yes. I know."

"Excellent. The quicker I can get an audience with the grand master on this matter, the better. It truly can't wait."

"Of course." The master sergeant smiled, but it was *not* a friendly smile. Far from it. "But you do understand the rules."

"Rules?" Laila suddenly asked. "What rules?"

"There's the question of whether Brother Gemma's a traitor or not. Many believe you are."

"But I'm not."

"That decision will be made by the grand master."

"Fine. Whatever. I need to talk to him anyway."

"But don't forget. You are on sanctified ground," the master sergeant pointed out. "That makes anyone in this territory subject to our rules and laws and punishments. None of which can be overruled by the laws of any king . . . or queen."

Eyes wide, Laila turned to Gemma. "Is that true?"

Gemma shrugged. "Pretty much."

"And you came here anyway?"

"Yes."

Laila glanced around before asking Gemma, "Even though they seem to think you're a traitor?"

"I'm not."

"But they think you are."

"But I'm not."

Quinn leaned down and said to Gemma, "I'd move if I were you."

"Why—*owwwww! What the fuck was that for?*" she yelled at Laila.

"Quinn, tell Gemma what that slap to the back of the head was for."

"Bad decision-making."

"And how do you know that, big Brother?"

"Because I've received many such slaps over the years for my own bad decision-making."

"Exactly." Laila turned her head, looked directly at Gemma. "*Exactly.*"

CHAPTER 7

Brother Katla led her battalion to the monastery. The draw-bridge was pulled up so Brother Shona called up to those on the ramparts to lower it. Her brother Kir—not just Brother Kir, but her twin brother Kir—rode on her left.

At one time Katla and Kir had been called Katla and Kir No One. They'd actually been grateful that No One was their surname. Because it was better than "Bastard," which some orphaned children had. But because they didn't know where they'd come from or who their parents had been, they had no idea if they were bastards or not. So they were called "no one" instead. Not exactly nice but not cruel either.

Then, one day, the pair had been discovered stealing food from a local merchant. Caught in the act as they say. They hadn't been caught by the local magistrate but, instead, by monks. Some monks, it was said, would simply feed young thieves and send them on their way. Some would chop off their hands. And some . . . some would give them jobs. The first few years, they were forced to live in the stables with the horses. Not that they minded. They loved the horses and didn't mind the smell of their shit. And while they lived with the horses they learned to care for them. They learned to feed them and brush them and tell when they weren't feeling well. They even learned when it was time to let them go, which was hard. Especially for Kir, who always cried. The monks hated that Kir cried but he kept getting bigger and stronger, so they learned to overlook those tears.

Then the twins learned to shoe the horses and ride them and defend them and help the monks with their weapons during battle and eventually how to fight themselves. They could have gone off on their own, made a life as warriors with no loyalty to any god. But they both felt it, Katla and Kir. They felt Morthwyl call to them. Felt they should wear his rune. Fight under his banner. They felt his power flow through their veins.

When they finally made their vows, Shona was with them. She wasn't an orphan. She came from a wealthy family in the east, but she'd left her life of privilege behind to fight as a war monk. Now they were all majors, fighting battles anywhere the brotherhood sent them.

"What's taking so long?" Katla asked Shona when the drawbridge didn't come down immediately.

Shona shrugged.

Katla looked up at the ramparts.

"I want that drawbridge down in five seconds or I'll rip it down with my bare hands!" she warned. She wasn't worried about what was in the moat either. Because she had trained what was in the moat. And they still adored her.

The drawbridge came down and she took the lead across it. The gates opened and she rode in. Once she was far enough inside so the entire battalion could follow, she dismounted, and her squire assisted her by removing the saddle and gear from her horse.

As Katla stopped to stretch her back and legs before finding a bath and food, Brother Julia came rushing to her side. Katla wasn't fond of Brother Julia. She seemed more of a lapdog than a warrior. And Katla had no time for lapdogs.

"Brother Katla!" Julia exclaimed. "So glad to have you back safely!"

Katla returned the greeting with a grunt.

"But," Julia continued, "unfortunately, you and your battalion must go right out again."

Katla stopped wiping some blood and brain off her white tunic and looked at the lapdog.

"What?"

Shona came to stand beside her. "Yeah? What?"

"Brother Shona," Julia said with a head nod.

"Fuck your nods. What's this about leaving again?"

"Unfortunately—"

"Stop saying unfortunately—"

"—Master General Pierce needs you and your battalion to go right out again to deal with land barons in the west. Immediately. It can't wait."

Katla felt an itch at the back of her neck. It was a feeling she'd heeded ever since she and her twin had lived on the streets. It had kept them safe. Kept them alive. Told her when something just wasn't right.

Like this moment. Something wasn't right.

"Shona. Find me something," Katla ordered.

Shona moved to Julia's side. Stood next to her. Towered over her, which at six-foot-two, wasn't hard for Shona to do. She leaned in but Julia kept her gaze on the ground.

"She's hiding something."

"I'm not. Just relaying a message." Julia's voice was calm but her eyes didn't move. Nor did her body. Normally Julia relayed orders, then stalked away, expecting those orders to be followed. The fact that she wasn't doing so now . . .

Shona sniffed Julia's hair before abruptly walking off, but Katla stood her ground and waited. A few seconds later her twin stepped closer.

"What are we doing?" he asked.

"Waiting."

"But I'm hungry."

Katla was sure he was. Her brother was three hundred pounds of muscle. When he wasn't praying or killing, he was eating.

"We'll eat soon, Brother."

"How soon?"

"You're irritating me."

"Enough to feed me?"

"No."

Shona walked out of one of the stables leading a horse. A gray stallion.

"Look familiar?" she called out to Katla.

Julia closed her eyes, cringing at Shona's question, but Katla didn't need that cringe as confirmation. Because she recognized that horse. She'd helped pull it out of its mother when it was born. Watched as it had taken its first wobbly steps, then as it grew strong and powerful. Then came the day she'd recommended it for placement among the warhorses.

Katla slapped her hand at the back of Julia's neck and yanked her close, pressing her lips against the monk's ear.

"Where *is* she?" Katla snarled.

They entered the Chamber of Valor, where many of the order's major decisions, rulings, laws, and judgments were made.

"I know," the master sergeant explained to the outsiders, "that you see all the weapons on these walls and think you'd like to handle them, but please understand that they are under the protection of ancient magicks. Touch them with the knowledge that you risk your very lives by doing so."

Of course, as he spoke those words, the centaur siblings had already grabbed two weapons off the walls and were looking them over. Gemma immediately yanked the double-headed battle axe and skull-headed mace from their hands just as the monks faced their group. The master sergeant scowled at her.

"What are you doing?" he demanded.

Gemma glanced at the weapons she held. "Just remembering how these used to feel in my hands . . . that's all."

She would have put the weapons back herself but they were quickly snatched from her grip by low-level monks and returned to their places of honor.

"Hands off, traitor," someone hissed at her.

"Only those without disgrace may touch these weapons," the master sergeant reminded her. And then he suddenly pointed at her. "And *that* I do not miss, Brother Gemma!"

"What?"

"That eye roll."

"Thought you only did that with your sister . . . and me," Quinn softly teased.

"Shut up," she replied. But not harshly. She was glad, for once, of his humor. She needed it at the moment. They kept her from reacting harshly to such rudeness.

The monks moved around the chamber, getting into place.

"I thought all these weapons were bewitched or something," Quinn remarked.

"They are. Which begs the question, why were you and your sister able to not only touch them but remove them from the wall and toy with them?"

He shrugged. "To most magicks, centaurs are considered animals."

"What?"

"Most magicks can't harm animals because in the eyes of most gods, they are innocents. So while spells and curses might cause you great harm, they do nothing to us."

"That makes sense."

"And, of course, every god has its favorites. Turns out, centaurs are the favorites of most if not all gods."

"How do you know that?"

"Look at us. We're gorgeous."

She glared at him. "Why do I bother talking to you at all?"

"I have *no* idea."

Quinn glanced at his sister and then at the room they were in. She gave a short nod, understanding him. This Room of Pestilence or Chamber Pot of Desecration or whatever the monks called it did not merely have a few weapons on the walls. Keeley's forge had a few weapons. This room, however . . .

The weapons not only covered the walls, they covered the ceiling as well. And all of them were usable. If necessary.

"Brother Gemma," the master sergeant called out. "Come forward."

It bothered Quinn that these monks who kept calling Gemma a traitor also insisted on calling her "Brother Gemma." Especially when she wasn't wearing her tunic. Quinn got the feeling they were doing that for a very specific reason and not a good one.

Gemma walked forward and Quinn motioned Samuel to his side.

"Tell me what's going on, Samuel."

"Tell *you*? Won't you just get bored?"

The boy had a point. Most things bored Quinn and monk-based

ceremonies would probably top the list if he'd been forced to go to any before.

"Fine. Go tell my sister then. Keep her apprised so nothing takes her off guard."

Samuel patted his shoulder. "That does make more sense."

Quinn glared at the hand on his shoulder and Samuel quickly removed it before turning to Laila and whispering to her.

Unable to make out what was being said, Quinn simply watched what was happening around him.

Gemma waited in front of a raised dais that the master sergeant stood upon. It took a moment to realize that she was positioned in the middle of the rune of their chosen god. Once again, something that Quinn felt wasn't necessarily a good thing, but perhaps not bad either.

"So," the master sergeant said, "tell us why you've decided to return here two years after abandoning our order."

"It wasn't abandonment, but that's neither here nor there. There have been brutal attacks on monasteries, temples, and churches throughout the lands. We're not sure who is behind the atrocities, but until we are, Queen Keeley of the Hill Lands is offering safe refuge for all religious orders."

"And you expect us to trust you? A traitor?"

"I'm not a traitor, but in this instance, you don't have to trust me. You can trust the queen."

"Which queen? I've heard there are two."

"Yes, but one comes with the son of the Old King attached."

"And the other comes with the Amichais and a treacherous cow."

Quinn glanced over at the wall. Saw a steel spear he liked the look of, that he could do a nice bit of damage with. Since it was starting to seem as if that would be necessary.

But he'd barely moved when the doors to the Alcove of Annihilation were flung open, startling everyone. Three monks—appearing as if they'd just stepped off a battlefield—stormed inside. They pushed past the monks attempting to stop them and crowded around Gemma.

"Wait—" was all Gemma got out before she was grabbed by the scruff of her chainmail and yanked back toward the doorway.

"Brother Katla!" the master sergeant yelled from his mighty dais.

"Back off!" was all one of the monks barked before absconding with Gemma.

Laila immediately went after Gemma, and the rest of their unit immediately went after Laila. The monks attempted to stop them, as well, but Farlan and Cadell easily shoved them aside so the rest of them could get through without much bother.

They didn't have to go far. The foursome were standing right outside the doors. A dark-haired woman, a little taller than Gemma, threw out her arms. At first, Quinn thought it was an open challenge. But then she said, "So where have you been?"

"Before you start yelling—" Gemma began.

"I'm not yelling."

"You have to let me explain, Katla."

"I don't have to do a gods-damn thing." She gestured to Gemma. "She's all yours, Kir."

"Katla, *no!*" Gemma cried.

The big man quickly moved forward, wrapped his arms around Gemma, and lifted her off the ground while he . . . sobbed?

Quinn leaned around the large man so he could look Gemma in the eyes and mouthed, *Is he crying?*

Gemma stroked the big monk's shoulders and soothed, "It's okay, Kir. It's okay."

"But you just left!" the big monk openly sobbed. "You just left us!"

He is! Quinn continued, shocked. *He's sobbing!*

Stop it! Gemma mouthed back.

But I love him. I love him, Gemma!

Quinn moved around so he could study the hugging monk. He was huge. Wide as a house. Quinn had hunted bears that were smaller. Had arm-wrestled dwarves that weren't as wide. But those big blue needy eyes filled with copious tears utterly confused Quinn. As did the nasty scar across his neck that said this sobbing monk had almost lost his life at least once. When their eyes met, Quinn smiled at him.

"Hello."

The hugger scowled. "Who are you?"

"I'm Quinn. I'm traveling with Gemma. Part of her protection unit."

"Brother Gemma needs no protection."

"That's very true. But she's *Princess* Gemma now."

"You're a princess now?" the sobbing monk asked Gemma.

Gemma didn't respond. She was too busy crawling onto the sobbing monk's shoulder so she could get into what appeared to be a whispering fight with the female monk called Katla. Quinn couldn't make out what they were saying to each other, but now Gemma was balancing herself on that massive shoulder so she could gesture at the female.

Unable to help himself, Quinn said to the monk, "You know what I'd like, Brother?"

"What's that?"

Quinn threw his arms open. "A hug."

The monk grinned and threw his own arms open, sending Gemma flipping off his shoulder to the ground as the two males happily embraced.

"Gods-dammit, Quinn!" Gemma exploded from the floor.

"What? I was getting a hug."

"Look at this, Katla," the monk said, turning to the female monk and lifting Quinn up a bit. "Amichai. I've always wanted to meet one of the Amichais!"

Brother Katla reached down and lifted Gemma to her feet by again grabbing the scruff of her chainmail shirt. Gemma slapped the hand away once she was standing.

"Get off! Get off! Get off!"

"Did it occur to you," Brother Katla asked in a tone that brooked no disagreement, "to tell us what was going on and to ask us for help?"

"I couldn't," Gemma said. "I had to move if I was going to get home in time. As it was, I barely made it before my family was attacked by one of the Old King's treacherous sons."

"You couldn't even get a message to us?"

"So you could what? Go with me?"

"Yes. That's exactly what we would have done."

"You're a traitor too, then, Brother Katla?" the master sergeant asked from inside the doorway.

"Oh, shut up, Alesandro," Katla shot back.

Confused, Quinn asked the tall female monk who'd walked in with the brother and sister, "Doesn't Brother Katla report to the master sergeant?"

"No. As master sergeant he runs the day-to-day operations of the monastery, but Katla's a major. She has control over an entire battalion. She outranks him. I'm Shona, by the way."

"Quinn. And what's your rank?"

"Major. So is Kir, Katla's brother."

"The sobber?"

She gave a dry chuckle. "Yes. Him."

"So higher ranks wear tunics that are—"

"White. Yes. Officers of higher rank wear white tunics. Black tunics are for lower ranks."

"You all trained together with Gemma." It wasn't really a question. Quinn could tell by their body language.

"More than that. We're battle-cohorts."

"I don't know what that means."

"We were linked together throughout our training. We ate together. Slept together. Fought together. Prayed together."

"Shit together?"

"No. But we had to keep watch while one went behind a tree. That requires a lot of trust."

"It does create a bond."

"A bond until death. That's why Katla's so pissed. Gemma never should have gone off on her own. But I know her. She was protecting us."

"Most likely."

Shona studied him for a moment. "You her friend?"

Quinn laughed. "Gods no. She hates me."

"I will not continue to have this argument with you," Gemma told Katla. Mostly because she knew Katla could keep an argument going until she lost her voice. It was a fact that had been written down in the journals of the monastery Note Takers.

"Because you have no excuse."

"Fine. You want to hear the reason why I left the way I did?

We'll take it to the grand master. Joshua can explain it to you in great detail. Will that satisfy you?"

It was as if the air had left the passageway. The three cohorts froze, gazing blindly at Gemma.

"What?" Gemma asked, feeling real fear for the first time since she'd entered the monastery walls. "What's wrong?"

Katla's face turned bright red but her anger was no longer directed at Gemma. Instead, she stormed to the chamber doorway and turned her rage on the master sergeant.

"You didn't tell her?" she demanded, her voice low but barely controlled.

The master sergeant forced himself to look at Katla, but Gemma could tell it was a battle for him. He was terrified of her. "I was not given leave to—"

"*You didn't tell her?*" Katla exploded. Kir appeared next to her, his big hand landing on his twin's shoulder. He wanted to soothe her, but knew he couldn't. So, Gemma knew, he was ready to grab her if he had to.

Gemma's right finger twitched but she held the rest of her body still as she asked, "Didn't tell me what, Katla?"

It was Shona who replied.

"Joshua is dead, Gemma." Her tone was flat, unemotional. The same way she always spoke unless she was in the midst of battle. But it didn't matter how she said it; Gemma didn't believe it. Not Joshua.

"That's not right. He can't be."

"It's true," Shona insisted. "He died nearly a year ago."

"But I would have heard if he'd died in war. That news would have spread faster than—"

"He didn't die in war. He died in Challenge."

Gemma's fingers curled into tight fists and she turned away from her battle-cohorts. She wanted to believe they were lying to her. That this was some fabrication. Or a grand scheme Joshua had concocted, and he was alive somewhere, ready to strike his enemies down. But grand schemes like that were not Joshua's way. They never had been. He believed in directness and honesty and valor.

"Before we go on," the master sergeant said into the silence, "perhaps Brother Gemma and her associates should be shown to private cells so they can get cleaned up before this goes any further."

Just hearing the master sergeant's voice and his attempts at placating her after he'd withheld the truth from the very beginning . . .

Gemma faced the chamber and slowly walked toward the master sergeant within. He saw her coming and began to back up.

The Challenge was the old way war monks used to fight for the title of grand master. But in the last five hundred years or so, after the Challenge ended up killing more monks than making them grand master, it became more common for a high-ranking monk to be voted in. But, like most of the Old Ways, it was still invoked every once in a while by some jackass.

Gemma didn't have a problem with the Challenge, especially where Joshua was concerned. He'd been her mentor. She knew what a fighter he was. Knew how good he was. Anyone who could truly take him deserved to be grand master. But the fact that no one was telling her the identity of the new grand master . . . that was a problem.

"Who is it?" she asked the master sergeant as she stalked him across the open space between them. He'd finally stopped moving when he realized how weak it made him look. Backing away from her like that.

"I have not been given leave—"

"Don't make me ask you more than once, Alesandro."

"You fail to realize the situation you're in, traitor. Perhaps I should point out to—"

Gemma wrapped her hand around his throat, lifted the master sergeant off his feet, and then dropped him to the ground. She squeezed until she knew his bones were about to start cracking.

"I am quickly running out of the patience I was never born with," she growled.

"It's Sprenger!" one of the lower-ranking monks screamed. "It's Sprenger!"

Eyes wide, Gemma released Alesandro and faced Katla, Kir, and Shona.

Katla stepped forward. "Gem—"

Gemma raised her fists, not wanting to hear any bullshit.

Instead, she barked, "With me! With me!"

She started walking but several of the monks quickly stepped in her way because—she was guessing—their orders had been to keep her in the chamber. So she tossed them out of the way with an angry slash of her hands, utilizing an energy spell she had never managed to master fully before. But she was just so angry at the moment, it worked beautifully. She sent her fellow monks flying and walked out with no one else attempting to stop her, her battle-cohorts right behind her.

Quinn and the others still outside the chamber watched as armed monks went flying. A few seconds later, Gemma stormed out with her friends.

"I've never seen her do *that* before," Keran laughed, gawking after her cousin. "That was amazing!"

"Whatever is going on," Laila whispered to him, "this is bad."

Quinn already knew that. He could see how bad it was just by looking at the stunned monks picking themselves off the ground.

"Move," he urged, pushing everyone down the passageway. "Everyone move."

"Where are we going?" Keran asked.

"I don't know, but I say we head down to the first floor."

"Why?"

"Because they can't throw us to our deaths from the first floor. That's why."

Keran blinked. "Excellent point."

CHAPTER 8

Gemma kneeled in front of Joshua's tunic and sword. All his other possessions had been burned on the funeral pyre after his death.

"I'm so sorry, Gemma," Katla said, sitting on the floor behind her and stretching out her legs. "I really thought you knew. I sent you a message. At least I thought I had."

"Sprenger must have stopped it," Shona said, her back resting against the wall of the Chamber of the Honored Dead, her knees raised, her arms resting on them.

"Sprenger knew I would have come back," Gemma guessed.

Because she would have. She would have come back for Sprenger. She wouldn't have let him remain grand master for two minutes much less a year. Not him. *Never* him. She'd rather have a large rat in the position than that reprehensible bastard.

"How bad has it been since he—"

"He's still on his best behavior," Katla assured her. "It's too soon for him to start all that again."

"But he will. He will start again. Men like him . . . they don't stop. Joshua knew that. He should have let me kill him when I had the chance."

"He didn't because you would have burned."

Gemma stood and began to pace, stopping briefly to stroke Kir's hair and kiss the top of his head. It was all she could do while he sobbed—again, she was sure—over the death of Joshua.

"There's no way that Challenge could have been fair. Were you here?"

"We were. Barely made it. Sprenger's allies did their best to make sure we weren't here for it. But Kir knew something was wrong."

"I just felt it," he sobbed out. "I just knew something was wrong."

Gemma went to kneel behind the big man to comfort him, but when she put her arms around his shoulders, she ended up hanging from him like a monkey from a tree. Her knees never touched the ground.

"We got back in time to see the beginning of it . . . and the end," Shona said.

"I tried to take Joshua's place," Katla admitted. As grand master, he was allowed a champion to fight for him.

"But, of course, he said no."

Katla sighed. Loud and long. "Of course he did. But, honestly, Gemma, I didn't see anything wrong with the Challenge. None of us did. We watched closely. It appeared to be a fair fight."

"Joshua was older," Shona added. "And he didn't go into battle the way he once did. He was running a monastery, probably didn't have time to train as he used to. Sprenger took advantage of that."

Gemma didn't want to hear logic. She wanted to hear the Challenge was all a vast plot to destroy the best thing that had ever happened to this monastery. But no one had loved Joshua the way she did, and she wouldn't hold that against them.

Gemma kissed Kir on his sweet face before releasing her hold and landing on the ground.

"What about those still loyal to Joshua?" she asked, standing up and pacing again.

"Sprenger plays nice with them. Even Thomassin, Bartholemew, and Brín."

The three elders that had been Joshua's battle-cohorts. The only three who understood exactly how Gemma felt at this very moment.

"I doubt they trust him," Shona went on, "but they also know that Sprenger has quite a few allies on his side as well."

"When it comes down to it," Katla ruminated, "it will be the Sprenger allies versus the Joshua allies."

"Monk against monk." Gemma shook her head. "The one thing Joshua never wanted. But he didn't want Sprenger in charge either."

"He didn't want him in charge? Or *you* don't want Sprenger in charge?"

"You know why he can't be in charge, Katla. He's a man who can *never* have power."

Shona watched her for a moment before asking, "But didn't you come here for another reason, Gemma?"

"What other reason?" Completely confused, Gemma gazed at her cohorts until she remembered why she had traveled so many miles back to her past. "Oh, gods! Yes! Uh . . . the destruction of monasteries, churches, temples, nunneries." She shook her head, trying to think like a representative of her sister and not a monk-knight loyal to Grand Master Joshua. "Ummm . . . Keeley is offering protection to any religious sect that wants it. You can stay in her territory. That's why I'm here. At least until we know who's doing this and how they can be stopped."

"Who's doing this?" Katla repeated. "We know who's doing this."

"It's Beatrix, isn't it?" Gemma immediately accused. "My father's not so sure, but I think it's Beatrix."

"It's not Beatrix."

Dammit! "It's not? Are you sure? It seems like something Beatrix would do."

"It's not Beatrix."

"Then who? It can't be those idiot twins. They can barely scratch their balls."

"It's Cyrus the Honored," Shona told her, stretching her arms over her head.

"It can't be," Gemma argued. "I thought he was the good brother."

"In that family, good is relative."

"There's something else you should know," Katla said, standing up and adjusting her weapons.

"What?"

"Sprenger's already made a deal for protection . . . with Beatrix and King Marius. In fact, she's made a protection deal under her husband's banner with religious sects all over this valley. From here to about five hundred leagues farther east."

Gemma stared at her battle-cohort until she finally raised her hands, balled them into tight fists, and, through gritted teeth, howled out, "*I. Hate. Herrrr!*"

Katla nodded. "I am aware. I believe it was one of the first things you ever told me. That and it was nice not having to share your bed with three other siblings. And a pig."

"Oh, yeah," Gemma said. Calm now that she'd gotten her hatred of Beatrix off her chest. "Tommy the Pig. My da loved that pig."

It seemed the safest place to wait. The stables. The horses didn't complain and the squires were too afraid to say anything at all about the Amichais as long as they didn't bother the horses.

Eventually, Gemma found them.

"There you are."

"I enjoy the way you make it sound as if *we* deserted *you*," Laila pointed out. Quinn's sister was more than annoyed.

"Have you seen Ainsley?" Quinn asked.

"Who?"

He frowned. "Your sister?"

"She's at home . . . isn't she?"

"She came with us."

"Oh . . . oh! That's right. I don't know where she is."

"Or that she's your sister?"

Keran stepped in front of Quinn. "I thought you lot were the drinking type of monks."

"We are," Gemma said.

"Then where's the ale?"

"I don't know. I haven't been here for two years," she added when her cousin's eyes grew wide. "Maybe they took a vow of celibacy since I've been gone."

"That's no sex," Laila corrected.

"Is it? Well . . . they wouldn't do that."

"What are the drinking rules here?" Keran pushed.

"No drinking if we're about to go to war. And maybe we are; I don't know."

Quinn, not in the mood for any of this, pushed, "Can we get back to your sister?"

"Which one?" Gemma asked.

"The missing one?"

"Which one's that?"

"Gemma!"

"Look, I'm sorry," she finally said. "This . . . isn't what I expected. I thought we'd be dealing with Grand Master Joshua."

"But we're not because he's dead," Laila said.

"Exactly. But there's an even worse problem."

"Which is?"

"Sprenger's in charge. And he shouldn't be. Even worse, he's already made a deal with Beatrix. She's offered protection to every religious order in this valley."

"Great!" Keran cheered. "Then we can find your sister and go back home."

"I can't go."

"I knew you were going to say that."

"You all can go. I've passed on Keeley's message. And now we know who is behind the attacks. It's Cyrus the Honored."

"I thought he was one of the good ones," Farlan pointed out.

"It seems he's a religious fanatic. Anyway, with that information, Keeley can make her plans."

"But you're staying here," Quinn said.

"Just for a little longer."

"But they keep calling you traitor."

"That's true."

"And you're staying where they call you traitor?"

"It's complicated."

"Can I talk to you for a moment?" Quinn asked politely, nodding toward the back stable doors.

"Actually, I have to—hey!"

He'd grabbed the back of her brown fur cape and dragged her toward the doors. When she began to put up a fight and the fur began to tear, he wrapped his arm around her waist and lifted her up, taking her out of the stables. Quinn looked around. He saw the monk who liked to hug everyone.

"Brother Kir!"

"Hello again, my new best friend!"

"I'd like to talk to Brother Gemma alone. Can you recommend a place?"

"Of course!"

"Kir!" Gemma barked.

"I'll show you where the armor room is!"

"Thanks, mate!"

Quinn followed Kir, carrying Gemma under his arm. She didn't say anything but he knew he'd be paying for this. But he needed answers.

When they arrived at the armory, Kir unlocked it and let them in.

"You know what?" Kir suggested. "To let you two have some privacy, I'll be right outside, blocking the way. No one gets past me."

"Because you're as big as a mountain."

"I *am* as big as a mountain!" Kir eagerly agreed.

"Thank you, my new friend."

"I know we haven't known each other long, Amichai, but I've decided I love you."

"And I love you!"

Kir threw his arms open, and Quinn tossed Gemma inside so he could embrace the monk.

"That's not funny, Quinn!" Gemma yelled from within the room.

They hugged and Quinn went inside while Kir closed the door behind them.

Confident the monk was blocking the door as he'd promised, Quinn was about to face Gemma but she slapped the back of his head before he could.

"Owwww! What was that for?"

"Don't toy with Kir!" she angrily whispered at him.

"That's your problem? I thought I'd get in trouble for carrying you around like a sack of grain."

"Kir is very sensitive. And you saying you love him?"

"I *do* love that man."

"Because he does whatever you say?"

"Yes. And he adores me, which shows he has excellent taste. Tell me, does he cry after every battle?"

"Yes, and why am I in this room with you?"

"So I can find out what the fuck is going on."

Quinn took Gemma's hand and pulled her deep into a large armory that was empty of monks but filled with nice weaponry. Not as nice as the work of Keeley and her mother, but not bad at all.

When he felt he was far enough away from the door so that even Kir couldn't overhear them, Quinn asked, "So what the fuck *is* going on?"

"You seriously dragged me all the way back here to ask me that again?"

"Now you can answer me."

"I don't have to answer you."

"Your silence confirms that you're going to do something incredibly stupid."

"What?"

"When you think you're going to do something smart, you brag. You tell everyone. But when you don't say anything . . . it's because you know the rest of us will think it's stupid. That's why you didn't tell us you were returning to the monastery in the first place. Because you knew we would think it was stupid."

"Stop saying stupid."

"Because what you're about to do is—"

"It's not stupid!" Gemma paced away from him. "You don't understand."

"Then explain it to me. Or I start stomping around this place in my hooves and take a serious shit right in the middle of your Chamber of Vagary."

She faced him. "The chamber of what?" She rolled her eyes. "And you will do no such thing."

"Try me." He stepped close to her, crossed his arms over his chest. "You do understand that I'm the crazy one in my family, don't you?"

"Pardon?"

"It's true. My father's the mean one. Caid's the gruff one. My mother's just the typical royal. Laila's the logical one. And I'm the nutter. There was a dark elf princess once who brought her entire entourage through our territory. Our mother arranged a very fancy dinner for her, but she was a dark elf, and to be blunt, she was an evil twat and rude to my mother and everyone else. Caid lasted about five minutes into the dinner before he couldn't stand it and left. My father was forced to stay because he had to protect my mother, but you could tell the entire time he just wanted to start killing elves. He was barely restraining himself. Laila spent the whole dinner debating whether servants should be beaten and whether slavery was right or wrong. I, however, spent the entire meal laughing and smiling and basically being a delight. Then, finally, the dinner came to an end. I got up to leave and as I passed the princess I stopped briefly in front of her, lifted my tail, and dropped a load right in her lap. She screamed in horror and disgust, and my father and mother made quite a show of chastising me, but I was never punished. So if you think I will not desecrate your little Chamber of Veneration, you're wrong."

"Stop renaming our chambers and threatening to desecrate them with your vile shit!"

"Then tell me the truth. All of it. Now."

Katla walked behind Shona toward her cell. She was just wondering where her twin had disappeared to when she heard a door open and someone grabbed her chainmail collar and yanked her inside. She started swinging but stopped when she realized she stood in front of three of the elders. There were nine elders who worked with the grand master on important decisions involving the monastery. The three who stood before her had been the closest confidants of Grand Master Joshua.

"Brother Katla."

"Brother Thomassin. Brother Bartholemew. Brother Brín. Is this about threatening the master sergeant? Because he definitely deserved it."

"Stop talking," Brother Thomassin told her, "and read this." He shoved a scroll into her hands.

Katla unrolled the parchment and began to read. When she had first arrived at the monastery, she couldn't read a word. All she knew how to do was count. She knew money. Had to so no one could cheat her or her brother. It was Brother Brín who'd made it his business to teach the twins how to read and write. She'd never been so grateful. A whole new world had opened up to them with these skills. She hadn't realized how much she'd been held back by lacking them.

But, as she read the scroll, written in the careful hand of Joshua himself, she was beginning to doubt her literacy for the first time in many years.

"Is this . . . accurate?" she finally asked when she'd read it through for the third time.

"What do you think?"

"But are all of you sure?"

"We've trusted him this long," Bartholemew said in that quiet way of his. "Why would we doubt him *now*?"

"Much has already been done," Thomassin said. "But there is still much left to do. Can you do it?"

"Of course. We'll get everything started right away."

"But remember, only those loyal to us. You know who that is, yes?"

"Absolutely. But you do know that Gemma will not like this. *At. All.* Besides, she's already—"

"Leave Gemma to us. Understand?"

"You don't want me to tell her anything?"

"*No*. Her painful and unreliable honesty is one random thing too many to deal with right now."

"But give her this . . . when the time is right." Brín handed Katla another scroll with Gemma's name on it.

Katla waved the scroll at them. "All of you do know this is insane, right? And what if you're all wrong—"

"A little late for that concern, isn't it, Brother Katla?" Thomassin asked with a smile.

Gemma knew that Quinn was not quite like his siblings, but by Morthwyl's sword, she'd had no idea he could be as difficult, as troublemaking, and as big a pain in the ass as any horse she'd ever had!

"I owe a debt," she finally admitted.

"Well, I could already tell that."

"Do you want to hear this or not?"

"Sorry, Princess. Go ahead."

She debated breaking his nose—again—but decided, instead, to continue with her story.

"Keeley was always wrong."

"About what?"

"When I first came here, it wasn't to be a monk. I came here to be an apprentice to the blacksmiths. I wanted to be as good as Keeley. And I knew war monks had great blacksmiths."

"But then you got here and you were recruited into the sect. They are a cult!"

Annoyed, Gemma picked up a wooden chair and slammed it down.

"Sit! And be quiet."

"Yes, ma'am," Quinn replied contritely as he sat.

"As I was saying . . . contrary to what my sister has always believed," Gemma went on, "I did not come to the Order of Righteous Valor to become a monk. I came here to study under their blacksmiths. It's known that war monks have some of the best blacksmiths next to the Old King. But I wasn't going to risk working for the Old King. When I got here, I started off like everyone else. As a lowly apprentice for the farrier, working mainly with the horses since I had a way with them. One day I was in the stables alone with a massive war horse named"—she suddenly smiled, remembering—"Sin Killer. I was bent over, cleaning Sin's hooves, when I sensed someone behind me and—"

"Stop." Quinn dropped his head.

"I thought you wanted to hear the story."

"And that's my fault," he admitted. "I never should have forced you to tell it. It's a story you should only tell if you want to." He looked her straight in the face. "I'm sorry, Gemma." Gemma was shocked to hear Quinn say that. Shocked to see him looking her right in the eyes when he did. Not only did he seem to realize his mistake, but he apologized for it, appearing to fully understand he'd crossed a line into territory most males could never fully grasp.

Gods, he was so *not* a human male. Which was why she was going to take this moment and tell him absolutely everything.

* * *

She locked her gaze with his and Quinn saw no forgiveness in those eyes. Not that he blamed her. He pushed when, for once, he truly should not have.

"You wanted to hear it, Amichai," she said, making him wince, "so you will."

She grabbed another wood chair and dropped it in front of his. She sat down across from him and rested her elbows on her knees, leaning in close.

"When I first got here, I didn't realize that Sprenger had a reputation. But his father was powerful and had very strong connections with the Old King. Brother Joshua—he wasn't a grand master then yet, of course—had been working hard to protect trainees from Sprenger. He was out of town at the time on a mission, but he had his closest allies keeping an eye on a new squire they all thought had piqued Sprenger's interest. The boy had, but Sprenger knew they were watching and I was alone in the stables."

Quinn was getting angry but reacting—ranting, throwing things—would do nothing for Gemma. It would just make *him* feel better. And this was her story to tell. Her nightmare. So, for once, he kept his mouth shut and listened. As hard as it was.

"They did eventually realize their mistake and came charging into the stables. Brother Thomassin, Brother Bartholemew, Brother Brín . . ." She stopped for a few moments, staring off. Took a breath. "They . . . had to . . . pry me off him."

Quinn blinked, glanced around. A bit confused.

Gemma looked down, gestured at her clothes. "I was covered in his blood. His . . . uh . . . arm." She pointed at the upper part of her left arm. "It was hanging by a tendon." Using the fingers of the same hand, she brushed her face. "I nearly had his jaw off . . . I had already unattached one side and I was working on the other side when they found us."

That's when Quinn could no longer stay silent. "His . . . his jaw . . . ?"

"It's a thing I used to do. I don't do it as much anymore. But when a man made me mad during a fight . . . I used to rip off his bottom jaw. It doesn't usually kill the person outright, so I'd make him, you know . . . look at it."

"Oh." Quinn nodded and wondered if that door Kir was standing in front of was the only way in or out of the room. "Okay."

"Anyway," she went on, rubbing her hands on her leggings, "they sent for Joshua and he rushed back from whatever battle he was at. They also got the best healers for Sprenger and saved his arm and jaw. Those healers did a really amazing job. Sprenger wanted me executed, of course. And if I'd killed him, I would have been. In fact, if not for Joshua, I would have been burned at the stake whether Sprenger had died or not. But Joshua wouldn't let that happen. You see, Joshua was a trainee when Sprenger was a young knight, and Sprenger liked to break the new boys in. Joshua was one of those boys. Many of the young trainees at that time were. It was just something that was never discussed, and nothing was ever done about it. Until Joshua came to the monastery. He didn't stay silent. He actually went to the grand master and complained. Formally. But still nothing was done. It was suggested by the elders that Joshua just . . . let it go. He couldn't. Not only for himself but because he knew it was happening to others. He simply couldn't let that continue to happen." She pushed her hair off her face and looked up at the ceiling. "He made protecting this monastery from Sprenger his ultimate goal."

"And you?"

"Joshua saved my life, and I went back to being a blacksmith apprentice. But I couldn't ignore the call of battle. The call of the war god. Should I make weapons of war or become one? Joshua took me under his wing, matched me with the best battle-cohorts any novitiate could ask for, and trained me to honor the gods of war every time I went onto the fields of battle. As soon as I put on my novitiate tunic, I knew this was where I was meant to be."

"And this . . . Sprenger?"

"He's the new grand master. He defeated Joshua in Challenge."

"And all these pious monks are okay with that?"

"Most of them are okay with it because a lot of them don't know what he used to do. A lot of the older ones have died in battle. Some have been hit in the head so many times, they barely remember their names. But I remember. And what I know is that now Sprenger is back in power, eventually he'll start again. Because men like that don't change. They never change. Because unless people like us continue to hold them to account, they never have to change."

"And you plan to stay here and hold him to account?"

"All I know, Quinn, is that there's no way I can let a rapist lead my monastery."

"Do you have any idea how many rapists rule towns? Cities? Countries?"

"I handle what I can handle, Amichai. And Sprenger is my debt to pay."

"They'll never let you near him."

Gemma nodded and stood, putting the chair back. "Maybe. I'm sure he's always surrounded by his allies. And he's smart enough to know he's still not in a safe position here. At least not while I'm alive. Because I'll never let him or anyone else forget what he did."

Quinn also stood and put his chair back against the wall. Probably not where it belonged but close enough.

"So what are you going to do? Run around telling everyone he's a rapist? I hate to say it, but they won't believe you. They'll think you're just being petty. A bunch of them already think you're a traitor. The others will think you're just upset about Joshua."

Gemma moved his chair back exactly where it had been before replying, "I know. I know all of that."

"Then what's your plan?"

"To do what I should have done that night when I was cleaning out Sin Killer's hooves," she told him before heading back to the door where Kir still stood guard. "Destroy that motherfucker."

CHAPTER 9

As the two suns set, Ainsley wondered if her sister had even realized she was gone. She doubted it since Gemma and Keeley seemed to constantly forget her existence.

Annoyed even thinking about the pair of them, she went back to simply watching everything that went on around her.

She'd found a nice spot in a very large tree hours ago and had been there ever since. She could look all around without being seen, which was just what she wanted. But as darkness grew, she began to hear strange noises. Sounds that she'd never heard before. Strange, since she'd heard most forest sounds. She'd grown up more in the forest than she had with her actual family. It was easier to fall asleep in trees than it was among her siblings or her amorous parents. So she thought she knew every sound. Every bird, every cat, every bear, every wolf. Even snakes and bugs. But the sound she heard moaning on the wind . . .

Ainsley leaned forward and let the sound lead her; head tilting one way, then another. Finally, she realized it came from a large mass of trees far in the distance. It almost looked like another forest surrounding a clearing but colors seemed to be rising from that clearing . . . which was just odd. Perhaps the monks were performing rituals or something in that clearing, but rituals that caused strange lights to rise from the darkness?

That sort of thing usually led to witches being burned alive.

Interested enough to leave her safe spot in the tree, Ainsley was about to get down when she heard a sound she knew quite well these days. The clanking of armored horses.

She leaned back to let the leaves hide her presence just as an army of blood-covered monks rode past on the path to the monastery.

Ainsley didn't think much about it. It was the third or fourth group of knights she'd seen ride into the monastery so far. Most had been smaller units. A battalion. A squad. But this was the first actual army, which meant it was being led by an actual general. She briefly wondered what a monk general was like. Like the generals that reported to her sister the queen? Or different? All gods and praying and sacrificing goats? She guessed she'd find out soon enough. But for now, she should probably get some sleep.

The army disappeared inside the monastery and she realized that the strange sound coming from that clearing had stopped. So had the even stranger light. Maybe she was just tired from all that riding and had started to see things. She didn't know. She just knew she was ready to take a break. She could think about strange sounds later.

And whether her gods-damn sister had even *noticed* that Ainsley was gone!

It didn't take Gemma long to realize that Sprenger wasn't in the mood to deal with her. As soon as she and Quinn walked out of the armory, several monks approached them to show the way to "your private cells."

Quinn had immediately panicked. "They're taking us to prison?"

Kir had laughed and slapped Quinn's back, sending the Amichai tumbling right into the other monks. Luckily they were all warriors so they kept their feet and were able to get the centaur back on his.

"No, no, my new friend!" Kir had said, oblivious as always to his own strength. "Cells are just what we call our rooms. Our sleeping chambers. Why would we put you in prison?"

Kir was also oblivious to the mood of the people around him. He didn't really see that the monastery was split right down the middle between the allies of Joshua and the allies of Sprenger. Poor, giant, crying bastard.

So the monks took Gemma and her traveling companions to the third floor, where each got a cell equipped with a good amount of food and water. Although Keran bellowing, "*Where the fuck is the ale, ya fanatic bastards?*" when the doors were closed made them no extra friends.

Yet after a hearty meal and the luxury of a hot bath, Gemma still couldn't relax. She paced her room like a caged jungle cat.

When she heard armored horses ride into the courtyard below, she moved to her stained-glass window and opened it so she could see below. It took her less than a second to recognize the general leading the army of knights.

Master General Ragna.

Each member of her army had been handpicked. Each member of her army answered to no one but Ragna. And Ragna answered to no one but the grand master himself. But everyone knew that her loyalty was to the war gods only. If Morthwyl asked her to burn down the monastery with everyone still inside it, everyone knew she would do it without asking one question.

What that meant, though, was that Ragna had no obvious loyalty to Joshua or Sprenger. She was a wild card none of them needed at the moment.

So, as soon as Gemma saw her riding into the courtyard, she said the only thing she could think of . . . "Oh, fuck."

Looking up from the book she was reading, Katla let out a deep sigh when she saw Ragna ride her massive stallion into the courtyard, and growled out the only thing she could think of, "Shit and balls!"

Shona was staring out into the night, not really thinking about anything, as she liked to do most nights, when she saw Master General Ragna ride into the courtyard below. The general gave a few orders to those who reported directly to her, then turned her stallion around and rode out of the courtyard again.

As Shona watched Ragna go—knowing she would return—she made note of their current situation: "We are so fucked."

* * *

Kir smiled happily in his sleep, dreaming his favorite dream about singing roses and dancing bunnies. He loved the dancing bunnies. They were just so cute!

"What do you mean I can't have that little bitch executed?" Sprenger demanded of the grand elder monks.

Thomassin glanced at the others before noting, "I'm not exactly sure how much clearer we can be than to say, 'You can't kill her.'"

"She's a traitor! A deserter!"

"She left on orders of the grand master."

"We have his signed orders here," Brín noted, gesturing to the documents with a lazy hand. "He logged these into the library with Mariello himself the day she left. Mariello will happily testify to that if you need him to."

"Making her *not* a traitor and *not* a deserter. More importantly—"

"Much more importantly," Bartholemew grumbled, his arms resting on the table, his head resting on his arms.

"—she came here with an offer of protection from the Queen of the Hill Lands. So not only would we be executing a princess—"

"A false princess," Sprenger felt the need to add.

The nine elders gazed at him blankly—even his allies—before Brín agreed with a sigh, "Okay."

"—but a princess who brought overtures of goodwill. I'm not sure that's a reputation we want. You know . . . as monks."

"Let's also keep in mind that Brother Gemma is the sister of"— Bartholemew held up his middle and forefinger—"*two* queens."

Sprenger spun away from them and Bartholemew kept his fingers raised but turned his hand and flicked it. Thomassin slammed his friend's hand down on the table just as Sprenger spun back around, his eyes narrowing on their falsely smiling faces.

"I know of at least one queen that will not cry at the loss of such a sister."

"Dearest Grand Master, I don't think any of us should guess

how deep the bond of blood truly goes between sisters. You may think you have permission to annihilate Brother Gemma, but then there are sisterly regrets and the blaming of those holding blood-covered swords."

"You always were the one with the pretty words, Thomassin."

"We strive to stick with our strengths, Brother."

"Fine. What do you suggest?"

"Suggest?"

"Yes. How do I get rid of her?"

"By letting her go?"

For a moment, the grand master's face became so red, Thomassin truly believed that his head would explode all over them. It took him several minutes before he could speak.

"Let her go?"

"You cannot kill her. You cannot keep her. So we send her back to the Queen of the Hill Lands with our kind regrets."

"*And that's it?*" Sprenger bellowed. "We don't even punish her?"

"For what?" Bartholemew wanted to know. "Following the orders of the grand master?"

"Maybe that's what she did then," Brother Peters interjected, "but what about now?"

"What about now?" Thomassin asked, unable to keep the aggravation out of his tone. Peters was one of Sprenger's supporters. He'd always liked "that boy's connections."

"She's been gone two years with no word to anyone. And when she does return, she does not wear her tunic and comes in the company of Amichais and a drunken cousin. She's no longer one of us. She's a princess now, as Brother Thomassin kindly pointed out, and the sister of two queens." His smile was like that of a pleased lizard sitting in the sand. "Strip her of her title and rank among our order. That way you take her power but you won't make her a martyr. Instead, Grand Master, you make her a cautionary tale for the trainees."

"Wait." Thomassin shook his head. "We're going to punish her because she's traveling with Amichais—a tribe we have no disagreement with—and a cousin who likes to drink too much ale?"

Sprenger's laugh was loud. "That's *exactly* what we're going to do."

Ainsley had just nodded off when she heard the snort of a horse. By the time she was fully awake, her bow was already in her hands, an arrow nocked, the bowstring pulled, and before she could stop herself . . . she let the arrow fly.

She was about to call out a warning when the rider turned and an arrow was released, slicing through Ainsley's arrow with ease. Ainsley had only a split second to react and roll out of the way. The metal head of the arrow sliced her cheek open just as she rolled off the branch, out of the tree, and she hit the ground hard.

As she tried to get her breath back, her opponent's horse slowly walked up to her. The blunt end of a spear jammed her shoulder, pushing her over.

The woman monk staring down at her sighed. "We're not taking recruits, child. And even if we were, this is not the way to apply."

"Not . . . recruit . . ." Ainsley panted out. "Wait . . . ing."

"Waiting? For who?"

"Gemma."

"Oh, for fuck's sake," the monk said with a massive eyeroll. "I should have known."

She slipped the spear back into a holster attached to the horse's saddle.

"What's your name?" the monk demanded.

"Ainsley," she got out in one breath. "My name's Ainsley."

"How long have you been out here?"

"Few hours."

"Are you sure? You *smell* like you've been out here for days."

"We've been on the road for days."

"This way." The monk gestured. "You need a bath and I need to treat that wound."

"I'm not going anywhere with you."

"Listen to me, little girl. You can stay here and hide in your tree. But if there's one thing lonely packs of men that have been riding for weeks can sniff out . . . it's a young girl. Especially one that hasn't bathed for a while. And if you don't treat that wound, you'll be too weak to fight them off. So you can let me help you, or you can sit here and wait to be a victim. Your choice."

Ainsley watched the woman ride off, her eyes wide. What kind of thing was that to say to . . . well . . . *anyone*? But horrified that the monk might be speaking the truth—a female soldier would know that sort of thing, wouldn't she?—Ainsley ran after her and her horse.

Gemma had just fallen into a fitful sleep when a hand slapped over her mouth. She had her thumbs against her attacker's eyes before she realized that it was Brother Thomassin. Thankfully she hadn't continued to shove her thumbs forward. That would not have ended well for either of them.

Throwing her arms around Thomassin's shoulders, she hugged the older monk tight.

"I'm so glad to see you," she whispered.

He pulled away from her and placed his forefinger against his lips. He motioned with a wave of his hand and she watched him climb onto her desk and easily haul himself into a small opening in the stone ceiling. She frowned at the ease with which he disappeared inside, but decided not to think too much on it. She just hoped she still moved like that when she was his age.

Gemma followed him through the narrow air shaft until they landed in a room she had never seen before. It took her a few seconds to realize they were in some part of the library. The most important part of any monastery. Even for war monks.

Once inside, she was happy to see Brothers Bartholemew and Brín. She hugged them both.

"I thought I'd never see any of you again."

"We don't have much time, Gemma," Thomassin told her.

"They're coming to execute me, aren't they?"

The brothers frowned.

"No, silly girl," Thomassin corrected. "We're just tired and need to sleep. We're old men."

"Oh."

"But I doubt we'll get a chance to talk to you again before you meet with Sprenger."

"He poisoned him, didn't he? Or tricked him. That's how he defeated Joshua."

"Sprenger was always a good fighter. You just never wanted to believe it," Bartholemew reminded her.

"I beat him. Even before I was trained."

"He expected no resistance from you that night. You were a sixteen-year-old peasant girl—"

"I was not a peasant."

"—alone in the stables. The last thing he expected from you was a fight. If he had, things might have been different."

"They might be different now," Thomassin said.

"What does that mean?"

"It means let us handle this, Gemma."

"You're going to let him get away with this, aren't you?"

"Gemma—"

"You're going to let him stay in power," she accused. "You're going to let him and his marauding penis terrorize this monastery once more! Well, I won't have it!"

Thomassin blew out a breath and looked at Brín, who immediately looked at Bartholemew.

"What?" Gemma asked. Then she guessed, "You're all planning to kill me now."

The three monks gawked at her until Thomassin admitted, "You are *the* most paranoid person I've ever known . . . and I've known kings. Several. But you're more paranoid than *any* of them. How is that possible?"

"We're not going to kill you," Bartholemew said. "Why would we kill you?"

"Because I won't fold to your persuasive tactics?" she weakly guessed.

"That's something."

After moving a stack of books and scrolls, Thomassin sat down on a chair. "Gemma, no one is planning to kill you. But there's a lot going on."

"Tell me. I want to help."

"You can help by doing what we need you to do."

"By letting Sprenger remain grand master?"

"It won't last. Trust me. But you have to play your part."

"And then?"

Thomassin glanced at his fellow elders. "The gods will do the rest."

Gemma threw up her hands. "Are you seriously expecting the *gods* to help us out of this? *Seriously?*"

"How did you manage to get through training?" Bartholemew asked. "Joshua couldn't have protected you *that* much."

She shrugged. "I mostly got hit a lot."

The elders nodded in agreement and Brín patted her shoulder. "That makes so much sense."

After what turned out to be a bath in a nearby lake that she'd needed more than she realized, Ainsley put on fresh clothes from her saddlebags. The war monk sat on a log a few feet away from the lake. She'd built a very small fire and already had equipment out so she could work on Ainsley's wound.

"Sit," she ordered, motioning to another log.

Ainsley moved cautiously toward her until the woman finally reminded her, "I could have killed you in the tree. Or when you'd fallen out of it. Now sit down."

She dropped onto the log. The monk grabbed her by the chin and turned her face so she could get a look at her cheek.

While watching her pull things out to tend to the wound, Ainsley asked, "How did you move so fast? With your bow, I mean."

"Training."

"I thought I was fast."

"You are. But with training, you could be faster."

"Faster than you?"

The monk glanced at her. "In time."

"You know my sister."

"Yes."

"Do you like her?"

"I don't like anyone." She wet a cloth with liquid from a small bottle and began to wipe it on Ainsley's cheek. It stung but Ainsley gritted her teeth against the pain. Then it burned, but still she gritted her teeth. She did let out a grunt, though, when the burning turned sharp and her eyes began to tear. But, just as abruptly, the pain stopped.

Able to speak again without screaming, Ainsley asked, "If you don't like anyone, why are you helping me?"

"I'm a monk."

"A war monk. It's not like you help the poor."

"War monks help the poor by destroying those who exploit them."

"Yes, I'm sure wiping out whole villages helps the poor who live in them."

The monk leaned back. "Do you want me to sew up your face or would you rather I let it get infected and ooze?"

"Sorry."

She threaded a needle and began the painful process of sewing up the open wound on Ainsley's face.

"Did Brother Gemma tell you all that?" she asked after a few minutes of silence.

"My sisters don't tell me anything."

"I see."

"But I can make up my own mind."

"And you've decided we're bad."

"I haven't decided anything. But keeping people away from their families—"

She stopped sewing to stare at Ainsley. "What are you talking about?"

"For ten years we never saw Gemma. You kept her away from her family."

"Ahh."

"Are you going to tell me it was her choice not to come see her family?"

"I wasn't going to tell you that. Because I have no idea." She began sewing again. "I can tell you I haven't seen my family since I walked out the door of our home. But they were glad to see me go."

"Why was that?"

"I frightened them. Because the love of my god was so strong."

"I don't understand."

She stopped sewing; leaned back again. "My earliest memory is not of my mother's voice. Or my father's. But of Morthwyl's. It's like he always spoke to me. Before I even knew about the gods. Any of them. And, like him, where I went . . . death followed."

Ainsley's horror at that statement must have shown on her face because the monk chuckled.

"It's not what you're thinking. I didn't kill puppies or strangle kittens. There's no challenge in that. Only weakness."

"So you killed your family instead?"

"Of course not. But I did hunt and kill my first adult bear by the time I was seven. I went with my uncle. I used a spear. I wasn't strong enough to drag it back through the snow. When I was nine, we were in the middle of a war. The enemy attacked my family's castle. All the children were hidden in the dungeons for safety. But Morthwyl called to me. I snuck out, went up to where all the fighting was. Grabbed a small fighting dagger off a body. I approached an enemy warrior. I knew I didn't have the skills to defeat him if I took him straight on. So as I walked toward him, I calculated. He was bigger, faster, much stronger. As I moved closer, he was hacking off a man's head with his broadsword. Still . . . I kept moving toward him. I knew there was only one thing to do."

"Run away?"

"No. That wasn't an option. Not for me. Not for my god. I approached and he saw me. With my long pigtails and my little-girl dress and the dagger I held before me. And he mocked me. Laughing with his friends about the little girl coming to attack him. And as he did, he looked away from me. That's when I slammed the blade into the top of his foot. And when he leaned over, screaming in pain, I rammed the blade into his open mouth. Killing him. And as the light went out in his eyes," she went on, "I smiled at him. Because I knew that I had made my first true offering to my god and that he would be pleased by it. Now do you understand?"

"Why your family never wanted to see you again . . . ? Yes."

"Why I never needed to see them. Because everything I need is here. Maybe that's how Brother Gemma felt."

"I really hope not. Because that's terrifying."

The monk tied a knot and cut off the end of the thread with a sharp knife. "Done. Don't toy with it. It'll itch. Don't scratch it. Blood will ooze, but don't panic. I'll check on it later, so don't worry if it oozes green."

"Green?"

"I said don't worry. If it oozes green, I'll fix it."

"Right. Well, thank you."

She put all her equipment back into her saddlebag but dropped a linen sack in Ainsley's lap. "Dried beef, bread. It should last a couple of days." Next she tossed in a canteen. "Fresh water. Stay in your tree during the day. You can travel at night but stay close by." She pointed in the direction where Ainsley had heard the sounds earlier. "Do *not* go anywhere over there. Understand?"

"Yes."

"Does that mean, 'yes, I'm going anyway.' Or, 'yes, I understand and I will do as you say'?"

Ainsley laughed. "You really do know my sister." The monk continued to stare at her, waiting for a proper answer. "I heard weird noises coming from that direction that I did find interesting. But after speaking with you . . . I'm not going anywhere near there."

"Good. Put the fire out in about an hour. If you don't, someone in the ramparts will notice. Understand?"

"Yes."

"Should I tell your sister where you are?"

"Don't bother. Her travel companions know where I am."

Without another word, the monk returned to her horse, mounted the beast, and rode off.

Ainsley didn't wait for another hour. She doused the fire and headed back to her tree in the dark. She climbed back to her spot, briefly stopping to yank out the arrow that was protruding from the trunk where her head had been before she moved. There was still blood on it.

She managed to keep the arrowhead attached, so she put it in her quiver with her other arrows and rested her head against the trunk. She worked hard to ignore the fact that the back of her head rested against the hole in the trunk that the monk's arrow had made. Considering how long that woman had been "killing for her god," Ainsley was feeling grateful that all she had to show for their encounter was a gash on her face that might or might not start oozing something green.

CHAPTER 10

The field of pretty flowers next to the monastery was a place many of the brothers used for meditation. This day, though, they had a lovely picnic with Gemma's battle-cohorts and those who'd traveled with her from her sister's queendom.

Yet despite all the interesting things the two extremely diverse groups could be discussing, there was only one topic on everyone's mind.

"Tell me, honestly," Quinn implored Gemma's cohorts, "how insane is she?"

Katla tore off a piece of wild boar from the bone and shrugged her shoulders. "We've never been able to settle on an actual number. A percentage. Is she seventy percent crazy? Eighty percent? Or should we just go with ninety-five and leave it there?"

"Why not a hundred percent?"

"As a monk, I am honor bound not to believe in absolutes. Like one hundred percent evil. We're taught to believe there's good in everything. So I'm sure there's some sanity in Gemma somewhere."

Gemma ripped a turkey leg from Farlan's hand before he could take his first bite.

"I don't appreciate this discussion," she informed them after she ate so much of the leg that Farlan dismissed the idea of taking it back. "I am not insane. You've met both Keeley and Beatrix," she reminded Quinn. "And my uncle Archie. He's the one who's insane."

"Is he though?" Quinn asked. "I mean, compared to you. Is he really?"

Annoyed, Gemma sucked the marrow from the turkey leg, then lobbed what remained at the centaur's head.

"Well, that was just rude!" he accused.

"I don't know why you always have to fight everyone," Katla complained. "You've been gone two years but you haven't changed."

Laila chuckled. "You sound like her sister."

"You too, Laila?" Gemma asked, mortally wounded.

"It is something Keeley would say!"

"And Sprenger's not going to kill you," Shona announced. She wasn't eating. Instead, she'd set up a blanket a bit away from them and spent her time sharpening her sword.

"You can't tell me he's not going to try. I'm positive. He's going to want to execute me."

"He's definitely not going to execute you."

"How can you be so sure?"

"Because he no longer makes decisions on his own. He and the elders have to agree."

"He'll override them. I'm sure of it. The man *needs* to execute me."

Laila finally threw up her hands. "What is this obsession you have with this man executing you? It's as if you *want* him to execute you."

Gemma smiled. "I do."

"My brother's right. You are insane."

"I told you," Quinn said, leaning back to stare up at the two suns, his hands behind his big head. "I told all of you."

"I'm not insane. I know exactly what I'm doing. Sprenger hates me, which means he'll want to look me right in the eyes before he sets me aflame. And that's when I'll do it."

"Do what?"

"Kill him."

"Won't you be tied up or something?" Keran asked.

"Eh. I can get past that." And then, when everyone stared at her, "What? You think no one's tried to execute me before?"

"She's right," Katla agreed. "If she was condemned to execution this time, it would be your . . . what, Gemma? Fourth?"

"Fifth."

"Fifth? Did I miss one?"

"You did," Shona said, looking over her sword carefully before going back to sharpening it a bit more. "You had an injury and stayed behind when we took on Lord Turnball at his mountain retreat. That was the fourth one."

"Has anyone *not* wanted you dead?" Quinn asked Gemma.

She glanced off, trying to remember, until Quinn finally sighed and said, "Forget I asked."

"And so it's true," a female voice said from behind her. Gemma felt that shudder go up her spine and her lip curl, and for once, she really wished her sister's demon wolves were around because they tended to randomly attack when they were startled.

Quinn had noticed the female monk walking toward them but hadn't thought much about it. Why should he? She hadn't seemed much different from the others wandering around the grounds. She was tall and strong, like all the female monks at the monastery. Well, they might not all be tall, but every one of them appeared strong. She had dark skin and black hair plaited into war braids. Scars littered her face, neck, and hands, the only parts of her Quinn could see.

Her eyes were dark brown and constantly scanned her surroundings. Whether they were searching for misbehavior or attacking enemies, Quinn couldn't tell. She wore the white tunic of high rank and a constant scowl of disappointment, but other than that . . . she seemed no different than the rest of her brethren.

She stopped behind Gemma and stared down at her as Gemma's battle-cohorts gawked up at the woman with something akin to fear. Strange since the three of them didn't seem to fear much of anything but more Kir-tears.

"And so it's true," the newcomer finally said to the top of Gemma's head, and Quinn saw Gemma cringe as if she'd just been caught stealing money by a town magistrate. "You really are back."

Katla opened her mouth to speak but the monk stopped her without doing more than glancing at her. Literally, that's all she did.

She lifted her gaze to Katla and the words died in Katla's throat. Then the monk moved her gaze back to the top of Gemma's head.

"I hear you're a princess now. How nice for you."

There was a beat . . . two . . . and then . . .

"So are you just going to sit there and not greet me properly, Brother Gemma?"

Gemma scrambled to her feet at the snapped question and faced the woman.

"Master General Ragna." Gemma briefly bowed her head. "How nice to see you again."

Hands behind her back, Master General Ragna began to walk around Gemma in a tight circle, looking her over as one might a prize bull. "I see you've been letting yourself go a bit. Not quite training like you used to."

"I actually have been training . . . Sir."

"Not like you should be." She slapped at Gemma's side. "Look at that flab."

Gemma's mouth dropped open but then she just as quickly closed it again.

"Your hair is ridiculously long too." It didn't even reach her shoulders.

"And what are you wearing?" she asked, feeling the chainmail between her fingers.

"I—"

"Have you taken a vow of poverty?"

"My mother made this chainmail."

"You're taking hand-me-downs from your mother now. That's pathetic."

"Master General—"

"Don't speak. I didn't give you leave to speak."

Impressive. Even Keeley—a queen!—couldn't get Gemma to shut up that easily.

The master general stopped in front of Gemma and stared her down again.

"So why are you back here?"

"I bring word from the queen."

"A princess bringing messages from the queen? Doesn't she have actual messengers for that sort of useless duty?"

"She does, but since I have a past relationship—"

Eyebrow peaking, the master general repeated, "Past relationship? So you no longer consider yourself one of our order?"

"I ... wouldn't say ... I ..."

"I asked you a question that should be easy enough for you to answer."

"It's complicated."

"Is it? Because the commitment you made was for life."

"I know but—"

"Are your commitments as weak as your back kick?"

"What's wrong with my back kick?"

"You know, Brother Gemma—"

"I feel like you're making a statement by calling me that."

"—there are some here that I'd let go without even a backward glance."

Shona frowned. "What are you looking at me for?"

"But there are others, like you, where I do believe ... that would be a mistake."

Now Gemma frowned. "Once you asked me if my parents knew when I was still in my crib if they'd created a disaster. Then you asked if they were closely related."

The master general pointed at the monastery. "You do know that right now, there are men, up there, making decisions about your life?"

"I'm aware."

"Because they seem to think that you've turned your back on our gods."

"That's not true. I just ... just ..."

"You just ... just ... just ... what? Tell me, Brother Gemma, what's more important than the commitment you swore to?" She stepped close to Gemma, standing over her, looking down at her.

"My family," Gemma finally said.

"Ahhh, yes," the master general said. "Your precious family. So important to you that you walked away from them all those years ago."

From the corner of his eye, Quinn saw Keran shoot past him, but Farlan was quick enough to catch her before she could tackle the master general to the ground and start pummeling.

"Is there something you want to say to me, Master General?" Gemma asked. "If not, I'd like to get back to my meal."

The master general grinned but Quinn took no solace from that grin. None at all.

"Actually, dear Brother Gemma, I'd like to show you something."

"Show me what?"

"You'll see." She glanced at each of them. "You'll all see."

No, no, no! Quinn did not like this *at all*.

Master General Ragna was a brilliant soldier, a brilliant general, and a brilliant tactician. But she was a bitch and Gemma hated her.

She didn't hate her for the same reason she hated Sprenger. How could she? Ragna had never once put her hands on any of the trainees inappropriately. But the monk was a ball-busting, cold-blooded, heartless female who had first been Gemma's trainer, then Gemma's first commanding officer. Those had been long, painful years.

It was clear to anyone with eyes that Ragna never liked Gemma nor had respect for her. The reasons why were plain. She thought that although Gemma was "fine" in battle, she did not truly uphold the dogma of their order. As far as Ragna was concerned, Gemma was vacuous, selfish, and—

"A complete chatterbox."

Quinn glanced back at Gemma. "A chatterbox? Gemma?"

Ragna nodded. "Yes. She never shuts up. Haven't you noticed? It shocks me that anyone talks as much as she does. She spends all day joking and distracting everyone from our true work and calling."

Quinn again looked back at Gemma, the confused expression on his face making him appear to be another person.

"*Gemma?*"

"Why do you keep repeating her name?"

"Because I've known her for two years. I've been in battle with her. Eaten meals with her. Hunted with her. And take it from someone who knows . . . the woman has no sense of humor."

"Perhaps you're just not humorous," Gemma noted.

"Perhaps you're just mean-spirited," Quinn guessed.

A mile or so later, Ragna silently called a stop with a raised fist.

Closing her eyes and clasping her hands together, she lowered her head and chanted a spell. A few seconds later, the air around them parted, revealing a large number of trees wound with twisted vines. She took out her sword and slashed at the vines until she'd opened up a small path.

She put her finger to her lips. "Shhhh," she said softly, and motioned them to follow.

The path only allowed them to move in two at a time. They were just about to enter a sizable clearing when Ragna stopped them all again and motioned for just Gemma to advance with her.

Once Gemma was inside the clearing, she saw a large, beautiful, dapple-gray horse with a black mane and tail on the far side grazing on some grass.

It seemed strange that Ragna would use her magick skills to hide a horse from the view of the other monks. Each brother was given two horses when they made their vows. Horses weren't something that war monks had to share with one another. Becoming one with the beast you rode into battle with was as important as learning how to use the sword strapped to your back. Meaning that there was no need to hide a horse you found if you took a true liking to it. And as a master general, Ragna could pick any horse she wanted. So why was this horse here?

The horse turned a little and Gemma saw the splotch of white on its hindquarter that almost looked like a hammer! She remembered when she'd first seen that marking and how she'd insisted that the horse had to be hers because "she's wearing my sister's hammer!"

"It's Kriegszorn!" Gemma happily cheered. "It's Kriegs—"

Ragna's hand slapped over her mouth and she was dragged back into the woods with the others.

Gemma was pushed into Quinn's arms and Ragna pulled out her sword. Then she silently waited. The horse moved around the clearing but eventually went back to grazing on the far side.

"What's going on?" Gemma whispered. "It's just Kriegszorn. My warhorse. She'd never hurt me. She . . . she . . . oh fuck."

* * *

Quinn had known Gemma for a while now . . . that was not her good "oh fuck."

"What?" he whispered.

Gemma faced him. "Kriegszorn's dead."

"When?"

"Couple of years ago."

"Is that her offspring?"

"She didn't have any offspring."

"Sibling?"

"No."

"Then that's a problem."

"How did she die?" Laila asked.

"In battle. A month or so before I left for home. A spear through the neck."

"I remember," Katla gasped, hands covering her mouth. "Oh, Gemma."

"What?" Quinn demanded while still keeping his voice at a whisper. "What's wrong?"

"Tell him, Brother Gemma," the master general insisted.

Gemma let out a sigh and rolled her eyes, but she finally began. "This particular battle wasn't going very well. We were getting pushed into a corner and it looked like we wouldn't be able to get out."

"And?" the master general prodded.

Gemma glared at the monk, but finally admitted, "So I raised Kriegszorn."

"*From the dead?*"

"Shhhhhh!" everyone hissed at Quinn's surprised yelp.

"Yes. From the dead," Gemma whispered. "But the spell should have only lasted twenty minutes. Maybe thirty." Gemma pointed toward the clearing. "Why is she still alive, Ragna?"

"It's Master General to you, defiler—"

"Hey!"

"—and I have no idea. She came here like that. Looking for *you*."

"That battle was a thousand leagues away."

"And yet here she is. In the decaying flesh."

"I don't understand," Shona said, trying to peer through the trees to get a better glimpse. "I've never heard of something like this before."

"It gets even stranger," the master general happily went on, much to Gemma's annoyance. "Parts of her are decaying while parts of her regenerate."

"What?"

"And, if you look at the clearing, some trees are dead and some are filled with beautiful, bizarre flowers I've never seen before. And on some nights, weird lights radiate from the area."

"What does any of that mean?" Laila asked.

"I have no idea," the master general said with a disturbing chuckle.

"What do the elders say?"

"Do you think I told *anyone* about this? Are you mad? If I had, I knew that Sprenger would have you burned as a witch as soon as you came back. Of course, that was my fear before I knew you'd become a princess."

"You do know you're actually saying prince-*ass*, don't you?" Gemma demanded.

"Only Joshua knew about your unholy horse and he had no answers either."

"She's not unholy," Gemma argued, "and none of this is her fault."

"No. It's *your* fault. *You* did this."

"I don't know how." Gemma looked at everyone. "Seriously. I have *no* idea how I did it. None." Gemma held up her hands, gazed at them in wonder. "Am I magickally gifted?"

"Doubt it," Keran muttered.

Gemma scowled at her cousin just as the horse finally turned away from its grazing spot so Quinn could get a really good look at it. What he saw horrified him.

There was no flesh on the right side of the creature's face, giving it a disturbing smile. Where its eye should have been, there was just a blob of blood. Chunks of its skin and flesh were missing from its neck, revealing rotting tendons that moved anytime it opened its mouth or moved its head. Pieces of it were dropping off its gut, and all that remained of its back right leg were tendons.

It didn't seem to be suffering. Yet Quinn didn't care. Pulling his sword, he started forward. He was going to end it now.

But Gemma grabbed his arm.

"Where are you going?" she asked.

"To kill that thing."

"You're not killing my horse."

"Gemma, it's an abomination."

"It's Kriegszorn."

He pointed. "Look at it. Did Kriegszorn have fangs? Because it seems to have fangs now." He pointed at another spot in the clearing. "There are bones over there of something that it has recently killed and, I'm guessing, eaten."

"That's wild boar. It doesn't mean she eats humans now."

"Are you listening to yourself?"

"I am not going to let you kill my horse and that's the end of the discussion!"

"Uh . . . Gemma?"

"What, Keran?"

Keran never got a chance to answer as the half-beautiful, half-horrifying horse's head poked its way through the trees inquisitively. And, like the mighty, fearless warriors they were, all of them—except Ragna—screamed hysterically and dove for cover.

"That was just embarrassing," Ragna complained. "You even scared the abomination."

"Stop calling her that," Gemma said as she brushed the dirt from her leggings, chest, and face.

"So what are you going to do with her?" Keran asked.

"I'm going to see exactly how dangerous she is."

"She's dangerous," Ragna insisted.

"We just scared her with our screams. How dangerous can she be?"

"When she was traveling here to find you, there were rumors of a devil horse killing people indiscriminately across the lands. When I secured her in here . . . those rumors stopped. So she's dangerous."

"That's not proof it was her." But even Gemma knew her argument was weak.

Gemma felt horrible. What had she done to her poor horse? Kriegszorn had been an amazing, loyal horse and she'd turned her into this horrible thing.

Before she made any decisions, she had to make sure putting the horse down was absolutely necessary.

Gemma stepped back into the clearing and called out to Kriegszorn. Well . . . she tried. What came out was a weak, squeaked-out whisper. She tried again. Still nothing. Finally, she got out, "Kriegszorn!"

The horse spun around and faced her.

Gemma cleared her voice again. "Kriegszorn, it's me. It's Gemma. Come here, girl. Come here. Come here . . . beautiful."

That last bit was kind of hard to get out, but she did it.

Kriegszorn stared at her from across the clearing; then she was suddenly charging Gemma.

"Uh-oh."

"Gemma!" Quinn barked at her from the tree line. "Get out of there!"

But Gemma refused to run. Kriegszorn had traveled all this way to find her. She must remember her. She must still love her. Gemma forced herself to stand her ground.

Kriegszorn came closer and closer, hooves tearing up the soil between them. When she was inches away, Gemma shut her eyes and waited to end up the way many enemies had ended up during battle when Gemma and Kriegszorn had run them down. She heard Kriegszorn whinny loudly and opened her eyes to see the massive horse on her hind legs, front legs high in the air.

A few seconds later, she came down, the ground around them seeming to shake with the impact. Kriegszorn moved closer and rested her big head on Gemma's shoulder. Just as she used to do when Gemma brushed her mane or stroked her neck.

She could feel blood from the open wounds on the right side dripping onto her chainmail-covered shoulder but it was the normal, left side that was pressed comfortably against Gemma's ear and neck.

"Oh, Kriegszorn. How I've missed you, my beautiful girl."

She stroked the horse's neck and ran her fingers through her mane, telling her, "Don't you worry. When this is all over, no matter what happens, you are going back home. My family will take care of you."

"*Have you lost your mind?*" Quinn demanded, now standing behind her.

Before Gemma could tell him to fuck off, as she liked to do when he overstepped his bounds, Kriegszorn suddenly pushed her aside with her large body, opened her mouth to reveal the large number of fangs she now had. And she roared at Quinn. Something horses didn't really do either.

That's when Quinn shifted to his battle-ready centaur form, with full antlers and fangs. He pulled his sword and axe.

Her battle-cohorts came out of the trees to stare at Quinn with their mouths open, but Ragna simply smirked at Gemma and flatly asked, "So now you're bringing *centaurs* to the monastery? What's next, Brother Gemma? Legions from one of the hells?"

Keran chuckled. "Wait until ya meet her sister's dogs— *owwwww! What the rude-fuck was that for, ya evil bitch?*"

"What do you think?" Thomassin asked his cohorts. The same men he'd trained with all those decades ago. They'd been through hell together, but hell hadn't mattered because they always had one another's backs. It was strange, though, planning all this without Joshua right by their side. Gods, how Thomassin missed him. But saving this order was the last thing he needed to do for his friend, and he'd make sure it was accomplished.

"He's going to make a move on her," Bartholemew guessed.

The three men watched Master General Ragna dismount from her horse and hand over the reins to her squire. She stopped to speak to several of her direct commands before sending them off.

"Joshua said he wasn't afraid of her," Brín reminded them.

Bartholemew shook his head. "Joshua lied. That woman is . . . that woman."

"If she sides with Sprenger . . ."

"We won't let her," Thomassin decided. "We'll go talk to her. Like calm, rational men."

Nodding in agreement, they all set off after Ragna but she abruptly stopped and turned toward them. They immediately stopped too and began to look . . . anywhere. The sky. The ground. Thomassin found a reason to stare at a broken fence. She watched them for a moment, then disappeared into the stables where her horses were kept.

"Remember that time I had to battle an army of demons?" Bartholemew asked. "And I was all alone until you three could get to me. And it took you nearly an hour?"

"Yes," Thomassin replied. "I remember."

"Still less scary than dealing with that woman."

Sprenger followed two of his guards into the stables. He knew Ragna was in here. She liked to wash off the grime of the day near her horses, so her army had set up a space for her within the stables. Then some dwarf engineer she knew had created an elaborate water system that with the assistance of a moving horse conducted water through tubing to spray down on her while she stood under it.

That's exactly where Ragna was when one of his guards grabbed her shoulder to alert her to Sprenger's presence. But before a word was spoken, Ragna's wet hand reached out and grabbed the monk's arm, twisting until the bone snapped at the shoulder. With her free hand, she grabbed the monk by the throat and lifted him off his feet, holding him high above her head.

"*Master General Ragna!*" Sprenger bellowed.

Unlike everyone else in the monastery, Ragna did not immediately drop her prey at Sprenger's command. Instead, her gaze simply shifted to him while she continued to hold the screaming man with both hands.

"Oh," she said in that calm voice of hers, "Grand Master. I didn't hear you come in."

"Release him this instant!"

"Why, of course. He just startled me." She released the monk and the second guard ran to his side.

"Take him to the healer," Sprenger ordered.

"But, Grand Master—"

"I'll be fine."

His protection detail quickly left and Sprenger moved closer to Ragna. But not too close. He knew better.

"I wanted to talk to you about Gemma Smythe."

"Ahhh, yes," she said, scrubbing her skin raw. "The return of the great Gemma Smythe. I really never thought she'd show her face here again."

"I want her executed but the elders do not agree with me."

"Why not? It sounds good to me."

"Excellent. So I can expect your support when the time comes?"

"Absolutely."

"Good." He turned to go.

"Of course . . . she hasn't actually done anything to warrant execution. Thus—"

"Thus?"

"—I would never feel right about her being executed. Is there another route we can go? You know . . . to get your point across?"

Sprenger turned back. "Well . . . is she even part of our order anymore? She doesn't wear her tunic. She travels with Amichai. She's a princess now, you know."

"All excellent points, Grand Master. And you're absolutely right. She comes in here with her hoity-toity ways, forgetting she's made a commitment to this monastery."

"Yes. But how can we demonstrate that she has greatly disappointed us without actually taking off her head or burning her at the stake?"

"Good question. Good question." They were silent for a moment while Ragna scrubbed and scrubbed, as if she was attempting to remove her skin completely. Finally, she said, "I have an idea. Maybe she needs to be stripped of her rank and tunic. Let her know that *you,* Grand Master Sprenger, are now in charge. Show her exactly who you are. And don't let her forget it for one damn second. How does that sound?"

He grinned. "Why, Master General, that's a perfect idea. How smart of you to think of it all on your own."

She nodded. "Yes, I knew you'd like that."

Ragna's second-in-command popped up from her own horse's stall, where she'd been checking her stallion's legs.

"What in all the hells are you doing?" she asked, laughing.

Grabbing a long linen cloth and wrapping it around her body, Ragna stepped away from the water.

"A long time ago, someone once said to me, 'It seems that your entire goal in life, Ragna, is to be nothing but the dark, unholy nightmare of man.'" She stopped the horse's movement and un-buckled him from the water system so she could return him to his stall. "Perhaps it's time I prove that belief correct."

"Did your father say that to you?"

"No. It was my mother that time. She sobbed when she said it. I laughed, which she took rather personally. My father did once ac-cuse me, though, of being the manifestation of true evil, which I felt was unnecessarily harsh."

Ragna held the horse's reins and asked, "Is everything ready?"

"Absolutely." Bowing her head, Ragna's second-in-command asked, "You sure it's going to be tonight, Commander?"

"I'm positive. I feel it in my bones." And her bones were never wrong. Not when it came to this sort of thing. "Make sure everyone is ready. We move on my orders. Understand?"

"Understood."

"Tonight our god starts all this anew," Ragna stated, leading the horse back to the safety of its stall. "And all we can do is announce his arrival with the blood of our brothers."

CHAPTER 11

Gemma initially worried that Ragna would tell the elders about Kriegszorn. She still had no idea what had happened there. She had done nothing different with her spell to raise the dead. A short-term necromancer chant that should have worked for her as it had in the past: raising the freshly killed horse to do Gemma's bidding, then twenty minutes later, releasing it to death. An hour or so after that, it would be nothing more than decrepit bones and decimated flesh. The spell had always gone that way and it continued so to this day.

Except for Kriegszorn.

The mare was the only one that had been unusual, but Gemma was positive she had done nothing different.

Except that ... well, except that Kriegszorn had not been an enemy. She had been Gemma's battle horse. As bound to her as one of her battle-cohorts.

Normally, Gemma would never have done such a thing as raise Kriegszorn, but she'd had little choice. They'd been in desperate straits. So she'd broken her own code and spoken the spell over the battle mare while tears had spilled from her eyes and her cohorts protected her back.

Could that be what made the difference? A broken heart and spilled tears?

It didn't matter. If Sprenger found out, he would definitely use the mare's existence to his advantage and have Gemma accused of witchery and unholy spell casting. And just the sight of the decaying but continually rejuvenating Kriegszorn might turn neutral monks firmly against Gemma.

But then Gemma remembered that in all this time, Ragna had not said one word about the horse to anyone but Joshua. Not even to Gemma's battle-cohorts. Eventually she stopped worrying about Ragna revealing Kriegszorn's existence and instead worried about her outing the centaurs. But that concern only lasted a few minutes. Ragna hadn't seemed to care too much about them either. She'd simply sealed up the area where she kept Kriegszorn and made her way back to the monastery. She didn't run back. She didn't even look at any of the Amichais any differently. If she had any concerns, she didn't show it.

And even after dismissing her main worries, Gemma couldn't stop the feeling that something was amiss.

Which made the knock at her window late in the evening almost a relief.

Gemma opened the window and found Quinn hanging from a rope outside it. "I'm not even going to ask what you're doing."

"You should see something."

She waited for him to climb back up and then followed him to the battlements on the monastery roof, where the rest of their group was waiting.

"There's no one up here? No one keeping a lookout?" she asked. "Wait, you didn't kill the lookouts, did you?"

Keran frowned. "Why are you looking at me?"

"You know why I'm looking at you."

"There was no one here when I came up," Quinn said. "Just needed some air. I find those tiny prison cells stifling."

"They're not prison cells."

"Look around."

"Look around at what?" Gemma asked.

"Everything."

She did. Walking to one end of the battlements, she saw what had caught Quinn's attention and what probably accounted for her having a hard time getting any sleep.

She gazed down at the amount of activity going on inside and outside the monastery walls. Everywhere, the monks were reinforcing what had stood for centuries.

Crossing the battlements, she watched the librarian monks—a special breed of fighting monks who would protect the monastery's books and artifacts with their very lives—removing various items wrapped in plain white cloth. She wondered if those were weapons from the Chamber of Valor.

"Cyrus is coming," she now realized.

"What?"

"Cyrus is coming. That's why they're taking out the artifacts. That's what all this preparation is for."

"Are you sure?"

"What else could it be?"

"Then why aren't they leaving?"

Gemma shook her head. "I don't know."

"Didn't you say Sprenger has already accepted Beatrix's help?"

"Yes, which means that if they're leaving, they should just be heading off to her castle. I don't know why they're not."

"Well, instead of standing around guessing, why don't we simply go down and join in?" Laila asked, always the helpful one.

"No," Gemma immediately replied.

"Why not?"

Gemma didn't bother to answer. She simply pointed, and they all turned to see what she'd spotted moments before from the corner of her eye. Several monks waiting for her at the roof door to take her back inside to the grand master . . .

"What is the plan here?" Quinn asked as they all followed the silent monks down the stairs and through the barely lit passageways to wherever the grand master and the elders awaited them.

"Why do you sound so worried?"

"Because when it comes to this lowlife—that even I have to admit deserves a death of unmeasurable pain—you're not the rational, calm Gemma I've come to respect and irritate. You're more like your uncle Archie. Easily agitated and slightly hysterical."

"I am *not* hysterical."

"You are *so* hysterical. At least for you. And if that only meant you cried a lot, I would be okay with it. But you don't cry. You're not a crier. You are, instead, a crazy person who, like your uncle, does crazy things."

"Such as?"

"That time you threw a fireball at your sister."

"It was *not* a fireball. It was a slightly lit log from the firepit."

"It set her clothes on fire."

"Barely!"

"Could you two have this conversation later?" Laila asked softly. "I think you're worrying the religious fanatics."

"See what you did?" Quinn demanded of Gemma. "My sister never called monks religious fanatics before. But now she does. And it's probably because of you."

"The first firepit I find," Gemma promised when they arrived at two large double doors deeply inscribed with her god's rune, "I'm setting you on fire."

"That is it!" Laila snapped. "I swear by the eight legs of Ofydd Naw, if you two don't stop it right now—"

The two doors swung open to reveal three older monks standing inside. But they weren't the only ones. The room was fairly stuffed with white tunic–clad monks. All waiting to see what would befall Gemma in the next few minutes.

"Brother Gemma," one of the monks greeted as he smoothly moved up next to her.

"Brother Thomassin."

"Starting shit as usual, I see," he quietly teased.

"He started it."

"I did not," Quinn replied.

"Later, children." He looked directly into Gemma's face. "Listen to me. You say 'yes' to whatever is said to you. Understand? 'Yes, yes, and more yes.' We'll take it from there. I promise it will work out for you in the end."

"But—"

"What part of that did you *not* understand?"

"All of it."

"For once, Gemma, follow directions."

"Fine."

"Good. Thank you. And tell your friends to keep calm. If everyone is rational, this should go exactly as Joshua wanted it to. Now let's go."

It was clear that last mention of her old mentor had filled Gemma with questions, but she didn't have a chance to ask anything before Brother Thomassin motioned her and the rest of them into the chamber. Monks lined the path that led to a five-pointed star in the middle of the floor. Gemma stood in the center, facing the raised dais and her nemesis. Grand Master Sprenger.

Quinn and the others moved off to the side. Laila stood on his right, her gaze searching the crowd for any signs of trouble. She trusted few humans, so this whole thing had her very uncomfortable. If she were in her natural form, her tail *and* ears would be constantly twitching with worry.

But while his sister studied everyone, Quinn studied Sprenger. He couldn't help it. Amazing the damage one human male could do to so many. Although his tunic and chainmail hid any scars on his body, Quinn could see the scar on his face well enough. Gemma really had fucked up that jaw of his. A double-sided scar stretched from his right ear, down along his jaw and across to about three inches from his left ear. There were no mirrors in this monastery, so Sprenger couldn't see that scar every day, but he must be able to feel it. Every time he touched his face. Every time he washed it. Every time he attempted to grow a beard and realized that hair wouldn't grow along those scars. Maybe even worse, when he talked or chewed or when it was extremely cold and the bone hurt or didn't sit right in the socket. Each time those things happened . . . he must remember what Gemma had done to him.

And the thought of his continued suffering did nothing but make Quinn smile.

Gemma didn't know what was going to happen but she was ready. She was ready for manipulation or lies or an outright assassination attempt by Sprenger and his minions. She'd never been so ready before. Not only had her training as a war monk prepared her for anything that bastard had to throw at her, but also her training as a Smythe. She had one sister who'd attempted to kill the other just so she could wear a stupid crown. An uncle who kept telling the children to be ready to kill each other should they be invaded by the enemy. And another sister who insisted on frolicking with demon dogs.

Gemma was more than ready for anything Sprenger could think of tossing at her.

So she lowered her gaze and she waited. Like a good little monk. For the false grand master to do what he planned to do.

"Brother Gemma, it's so good to have you back," he began, and Gemma was glad that she had her gaze lowered because she rolled her eyes *so hard.* "We have missed having you here among us. But I think all of us can admit things have changed since you last graced our humble monastery. And decisions have been made that affect your relationship to the order directly."

Under her lashes she glanced at Thomassin, now sitting on the dais behind Sprenger. He gave a very small nod, urging her to remain calm and just remember, "yes, yes, yes."

"Yes," she replied.

Sprenger smiled as if that was exactly what he wanted to hear, which annoyed her greatly, but she'd promised.

"And after much thoughtful and painful consideration, a decision has been made. Since you are now a princess of Queen Keeley's court, while the Order of Righteous Valor will be falling under the banner of King Marius . . . it is impossible for you to continue as one of our order."

Gemma would admit that it took her a considerable amount of time to understand what Sprenger was actually saying to her.

Lifting her gaze, she first looked at Thomassin, Bartholemew, and Brín. Silently and with as little obvious movement as possible, they all frowned and nodded toward her. Wanting her to agree. But she was still a little confused, which horrified her. She'd always considered herself the "smart one" of her family.

She shifted her gaze to Sprenger and asked, "What?"

"What don't you understand, dear?"

Dear? Did he just call her dear?

"All of it."

"Oy," he muttered under his breath. "I forgot about this part of dealing with you." He cleared his throat and began again. "As of tonight, you will agree to no longer call yourself a monk of the Order of Righteous Valor. Instead, you will simply be Princess Gemma of Queen Keeley's court. Or, if you'd like, you could find another war monk order somewhere closer to your sister's queendom. I'm sure several of the elders will be more than happy to write you a glowing recommendation to help you secure a position. This has already been discussed with the grand elders and Master General Ragna. They all believe it is the best course. Now, if you agree, we can finish this conclave, and move on to a delightful evening of feasting—"

"And ale?" Keran called out, ever hopeful. When she realized that now everyone was gawking at her, she raised her hands, palms out, and said, "Sorry. Sorry. Forgot where I was. Sorry."

"Do you agree to that . . . Your Highness?"

Again, Gemma looked at the three elders. They were no longer trying to be subtle. Instead, they were mouthing, *Say yes! Now!*

She looked at her travel companions. Quinn and Laila were loudly whispering, "Just say yes. What are you doing?" while Keran was begging, "Please say yes so I can get to a gods-damn pub, woman!" Poor Cadell and Farlan appeared overwhelmingly bored. Samuel said nothing; he appeared . . . terrified. She had no idea if he was afraid she'd say yes or no. He just seemed scared to death. Not that she blamed him.

Gemma glanced at her battle-cohorts and they shrugged, leaving the choice up to her. A decision this momentous had to come from her heart and soul.

Finally, she scanned the crowd for one more person and found her standing at the far side of the dais, simply watching Gemma.

Gemma stared at Ragna but all Ragna did was exactly what she used to do when Gemma was in training and was confused by a question. She just raised that damn eyebrow. Just the one. Her left one. That simple, single move used to irritate Gemma to her very being. To her very core!

And that's what it did right now. Because that gesture always seemed to say the same thing to her. "Don't you already *know* the answer to this question? Must I actually *give* you the answer? Are you really *that* worthless?"

She knew that was a lot for one eyebrow to say, but she knew that's exactly what that one eyebrow was saying to her. And in that moment, in that second, Gemma had her answer.

She returned her gaze to Sprenger. Lifted her chin and with pride said loudly for everyone to hear . . .

"Fuck *you!*" she bellowed at the grand master of the Order of Righteous Valor. "*Fuck you, fuck you, fuck you!*"

"This is your fault!" his sister hissed at him.

"How is this *my* fault?"

"It just is!"

Quinn didn't know how that was possible, but he was glad Laila had said something. Because if she hadn't, he would have started laughing. Especially when he'd locked eyes with the master general across the room. He'd never really seen her shocked up to this point, and her shocked face was hilarious. She looked like a startled bird. Her body straightened, her head snapped up, her eyes widened, and she almost smiled. It was as if she'd expected something from Gemma, but not quite *this*.

Of course, none of them looked as if they'd expected this from Gemma. Even he hadn't expected this from Gemma. Then again . . . it was just so Gemma, wasn't it?

Sprenger sat forward in his big chair, hands gripping the arms, his rage barely contained.

"What did you say to me?" Did he really want her to repeat it? Because . . . that seemed a mistake. Quinn knew Gemma. She would definitely say it all again. Happily.

"I said fuck you!" *See?* "Want me to say it a few more times?"

By the unholiest of gods, this was going to get nasty. And to be honest, Quinn couldn't wait.

"I was going to give you a chance—" Sprenger began.

"Give me a chance for what? I did nothing wrong. It was a grand master—a *true* grand master, by the way—who sent me out. I was following orders as I've always been trained to do. So there's nothing to punish me for. And if you think Beatrix is really an ally, you're a fool. She will take from you everything she can, and then she will destroy you."

"You know nothing about her."

"Very true. She's just my *sister*," Gemma said with great sarcasm, then tilted her head to the side and opened her eyes wide to illustrate how stupid Sprenger was being. A move he didn't appreciate at all.

"This discussion is over," Sprenger announced. "I have made my decision."

"You can't just remove me from the order without due cause."

"I can do anything I want."

"Really? Is that written down somewhere? Brothers?" she called out to a group of well-armed monks clustered around a desk filled with parchments, scrolls, and ancient tomes. "Is it written down somewhere that the grand master can do just anything he wants?"

"That is it!" Sprenger launched himself from his chair and marched down the steps until he was standing in front of Gemma, towering over her. "You are out!"

"You can't throw me out without justification. Trust me, that was one of the first things I checked when I committed my heart and soul to Morthwyl."

"Except that's just what I did! I've thrown you out! For gross insubordination."

"This isn't the Order of Silent Prayer and Sacrifice, Grand Master. You need more than that to toss me out on my ass."

"I'll think of something."

"You want something, you arrogant fuck—"

Thomassin buried his head in his hands and moaned, "Oh, Gemma."

"—then . . . Challenge."

There were shocked gasps around the room and more elders dropped their heads in their hands or rolled their eyes or simply closed their eyes and shook their heads.

Sprenger gawked down at Gemma. "What did you say?"

"Challenge."

"You can't challenge me. You're not of high enough rank."

"So? You can't just throw me out. And yet here we are!"

With no answer, the grand master just stared at her.

That's when Gemma asked, "What's the matter? Afraid I'll finish taking off that jaw?"

The backhand took them all by surprise. Blood from Gemma's

mouth and nose splattered Quinn and Laila, but they still managed to catch Keran before she could get her hands on Sprenger.

Slowly, ignoring the blood pouring down her lips and chin, Gemma looked up at the grand master and spat out, "Challenge."

"I will *not* accept a challenge from some low-born, low-rank no-body!"

"Hey!" Gemma was quick to remind him. "I'm a princess now, bitch!"

"Brother Gemma!" Thomassin barked again.

"There's another option," Master General Ragna said as she made her slow, methodical way across the room, inserting herself between Gemma and Sprenger to prevent any more unnecessary hitting. "Brother Gemma's rank doesn't matter if she's someone else's champion."

The anger that now flashed across Sprenger's face was white hot and dangerous and, Quinn was guessing, much deeper than what he'd felt toward Gemma. He was so angry that he grabbed Ragna's upper arm and yanked her close.

He snarled between his teeth, "What do you think you're doing? We discussed this."

A few of Ragna's soldiers were in the chamber with her and the ends of their spears hit the ground. It was a simple gesture but most of the monks backed away. Sprenger didn't seem to notice; his gaze was locked on Ragna's face. She, however, was too busy staring at where his fingers gripped her arm.

"I would strongly suggest," Ragna said, "that you think about where you put your hands . . . Grand Master."

It was a simple statement, quietly made in her effortless, calm way. But that was where the threat came from. In that calm way that told Sprenger she would destroy him in ways that the rest of them could only dream about. Sprenger wisely released her and turned his back. A risky move, but Quinn sensed that Ragna was too proud to attack such a man from behind.

Without even acknowledging him, she went on. "Elder Thomassin, is Brother Gemma a worthy champion for you?"

Thomassin looked at the two elders on either side of him. First one, then the other. They both nodded and he returned his gaze to Ragna. But before he said anything, he sighed. Loud and long. Not in anger or disgust. Just in frustrated acceptance. Whatever these three monks had planned, Gemma had fucked it up as only Gemma could. It was something about the Smythe family. They tended to fuck things up. Whether it was for their own siblings or for kings. They never meant to, but fuck things up they did.

"Yes," he finally stated. "She is a worthy champion."

"Then we have Challenge, Grand Master. One you cannot turn down. As you so wisely pointed out to Grand Master Joshua when you challenged him."

"Fine." Sprenger faced them. "Three days hence—"

"Now," Gemma said.

Ragna shrugged. "As the *weaker* of the challengers, Grand Master, Brother Gemma chooses the time. She says now. So it's now. Weapons?"

"Swords," Gemma announced.

"Swords it is."

"Do I get any say?" Sprenger demanded.

"Not really."

"Hold!" one of the monks called, stepping forward.

"Yes, Brother James?" Ragna asked.

"I offer to be the grand master's champion," Brother James announced proudly.

Gemma cracked her knuckles before opening her arms wide and demanding, "Let's go!"

"No," Ragna quickly interjected. "There will be no champion for the grand master."

"Why not?" Brother James wanted to know.

"Because Grand Master Sprenger did not allow one for Grand Master Joshua. So it seems only fair, does it not? Good!" she finished when Brother James attempted to argue.

"Now," Ragna said, looking at both parties, "five minutes and then we begin."

Ragna briefly stopped next to Gemma and told her, "For once, attempt to remember what I taught you."

Sprenger, however, looked at Thomassin and threatened, "Once I kill her . . . I kill you."

"Oh, dearest Brother," Thomassin replied with a smirk, "we've had so many experiences together . . . what's one more?"

* * *

Gemma removed her fur cape and the chainmail shirt her mother had made for her, leaving only the thick white shirt she wore under it. She moved her arms and shoulders, twisted her head from side to side.

Shona looked over the weapons she had on her sword belt. "Long sword or—"

"Not sure yet."

"Better think fast."

"Don't start with me, Shona."

"Thomassin and the others had different plans," Katla needlessly pointed out.

"Yes, I figured that out."

"Then why didn't you—"

"Just go along? I'm a war monk. We were never trained to just go along. Joshua's ashes would be swirling around in his . . . wherever they are."

Shona moved closer. "Don't make the mistake of thinking that Sprenger is not a good fighter, Brother. He's always been a good fighter. And over the years he's only gotten better."

"Do either of you really consider this a pep talk?"

"If you want a pep talk, we'd suggest Kir. But he's too busy crying."

"We just got you back," Kir sobbed when the women looked at him.

"The faith all of you have in me is overwhelming."

"Which sword?" Shona asked again.

"I'm still thinking."

"Still?"

Katla put her hand on Gemma's shoulder. "Just . . . don't fuck up."

"Ahhh, how I've missed the brotherhood of it all."

It was worrisome. First, he saw Farlan whisper to Samuel, "Go down to the stables and get the horses ready. Be ready to move. Understand?"

And off the boy went, to get the horses and supplies they'd need. No one stopped him. None of these monks paid the least bit of attention to Samuel. Of course, Quinn had the feeling they'd paid little attention to the poor kid when he'd been an actual squire wearing the tunic of the monastery.

That wasn't what was worrisome, though. It was what he saw after that. Ragna spotted Samuel moving through the crowd and with a subtle nod, she sent one of her own warriors to follow. Why? Why was Ragna sending one of her rather fanatical soldiers to follow a kid? What was really going on? And what did Sprenger mean when he said something about their having "talked about this"? What had they talked about? Gemma? Thomassin? This Challenge? What exactly was happening here?

But before Quinn could decide what his next move should be, his sister grabbed his arm. And it was the urgency with which Laila grabbed him that pushed all other thoughts temporarily out of his head.

"You need to irritate Gemma," she whispered to him.

"You just told me to stop irritating her."

"That was before," Laila insisted. "When I thought we might get out of here without a fight. Now that's obviously *not* going to happen. So now you need to irritate her."

"You're serious?"

"What do you think?"

"You know, this isn't something I can just make up on the spot."

"You are kidding right now, aren't you?"

"No. I don't just irritate her to irritate her. She's irritated by me for some unknown reason. So I have no idea what I could possibly say at the moment that would annoy her so much it would distract her from something as serious as what is about to happen here at this very—ohhhh! You know what? I have something."

Quinn shook off his sister's grip and made his way over to Gemma's side. She stood alone with two swords in her hands. A long sword and a broad sword. She swung both, stretching her arms and shoulders.

"Is this to the death?" he asked.

Gemma stopped moving, turned to face him. "What?"

"Is this a fight to the death?"

"Why are you asking?"

"No reason. Just wondering."

"Stop being an ass and just tell me."

"It's nothing. Go fight."

"Fine. I'm not going to waste my time playing your little games, Amichai."

She took several test swings with each sword before turning back to him and asking, "Does this have anything to do with my horse?"

"Dagger? Dagger will be fine."

"Not Dagger. And you know I don't mean Dagger."

"You're calling that abomination your horse?"

"You're calling her an abomination?"

"It *is* an abomination and that's why if you don't make it, I'm putting it down."

Her back straightened. "You will do no such thing."

"I'm not leaving that thing to roam the earth half-dead."

"Of course you won't. You will take it back to Keeley—"

"I am *not* taking that thing back to Keeley! And I am not going to have it around your family!"

"Brother Gemma," a monk called out, "please join us here—"

"In a minute!" she barked.

"I don't know why you're getting hysterical."

"I am not *hysterical*." But she spit that out between her teeth.

Moving over to their traveling companions and gesturing to Laila with both swords, Gemma wanted to know, "And you, Laila . . . ? Would you protect Kriegszorn?"

"Oh!" Laila replied, forcing a smile she clearly did not feel. "That's right. It has a name."

"None of you would protect Kriegszorn?" she demanded of the whole group. "Keran?"

"The bloody thing has fangs. And it's rotting. It's rotting with fangs."

"All I have to say . . . is that I am *very* disappointed in all of you. Very. Disa. Pointed."

Gemma turned to walk away, but Quinn just had to point out, "Aren't you being just a bit of a hypocrite?"

She spun back around so quickly, their entire group took a step back.

"Excuse me?"

"Are you coming or not?" Sprenger demanded.

"Shut up!" She stepped closer to Quinn. "What did you say?"

"I said, aren't you being a bit of a hypocrite?"

"About what?"

"About your demon horse."

"It . . ." She closed her eyes for a moment. "*She* is not a demon."

"Fine. Abomination then. You've given Keeley such a hard time about her wolves, going on and on about them but now, when that thing is *clearly* unholy . . . suddenly you have some moral objection to doing what is obviously right, which is chopping it into the tiniest pieces, salting them, and performing whatever banishing spell is necessary to send it back wherever it came from."

Gemma was silent for so long that Quinn thought she was simply going to walk away. Perhaps *never* speak to him again. But after several very long seconds of staring at him, she finally said with extreme, absolutely terrifying calm, "I am going to go over there and kill Sprenger. And when I'm done with him, I'm going to come back over here, cut your centaur balls off, and feed them to Kriegszorn."

There were several more moments of brutal, silent staring until she exploded with, "*Is that hypocritical too?*"

Laila stepped in front of Quinn to protect him but Gemma had already stomped away.

"Was that the kind of irritation you were talking about?" he asked his sister.

She lovingly patted his back. "One day the elders of our tribes will tell tales of your sacrifice, Brother. And your sad, early death."

CHAPTER 12

"Are you done chatting with your friends?" Sprenger asked with more sarcasm than Gemma could take at the moment.

So she handled her fury more like a Smythe than a brother of the Order of Righteous Valor, barking, "Oh, shut up!"

"Brother Gemma!" Brother Thomassin scolded from where he stood with the other elders. They were no longer on the raised dais, but grouped with Ragna and the other generals. The highest-ranking monks created a half circle around the Challenge pair.

"Sorry," Gemma muttered. But she wasn't. Not really. Because she was thinking.

"You both know the rules of Challenge," Thomassin reminded them. "And . . . and . . . Brother Gemma . . . are you going to pick a sword?"

"Pardon?"

"One sword. Not two."

She looked down at the two swords she had in her hands. A long sword and a broad sword. She spun around and stared over at her traveling companions. Actually . . . she was staring at Quinn. He knew it too. He picked up Keran and lifted her so that she blocked his face.

"I don't appreciate this," her cousin told the centaur.

"Brother Gemma?" Thomassin pushed.

"Yeah. Sorry."

Biting her lip, she looked down at the two swords and decided. "Shona. Gladius."

Shona reached back, pulled the short sword from the sheath tied to her back, and tossed it to Gemma. She caught it and chucked the other two swords back. Shona caught the broad sword. Laila caught the long sword. And everyone else ducked. It was not pretty.

"Okay. Made my choice," Gemma said.

"Excellent."

"Only took you two hours," Sprenger muttered.

Gemma held the weapon in her hand and it felt right. But still, she felt annoyed. Irritated. She looked at Quinn over her shoulder. He immediately noticed.

"Are you listening to me, Brother Gemma?" Thomassin asked.

"Yes. Of course. Challenge. Rules. Blah blah blah."

It wasn't that she wasn't listening to Brother Thomassin. It was that she was staring at Quinn and thinking about everything he'd said to her in those last ten minutes. He'd managed to irritate her in a way that had her completely livid in seconds. If the two of them were about to fight, it would have been smart.

"Is your disgusting Amichai lover distracting you, Princess?" Sprenger loudly mocked, his group of sycophants laughing along with him.

Gemma focused on Sprenger again, taking a moment to examine him closely. He was taller than her by several inches. Taller than Keeley. Not taller than Quinn or his brother, though. He was also not wider or nearly as fast as Quinn and the other centaurs, but the bastard was quick in battle. She'd seen him fight. She remembered now. He was brutal. Especially when starting out. He moved well too, considering his size. And he knew how to use a sword, his blade picking up momentum and power as he slashed again and again.

So maybe everyone else had been right and she'd been wrong. Maybe Sprenger hadn't tricked Joshua during the fight. Maybe Joshua had simply lost.

Of course, none of that changed Gemma's desire to destroy Sprenger; it simply changed her approach to killing him.

Again, she turned and looked directly at Quinn. If he could piss her off that quickly, maybe she could piss off Sprenger that quickly. She just had to find the right thing to set him off.

* * *

"That woman is going to chop my balls off."

"The way she's staring at you, Brother . . . it's possible."

"You could sound a little more concerned, Laila. She's planning to geld your brother."

"I told you to irritate her. Not send her spiraling into a universe of raging insanity. She's not even paying attention to her opponent! He's going to cut her head off. How are we supposed to go back to Keeley with just her sister's head?"

Laila was right. Gemma was so busy glaring at him, she was completely ignoring the man she was actually supposed to be fighting. And the more Quinn watched Sprenger, the more Quinn was convinced that Gemma had underestimated the grand master's skill level.

Quinn could also see that he and his sister weren't the only ones beginning to feel this way. Thomassin was watching Gemma with great concern. "Brother Gemma," he asked, "are you sure about this?"

"She's sure! Aren't you, Princess?" Sprenger asked. "Although you must be disappointed, yes? That your fondest dreams won't come true tonight."

Gemma blinked and looked at Sprenger over her shoulder. "My fondest dreams?"

"To become grand master of this monastery. To take over all this and finally be in charge of the brotherhood. That is what you want, isn't it? What you've always wanted," he brazenly taunted. He knew she was angry about something. He was trying to tip her over into careless anger by insulting her honor. And with Quinn already pissing her off, it would probably work.

Fuck. Caid was going to kill Quinn when he came home with just Gemma's head.

Gemma faced Sprenger and gripped the gladius by the hilt, adjusting it carefully.

She now stared at the grand master the way she'd been staring at Quinn. That terrifying, blank, "I'm-about-to-cut-your-balls-off" stare.

Finally, after a few long seconds, she calmly announced, "I've never wanted to be grand master." She briefly stopped and looked down at the sword in her hand, tightened and released her fingers around the hilt once, twice. Then finished with, "I just couldn't allow a vile rapist to run the brotherhood I love so much."

It was as if time itself froze.

Everyone stopped moving. Stopped speaking. Stopped breathing.

Quinn realized in that moment Gemma had said the one thing no one in this monastery had ever spoken out loud before. And by doing so, she'd unleashed something very ugly. Not among the other monks, but within Sprenger himself.

His joking expression faded, his eyes grew wide and black in their anger and slowly swiveled in their sockets until they locked on Gemma. She didn't seem to notice, busy as she was, still adjusting her hand around the hilt of her sword.

"What . . . what did you say to me?" he barely managed to ask; his voice was a low, panting growl.

"What did I say?" she asked; still so calm. "I called you a vile rapist. Because that is all you are. That is all you have ever been. That is all you shall ever be." She lifted her gaze to his. "And you shall remain so upon death. Is that clear enough for your understanding? Or is more necessary?"

Sprenger's rage was so strong, his entire body began to vibrate. And Quinn was sure the man had yet to blink. His eyes were wide black pits of unspoken evil and fury.

When the explosion came, it was mighty. His roar of rage reverberated off the stone chamber walls. Sprenger slashed his sword down with one hand, aiming for Gemma's neck. She brought her weapon up, and Quinn waited for the blades to clash.

But then Gemma twisted to the side. A spin, like a dance move. To the grand master's exposed right. His blade stopped in midair. As all of them watched, he finally blinked, dazed, his anger seeming to drain away.

Quinn focused on Gemma and that's when he realized she'd buried her blade deep into Sprenger's right side, just above his waist. Her other arm wrapped around Sprenger's chest and held him tight; then she pulled the weapon out, and shoved it back in. Yanked it up a bit, tearing the flesh along the way, pulled it out, and shoved it in a few more times.

Sprenger dropped to his knees. He was trying to breathe. His blade was still gripped in his hand, but he was no longer able to lift it.

Gemma pulled her arms away and stepped back—the gladius now buried up to the hilt in Sprenger's side—and held her hand out. Katla tossed a dagger to her and Gemma easily caught it. Then she moved behind Sprenger and grabbed him by his gray hair. She pulled his head back and put the blade to his throat. She didn't quickly slash as she had been taught to do. As Quinn had seen her do in battle many, many times before. Instead, she rammed the tip of the blade into the major artery on one side of his neck and dragged the blade from one side to the other, nearly cutting his head off.

When enough blood had flowed from him that the only one who could possibly bring him back was Gemma herself, and that was only as an undead thing, she shoved him to the ground.

Still gripping the dagger in one hand, Gemma pulled the sword from Sprenger's carcass with the other. She looked at the remaining monks, slowly turning in a circle.

"Anyone else, Brothers?" she called, which seemed strange. Wasn't the Challenge over now? She'd defeated Sprenger in what seemed to Quinn a fair fight. But just as he had that thought, a monk broke free from those surrounding Gemma. He charged toward her, swinging a sword, but she ducked and slashed her own up, cutting him across the chest and throat. He went down and another attacked. A woman monk with an axe. Gemma blocked the oncoming blow with her sword and stabbed the monk in the neck.

"That's it," Laila said, moving forward. But Shona grabbed her shoulder just as several monks moved in front of them to keep them from helping.

"Sprenger's allies," Shona said in that flat, emotionless way of hers.

"They're still loyal," Katla explained. "They won't let Thomassin take over."

Laila searched out Ragna. She now stood in front of Thomassin and the other elders, a double-headed battle axe in her hands. Her team of loyal soldiers with her. The two females exchanged long glances and Ragna finally nodded. Laila turned to Quinn, and she didn't have to give him any sign. They'd been speaking to each other without words since the day she'd dropped from their mother. He, in turn, signaled Farlan and Cadell.

They didn't have their weapons but they didn't need them. They had weapons all around them. They simply had to take them.

Quinn moved first, shifting into his natural battle-ready form and rising up on his hind legs. The monks in front of him were so shocked, he was able to bring down his front legs on them, crushing their skulls in the process. Cadell and Farlan took swords and war hammers from the bodies before shifting themselves and moving toward Gemma. Laila kept her human form but took the spear casually tossed to her by Shona and speared the first monk who attempted to strike.

That's when all hells broke loose. Sprenger loyalists fought everyone else while Gemma stood at the center of it all since it was she who had killed Sprenger.

Quinn made his way to her side. They'd fought side by side more than once in their time together. But their space was tight here and it was hard to know who was friend and who was foe when everyone was wearing the same thing, down to their short haircuts.

So Quinn stuck with defense rather than offense. He kept the monks off Gemma's back rather than going after anyone. He didn't want to accidentally kill a loyal friend she hadn't mentioned to him.

Laila, Farlan, and Cadell had taken up position by Thomassin and the other elders, alongside Ragna and her troops. A good thing, because they were getting hit hard as well. There seemed to be a new leader among them now that Sprenger was gone. A woman monk filled with rage that someone had taken her messiah from her. She was calling out orders that had the allies attacking the two groups again and again.

"We need to take her down," Quinn said against Gemma's ear during a very brief lull in attacks.

"That's Brother Millie. She adored Sprenger." Gemma briefly stopped to cut off the leg of one monk and the arm of another by swinging her blade back the other way. The benefit of pure momentum. "She won't go down easy. And the loyalists won't let us near her."

"We need to do something. There's more of them than I realized."

"And the rest of our supporters are outside reinforcing the battlements. We need to get word to them."

A spear aimed for his front legs had Quinn shifting back to human, flipping over the spear, and returning to his natural form. He kicked out his back legs and sent the spear handler flying into several of his brothers.

Before they could decide what move they should make next, Laila walked between them and stared up at the very high windows.

"What the fuck are you doing?" Gemma asked her.

"Do you hear that noise?"

"I don't hear anything."

But Quinn heard it. It was a strange, moaning wail and he detested it more than anything he'd ever heard.

There it was again. So distracting, she looked away from whatever was happening at the monastery. And something was definitely happening at the monastery.

Ainsley turned toward the noise and as she had suspected . . . it came from the clearing. The one that knight had warned her to stay away from. An order she intended to follow. But she still climbed higher in the tree, trying to get a better view. Because she knew something was definitely wrong. All the animals had fled. Birds no longer sang. Foxes no longer hunted. Wolves no longer howled. Even the snakes had slithered away.

That only happened when the earth was about to shake, when the wind was about to blow, or the forest was about to burn. Or . . . when armies marched.

Standing as high as she could, Ainsley looked out. She still saw nothing, but the wailing became so loud she nearly covered her ears. Something was in distress. She knew that.

She climbed down until she reached the ground. She whistled between two fingers and heard her horse gallop toward her. As she gathered her things, she stopped briefly to touch her hand to the earth. It was still distant, but it was there. The rumble of many hooves pounding the ground, coming closer. And whatever was making that horrible sound was in that army's way.

Ainsley mounted her horse and briefly debated her next move.

She rode toward the sound, frowning as she got nearer. It took her a second to realize that a scouting party had already reached the clearing. And they'd used wizards to break through whatever protective barrier had surrounded it. Now they were torturing whatever was inside. When she was close enough, she dismounted from her horse and pulled her bow. She nocked her arrows and shot the scouts who were supposed to be standing guard at the opening, but were so fascinated by whatever nightmare was going on inside, they'd turned their backs.

Ainsley crept close and peeked inside. Wizards surrounded the tormented beast while seven soldiers held ropes around its throat in an attempt to keep it steady. The wizards chanted spells, but she honestly didn't know if they were trying to trap it or kill it.

She didn't wait to find out.

She nocked three arrows in her bow, aimed, and let them fly. She took out two of the wizards and one of the soldiers. She immediately nocked two more arrows while running to a new position. She was able to fire again. Two more soldiers. Soldiers came at her and she ran. With several of the ropes now unmanned, the beast was able to break free. It took off running, but it didn't run away. It attacked. Charging the soldiers, picking up one in its mouth and biting him in half, then spitting him out before trampling over several others.

While the creature ran, it grew tusks on either side of its bottom jaw. Ridiculously long ones aiming up that it used to impale the wizards throwing fireballs and lightning at it. When it did get hit by magick, it seemed to absorb the damage and spit it back out. Its back legs sent other soldiers flying, possibly miles away.

Ainsley used her bow to block further attacks, but then the beast was there, dragging off a soldier who'd gotten Ainsley on her back and was about to impale her with his sword. It dragged the soldier off and proceeded to toss him around like a limp doll. Banging the man from side to side, up and down, until it tossed the decimated carcass away.

When it was done, the tusks vanished but it was still some half-dead thing that Ainsley had never seen before. Horrifying to look at. She still felt bad for it. And it had still saved her.

If nothing else, it hadn't tried to eat her. That was something, right?

Eyes wide, she remembered that the ones the beast had killed were only a scouting party.

"You need to run," she told him. "Run! I have to warn the others." She scrambled to her feet and took off, stopping to mount her horse along the way and riding hard toward the monastery.

"It's stopped," Laila said.

"What was it?"

"I don't know. It was strange. Like an animal but . . ." She lifted her gaze to Quinn, and then the siblings looked at Gemma.

Gemma knew that expression. "It wasn't necessarily her."

"Are you sure?" Quinn leaned in. "What if she got out? What are you going to do then?"

"Don't we have bigger issues to deal with right now?"

"Do we?"

They did. Although Thomassin, Bartholemew, and Brín had their weapons drawn and stood with Ragna and her small group of troops, Millie held the remainder of the ancient elders hostage at the moment.

"Release them, Brother Millie!" Thomassin ordered.

"I don't take orders from you, false Grand Master."

Quinn rolled his eyes. "By the gods, this could take all fucking night."

The double doors to the chamber opened and more of Ragna's troops rushed in. How they'd been alerted to the troubles here, Gemma wasn't sure, but she was grateful.

"Commander! We have . . ." The words of Ragna's second commander faded away as she took in the sight before her.

But Ragna ignored her own troops for the thin girl who'd been following them.

Ragna pointed at Millie and barked, "Ainsley! Her!"

Without question, Ainsley raised her already nocked bow and released. The arrow flew true and slammed Millie in the throat, sending her entire body jerking back several feet.

"And those two!" Ragna added.

Ainsley let two more arrows fly and she hit her marks without error.

Shocked at her sister's presence and Ragna's ordering her around, Gemma asked Quinn, "When did Ainsley get here?"

Quinn threw up his hands. "Woman! She's *been* here!"

CHAPTER 13

Laila heard it first, wrapping her arm around Ainsley's shoulders and dropping them both to the ground.

"*Down!*" Quinn bellowed. "*Everyone down!*"

Gemma dropped to her side as the entire monastery shook around her. She knew why. Her parents had built plenty of trebuchets and used them. They were being bombarded by fireballs.

"They're here!" Ragna called out when everyone got their bearings and scrambled to their feet. "Cyrus's army is here! You all know your orders! Move!"

"What orders?" a few monks demanded. Of course, the ones asking those questions had all been loyal to Sprenger. There were only a few of them left and with a nod from Ragna, her knights killed them quickly with a sword to the belly or a blade to the throat.

Gemma jumped up. "*What the hells are you doing?*"

The ones killed hadn't joined in the attack with the others. They appeared ready to follow Thomassin's orders. Why would Ragna kill them?

Thomassin tapped Ragna on the shoulder. "Do what you must, Ragna. You know your orders."

"Her orders? How could she already have orders?"

"The orders Joshua gave her a long time ago."

More fireballs hit the monastery and Gemma could hear her fellow knights below calling out orders to one another as they readied themselves for another attack.

"I didn't think they'd come so soon," Thomassin told Gemma. "I thought we'd have more time. But our god Morthwyl will have his way."

"What are you talking about?"

"Tonight we fight against Cyrus and his army."

"Of course we do." Gemma would expect no less. "I'll get my—"

"Not you, Gemma."

"What do you mean not me? I will fight by your side. I will defend all of you with my life."

"Joshua had other plans for you."

"What other plans? You need me with you if we're going to fight Cyrus."

"We're not fighting Cyrus. He's somewhere else. Instead, we face several of his best legions. And tonight they will wipe the Order of Righteous Valor from the face of this earth."

Gemma closed her eyes and asked her question, but she already knew the answer. "And you're going to let him . . . aren't you?"

A monk Quinn didn't know shoved the Amichai's weapons into his arms along with a terrified Samuel.

"Are you all right?" Quinn asked the boy.

"Yes." But each time another projectile hit the monastery, Samuel looked ready to pass out.

"Where are the horses?" Quinn asked, hoping to keep him focused and alert.

"Waiting for us at an exit that we will use to escape." Samuel swallowed. "Apparently, we are going to escape?"

"Yes. I'm starting to think that is the plan, which Gemma will not like. So be ready. I will have to move fast. Understand?"

"Yes. And you will definitely have to move fast."

Quinn walked over to Gemma while quickly attaching his weapons to the sword belt on his kilt.

"You can't do this!" she argued with the elders.

"Gemma—"

"You can't!"

Thomassin, Bartholemew, and Brín were working hard to talk to her, but Quinn knew that look on Gemma's face.

"We're war monks," she argued. "Not some suicide cult."

"We're going to go out there and fight as hard as we can. Fight as we always have. We all are. But we're going to die. With honor."

"Then I'll die with you."

"Like hells you will." Thomassin grinned. "Joshua said you'd insist, but no."

"And what do you expect me to do? Spend the rest of my life mourning all my brothers?"

"You'll have no time for mourning," Bartholemew promised. "Because what is destroyed here, will rise again."

Quinn sneered. "By Ofydd Naw's cock, they want you to raise them all from the dead."

Brín rolled his eyes. "No, we don't."

"Brín's right," Thomassin explained to Gemma. "It's not us you'll be bringing back. We'll be feasting at our god's table with Joshua." He wiped a tear even as he smiled at the thought. "But you will be the one who leads Ragna, her army, and the librarians out through the tunnels and to your sister's territory. There, our order will find new life."

Gemma shook her head. "I won't do that. I won't. I won't leave you. I won't—"

Thomassin pulled his sword, ignoring Gemma's words. He took the tip and used it to tap each of her shoulders.

"I now bestow upon you the rank of general. Along with your battle-cohorts. They too will be going with you to your sister's territory to teach and lead the next generation of our order. Understand."

"I don't care if you make me queen of the universe and they're coming with me to hell. I'm not leaving you."

Thomassin cupped her cheek. "You are leaving us, you pain-in-the-ass farmer's brat. You are. And you will live and thrive and make us all so very proud. Now take her, Amichai. Take her and don't stop."

"No! Thomassin, please! No!"

But Quinn already had Gemma around the waist, shifting into his natural form as he lifted her off the ground. He nodded his head at the elders before he went up on his hind legs, turned, and charged through the open chamber doorway.

"*Let me go, Quinn! Let me go!*"

He heard the pain, the absolute *agony* in Gemma's voice. Knew that at this moment, at this very second, he was destroying her in a way he'd never thought he could. But he knew in his heart, in his soul, that it was the only choice he had. This wasn't about honor. This wasn't about courage. This was about survival. Not just hers, but the survival of her precious brotherhood. Of all that she believed. That's what Thomassin wanted and he was ordering her to make that happen. She couldn't ignore her duty so she could die with honor.

She tried to fight him, but he held her tight as he went down several flights of stairs. Farlan waited for them at the bottom.

"This way!" he yelled over the invading army's attack.

He pushed past monks heading in the opposite direction. Some were already on horseback, making ready for their counterattack while ducking flying fireballs and falling pieces of building.

Gemma almost got away from him twice, but still, Quinn didn't let go. It cost him some torn flesh on his arm and he was sure at least one broken rib, but nothing that couldn't heal.

But he had to admit he was grateful to see the others. If anyone could talk some sense into Gemma, it was his sister. He practically threw the woman in front of Laila and she immediately grabbed Gemma's arm to prevent her escaping.

"Let me go, Laila! I'm going back!"

"Just listen to—"

Laila didn't get a chance to finish her sentence, because Gemma was wrenched from her grip by Ragna. The master general spun Gemma around and punched her once in the face.

Quinn and his sister both cringed, and Gemma's entire head snapped to the side. Quinn worried her jaw might have been broken.

"Listen to me, little girl," Ragna said, holding a dazed Gemma with one hand while pointing at her with the other. "I don't have time for your dramatic bullshit. Our brothers are going out to meet that army to give us time to get a safe distance from here. You're a general now. Act like one. So dry your fucking tears. Gird your loins. And *lead.* Or I'll cut you open from cunt to throat and then I'll tell your precious queen sister why I did it: because you're being as whiny as a lovesick man. Do you understand me?"

Gemma moved her jaw around a bit, as if she also wasn't quite sure whether it was broken or not, before finally replying, "Yes, I understand."

"Good. Then go."

Gemma strode through the mostly empty stables—the last of the horses had been taken out by their riders—and over to Samuel. She grabbed the reins of her own horse and started down the tunnel, moving around the knights still entering. When she was gone, Ragna turned to Quinn and Laila.

"Stop babying her," she admonished.

"We don't report to you," Laila instantly shot back. "You got a problem with how we deal with Gemma? Take it up with her."

The two females began to bicker but heard the whistling sound of an incoming projectile just above their heads. Quinn waited a beat to see if it would pass them, but no. It wasn't passing them. It was coming right at them.

Quinn grabbed both females and charged toward the tunnel entrance, diving in just as the stables were destroyed.

Gemma rode back after she heard the explosion and quickly dismounted from her horse. Farlan and Cadell helped her move the dirt off Quinn and Laila, but it was Quinn who dug out Ragna. Good thing since Gemma hadn't realized the woman was with them.

"Are you all right?" Gemma asked Laila, brushing the dirt from her friend's face.

"I'm fine. I'm fine. Quinn?"

"Yeah," he said with a cough that mostly brought up dirt.

Ragna, however, just wiped her eyes, gave one cough, and walked off to find her horse, which had thankfully gone in ahead of her.

"Do you guys need help?" Gemma asked the siblings.

"We're fine. You go."

Gemma again mounted Dagger and rode ahead.

"Pick up the pace!" she urged. "Let's go!"

She wasn't sure how long the rest of the brotherhood could hold Cyrus's legions at bay. And the tunnels were only big enough for seven or eight mounted knights to pass. So she and Katla, Shona, and Kir kept everyone moving while Ragna rode ahead to meet with her army, the bulk of which had been sent off four days before, according to Shona.

The desire to go back was still there for Gemma, but she knew it wasn't what Thomassin and the others wanted. So she pushed on into the same tunnel she'd taken when she'd returned to her family the first time two years ago. She pushed on even though this time it felt like it was killing her inside.

Thomassin sat on his horse and looked at his two battle-cohorts. He was glad to be riding into battle with them again. Glad to again be bringing honor to their god in a sacrifice of blood and death.

He nodded once and Brín raised the banner attached to his steel spear.

Thomassin took in a deep breath and then gave the Order of Righteous Valor charge command one last time: "*Kill everyone!*"

Quinn was bringing up the rear when he found Gemma standing in front of a smaller, unlit tunnel that shot off the main one everyone else was traveling. She was just standing in front of it, not moving.

He stopped and stared down at her.

"What are you doing?" he finally asked.

"This should have been closed off."

"It's a little late for that, isn't it?"

"I guess. But Cyrus's men could come up behind us now."

"Where does this go?"

"To a ritual site under a sacrificial altar outside the monastery."

"Do a lot of sacrificing, do you?"

"Just bulls before certain battles," she said with a dismissive wave.

"Do you want to take a look?"

"No." She shrugged. "But we'd better."

He grabbed a torch from the wall and together they began walking. They didn't speak. Both of them had a lot on their minds, Quinn was guessing. He just wanted to get out of these tunnels. He hated tunnels. He liked being outside. With fresh air. Besides, he'd already been trapped once by a falling ceiling; he'd prefer not to test his luck a second time.

The tunnel abruptly turned up ahead and as they went around the corner they stopped, coming face-to-face with a small unit of Cyrus's soldiers. It was almost comical, the way they all stared at one another. Clearly neither expected the other to be there. But then the leader of the other group pulled his sword and Quinn pushed his burning torch into the man's face. He screamed in pain and Gemma pulled out the gladius she still carried and immediately started stabbing those closest to her.

The other soldiers stabbed back. Quinn was able to block most of them, but one blade made it through, slashing Gemma's arm. She hadn't been able to put her chainmail back on after her earlier fight with Sprenger so she wore only her cotton shirt. The blade cut through the material easily and straight across her flesh.

Startled, Gemma yelped from the pain but it was the explosion from the wall that had her and Quinn falling back, raised arms blocking their eyes to protect them from rocks and dirt.

Quinn heard horrifying screams, tearing flesh, and bones being crushed.

He forced his eyes open to find that half-dead horse thing standing there with someone's head in its mouth.

"Gemma."

Gemma lowered her arm. "Kriegszorn." She glanced at Quinn. "See? Value."

"See? Head in her mouth."

There was something farther up the tunnel that caught the creature's attention. It growled and barreled off toward whatever it was.

"Kriegszorn!" Gemma called out.

"What are you doing? If it wants to kill something that's not us, let it kill something that's not us. Now come on!"

He brought Gemma up with him and pulled her onto his back.

"Hold on!" he ordered, racing back to the main tunnel and then catching up to the others.

They reached Gemma's horse Dagger and she quickly jumped off Quinn's back and mounted her horse. Together, they continued down the tunnel, eventually reaching the others.

Quinn looked back but didn't see anyone following them. But that half-dead thing had heard something. She'd gone after something. He was afraid to know exactly what it was.

* * *

The battle had raged on for longer than either side had expected. Thomassin knew that all those who had died this night could go to their god with honor.

Pleased that he'd done all he could possibly do, he dropped to his knees and looked down at the spear that had pierced his chest. Bartholemew and Brín had gone to meet Joshua minutes before. So it was his turn to follow the others into the next world.

He saw Cyrus's precious wizards moving toward him. They wanted his soul apparently, but he wasn't going to let them get it. Both Bartholemew and Brín had died before the wizards had a chance to take theirs and he would make sure he did the same. He reached for a blade that was close by but a general slammed his foot onto Thomassin's hand, stopping him from doing what he needed to do.

"Sorry, heretic, but there is no easy escape for you," the general told him. "So just accept it and—"

It came out of nowhere. A thing Thomassin had never seen before. Half of it looked like any normal horse, but the other side . . .

The other side just looked dead. Extremely dead. But as dead as it might look, it fought like it was still alive and very pissed. First, it impaled one of the wizards on what appeared to be a tusk. Then it bit the arm off another wizard before impaling him too. It stomped the third wizard into the ground. When it was done with them, it turned on the general still holding down Thomassin's hand.

"Unclean thing!" the general cried. "I shall destroy you in the name of my god!"

It studied the general a brief moment before looking down at Thomassin, making him feel as if it was asking permission to do what he could not do for himself.

Smiling, Thomassin nodded his approval and the thing that had saved his soul from these bastards unleashed a cleansing fire that released his soul to the war gods he had fought for until his very death.

When Gemma finally made it out of the tunnel, she and the remainder of her entire order were miles from the monastery. And yet . . . they could still see it burning even from where they stood.

She climbed a large rock and stood staring, gawking really as the flames and smoke rose high into the night sky and the life she'd known for a decade was destroyed.

She wanted to cry. To scream. To destroy the world with her rage and pain and heartache. But she couldn't do any of that. Not now.

"You have a job to do," Ragna reminded her.

Gemma closed her eyes, wishing that of all those who had died this night, one of them had been gods-damn Ragna.

"I know. To get everyone to Keeley's territory."

"No. Ainsley can do that. Or Samuel. You have another job."

Gemma jumped off the boulder in front of Ragna. "And what's that?"

Ragna handed her a scroll with a map printed on it. "Go here. See if any of the representatives of these sects arrive and provide them protection on the journey back to your sister's castle. I'll meet you there."

Gemma looked at the list on the back of the map. "Wait a minute. These sects you have listed. These are all our enemies."

"Yes."

"We've actually burned these witches at stakes."

"At least six times in the last two hundred years."

"And didn't we annihilate these temple virgins?"

"Don't be silly. We just burned their temple to the ground. But now we can say we know how they feel, can't we?"

"And these truce vicars—"

"We cut out their tongues because we accused them of lying about us. Yes, that was an ugly period between our two groups. But all these sects are in as much danger as we are from Cyrus's men. So I'm sure they'll be more than willing to overlook our unfortunate history in order to move on to a bright and prosperous future. Together!"

With a brusque pat to Gemma's shoulder, Ragna mounted her horse and ordered everyone to move out. And she meant everyone. When Laila attempted to stay behind with the rest of Gemma's original travel group, Ragna made it very clear that would not be permitted.

Not wanting any more drama, Gemma told them all to go. Of course, Laila tried to argue, but Gemma wasn't in the mood for well-reasoned centaur arguments. Nor was she in the mood for Samuel's loyalty or her battle-cohorts' willingness to risk Ragna's wrath so they could stay by Gemma's side. She wanted them all gone.

The last thing Ragna did before she rode off with her entire army and all of Gemma's friends was toss her a second travel bag. It wasn't until Gemma opened it and found a white tunic with Morthwyl's rune emblazoned on the front and back in bright red that she burst into tears and allowed herself to cry.

By the time the two suns came up, her tears were gone and she was finally back in her chainmail, wearing the tunic of a high-ranking monk.

She mounted Dagger and rode for about two hours until she pulled to a stop at the sight of the idiot sitting under a tree. Eating apples.

"Took you long enough," he complained between bites.

"What are you doing here, Quinn?"

"Couldn't let you go alone. Poor sweet thing like you. All alone out here? Men might take advantage. You're so weak and frail. Just look at you. Can you even walk on those tiny little feet of yours or does that horse have to carry you?"

Only Quinn of the Scarred Earth Clan could make her crack a smile after the last few hours. Only him. And they both knew it.

"Only when I ask him nicely." She held her hand out and he tossed her one of the apples from a small bag. Where he'd found that bag out here, where she knew of no nearby towns, she had no idea.

"I see you dragged poor Scandal with you," she pointed out before taking a bite.

He glanced over at the big warhorse few men dared to ride. Not only was he too big for most but he was also mean. Very mean.

"We have an agreement. I ride him as little as possible and he takes me where I need to go when I have to pretend to be human."

"So . . . did Laila order you to come with me?"

"No. She just gave me the nod. And I slipped away when Ragna wasn't looking."

"Ragna is always looking. Never forget that."

"Besides, I am dying to meet these other sects you mentioned. They sound fascinating."

"If any show up. Trust me when I say they are definitely our enemies."

Quinn stood. "Enemies today. Friends tomorrow. Especially when a fanatic is trying to kill all of you."

"And he's doing a damn good job of it."

"Don't be so negative. I have faith all will balance out in the end."

Tossing the core to the ground, Gemma asked, "Why are you staring at me that way, Amichai?"

"I have a favor to ask you, but you won't like it. But after the night we've had . . . I have no choice."

"After the night we've had, I'm too tired to slap you around if the request annoys me. So ask away."

"I need a hug and Kir isn't here."

Gemma couldn't help but frown. "Are you serious?"

"Honestly? More serious than I've ever been."

Willing to play along, Gemma swung her leg over her saddle so she was still on it but facing the Amichai. She opened her arms to him and he leaned in, putting his own arms around her and resting his head on her shoulder.

At first, Gemma felt very little. She simply gazed off behind Quinn, staring into the trees that lined the pathway. But his heavy head resting on her shoulder and his arms around her back . . .

She thought about all she had lost, but she hadn't lost everything. She still had her family. She still had her friends. And Thomassin, Bartholemew, Brín, and even Joshua had entrusted her with what was left of the brotherhood.

Even this hug was better than nothing. It may have been with one of the most annoying beings in the universe but he always had her back, he was a damn good fighter, and he was one of the few who knew how to find humor even at the absolute worst moments.

Before Gemma knew it, she was off her horse and the only thing holding her up was her grip on Quinn's neck and his hold on her waist.

"Can we just stay here like this?" Quinn asked. "At least for a few more years?"

"Sadly, no." Gemma turned her head to the side and rested it on Quinn's shoulder. "But I think we can at least get away with a few more minutes."

"I guess that's something."

For now, it would have to be.

PART 2

CHAPTER 14

For four days they waited at the appointed location. For four days, they kept a lookout for any messengers or black crows or white doves with notes tied to their legs. But there was nothing.

"Think they're all dead?" Quinn finally had to ask when the fourth day was reaching its end.

"I don't know. But I'm ready to leave." She began to pace. While the Amichai had been quite patient, she had grown restless after the first day. Mostly because Ragna had given her so little information. How long was Gemma supposed to wait? Days? Weeks? Years?

She'd forgotten how frustrating that woman could be to report to. You never knew exactly what she wanted. Sometimes she wanted you to follow your instincts and make solid, logical decisions. Other times she wanted you to ask follow-up questions and when you didn't, she assumed you were stupid or trying to "take over."

Gemma didn't have time to play Ragna's mind games.

"Come on. We're leaving."

"Now?"

"Yes. Now."

They packed up their saddlebags, mounted their horses, and rode off. They'd only traveled a few miles when lightning struck so close to Gemma's horse that it reared to the side and began to go down.

Gemma rolled off so Dagger didn't fall on her legs, possibly crushing one or both. By the time she got back to her feet, she saw more lightning strikes, hitting the ground randomly. But there were no clouds in the sky. No rumbles of thunder. No signs of storms.

Dagger did fall to his side but was also unharmed. Gemma got the horse back on his feet and slapped his rump to send him off at a run. Then she pulled her sword and caught the shield that Quinn tossed her. They took cover behind a big tree just as massive winds began to blow.

"What's going on?" Quinn yelled over the screaming wind.

"A battle of the idiots!" She pointed at two black-robed men. "War priests against"—she gestured at two young women in flowing white gowns—"temple virgins"—she leaned around Quinn and motioned to men in bright gray satin robes, the lower halves of their faces covered by black cloth—"against divine assassins."

"They're not the ones we're supposed to be—"

"Of course they are!"

"Perfect. Now what?"

"You go out there."

"*Me?* Why the fuck would I go out there?"

"You said centaurs can't be touched by magicks, right?"

"Charms. Curses. Spells. They don't harm my kind. But bolts of lightning and massive windstorms and . . . ?"

They silently watched an elk spin by, carried by the insane wind one of the fighting pairs had unleashed.

"Yeah," Quinn admitted, still watching that poor elk, "I can't fight that."

Ragna couldn't believe how easy it was to walk into the queen's castle. No one stopped her. No one questioned her. Her army was still several leagues away, but she wanted to see what she was dealing with before bringing her monk-knights here.

Of course, she was wrapped in the robes of a healer nun, but still . . . during wartime, questions should be asked. But no. Nothing.

Disgusted by the lack of castle security, she turned to walk back out but stopped when a metal hammer hit her in the back of the leg.

"Who dares invade my queendom, foul beast?"

Ragna looked down at the chubby child attacking her with what appeared to be a baby-sized blacksmith hammer.

"Speak before I destroy you and all you love!"

"Sorry! Sorry!" An older child ran into the hall and grabbed at the hammer but the younger one ran around Ragna, using her as a shield. "Give me that hammer, you little cretin!"

"Come get it, demon!"

"Mum! Endelyon is threatening the nuns again with her hammer!"

"Your mum is at the forge!" someone yelled back from deep within the castle. "Want me to get your father?"

The elder girl rolled her eyes. "Don't bother."

"Ha! No one will stop me! For I am ruler of—*oof!*"

A little boy, near the age of the younger girl, tackled her to the ground with such force that Ragna wondered if he'd possibly broken her bones. He yanked the hammer from the child's hand, waved it in her face, then ran from her. The girl scrambled to her feet and went after her brother, screaming, "I cannot rule without my hammer! Give me back my hammer!"

"Sorry, Sister," the older girl said with a quick curtsey before she followed the smaller children.

Now Ragna was doubly disgusted. A child taking care of a child? Who was overseeing this place? Who was on guard? And where was this precious Queen Keeley she'd been hearing so much about?

"Can't you fight them with your own magicks?" Quinn asked as the winds finally died down but the lightning strikes increased.

"What magicks?"

"You're a war monk!"

"I raise the dead!"

"Is that all you can do?"

"Nooo. Of course not!" Gemma shrugged. "But studying magicks never interested me as much as my combat lessons."

"So what can you use against them?"

"Well...I can throw enemies around a little bit. I can, uh... um..."

The pause went on for so long that Quinn finally snapped, "*That's it?*"

"Not so loud!"

"Ragna sent you here alone to prove a point, didn't she?" Quinn guessed. "Because I honestly don't know how we're going to handle these people without any magick skills at our fingertips. No wonder she didn't stop me from riding after you."

"Oh, calm down. We just need to distract them. That's all you ever need to do with magick—distract those wielding it."

"And how do you propose we do that, O brilliant one?"

The fight behind them began to pick up again. Boulders flying, lightning striking, the wind increasing once more. That's when Gemma spotted the elk again. Quinn saw her smile and he immediately shook his head.

"No," he said. "No. We're not using him."

"He's perfect."

"The fact that he survived the first round is enough. We're not torturing that poor animal again."

"Don't be a big baby."

"Stop going out of your way to be the opposite of Keeley. Because we both know your sister would never do this."

"Fine," she said, no longer smiling, but smirking. Smirking at *his* expense. "You know what that leaves us."

"Yes!" he snapped. "I'm aware."

Ragna decided to search the queen out. She'd heard the new royal had started off as a blacksmith, so she headed first to the forge. There she found a big-shouldered woman who matched the description of Queen Keeley. Long dark hair. Giant shoulders. Large muscles. And a way with steel. When Ragna entered the forge, the woman held up a sword that had the monk pausing for a moment. She'd never seen such a beautiful weapon. It was true. She preferred her weapons plain and deadly. She didn't need fancy markings on the blade or jewels on the hilt. She was a monk, after all.

But still . . . that sword was a thing of beauty.

"Queen Keeley?" Ragna asked.

The woman laughed. "Sorry, Sister. You're looking for my daughter. Anyone seen me girl?" she called out to the other blacksmiths and apprentices working with her.

When the answers were all "No," the woman tossed that beautiful weapon into a barrel filled with other beautiful swords. "I'm sure she's around somewhere, though, Sister."

"You're the queen mother?" Ragna had to ask.

"Guess I am," she said with another laugh, turning back to her forge and all that heat.

Ragna was a few feet away from the forge when she heard a bellowed "Oy!"

She froze, her shoulders locking, left eye twitching. Had the queen mother just "oyed" her?

Looking over her shoulder, she said, "Yes, Your Highness?"

"Try that unfinished building over on the east lawn, yeah? She might be over there. That's where the pack stays."

"The pack?"

"Of her wolves. That's where they've started keeping their pups the last few days. Since the dwarves don't seem to mind 'em."

"Dwarves?"

"Yeah. You'll probably find her there."

Ragna forced a polite, saintly smile. "Thank you."

"Sure," the royal said with a hammer wave before disappearing back into her forge.

"This is humiliating," Quinn complained, arms folded across his massive chainmail-covered chest.

"I know," Gemma soothed. "I know."

"You're enjoying this, aren't you?" he accused. "You're enjoying my humiliation!"

"Of course not! But I don't see any other option."

As if to push that point home, the elk leaned up against Quinn as he fearlessly grazed on the grass at the centaur's feet.

"You're both in on this together . . . aren't you?"

"That's silly." Gemma grabbed Quinn's hand and gazed deeply into his eyes. "Now you just need to trust me."

"Except you know I *don't* trust you."

"That's what makes this so wonderful."

Ragna headed east until she found a half-finished building. There was a lot of hammering coming from inside, so she entered.

Although she could hear continued work, Ragna saw only two people inside the main room. One was another big-shouldered woman with massive muscles exposed by a sleeveless shirt and a long dark braid that reached down her back. She was facing away from Ragna and was deep in conversation with a monk. A pacifist monk based on his bright yellow robes.

Robes so bright, Ragna felt as if she was gazing directly into one of the suns. She felt an urge to shield her eyes.

She didn't want to interrupt the hushed conversation going on between the pair, so she patiently waited.

Examining the building she was in, she wondered if it was being built or destroyed. She wasn't sure. There were stone pieces of rubble littering the floor as if someone had already come in and knocked parts of the walls down. Hammering continued in distant parts of the building but Ragna saw no evidence of builders or stonemasons wandering around. Perhaps they were avoiding the queen.

Which begged the question . . . could the queen not find a better place to have her conversation with the monk?

Finally, Ragna spotted the first sign of the "pack" that the queen mother had mentioned. Two wolf pups scrambled through the rubble before climbing into the queen's lap. She'd thought the queen mother had meant dogs, but Ragna had known some royals who made wild animals their "pets." Wolves or jungle cats or sometimes the occasional bear. Although that was always risky.

But these wild wolf pups didn't interrupt the queen's flowing conversation with the peace monk, even when one of them climbed up her bare arm onto her shoulder.

The pup pawed at stray hairs hanging from her braid, rubbed its face into her neck, and licked her ear before finally settling onto her shoulder. Ragna thought it had fallen asleep until it blinked open its lids and looked at Ragna with eyes of flame. Actual flame.

That's when it struck her like a lightning bolt. This was no mere wild animal that the queen had managed to tame with treats and a soothing voice. That wasn't what this *thing* was at all.

Ragna had been holding her hands clasped demurely together, but she now separated them, moving them to her sides. She lowered her head, her gaze locking on the thing that rested on the queen's shoulder.

The pup, barely a few weeks old, watched Ragna closely and, as she moved, it slowly rose up on its paws and bared its fangs. Blood dripped from its mouth rather than drool and it gave a low warning growl. The other pup jumped from the queen's lap to the ground and mirrored its sibling's stance.

The peace monk leaned past the queen's massive shoulders. "Ahhh, Sister, let's be calm, shall we?" the monk urged Ragna.

She pointed at the unholy beasts with one finger. "You allow those things here, Brother?"

The queen's head turned slightly, so she caught sight of Ragna from the corner of her eye.

"You understood the agreement when you came here," the monk went on. "We are safe on the queen's territory, and we may worship as we like, but no human sacrifices, and we *must* leave the wolves alone."

"And all of you agreed to this . . . heresy?"

"It's a small price to pay," the monk argued, "considering the alternative."

"It would be better to die with honor, *Monk,* than live with such depravity."

"How could a sister of acceptance and love be so closed-minded?"

"That's because," the queen said, finally standing and facing Ragna—Blessed Morthwyl, the size of her—"she's *not* a sister of acceptance and love, Brother Emmanuel. She's not a nun at all.

"Isn't that right"—the queen looked Ragna over from head to foot—"*War Monk?*"

Father Aubin lifted his fist and dragged the temple virgin off the ground, choking the unholy little pagan with the power of his god. But before he could finish her off, the other temple virgin slammed him from the side with a blast of swirling wind so powerful, it knocked him into the two divine assassins. The three men hit the ground but Aubin was able to quickly sit up, only to come face-to-face with a poisonous snake one of the assassins had called forth.

Aubin tried to move but the snake followed, fangs bared, poison dripping from the tips. Then Father Léandre's black spear swiped its head off in one move and he pulled Aubin to his feet.

The three groups faced one another, hands raised, spells and chants and curses on their lips.

Aubin knew that he and Léandre could destroy these treacherous bastards. They just needed one good—

Blinking, Aubin looked at his enemies and asked them what he was sure they were all thinking. "Was it just me ... or did anyone else see a *hoof* go by?"

The eyes of the pacifist monk grew impossibly wide at the queen's words, and Ragna was shocked that he didn't run. He just stood there, fussing with the gratuitous gold medallion he wore around his neck.

"Would you excuse us, Brother Emmanuel?" the queen asked when he didn't leave.

"Your Majesty ... I ... uh ..."

"It's all right. I'll be fine."

"Should I get your guards? Do you have guards?"

"I have my wolves. And I have my hammer. I'll be fine. Now go. We'll finish our talk later."

He bowed—which made the queen cross her eyes—then backed out of the room. Not because he was wary of the queen, Ragna guessed, but because of Ragna.

Not that she blamed him.

"These abominations?" Ragna asked when the monk was gone. "They're yours?"

"These *animals* belong to no one. They come and go as they please."

"I'm sure they kill as they please too."

"Out of respect for me, they don't."

Ragna laughed. "You can't be that stupid."

The royal raised a dark brow. "You can't be stupid enough to call me stupid on my own territory."

"How about we make this simple? I have an army of unbeliev-ably well-trained monk-knights. I put down these"—she motioned to the tiny atrocities standing by the queen's long legs—"errors in judgment, and my knights become an indispensable part of your fight against Queen Beatrix."

"Or," the queen said with a wry smile, "I let these pups' father and his friends have a very filling dinner."

Ragna finally heard the growls behind her and slowly turned to find the adult abominations surrounding her. All of them with flames for eyes and blood for drool. All of them nightmares from the very pits of one or all of the hells.

Screaming her favored war god's name, she tore off the nun robes and yanked swords from sheaths. But suddenly the ground shook and she briefly thought it was going to open up and swallow her into hell itself. Perhaps that was what these demon beasts did to those who challenged their favored queen.

But when Ragna spun around at a simultaneous clanging sound, she realized it was the queen and her ridiculously oversized ham-mer that had caused the disturbing jolt. She knew this because the queen swung the hammer again, lifting the enormous thing up and over her head and slamming it into the stone floor.

"*That is enough!*" the queen bellowed, now pointing that ham-mer at Ragna with just one hand. "You will not come to my terri-tory and brandish your weapons without orders from me! *Do I make myself clear?*"

Ragna was about to tell her "no" when the room suddenly filled with centaurs. So many centaurs. Three of them Ragna knew for a fact she had left with her army but the rest she had never seen be-fore. Bravely, they put their hideous half-human and half-horse bodies between the two armed and dangerous women.

Laila glared directly at Ragna, panting as if she'd run the entire way from the spot where Ragna had left them to this building.

"Really?" Laila demanded of Ragna. "You *really* thought this was a good idea?"

"I didn't know she had demons as pets."

The queen started to push her way through the crowd but a black-haired centaur grabbed her and pulled her back. "Keeley, no."

"I don't like her. And I like everyone!"

"She really does," another centaur muttered.

"If you just let me humanely crush their skulls, we could be the best of friends," Ragna gently reminded her.

That's when the black-haired centaur was forced to pick the queen up. "Off we go," he told her. "Far away from here."

"Not until I smash her brains all over the floor." The queen again pointed her hammer at Ragna. "*You war monk cunt!*"

"And a *classy* queen at that!" Ragna shot back.

That's when the queen attempted to *throw* her big hammer across the room but Farlan wrestled it from her and held it against his chest. The black-haired centaur started to carry the queen out of the building, but he abruptly stopped and gawked across the empty space. And then Ragna saw them. Dwarves. Stonemason dwarves. Ragna had met a few in her time.

"What are you doing?" the centaur asked the leader of their group.

"Watching your beautiful queen work her hammer." The dwarf grinned. "Think she'll do it again? Maybe without her shirt this time?"

The centaur went up on his hind legs, the queen still held in one arm, but Cadell used his own horse body to force the other centaur out of the building and, laughing, the dwarves returned to their work.

Ragna stared at a still-seething Laila. "I don't know why you're glaring at me so, centaur. You had to know I was not going to react well to your queen's demon pets."

Laila opened her mouth as if to argue that point, but finally, she shook her head and admitted, "Yes. I did."

CHAPTER 15

"You did that on purpose!" the centaur accused, climbing the giant boulder he'd been tossed over just a minute before.

Balla grabbed her assistant, Priska, and pulled her away before the war monk could brush against her. It was said in the Old Text that even touching a war monk could taint a temple virgin's innocence.

"I did no such thing!" the war monk argued. "I was aiming for them; I just overthrew!"

"That's such a lie! You're such a liar!" The centaur wiped blood from the scrapes on his now human legs. "You could have broken something, you know? Throwing me like that."

"Are you really that brittle?" She gestured to Balla and the rest of them. "And look! We stopped them from fighting without killing anyone. That's exactly what we wanted."

"'That's exactly what we wanted,'" he repeated in a mocking tone. "You flung me!" he accused. "Randomly into the universe!"

"I did no such—you're just walking away?"

"I'm walking away from *you*!"

"Perhaps if you apologized for being such a heartless cow, War Monk, he'd be more inclined to listen to you."

Slowly, the war monk looked at Balla. "You know, virgin . . . I don't have to return to my brothers with *all* of you."

Three groups had shown up to meet the representative of the Order of Righteous Valor and three groups had gotten into a nasty battle that almost destroyed a poor elk and Quinn.

The war priests, Father Aubin and Father Léandre. The head priestess of the temple virgins, Balla, and her assistant, Priska. And two divine assassins, Tadesse of the High Plains and Faraji of the Low Mountains.

The remaining members of these three groups had gone into hiding, leaving everything they had behind. Then, to ensure that Cyrus's wizards and sorcerers could not follow those who'd managed to escape, their gods had closed all mystical doorways behind their most devoted. Meaning that all had to travel by horse and foot. It slowed things down painfully, but it was the only way to ensure they didn't end up like the Order of Righteous Valor. With Cyrus's legions burning that order's monastery down to the ground and destroying at least half the brotherhood, it was clear that no one was safe. Absolutely no one.

Even worse, after stopping at a nearby town for a few supplies, Quinn had picked up rumors that Cyrus's wizards had worked together to meld all the artifacts stolen from the monasteries and churches so that the combined power would ward off any magicks anyone attempted to use against Cyrus himself. If this rumor was true, a direct attack against Cyrus the Honored by any of the sects or even a combined attack by the sects might be impossible. At least not without knowing each and every artifact he had access to. And why in the world would Cyrus tell anyone that?

Although Gemma would never admit it, Ragna might have been right to send Gemma on this odious task. It would be good to have the assistance of other war sects. Gods knew they would need it.

At the moment, however, every order was reevaluating what its options now were. Some were relying on King Marius and Queen Beatrix to turn things around. But the groups standing with Gemma were relying on the remaining war monks and Queen Keeley.

Possibly.

"She'll have to prove herself."

Quinn winced at that, knowing Gemma would not take well to that particular phrasing.

And, of course . . . she didn't.

"Queen Keeley doesn't have to prove shit all to you, *Balla*. Or anyone for that matter." She pointed at the entire group. "That goes for all of you."

"We don't know this Queen Keeley," the war priest Aubin argued. "Who are her gods? Who does her soul belong to?"

"All you need to know is that she has a soul. Because I can promise you, Beatrix does not."

"Beatrix doesn't rule. Marius does."

Gemma and the temple virgins laughed at that, insulting the priests. "What's so funny, whore?"

"I think the women find your belief that Beatrix has no say in the rule of her lands a humorous one," Tadesse said as he saddled his horse.

"Your Queen Keeley may have no man at her side to rule, but Marius does not need to let Beatrix do anything but raise his heirs."

"Beatrix will never raise a child," Gemma told them, "because she will have to kill it before it kills her."

"How do you know so much about Marius's queen?" Father Léandre asked.

"Because I'm her sister. And I'm Keeley's sister. And trust me . . . you really want to stick with Keeley. If you prefer to go on breathing, I mean."

Gemma put two fingers to her mouth and whistled. A moment later, Dagger galloped to her side. She mounted the horse and looked over the others.

"Your choice," she said to them. "You can go to Beatrix, who will welcome you. And use you. Because that's what my younger sister does. Or you can go to Keeley, who finds everyone interesting and can't wait to help them. As for me, I'm tired. I'm mourning. And I don't really give a fuck what you do. But if you do come with me, no fighting each other, no calling me a *whore*"—she said, glaring at the priests—"no avoiding physical contact with me like I'm carrying some fatal plague"—she glared at the temple virgins— "and no . . . wait . . . actually, you two have been perfect gentlemen"—she said to the divine assassins—"and thank you for that. But if either of you quiet-moving bastards tries to kill me in my sleep, I will cut your throats and bring you back from the dead. And all of you know what that means."

Lip curling in disgust, Aubin took a step away from Gemma and her horse. "You . . . you're a necromancer?"

"A good one. So I warn all of you. Fuck with me, my sister Keeley"—and that's when Quinn caught her glancing at him—"or my friend Quinn of the Scarred Earth Clan at your peril. Understand me? Good!" she said before any of them actually answered.

Without another word, she rode off, leaving the others to follow or not as they saw fit.

Quinn stood there, fighting a smile when Scandal hit him in the back with his big horse head, urging him to follow.

"I'm going," he told the big horse. "I'm going. But let her think I'm not for a minute. You know . . . let her know that I'm still expecting that apology."

Scandal snorted at him and trotted past. He hated to say it, but as a centaur, he knew that was a mocking snort.

The remaining war monks of the Order of Righteous Valor made their new home outside the massive steel ramparts of Keeley's queendom. She watched them build their forts from the ground up. They'd brought the wood with them and began using them to build forts as if they were throwing together simple tents.

It was fascinating but worrying. Keeley didn't know how she felt about an army of war monks taking up residence in her queendom. Not because of her wolves. She knew they could take care of themselves. And if things got too dangerous for them, they could return to their original home. But she didn't want one fanatic replacing another. Cyrus was a nightmare but were the war monks any better?

Was Ragna?

"Keeley?"

Gods, what she wouldn't give to be back in the forge with her mum. How she missed the steel. The heat. The infernal banging of her hammer.

"Keeley?"

Realizing she'd gotten lost in daydreams again, Keeley faced her sister. "Ainsley. What do you need?"

"I'm back."

"Right. You're back. And we are all so glad you're back."

Ainsley's eyes narrowed the slightest bit. "You didn't know I was gone, did you?"

"Of course I knew you were gone. You're my little sister. How could I not know you were gone?"

"Then where did I go?"

Feeling certain this was a trick question, Keeley didn't answer right away, which led to Ainsley rolling her eyes and asking that question she'd been asking since she could speak whole sentences.

"Am I invisible? Does anyone know I exist? Did I die when I was a small child and I'm just a phantom that follows the rest of the family around?"

"That's a horrible thing to say and of course not! We know you're here. I can see you!"

"Can you? Because it doesn't feel like it! I was gone for days and you didn't even notice!"

"Do you realize how busy I am? I'm queen. There are things I have to do all day, every day and I'm sorry if I can't spend each and every minute worrying where my *adult* sister is."

"Excellent point. But remember when I was living in that tree—"

"I knew you were going to bring that up."

"—and no one noticed for nearly three weeks?"

"I told you—"

"I was only ten. No one noticed. Mum and Da didn't even ask about me. You went to work—not as a queen, but as a blacksmith— came home, didn't notice. Why? Because as far as this family is concerned, I'm invisible. So don't give me that I'm-an-adult-and-a-queen thing. Because we both know that's horseshit."

Not wanting to rehash the living-in-a-tree story yet again, Keeley asked, "Other than letting me know you're back home—"

"Even though you didn't notice I was gone in the first place."

"—is there any other reason you needed to talk to me?"

Ainsley gestured with her thumb to the three monks standing behind her. "This lot wanted to speak with you."

Unlike Gemma, these three monks wore white tunics instead of black. Just like Brother Ragna, which meant Keeley already didn't like them.

"Queen Keeley," a female monk said. "I'm Brother Katla, this is Brother Shona, and this is Brother Kir. We are Brother Gemma's battle-cohorts and she's asked that—"

"You're her what?"

"Battle-cohorts. We trained with her from when we were novitiates. The four of us are bound together in friendship and blood."

Disturbed by all that, Keeley took a small step back. "What exactly does *that* mean?"

"It just means that our loyalty to one another is unto death."

Now Keeley rubbed her suddenly aching forehead because . . . what? "Is it possible for you war monks ever to talk about each other without bringing in death and blood?"

"Not when you're a war monk. Anyone can be a monk. But we're *war* monks, which means there's always blood and death involved in what we do."

Brother Shona rested her hand on Brother Katla's shoulder. "I don't think you're making this better."

"I know, but," the other female monk pushed on, "I do want to say how amazing your Ainsley was during the final battles at the monastery. She's an incredible archer, your sister. Her aim is true. She was *not* invisible to us."

Keeley's gaze moved to her sister's, catching her mid-grimace.

"Wait. I don't understand. Ainsley, you were part of that battle against Cyrus's legion?" Keeley asked. "Gemma didn't keep you out of that?"

"Well, it's just . . . um . . ." Ainsley cleared her throat. "I mean, I did face some of Cyrus's soldiers and a few of the war monks fighting Gemma."

Whatever her sister might believe about her role in the family, Ainsley was still too young and naïve to be in the middle of life-and-death battles! And Gemma, of all people, should have known that!

Instead of exploding at Ainsley about being in battle—since Gemma wasn't there to explode at instead—Keeley demanded,

"Why were loyal war monks fighting other loyal war monks? I thought all of you were loyal unto death and blood and all that. What happened to all that fucking loyalty Gemma bragged about?"

"It's a complicated story," Ainsley admitted.

"I'm sure it is." Keeley looked at the monks. "Maybe you three can explain it to me?"

Instead of lying—which was what Keeley was expecting from them—Brother Katla just told the big male, "Do not start crying, Kir."

But a tear was already sliding down his cheek before he said, "We should not have been fighting amongst ourselves. I will always blame Sprenger for what happened to us. We should not have been fighting each other there at the end before half of what remained of us went off to die in glorious battle. We should have been united as one, *then* gone off to die in glorious battle. That's the way it was *before* Sprenger and that's how it should have been until the end. But he destroyed our unity, and I hope he burns in hell for it."

Brother Katla closed her eyes, shook her head. Brother Shona simply grimaced.

Keeley, however, grabbed Ainsley's arm and yanked her close. "I see what's going on here."

"You do?" Shona asked.

"You're trying to recruit another sister of mine to your death cult. Is that it?" Keeley accused.

Ainsley held up her hand in front of Keeley's face. "You do understand that I can take care of myself, don't you?"

"Since when?"

"Well, since all of you keep forgetting I exist—"

"Can we discuss that later?" Keeley quickly cut in.

"And just so we're clear, we're not a death cult," Brother Katla argued. "Death cults only care about their own deaths and, of course, the end of the world. We, however, kill everyone else." Now she grimaced. "That came out wrong."

"Truly? Because it sounded so *perfect* from here," Keeley replied with an intense amount of sarcasm. Even for her.

Brother Shona stepped in front of Brother Katla. "Look, I see that we've gotten off on the wrong foot. We're not attempting to recruit anyone. Gemma just asked us to introduce ourselves. So you could get to know us."

"Why in the fuck would she do that?"

"She actually did think it would be a good idea in the hopes that you'd feel more comfortable with all these war monks here at your doorstep. At the time. Of course, our monastery had just burned down. So maybe she was still in shock."

Keeley jerked her chin at the giant male, unwilling to release Ainsley for fear they'd steal away with her. "Why is he still crying?"

"We didn't mean to upset you so!" he sobbed out.

"You know what?" Keeley finally admitted. "I now understand something. Why none of you are like Brother Emmanuel. He's a pacifist monk I met very recently. He goes out and makes people feel better. He's been doing it for days. I've watched him. No matter the sect or the god worshipped, he puts all at ease." Keeley shook her head. "But I think we can all agree. That is *not* a job you three should ever have."

Shona let out a long sigh. "I wish we could argue that point with you, Your Majesty . . . but we cannot."

Gemma decided to pass through a town to pick up a few supplies. That was where she caught sight of three witches standing outside a pub. She only knew they were witches because her order had battled their coven several years back. It had been an ugly, violent conflict that hadn't ended well for the nearby townspeople, who were left with nothing but a burnt-out husk of a village, a lot of dead farm animals and, most likely, a never-ending hatred of war monks and witches.

Immediately, Gemma pulled the list of names out of her boot and studied it.

"Shit."

"What's wrong?" Quinn asked.

"They're on the list."

"Who is?"

Too annoyed even to answer, Gemma dismounted Dagger's back and walked over to the three witches.

"Ladies," she coldly greeted.

"They sent *you*?" Adela demanded.

"It could be worse," Gemma shot back. "Ragna could have come. She's the one who burned your grandmother, I believe."

Adela raised her gloved hand and Gemma had her sword out when a man's explosive laugh had all of them looking around.

"Now, now, my lovelies! No need to be so angry! We can all get along! And I guess we're all here for the same thing!"

"Who are you?" another witch demanded.

"I am Vicar Ferdinand," he said grandly, bowing at the waist. "At your service."

"Oh, no," Father Aubin said from behind Gemma. "A truce vicar."

There was nothing but sighs and groans except from Quinn, who asked, "What's a truce vicar?"

"Hell on earth," Faraji of the Low Mountains drily complained from behind his assassin mask.

"I, young man, am here to bring healing and peace among all the different factions," Vicar Ferdinand explained to Quinn.

"That seems helpful."

"It's not," Gemma muttered, putting her sword back in its sheath.

"The war lovers among us," Ferdinand went on, "feel I get in the way of their glorious deaths."

"Do you?"

"If I'm lucky! Because the work of a truce vicar is to stop all this unnecessary killing! That's why I'm here. To help Cyrus see the many wrongs of his ways."

"Good luck with that," Father Aubin told him. "You should go find him and start talking."

"I think it would be better to meet with the great Queen Keeley first. I've heard wonderful things about her. So let us be off!"

"We're not staying here for the night?" one of the witches complained, looking at the pub longingly.

"No," Gemma said without an ounce of pity. "So get what supplies you need. We leave in ten minutes."

"Fine," another witch said. "Have my bags brought along, War Monk."

Quinn saw Gemma reaching for her sword again, but he caught her arm. She didn't fight him this time and instead said to the witch, "I'm not your servant, Adela. You want your bags, you fucking carry them yourself. That goes for all of you."

After Gemma went to get supplies, the truce vicar slapped Quinn on the back. "You'd make a good truce vicar, my boy. You have a knack for keeping the peace."

"Does it matter that I actually have four legs?" The vicar frowned. "I'm a centaur."

"Ahh. No. Not to the truce vicars. We welcome all!"

"That's nice."

"Except for those evil divine assassins who should burn for eternity in the pits of all the hells."

Quinn stopped and let out a sigh. "Seriously?"

That laughter exploded again. "I'm just joking, my four-legged friend! Truce vicars deal with all! I promise." He again patted Quinn's back. "And that includes even those we find to be pure evil like the divine assassins."

The entire group rode for a few hours until it was late in the evening. Then Gemma led them into the trees and found a relatively safe spot for them to camp for the night. Quinn built a fire and one of the priests returned with a few rabbits they could roast over the fire.

Gemma had also picked up some fresh bread from the baker in town and handed out loaves to everyone. As they ate, no one spoke. And, once they finished eating . . . no one spoke. Not even Quinn.

Quinn always had something to say. Of course, he probably wasn't used to this much silent animosity. He was used to sisterly fights about past bullshit. He was used to two brothers arguing over Gemma's mother. What no one was used to was sitting with members of religious sects that loathed one another and, on more than one occasion, had attempted to destroy the other's sect over the centuries.

And, of course, when the silence was finally broken, it was in the worst way possible.

"So," Father Aubin finally asked a silent Quinn, "do you *feel* unholy?"

Quinn shook his head. "No. I do not."

"Unclean?"

"No. I feel blessed."

"Huh. Interesting."

"Do you feel like a dick?" Gemma asked the priest. "Because, you know, you are."

"Do you have something to say to me, War Monk?"

"I think I just said it."

"Now, now, my friends!" the truce vicar cut in, making everyone but Quinn roll their eyes. "Why must we argue and bicker and make the unholy one feel uncomfortable?"

Quinn dropped his head but Gemma could see he was grinning, because the centaur had no sense.

"First off, he's not unholy. He's a centaur. He's annoying and a pain in my ass, but he's not unholy."

Adela the witch lifted her head and asked, "Are you looking at me, War Monk?"

"I guess I'm just wondering why *you're* here?"

"Fear of Cyrus the Honored?"

"Oh, please. Try again."

"She's right," Balla agreed. "I can't think of any reason why *you* would be here, witch."

"Shut up, virgin. What do you know anyway?"

"Yes, I'm sure I've missed much in my life because I haven't had a cock in my mouth."

"Ladies!" the truce vicar exploded. "Can we all please remember our manners?"

"The vicar's absolutely right," the divine assassin Tadesse chimed in. "You don't want to disturb the priests by talking about sex they will *never* have."

"It's a sacrifice we are willing to make for our god," Father Léandre snapped. "What sacrifice are you willing to make?"

"Our god never asked us to make *that* particular sacrifice," Faraji of the Low Mountains calmly replied. "Because our god actually likes us."

That's when poor Quinn lost it, laughing so hard he had to get up and leave. He walked off into the surrounding trees, his laughter echoing back to them for a very long time before it finally tapered off.

"What was that all about?" Aubin finally asked.

Gemma shrugged. "I'm guessing he found all of you fucking ridiculous."

"But not you?" Balla asked.

"No," Gemma answered in all seriousness. "Not me."

CHAPTER 16

The first day of travel and already Balla was annoyed by . . . well . . . everyone. Absolutely everyone. The witches. The priests. The divine assassins. And that truce vicar. She wanted to stab him in the throat if only to shut him the fuck up. Goddess, the price she paid for her powers. She didn't mind keeping her virginity. For her, sex wasn't really that big a loss. Men in general annoyed her and she found offensive the way many of them insisted on waving their cocks around. But being forced to leave her precious temple, where she'd been in complete control for the last decade, to travel not only with whorish witches; overbearing priests; dangerous assassins; a disgusting, foul-mouthed war monk; and a never quiet truce vicar was her goddess asking entirely too much of her.

All she could hope was that they arrived at Queen Keeley's castle sooner rather than later. Balla longed for a bath and a few minutes of silence.

The centaur, who traveled with a horse he did not ride, suddenly stopped, his head moving one way then another, before galloping off; the war monk chased after him. Balla was more than happy to let them go but everyone else went after them so she felt she had to as well. Of course, Priska waited for her to make the decision for both of them as she should.

She followed the others and ended up at a ledge that overlooked a drop of at least sixty feet. The others had dismounted from their animals and were staring down at something, so Balla also dismounted and went to the edge to see what they were looking at.

It was a fairly large company of soldiers surrounding a woman. It seemed an excessive number of soldiers to guard one lone woman or one lone man until she noticed the soldiers' colors. Cyrus's green and gray.

"All that for one woman?" the centaur asked.

"A nun," the war monk pointed out.

"One for you to pick up?"

"No. There were no nuns on the list."

"Excellent," Balla said. "Then we should be off."

She turned to go but when she had nearly reached her horse she realized she was walking alone. With a sigh, she faced the others. "Do we really have time for this? She's just a nun. Don't you agree, War Monk? Don't we need to go?"

The monk looked at the centaur and together, the pair began to walk toward Balla. But when they drew near her, they pulled their swords, turned, and charged toward the ledge. When they reached the edge, they both jumped.

Balla stomped her foot. "This is why I *hate war monks*!" she bellowed.

Gemma landed hard on the back of a soldier, slamming her blade into his spine and using his body to break her landing. When he hit the ground, she rolled off him, dragging her sword out of his back at the same time, and got to her feet.

She quickly moved until she was on the nun's left and Quinn was on her right.

"War Monk," the nun greeted, holding tightly onto a steel walking stick. "I have to say I'm most heartened to see you."

"Sister."

"Stay behind us, Sister," Quinn said, his long sword out.

"Unholy four-legged thing!" one of the soldiers cursed at Quinn even though Quinn had quickly shifted back into his human form, and the nun seemed confused by the insult.

In response, Quinn dramatically pointed his sword at the man and promised, "I'm going to shit on you."

The expression on the soldier's face was so horrified that Gemma started to laugh and then she charged, killing the soldier closest to her. It was the last thing anyone was expecting from her, which was why it worked so well. She'd hacked her way through nearly ten soldiers when she noticed that Quinn was just standing there.

"What the fuck are you doing?" she demanded, but he didn't answer her. He just continued to stand there, staring . . .

She turned and . . .

The nun tore through soldiers. One after another after another. Gemma could not say she'd never seen such a thing before. She had. But never from a nun. And this was definitely a nun. Not a war monk dressed as a nun, but a true nun.

And yet . . . she ripped through those soldiers like they were nothing. It wasn't a steel walking stick she'd held but a steel battle staff. A battle staff that was designed so the nun could easily pull it into two pieces, each of those pieces equipped with a spike on the end. She used those spikes to rip open throats, abdomens, inner thighs, spines, and to tear out eyes. She never said a word, she never made a sound as she did her brutal work. There were no war cries, no curses, no spells cast. She just decimated.

She butchered.

That's when Gemma knew who this woman was! The Abbess Butcher!

She'd always thought the Abbess Butcher—called just the Abbess among the sects—was a tale told to scare novitiates. But her existence made sense. How else would a convent filled with virginal, defenseless women be able to protect itself except to choose one nun to be trained in the art of killing? So while her sisters were lost in peaceful love, prayer, and contemplation of their god, there was one among them who was prepared to destroy any man or men who thought a convent in the middle of nowhere might be ripe for the plucking.

"Behind you," Gemma told Quinn.

"Huh?"

The centaur couldn't stop watching the white-robed nun brutally killing everyone around her, but he really needed to stop. Because their job was not nearly done.

Gemma grabbed Quinn's shoulders and spun him around. He raised his sword in time to stop the axe aimed for his head.

"Thanks!" he yelled at her before diving into the soldiers coming for him.

Gemma buried her own sword in the belly of another soldier, then took his weapon. She used both swords to slash her way through the soldiers closest to her. She kept an eye out for the wizards that usually accompanied Cyrus's soldiers, but that must be only for the legions and field armies.

Still, there were more than a hundred soldiers to battle and they'd only gone through about fifty. But before she could worry about the next fifty, Gemma saw ten abruptly drop. Quickly and without warning. She stepped back, her swords raised and ready.

Something whizzed under and near her before sliding up and around the legs and bodies of several soldiers she'd been facing. The creatures were inky black and once they were near their victims' faces, they pulled back enough to reveal snake heads. The soldiers screamed but the snakes bit into their necks or lips or eyeballs. The soldiers died quickly from the poison but the deaths were painful. Seconds later, the snakes were gone, turning to liquid and evaporating into the ground beneath the bodies of the dead.

Lightning lashed from the sky and skittered across the ground, striking three more soldiers and roasting them to death.

Aubin and Léandre appeared next to the Abbess with their black spears. She'd already put the two pieces of her staff back together, allowing the priests to decimate the remainder of the soldiers, while she batted away any that came too close. That way, it was the priests who could claim the glory; their male pride would not be harmed by a woman possibly showing them up with her battle skills. *How nice for them.*

"Now can we leave?" Balla demanded once the soldiers were all dead.

"Where are the witches?" Gemma asked Balla.

"You are joking, aren't you?" Disgusted that the witches didn't even attempt to help, Gemma moved toward the Abbess.

"Come with us," she urged the nun.

She glanced at Balla, raised an eyebrow. "You travel with pagans."

"True. As well as witches and assassins. But it would still be good if you come. Safer for you at least."

"Come where?"

"To Queen Keeley." Gemma grinned. "Actually . . . I would *love* for her to meet you. I don't think she's ever met a nun. At least not a *real* nun."

Quinn snorted, covered it with a cough, and quickly turned away.

"I appreciate the offer," the Abbess replied. "And gladly accept. Unfortunately, I don't have a horse. I've been traveling on foot."

"You can take my horse," Quinn offered. "Scandal. He'll appreciate how lightweight you are."

"But if I take your horse, what will you ride, good sir?"

Quinn paused, realizing she hadn't seen him in his true form, so how direct should he be in answering that question?

Balla stared at him and asked, "Yes, good sir, how will *you* ride?"

Now the priests and the assassins were staring at him too. Even Gemma was staring. It was uncomfortable because they were all waiting for him to be the one to tell this poor nun what he was, and he wasn't sure how she would take it. Just because the nun was good in a fight didn't mean she was worldly enough to have met centaurs. For all he knew, she might never have been outside her convent before now. And it was traumatic enough to see her white robes covered in all that blood. Now this!

"Well, good lady . . ." He paused again, still unsure. He wasn't used to being unsure about anything.

"Yes?" the nun said, innocently blinking up at him.

"Yes . . . ?" Gemma pushed and he thought about dumping the war monk on her ass. Maybe later, though.

"I don't want you to worry, Sister, when I say this . . . um . . . the reason I don't have to be concerned about my horse is because I am a centaur. So I'm actually half horse."

The nun blinked a few more times before responding with, "I see."

"But like I said, you don't have to worry. You're safe with me," Quinn earnestly promised.

The nun gave the sweetest smile and patted his arm. "And I want you to know that the centaur I disemboweled about seven years back was attacking *me*, and as long as I'm safe with you, you are absolutely safe with me. I would never disembowel a friend. Okay?"

"Uhhhh . . . oooookay."

She reached up and rubbed his shoulder. "Good. Very good."

The nun followed the priests to their horses. Balla and Priska rushed off after them, both women giggling. The divine assassins trailed behind both women, and even with the lower half of their faces covered, Quinn knew they were also laughing at him.

When the rest of their companions were gone, Quinn turned to Gemma and asked, "What the fuck was that?"

Gemma shook her head. "I . . . uh . . . wish I could tell you." She playfully punched his chest. "But, hey. At least she wasn't shocked by what you are."

"Really? That's the best you can come up with?"

She grabbed his arm and tugged him back toward the horses.

"These days, centaur, it really is."

CHAPTER 17

It was a long, hard ride home with only a few hours of sleep at night and only a few breaks during the day, breaks that were more for the horses than for the rest of them.

But the hard ride also kept their small group from one another's throats. With all of them devout practitioners of one religion or another, if they weren't riding, eating, or sleeping, they were praying or meditating.

But war monks didn't pray or meditate when they were on a mission. They felt their battle-ready gods would want them to remain alert and ready for any attacks from enemies.

Yet Gemma didn't notice anything unusual when they were about ten miles from the castle gates. Nor did the witches or the priests or the temple virgins. It was none of the humans that noticed anything.

It was Quinn.

They'd briefly stopped at a stream to let their horses get some water when Quinn's centaur body began to turn in circles, his hooves stomping as he gawked at the ground.

"What's wrong with him?" Aubin demanded.

Gemma didn't know, but this wasn't like Quinn.

"Stop!" the centaur ordered when she came near. He shook his head and massive antlers exploded from his skull, fangs from his gums.

Gemma had seen Quinn's battle form before. She'd fought beside him like this many times, so she wasn't exactly shocked by it. The others, however . . .

Weapons were unleashed, spells readied, but she raised her fist. "Hold!" she commanded.

"What is he doing?" Aubin wanted to know.

"Just back off!"

Quinn stopped moving, stared at Gemma. "You really don't see it? None of you see it?"

"Don't see what?"

"The tracks. Horses. Carts. I'm counting"—he looked down at the ground again—"I don't know. Hundreds of soldiers. And not our soldiers."

Gemma immediately gazed down at her feet but she saw nothing. She knew Quinn wasn't insane. He also wasn't human.

"Balla," she called out.

"Wouldn't the witch be better . . . ?" the vicar began to suggest.

She wasn't going to waste her time. "Balla."

The temple virgin moved forward until she was near Quinn. She raised her hands, closed her eyes.

"Some power has been used here," she finally muttered after many minutes of silence, her voice dragging out. "Something very powerful. It's blocking our sight." She turned in a circle. "It's . . . like it's . . . almost fighting me. Fighting us. Fighting—"

Her eyes snapped open, her gaze locked on a spot behind Gemma.

Gemma turned and saw a figure standing by some trees. She should have noticed him before. How could she have missed him in those dark red robes that covered him from head to toe with gloves covering his hands and a hood covering his face?

Balla growled and began to unleash a spell but her enemy was faster, lifting the priestess off the ground without touching her and starting to wring her neck. Priska ran to Balla's side, grabbing her around the legs and attempting to bring her to the ground.

The priests, assassins, and even the witches quickly moved forward to counterattack but they were tossed back so quickly and violently that Gemma could do nothing but pull her sword and take a battle stance. She had to admit, she didn't feel that would do much at the moment.

Thankfully, Quinn took his place beside her. The hooded head moved, but without being able to see their attacker's face, they had no idea where he was looking and no way to guess what he might be planning next.

Quinn's tail twitched and Gemma knew he was about to make a move, but before he could, the Abbess slowly stepped between their group and the red-robed man.

"Ahhhh," a low voice said from inside that red hood. "Abbess Hurik."

"Ludolf."

"It's been a long time."

"It has."

The Abbess barely gestured behind her, and Ludolf fanned his hands across each other, releasing Balla.

"I'm surprised, Hurik," he said, ignoring the gasping and coughing of the temple virgin on the ground, "to see you traveling with heretics."

"Don't worry about what I'm doing, Ludolf. What are *you* doing?" She gestured at the ground. "Is this all because of you? What the centaur sees?"

"This?" He studied the ground and Gemma realized he could see what the rest of them could not. "I wish my powers extended to such feats but no. This was not me." He seemed to study their group as some helped Balla and the others held up their weapons, ready to charge. "Such an interesting . . . team, you have. And so close to the newish queen. Maybe you can help her."

"Help her?" Gemma scoffed. "To do what? Fight an invisible army?"

"The ones that left the tracks only I and your horse-man can see are long gone, War Monk. But the friends that Cyrus the Honored left behind are still here."

He had the attention of all of them. Even Balla, with her hand around her throat, stared at the red-robed man.

"What friends?" the Abbess asked.

"Why fight two armies when you can fight just one? Cyrus does not see your queen as a challenge. That would be his brother and the new wife, Beatrix." His head moved slightly and Gemma knew he now looked at her. "Your sister, I believe, War Monk. But still,

Queen Keeley's army grows. People flock to her. Cyrus feels if he gets rid of her, he won't have to worry about her and he can have all her territory. So those loyal to Cyrus move through the little town, unseen, unheard. Waiting to strike your queen. I could be wrong, but with your upcoming return, they probably feel the time for your older sister to continue living has come to an end, and—"

Gemma didn't wait to hear any more. Didn't wait to see if anyone followed. She just mounted Dagger and took off for home.

Someone was pulling a cart of firewood past the open gates of the battlements but Quinn cleared it. Not surprisingly, Gemma was ahead of him. What shocked him, though, was that right behind them were all those who'd traveled with them. All of them. Even the Abbess.

"Mum!" Gemma called out as she thundered up to the forge. "Mum! Where's Keeley?!"

Emma pointed. "The woods! Near the north field!"

They barreled on, none of them stopping, and Gemma's mother knew not to stop them. The travelers maneuvered their horses around merchants, locals, and members of the religious sects that had come to town for safety.

They made their way through the pasture and into the woods. Once inside, the trees became thicker and the ground more perilous. Soon, the humans abandoned their horses and Quinn tracked Keeley by her scent.

They found her by the base of a large, ancient tree. She stood with her back to them. And just as Gemma began to call out to her sister, a woman appeared, becoming visible among the leaves and trees where she'd camouflaged herself, and charging at Keeley's back.

Keeley turned fast, snatching the woman up by her throat and slamming her against the tree twice. Another woman came at her and Keeley caught her head and twisted, snapping her neck with the brutal move. When the third attacked, Keeley dropped both women and pulled her sword. She rammed it into the woman's belly; their eyes met and Keeley dragged the blade up.

She pushed the woman off, then threw the weapon down so the tip was buried in the dirt and it stood tall.

Reaching back, she picked up her hammer and gave a few practice swings.

Quinn, confused by that move, started forward, but Gemma grabbed his forearm tight and pulled him back.

As Keeley gripped the handle of her ridiculous hammer with both hands, Father Aubin leaned forward and asked Gemma very softly, "Should we be running?"

"Honestly," she quietly replied, "I don't know what's happening."

Without moving her head, Keeley looked from side to side with just her eyes, then barked, "Ainsley . . . *now!*"

Arrows came from the treetops and Gemma yelled, "*Down!*"

But the arrows weren't for the travelers Gemma and Quinn had brought with them.

Quinn heard male grunts and saw bodies fall. Male bodies that he hadn't seen before. It seemed that as long as these men stayed still, they could remain hidden by the trees and leaves, but as soon as they changed position, they were easy enough to spot. Especially by someone like Ainsley.

More arrows came down and more men fell. Ainsley was guessing now where these men stood, but her guesses were good enough, and now they no longer had a reason to remain hidden.

Cyrus's soldiers charged at Keeley, weapons out, their battle cries loud. And she began to swing her hammer.

"By the almighty gods of war," Léandre gasped when he saw her cave in the chests of the first men who came for her.

She turned her weapon and swung the other way, only higher, smashing heads like pumpkins.

Some of the soldiers, perhaps not as fanatical as those that had already lost their lives, began to run off into the trees.

"Ainsley!" Keeley barked.

More arrows flew, hitting the fleeing soldiers in the back. But several escaped and kept running.

"You missed—"

"I know!" Ainsley barked back. She inched out onto the tree limb she'd been sitting on. She raised her bow with three arrows nocked, breathed, and released. The arrows flew, hitting each of the targets. Two in the back of the neck and one right in the back of the head.

"Don't look so proud of yourself, Lady I Can Take Care of Myself," Keeley chastised. "You almost lost them."

"But I didn't."

"But you almost did."

Quinn heard moaning and realized Keeley's first victim was still alive and attempting to crawl away.

Ainsley flipped out of the tree, nocked an arrow in her bow, and aimed at the woman's back. But before she could let her arrow fly, blood flew, splashing them all as the head of Keeley's hammer smashed into the head on the ground.

Gemma gasped at what her sister had done, her eyes wide in horror, blood and gore covering her face and chest.

"What the unholy fuck *was that*?" she exploded at Keeley.

Keeley lifted the hammer onto her shoulder and glared at her war monk sister. "Don't yell at me," she told Gemma. "I am in a bad mood."

With that, Keeley headed back into town.

"Bad mood!" she growled over her shoulder one more time. As if unsure whether her sister had heard her the first time.

Ferdinand wiped gore off his chin. "So...that's the queen then?"

"Oh, shut up, Vicar!"

CHAPTER 18

"You can't really expect us to deal with *her*, can you?"

Gemma continued to scrape sorcerers' remains off her face while trying to scare off Balla with one of her looks. Unfortunately, the temple virgin was not frightened away by Gemma's terrifying glare.

"Are you going to answer me?" Balla demanded.

She wasn't and proved that by focusing on Ainsley.

"And you," Gemma snapped, turning toward her younger sister. "What the fuck do you think you're doing?"

Her sister stood tall, indignant. "That's all you have to say to me?"

"What do you want me to say?"

"How about commenting on my beautiful bow work? I made every shot count. Each one a kill. You should be proud. Instead, you just complain."

"I haven't complained."

"You're complaining with your eyes."

"You're right. I am."

Quinn, who'd abruptly walked off, returned with his siblings Laila and Caid in tow.

"Holy shit," Laila gasped out when she saw the carnage. "What the fuck did she do?"

But Caid simply snarled and galloped back the way he'd come in search of Keeley. At least that's what Gemma was guessing.

"She didn't tell you about this?" Gemma asked.

Laila shook her head. "Not a word."

"How did she even know? Because trust me, Laila, she knew that attack was coming. The question is how did she know and why didn't she tell anyone else about it?"

"She told me," Ainsley piped in.

"Oh, shut up."

"You shut up!"

"Ainsley!" Gemma snapped before focusing again on Laila. "Any idea how she knew?" Gemma pushed, which she immediately regretted.

Because she realized what the answer would be, and she immediately knew what would appear. And they did appear, as if purposely timing their appearance for maximum damage to her reputation.

The priests noticed them first.

"What unholiness is *that*?" Aubin demanded, brandishing his black spear.

Keeley's demon wolves inched closer to the dead, sniffing them while keeping their eyes of fire on the humans that still lived.

"If you hope to keep the queen's favor, Priest," Quinn warned, "you'd best put your weapon away."

"If you hope to keep your *life*, you'd best put that weapon away," Laila muttered.

Balla stepped back. "What haven of ungodliness have you brought us to, War Monk?"

"I think they're adorable," Adela announced. She moved closer to one of the wolves but it snarled and snapped at her.

The Abbess laughed. "Even pure evil wants nothing to do with you, witch."

The witch hissed in warning at the nun and Gemma began to rub her forehead. But her skin was sticky from all the blood her sister had splattered on her.

She pulled her hand away just as each of the wolves began to drag off a body to devour on its own. A couple of the younger ones fought over a sorceress, tearing her into pieces and charging off with an arm and a leg. That's when their little travel party turned to stare at her in mute horror. She didn't blame them. Gemma also decided she didn't have to put up with it.

She reached down to pick up her sword. She'd stuck it into the ground when she and Keeley had gotten into it. She had it by the hilt when Quinn grabbed her around the waist and carried her off.

Gemma had no idea where the centaur was taking her. But even one of the hells had to be better than this.

Keeley sat with her back against a tree, her knees raised, and her elbows resting on them. She didn't know she was not alone until she heard his voice.

"May I join you, Your Majesty?"

He wore red robes that covered him from head to foot. She couldn't see any part of his face. Not even his hands because he wore red leather gloves.

"Only if you don't call me 'Your Majesty,'" Keeley practically snarled and she immediately winced. She knew she sounded petulant and bitter. And fucking whiny. When had she become whiny?

"Sorry. Sorry about that," she immediately apologized. "That was pathetic and you didn't deserve that tone." She gestured to a nearby stump. "Please. Sit."

He did. "I have never heard a royal admit he or she sounded pathetic before. Nor apologize. I feel truly confused."

"I've only been a royal for two years. I'm sure I'm doing it all wrong." She gazed at the man now sitting across from her. "I have to admit, though, I'd feel much better if I could see your face."

"Everyone believes that . . . until they actually *see* my face."

"Don't flatter yourself. I've made armor and weapons for men and women who've been through the hell of battle and went back for more. I doubt you'll show me anything I haven't seen before."

Quinn scrubbed the blood and gore from Gemma's face, neck, and hands while she sat near the river and silently seethed.

He could tell she was seething by the way her brows were pulled together. In order to get the blood off her forehead, he'd had to pull the skin so he could clean it properly. It wasn't easy. The muscles were so tight, he'd had to force her brows apart.

"Are you really going to sit there all day . . . glowering?"

"That is my plan."

Quinn sat down and began to wipe his own face but Gemma snatched the clean cloth from him and began to clean him herself. Apparently, he wasn't "doing it right." He didn't know what that meant, but he was too afraid to ask when she was like this. He should have grabbed her before she'd picked up her sword but he'd been slow to react. That was his fault. Because he knew better than most that once she picked up her sword, she was already too pissed for rational thought.

"She bashed in that woman's head like it was nothing," Gemma suddenly announced.

"That woman was a sorceress and she did try to kill Keeley."

"But Keeley should have still talked to her first or at least—"

"Don't you mean the old Keeley?"

"What?"

"The old Keeley? The one that Caid first met before I even came along. The one that Beatrix hadn't stabbed yet. That Keeley would have asked questions first and would have tried to stop you from cutting off the sorceress's head until she saw there was no other option. But this Keeley doesn't wait. She asks fewer questions. She's quicker to react. And you're worried what that means."

Gemma sat back on her heels, her head dropping.

"She's not turning into Beatrix, Gemma," he said, which was the question she was truly asking herself.

And after a long moment of contemplative silence—something these religious types were known for—Gemma asked in a low voice, "But what if she's becoming something far worse?"

That's when Quinn laughed. He had to. It was so ridiculous!

Gemma glared at him. "What the fuck's so funny?"

"You say something so stupid after asking me that question? About Keeley?"

"Well—"

"Not only do you ask it about Keeley but you're comparing her to gods-damn *Beatrix*!"

"You forget that Beatrix hasn't actually done anything evil since she's been queen."

"It's only been two years."

"Yes, but everyone thought that as soon as she got the crown, the skies would turn to blood and the earth would crack open and unleash all sorts of hell beasts. None of that has happened. In fact, the only one with actual hell beasts is Keeley!"

"Is that what you were hoping for?" he laughed. "The earth to crack open when Beatrix became queen?"

"No! Of course not. But I thought we were fighting against pure evil. Not stopping my sister from sitting on a throne in some fancy dress."

"Is that really what you think we're doing?"

"I'm starting to think maybe we should have had our focus on Cyrus all this time. He's managed to destroy monasteries and churches and sneak onto our land unseen, and nearly kill my sister."

"He did not nearly kill your sister. We have absolutely no idea how long they were here watching her, but Keeley has known the entire time. She was not surprised when they attacked her."

"I know." She briefly looked away before asking, "And that doesn't bother you? If she knew about them, why didn't she kill them right away?"

Quinn couldn't help it, he laughed again.

"What's so funny?"

"You and my sister. Either you're yelling at Keeley because she's making snap decisions and not thinking things through. Or you're yelling at her because she's not moving fast enough."

"That's not true."

"It is true. The only thing you two ever consistently tell her is that she should kill Beatrix as soon as she sees the whites of her eyes, which you both know she won't ever do."

"Which is a mistake."

He laughed again and stood, stripping off his kilt and chainmail shirt.

"Why am I seeing you naked? I don't want to see you naked."

"Of course you do. And I'm getting in the river. I still have blood in my hair."

"And a little bit of brain at the temples."

"That's nice."

* * *

The man sat down across from Keeley and began to carefully dismantle the hood of his robe. It took some time because it was a complicated endeavor; she assumed it had been arranged so no one could simply rip it off. When he was done and Keeley could see him clearly, she asked, "Did someone do that to you or did you do that to yourself?"

"A combination, I'm afraid. It's the price one pays for power."

"Steep price."

"Yes, but now I have a lot of power."

"And you've brought it here . . . for what reason?"

"I wasn't sure." He went through the process of putting his hood back into place. When he was done, he said, "I met your sister. Beatrix. She's cold. Calculating. I like that."

"She's smart too. Smarter than everybody."

"And she knows it."

"She does."

Keeley had nothing else to say to this man, but before she could tell him to go, the only companions guaranteed to cheer her up ran to her side. The pack jumped around her, licking her face and neck, rubbing against her. They'd eaten well today. She didn't allow them to eat humans, except enemy soldiers during battle and enemies that attacked her like the ones this afternoon. So the wolves were in a very good mood, which cheered her up immensely. In fact, she was so busy laughing and petting them that it took her a few minutes to realize that the man had gone quiet.

"What?" she finally asked, smiling.

"Do you know what you have there?"

She let out a pained sigh. "Not you too. I thought with that face of yours, you'd be a tad less judgmental. But, since you're not, I'll tell you what I tell my self-righteous war monk sister. They may come from one of the hells, but they're animals. And animals are innocent. Even if their eyes are made of flames and their drool is made of blood. It's not their fault they are what they are. They did not choose this life, and I'm not going to blame them for it. They are my friends and they are welcome here for as long as they want to stay."

She heard the man sniffing the air. "You do know they've recently eaten humans?"

"The ones who tried to kill me. I told them they could. The humans were dead anyway. And the wolves have been very good. At my request, they don't kill the villagers. So letting them eat my enemies is the least I can do."

The man abruptly got to his feet. Keeley thought he was going to storm off. Something she was used to from Gemma. But instead, he brushed off his robes, and then he bowed.

"Queen Keeley, I am Ludolf of the Eastern Shores. A blood warlock and at your service." He took a step closer. "I believe I can be of great assistance to you and your reign."

Keeley, still petting one of her wolves, stared up at the robed man for at least a minute before she finally asked, "What's a blood warlock?"

"Uh . . . that's your question? I offer you the assistance of a warlock and you want to know what a blood warlock is?"

"I've never heard of one before. It sounds fascinating."

"Well . . . let's see . . . the best way I can explain what I do is to tell you that a blood warlock is something that will greatly annoy your war monk sister."

"Oh!" Keeley nodded. "Then, Lord Ludolf, which is what I will now call you, we're already off to a great start."

Gemma paced at the river's edge. "Are you even listening to me?"

"You're ranting."

"I am not ranting. I'm just concerned."

"Concerned about what?"

"That we're making a mistake."

Quinn finished rinsing his hair and when he rose from the water, he was centaur. The top half of his horse body was above the water, his tail swinging.

"A mistake about what?"

"Beatrix."

He started laughing again and Gemma couldn't stand it anymore.

"What is so fucking funny?"

"She stabbed her own sister in the gut! For a crown. And you think you made a mistake about her? So the war monks...? Not big readers... or thinkers...? You left that to the priests? Maybe the nuns?"

"I just expected her evil to be more... obvious."

"Can you get more obvious than stabbing your sister? Keep in mind that she wasn't positive she'd become queen. She was just really hoping."

"Maybe we need to rethink our whole plan."

"I didn't know we had a plan. I mean... not a specific plan."

Gripping her hands together, she faced Quinn. "Maybe we should consider joining forces with Beatrix and Marius so we can challenge Cyrus together."

"Huh," he said before he waded through the water toward her. Massive, majestic, all four legs moving easily through the water as he made his way over to her. His arms reached down and he grabbed her, lifted her up, and heaved Gemma several feet into the river.

"Perhaps we made a mistake. Coming here."

"It's not like we had many choices, Balla." Aubin took several hot rolls from a plate and sat down on a bench. None of them were comfortable in this pub, but they'd had little choice. Making themselves at home in the queen's castle didn't seem like a good idea at the moment and they didn't know where any survivors of their own sects might have settled in the town. If any of their colleagues had made it this far.

The pub just seemed like the safest place.

"I think we should still speak with the queen ourselves," Tadesse remarked, sipping his ale.

"Of course, *you* do, Assassin. I'm sure you find nothing wrong with that giant woman."

"My people would adorn her with our finest jewels and silk and beg her to breed with our strongest men so we could harness the mad strength of her oversized babies."

Balla threw her food down. "And now we know why I've happily remained a virgin."

* * *

By the time Gemma swam back to the surface, Quinn was swimming beside her. All four legs happily moving along in the water.

"What is wrong with you?" she demanded. As she *always* demanded. Because she had become convinced that he'd been damaged while still in his mother's womb!

"Nothing. Why do you ask?"

"Why did you toss me into the water?"

"Because you needed a bath and because you were clearly not thinking rationally."

"What?"

"If your plan is to join forces with Beatrix, you are *not* thinking rationally, Gemma. Trust me. And swift-moving river water is good for waking up those that have lost their senses, which you clearly have."

"I have not lost my—"

"Come on!" he cheered. "Let's wash your hair!"

Then he dunked her again.

"Gods-dammit, Quinn!" she screamed when he finally let her back up.

"Is anyone else concerned the witches are not here?" Priska asked in the softest voice, shocking Aubin. He didn't think she was allowed to speak.

Balla looked around the pub. "Weren't they with us when we walked in?"

"They were," Ferdinand said. "But you shouldn't all be so paranoid! I'm sure they're just looking around this beautiful town! And I'm sure the queen is quite worthy of our loyalty!"

"Could you keep your voice down?" Balla nearly begged while the rest of them cringed. "We are in her territory."

"Sorry. Sorry. I just feel you're all overthinking this."

"Or perhaps you're not thinking at all," Léandre sneered, his tolerance for the truce vicar's cheery countenance waning with each day.

"I'll just ask someone," Ferdinand suggested.

"Ask someone what?" Balla demanded.

"How they feel about their queen."

"Have you lost your mind?"

"We'll be smart about it."

"But you're not smart," Aubin reminded the vicar. "You're, in fact, very dumb."

"There—" He pointed at someone standing at the bar. "I'll ask that very large young man there."

"That's not a man!" Balla whispered desperately as the vicar walked away. "That's a very large woman!"

Her chainmail weighed her down but Gemma still wouldn't let Quinn help her out of the water. Yes! She was being ridiculous, but she didn't care. She was too angry to be rational.

"*Why can't you be normal?*" she raged at him once she'd made it safely back onto land.

"I am normal," he said, relaxing casually on the ground. He was back in his kilt, his chainmail shirt tossed over his shoulder, unworn boots leaning against his side. His arms rested against his raised knees, his fingers interlaced. "Half man. Half horse. How much more normal can I be?"

He grinned and she wanted to slap that grin off his face.

"Are we rational now?" he asked in the most annoying tone she'd ever heard from him. "Are we having rational, calm thoughts? Or do we need to be dunked again?"

"I should beat you until there's nothing left but bone!"

"That would be fine as long as you don't keep thinking it's a good idea to join forces with Beatrix."

"Why?"

"Beatrix may not be running around raping novitiates, but she tried to kill your sister. And all Keeley ever did was love and protect her the way a big sister does. That's not someone you can ever trust. Ever believe. Ever risk your sister's queendom by trusting. Don't you see that?"

"What I see is that we have a real problem."

He shrugged. "All we have are real problems. Why add to them by trusting Beatrix?"

Gemma dropped down next to Quinn and admitted the truth. "I don't know what we're going to do. I don't know how we're going to fight Cyrus. How we're going to stop this war before it all gets out of hand. And right now, I just feel drained."

"Gemma, you've just been through hell. Of *course* you're drained. But my question is why do you think this is all on you? It's not. Right now we've got war priests, divine assassins, temple virgins, and the Abbess. You can't tell me they won't have ideas to get us through this."

"But they just saw the queen bash a sorceress's head in."

"You can't tell me that's the worst they've ever seen. Especially that abbess."

She shrugged. "I guess you have a point."

"Let's talk to them. The worst they can do is walk away. And if they do, so what? We still have Laila, Caid, Cadell, and Farlan. Do you know how much damage they've done in their lives? Long before we ever got here? They'll do whatever is necessary to protect your sister and her queendom."

Quinn suddenly reached out and took Gemma's hand. Her first instinct was to snatch it back and punch him in the face, but she fought that instinct and waited to see what he'd say and do.

"Just for once," he went on, gently, "instead of trying to fix this all on your own . . . instead of trying to come up with a plan when you have absolutely no idea what's going on and you just saw the destruction of your entire brotherhood, maybe you sit back and you just let Keeley lead. Just this once you trust her to do the right thing, not just for herself, but for her people."

Gemma hated to admit it to herself, but Quinn was right. She'd been through too much. Had seen too much. And she couldn't keep trying to rule *for* Keeley. That wasn't her place or her right. Keeley was queen, not Gemma.

"Or," Quinn continued, "you can simply burn Keeley as a witch. Whichever you feel more comfortable with."

Gemma shook her head and tried not to laugh. "Why are you such a bastard?"

"I was giving you options."

"Bastard."

"Come on," he said, chuckling. "Let's get back. You must be starving."

"No. *You're* starving."

"I am. I am starving. I need to feed."

"Fair enough. And if nothing else, I need to get this chainmail off for a bit. I feel like I'm wearing my bag of rocks right now."

They headed back to town but saw some of Ragna's monk-knights training. Gemma was in no mood to deal with any of them at the moment.

Quinn motioned behind them. "We'll cut through the hot springs and loop around."

"There are hot springs?"

"There were when we were done."

"You built hot springs?"

He shrugged. "Centaurs love hot springs."

They silently walked, cutting around big boulders and massive trees. Gemma saw several small hot springs and knew she was going to come back at a later time to indulge, because centaurs weren't the only ones that loved hot springs. The thought of soaking her sore muscles almost had her moaning out loud, which was why she was surprised when she thought she heard someone moaning.

She stopped and so did Quinn; she realized he'd heard it too. They looked at each other and slowly took several steps backward, past a boulder, not bothering to actually turn around, and looked into the hot spring they'd just passed.

"Gods!" Quinn immediately covered his eyes. "I don't need to see this!"

"Really, Shona?" Gemma demanded of her battle-cohort. "Everything is falling apart and you take time out for fucking?"

Shona rolled her eyes and moved away from her latest conquest.

"And I'm telling Mum!" Quinn promised.

"Telling her what?" Laila wanted to know.

"That you're being a very disreputable princess."

"Oh, please! That's not exactly going to surprise *our* mother."

"You can do better, Laila," Gemma told her.

"Oy! Where's the loyalty, friend?" Shona wanted to know.

"I don't understand!" Quinn finally admitted, gesturing between the two war monks. "I thought you lot were virgins."

It was a long pause, born out of surprise. But when the laughter exploded out of them, it lasted for ages and felt so very good. Gemma didn't realize how much she'd needed that laugh. More than she needed to soak her sore muscles in a hot spring.

"What, in all the universes, made you think we were virgins?" she finally managed to ask.

"You're religious monks, yes?"

"We're *war* monks, centaur. After a bloody, violent, destructive battle, the last thing you want is a moment of prayer. You want ale, you want food, and you want a lusty—"

"Yes!" he cut in. "I get it."

"Do you?"

"I do now," he muttered, walking away. Calling back to his sister, "I'm still telling Mum!"

"Virgin," Gemma laughed, following him. "What made you think *I* was a—"

"Shut up!"

Katla walked into the pub with her brother and several of her fellow war monks. She'd been going out of her way to avoid the queen the last few days. After their unfortunate conversation, she'd decided not to meet with Keeley again until Gemma's return.

Of course, Gemma was back but now there were new . . . issues. Issues that were best dealt with by the sisters. Until then, Katla would just keep herself and her brother out of the queen's way until they were needed.

At least that was the plan until she walked into the pub and saw some of the worst enemies of her brotherhood listening to the one person they shouldn't be listening to. The queen's cousin. Keran Smythe. A woman of great skill in battle and in hand-to-hand combat, but a right mess in life.

Grabbing her brother by the arm, Katla dragged Kir across the pub, followed by the other monks, until they all stood next to the table that held the group Gemma had brought back to meet with Keeley.

What was disturbing Katla was what she heard when she came to a stop.

"Then, of course, came the goat incident," Keran announced.

"Keran!" Katla said, her voice much sharper than she'd meant it to be. She cleared her throat, tried again. "Why don't we go with you back to the castle?"

"Why? They're all probably just arguing there. I can't drink enough ale to sit through that much arguing. Unless it turns physical." She chuckled. "Then it turns funny."

She looked off, stopped talking, and . . . nothing. For a good minute.

"Are . . . are you all right?" a war priest finally asked.

She seemed to come back into the moment, her gaze moving back to those at the table. "Huh?"

By Morthwyl's cock! This woman!

"Are you all right?" the priest asked again.

"Oh, yeah. Been like this for years. I was in a fight guild. You get hit in the head enough and . . ."

They all waited a bit for her to continue until Katla finally leaned in and slapped her hands in front of Keran's face.

". . . you forget what you were saying," Keran went on without realizing she'd stopped.

Then it got worse.

Keran looked at Katla and greeted her with a "Hey!" as if seeing her for the first time. "Did you just get here?"

"No. I've been standing here for five minutes."

"Oh. Well, I need to tell you something before I forget. I know I'll forget, because I don't care."

"That sounds great," Katla quickly said, taking Keran by the arm and attempting to lift her from her chair. "Let's go to the bar and get you a nice, cool ale."

"I'd love an ale."

"Of course you would."

"But first," she said, sitting back in her chair, "I need to remember what I'm supposed to tell you. Just give me a minute." She stared up at Katla. And stared. And stared. Finally, she snapped her fingers. "Now I remember."

"Thank the gods."

"I need to tell you that you should keep Brother Ragna away from Keeley because I think that war monk is inches away from losing her tit to the queen's sword."

The brothers near Katla cringed at that description and looked away; Kir just groaned.

"Why do you hate me?" Katla asked the woman.

"If I hated you, I would have torn your arm off by now because you're still touching me. I'm not a fan of being touched, except by close friends. Anyway, your Ragna—"

"She's not my Ragna."

"—made the mistake of suggesting to Keeley that her younger siblings might be better taken care of by your brotherhood than by her parents. That is a very good way to get your head bashed in. Anyway, Gemma told me when we separated outside the monastery that if it looked like Ragna was starting any shit with Keeley, I should tell you. So, I'm telling you." She stood. "Now how about that ale?"

"I'm busy."

"You promised me an ale." Then Keran cracked her neck, apparently making a threat with that little move.

Katla faced her battle-cohort's cousin. "You do know I'm an impoverished monk, don't you?"

"Really? Because those are nice weapons you have, impoverished monk."

Growling, Katla dug out the few coins she had in her purse and slapped them into the held-out hand of the queen's *cousin*, who never seemed to be without coin of her own.

"Thanks, mate!"

Once the onetime fight champion was gone, it was the temple virgin who asked, "So the queen doesn't get along with Brother Ragna?"

"I wouldn't say they don't get along."

"It *sounds* like they don't get along."

Katla gave a helpless shrug. "We all know how Ragna is. I'm sure she didn't mean to be—"

"Herself?" one of the priests asked.

"I was going to say difficult."

"Ragna loves being difficult," the temple virgin insisted.

"Let's go talk to her," another priest said, standing up.

"Good idea," Katla agreed. "I can take you to Ragna right now."

"Not Ragna, War Monk," the temple virgin practically barked at Katla. "Take us to the queen. We want to talk to *her*."

CHAPTER 19

They all met right outside the doors leading to the main hall. To say it was awkward would be downplaying it considerably. Because Ragna was already standing there when Quinn and Gemma walked up from one direction and the rest of their travel party walked up from the other. And she was acting as if she was the official greeter for the queen herself, lurking in front of the open doors, forcing each of the travelers to pass by her before they could enter.

"Oh, Ragna. I wish I could say it was good to see you again but, of course, I'd be lying," Priestess Balla taunted.

"Balla," Ragna replied. "How nice . . . for someone, I'm sure . . . that you survived."

"Now, now, ladies," Vicar Ferdinand chastised with his booming voice. "No need to peck at each other as you females always like to do. Let's be friends instead!"

Ragna let out the first frustrated sigh Quinn had ever heard from her before she asked the vicar, "Good gods, why are *you* here?"

"The gods have blessed us all!" he happily replied, slapping Ragna on the back and following the temple virgins into the main hall.

"Was a truce vicar actually on the list," Ragna asked Quinn and Gemma, "or are you simply attempting to make my life hell?"

"Well—" Gemma began, but Quinn quickly cut her off.

"He was on the list. And why don't I make introductions?"

"We need no introductions," Father Aubin sneered, pushing past the master general. "We all know Ragna."

"And she knows all of us," Tadesse of the High Plains said, following the priest.

Ragna smirked as the representatives of the other sects passed her, only speaking again when the witch Adela was close.

"How's your grandmother, Adela?" she asked with what seemed to be an attempt at a smile.

It took the witch's two associates to drag the coven leader away as she desperately attempted to get her hands around Ragna's throat.

"What was that about?" Quinn asked.

"She burned Adela's grandmother at the stake," Gemma explained, shaking her head.

"Then why would you ask how the woman was?"

"Because it amused me to do so," Ragna answered honestly. "And don't give me that look, Brother Gemma. Her grandmother used to sacrifice babies."

"Are you saying you wouldn't have burned her if she didn't sacrifice babies?" Quinn wanted to know.

"Of course I would have burned her, but that particular coven doesn't sacrifice babies anymore, now do they? See? It all worked out in the end. So stop being such a bloody—"

"Blessings of the day to you, Ragna."

It was the Abbess sweetly greeting Ragna, her hands tucked into the sleeves of her white robes, a soft smile on her lips.

Ragna's entire body tightened as her gaze shifted to the nun.

"She was on the list?" she demanded of Gemma.

Her tone was so different, so livid, that Gemma didn't hesitate. "No. She wasn't. We picked her up along the way."

"And you brought her *here*?"

"They saw I was in danger and they saved me," the Abbess explained.

"You? In danger?"

"Cyrus's men were trying to kill her," Gemma explained.

"You should have let them."

"Ragna!" Gemma gasped. "We always protect the sisterhood."

"It's all right, Brother Gemma. I'm used to Brother Ragna forgetting her oath . . . especially to her precious god."

A blade slashed and Quinn leaned back barely in time to avoid it cutting his face as he pushed Gemma into the arms of Shona and Laila, who'd just walked up. But the blade hadn't been aimed at him. It was aimed at the nun.

The Abbess caught Ragna's wrist and held it, smirking at the war monk seconds before she twisted, flipping the other woman. Ragna landed in a crouch, the blade still tight in her grip.

The Abbess yanked Ragna's arm under her own. She bent the wrist back until she forced the monk to drop the blade, then turned to face Ragna again. She grabbed the monk's tunic, dragged her forward, and head-butted her with a roar that had Quinn shifting into his battle centaur form.

He moved to shove the two women apart but they were separated by an unseen force, each woman landing hard on the ground, feet apart.

The red-robed man appeared. Ludolf the warlock. He stepped from inside the castle, gazing down at each woman before nodding at Quinn.

"Centaur."

"Ludolf."

Ragna picked herself up. "You? I thought I killed you, Ludolf."

"It's good to see you too, Ragna."

"Woman, is there *anyone* you get along with?" Quinn felt the need to ask the war monk.

"Ragna is a true follower of Morthwyl, centaur. War is a creator of chaos and that's what Ragna enjoys doing. Isn't that right, War Monk?"

Ludolf held his gloved hand out for the Abbess but she ignored it and got up on her own.

"Thank you anyway, Ludolf."

"Of course. Now if you'll excuse me . . . the queen should be arriving soon."

"You know my sister?" Gemma demanded.

"I introduced myself. We talked. Did you think I'd wait for you to introduce us, Brother Gemma? I know better than to trust a war monk to do anything for a blood warlock. Ragna made it perfectly clear we should never trust a war monk to do anything for us. No matter what our intent."

"What does that mean?"

"Maybe Ragna will tell you one day. Until then . . . I've got other business." He turned to the Abbess. "Hurik? After you?"

"Thank you, Ludolf." The nun again smirked at Ragna, before heading inside ahead of him.

Ragna slipped her sword back into her sheath and started toward the main hall but Gemma grabbed her arm and yanked her back.

The master general looked down at the hand clutching her and then at the woman it was attached to. "I know you didn't just grab me," she said.

"You need to tell me what's going on."

"You need to get your hands off me."

"Gemma's right," Katla announced. "You need to tell us everything, Ragna."

Ragna smirked and in that moment, the calm and determined war monk returned. She gazed at the battle-cohorts she'd once trained and asked easily, "And who is going to make me do that, dear girl? You?"

Then, with a soft chuckle, she made her way into the main hall.

The small group of people who were left faced one another.

"What *was* that?" Kir whispered.

"At least you're not crying," Katla noted.

"I'm too fascinated to cry."

"You know what?" Gemma reasoned. "We'll deal with this later. We have bigger issues to worry about. Let's just head inside."

"Wait." Katla held out a scroll.

"What's that?" Gemma asked, reaching for it.

"It's from Joshua. Thomassin—"

Gemma snatched her hand back so quickly everyone froze.

"Have you lost your mind?" Gemma demanded.

"What?"

"I can't read that now!"

"Why not?"

"Everything that's going on and you take this moment to hand me Joshua's missive from beyond the funeral pyre and then you have the nerve to ask me why I can't read it now? Really? It's like you don't think at all, Katla!" With that, Gemma stormed inside, shaking her head.

"Well, she's tense," Katla sarcastically noted.

"If I were you," Quinn suggested, "I'd wait until things here settle down a bit and then give it to one of the servants to give to her."

"Why?"

"Because Gemma will never yell at a servant. You, though? She'll yell at you all day long."

Katla thought on it a moment before nodding. "Good plan."

The others started to head inside but Quinn noticed that Shona was staring at him.

"What?" he asked.

"I like your horns."

"These are antlers. And compliment me all you want. Hurt my sister, and I'll tear your legs off."

"*Quinn.*"

"What?" he asked Laila. "*What?*"

"You're embarrassing me."

"Make better choices then." Laila grabbed his arm and pulled him off to the side.

"You're actually telling *me* to make better choices?"

"Yes. What about that nice merchant in town?" he suggested.

"You just like her because she gives you all those extra cooked chickens!"

"And she's *nice*. Not some *soldier nailing every innocent girl she meets*!" he finished on a yell in Shona's direction, prompting her to walk inside.

"Innocent girl?" Laila asked.

"Yes. That's you. Mostly. You're nice and innocent. And you deserve nice and innocent."

He went toward the main hall.

"But, Quinn, in what world am I an innocent—"

"Don't want to hear it!"

* * *

As the warlock had said, Keeley was not in the main hall yet. So everyone stood around and waited for her. Not surprisingly, the longer they waited, the more tense everyone became.

Until Keeley's demon wolves came in. The priests, temple virgins, and the Abbess were immediately uncomfortable when the creatures trotted in from the kitchens. Adela attempted to approach the wolves again, but they went around her in a way that had Gemma smirking. She enjoyed that they completely ignored the witch. What she *didn't* like was how they went right to the blood warlock, circling his legs and then sitting on either side of him. He reached down and petted two of them on the head and all of those who'd traveled back to the castle with her turned to stare at Gemma.

"What's going on there?" Ragna asked Gemma.

She leaned in close to the master general and confided, "I'll tell you what's going on between him and those dogs when you tell me what's going on between you and the Abbess."

Ragna's eyes narrowed the slightest bit. "Don't forget whom you're speaking to, Brother Gemma."

"Don't forget that we're the last of our order. We're starting over. *You're* starting over."

"That just means I'm in charge. Not a novitiate."

Gemma stepped closer to Ragna. "Would you like to test that point?"

Ragna appeared ready to do just that when a massive horse body wedged its way between them.

"Gods-dammit, Quinn!"

"Don't make me lift my tail," he warned.

"I have no idea what that means," Ragna said with an eye roll.

"You've worked with enough horses, Master General. You know *exactly* what I mean."

Quinn stomped off, tail swishing, but Ragna didn't watch him go. She had her eyes closed.

"That's disgusting," she complained.

"At least he warned you," Gemma said with a shrug. "From what he's told me . . . there are others he has *not* warned."

"These are the people you're associating with, Brother Gemma?"

"At least they like me. Sadly, you cannot say the same."

Keeley finally made an entrance as only Keeley could. While yelling at her uncle.

"Mention the family axe again, old man, and I'll use the ones I do have to *split your head open*!"

"Should have killed him when I had the chance," her father tossed in while petting a baby goat. He put his feet up on a table that Quinn had just noticed was brand-new. What had happened to the old dining table?

"*Daddy*," Ainsley chided.

"What? He's an asshole. Bothering my baby girl."

His "baby girl" stalked across the room. She'd wiped the blood of the earlier battle off her face, neck, and arms but it was still on her sleeveless brown leather jerkin.

Keeley stepped on the chair and from the chair onto the table in one easy movement. Without preamble, she launched into what she had to say.

"Cyrus the Honored is doing exactly what we all suspected he's been doing. Simply annihilating the other religions so he can make his god's religion the one and only. That's why he wants to be king. Not for himself, but for his god. I don't know about you, but I find that more frightening than if he wanted to be king for himself. Nothing is worse than a fanatic."

Keeley walked across the table, appearing strong and ready.

"That leaves us with only one option for Cyrus. He has to die."

Ragna crossed her arms over her chest. "And you want my knight-monks to ride into battle against Cyrus's army to do the killing, is that it?"

"As a matter of fact . . . no, I don't, Lady Bitch-en-son."

Katla snorted a laugh, but it quickly turned into a throat-clearing cough when Ragna glanced at her.

"At the moment, I want nothing from your war monks." She re-focused on everyone else. "I plan to focus on finding Cyrus the Honored."

"Finding him?" Gemma asked. "Finding him for what?"

Keeley tossed her hands out in frustration. "Why do you *think* I'm looking for him? So we can become best of friends and start braiding each other's hair?"

"Is the tone absolutely necessary?"

"Clearly it is. I'm going to find him, Gemma, so we can kill him. Why else would I be looking for him?"

"Fine. I just wanted to make sure."

"I do have a concern."

"And you are?" Keeley asked.

"Father Aubin."

"And your concern is?"

Aubin looked across the room directly at Ludolf. "That you would trust *him*. The warlock."

Keeley looked back and forth between the two men several times before asking Aubin, "And you don't think I should trust him?"

"Absolutely not."

"And what exactly is the difference between you two?"

Léandre caught his associate's arm and held him tight as the other travel companions quietly laughed and Gemma grimaced and lowered her head.

"What?" Keeley asked. "No offense but I don't really know the difference between warlocks and priests and monks and witches and . . . and . . . virgins? Why are there virgins? No. None of my business. Personal choice. Anyway, other than color scheme in robe choice, I have yet to see differences between any of you. And I promised I wasn't going to judge. Besides"—she smiled at Ludolf—"my wolves love him."

Again, Gemma shook her head and muttered, "That is not helpful."

"Anyway, I have something else I need all of you to do for me while we're searching for Cyrus. If you're up to it."

"Wait, wait, wait," Gemma said, quickly stepping forward.

Quinn rubbed his eyes. Gemma just couldn't help herself, could she?

"Keeley, what are you doing?"

"Asking your friends for their assistance."

"They are not my friends."

"That's hurtful!" the truce vicar announced. "And we've all been getting along so well, I thought!"

Gemma crossed her eyes but she kept her focus on her sister.

"Perhaps we should discuss this privately."

"Why?"

"Yes, why?"

"Balla . . . what are you doing?"

"I have no idea, but I am fascinated by this entire thing."

"I'd like to know what the queen wants from us."

Gemma folded her arms over her chest and faced Adela the witch.

"You? You want to know what the queen wants from us? *You?*"

"Yes. Anything you want from us, Queen Keeley. Please. Just ask."

Gemma and Balla exchanged openmouthed glances, but Quinn didn't blame them. Adela hadn't shown any interest in helping anyone at all since they'd met her. But here she was . . . offering the services of not only herself but all her travel companions to a queen she did not know.

It was strange. Shocked expressions were to be expected.

"I've been told by Lord Ludolf that all of you are very good at the stealth arts."

"Well," one of the assassins noted, looking directly at the truce vicar, "most of us are."

"Then, if you're interested, I need you to do something very dangerous for me." Keeley looked at each of those who'd traveled with Gemma. "I need you to find a way into the Old King's castle and discover exactly what my sister Beatrix is up to."

"What are you doing?" Caid asked Quinn.

"Counting down to one."

"For what?"

"You'll see," Quinn said. "Four, three, two, and—"

Gemma lifted two wooden chairs and threw them against the wall, shattering them into pieces before facing her sister and screaming, "*Have you lost your bloody mind?*"

"One," he told his brother. "That was one."

* * *

Gemma knew she was supposed to let her sister lead but lead where? To hell? Was she supposed to let her sister lead them all to hell?

"I liked those chairs," Keeley complained.

"Fuck the chairs!"

"All right," their mother said, "that's it. You lot upstairs."

"Mum, I'm too old for you to send me upstairs because I upset you," Gemma said.

"I'm not talking to you."

Gemma looked at the stairs and realized that all her much younger siblings were sitting on the stairs, watching.

"Isadora," Keeley said. "Please."

Isadora led the kids to their bedrooms. Gemma waited until she heard the children's doors close before turning back to her sister.

"All right, what did this . . ." She gestured to the warlock. ". . . this . . ."

"Friend?" Ludolf offered.

"Shut up."

"Now, now, friends," the vicar immediately jumped in. "Perhaps we should all calm down. Talk about this rationally."

Gemma ignored the vicar. "Is the warlock the one telling you to go sneaking into Beatrix's castle? Does that really sound like a good idea to you? Or does that sound more like a trap? Because to me it sounds like a trap."

"Because any time it involves Beatrix, you assume I'm stupid and it's a trap."

"That's not true."

"You did it just now!"

"I just want you to think! Instead of listening to the first warlock you meet! Whose face you've never even seen."

"I did see his face."

Gemma was stunned. "You saw his face?"

"Yes." Keeley looked around. "Why is everyone staring at me?"

"You saw his *face*?" Gemma asked again.

"Yes."

"All of it?"

"Did I see *all* of his face? As opposed to what? Exactly?"

Gemma moved across the room, pointing a finger at Ludolf. "What did you do to my sister?"

The warlock immediately raised his gloved hands, palms out. "Nothing. I wouldn't dare."

Gemma slowed to a stop. "You wouldn't dare? Why not?"

He glanced down at the wolves resting at his feet.

"I thought they liked you."

"They tolerate me. They tolerate us all. Some more than others. And some extremely less."

They all discreetly glanced at Ragna but without even lifting her head, she replied, "I am aware."

"So," the warlock went on, "I can assure you. I have not discussed Beatrix with the queen other than to say I met her."

"But you have discussed Beatrix with someone. Haven't you?"

"My fellow warlocks and I were very curious about Queen Beatrix. About where our ultimate loyalties should lie. We knew we could never side with Cyrus. His fanaticism is tiresome. But we knew nothing about either queen. Some of my brothers have already aligned themselves with Beatrix."

"But not you."

"No."

"Why not?"

"That's obvious, isn't it?" a voice chimed in.

Gemma briefly closed her eyes. "No one asked you, Ragna."

"Come now, don't you see? The warlock is here because he knows that *here* he can manipulate. He can control. Here he can do what he likes and the queen with the hell beasts that she seems to think are friends will let him. The question, Brother Gemma, is whether you are going to let her get away with it?"

Gemma turned from the warlock and looked up at the table her sister still stood upon. In silence, they gazed at each other as Ragna continued.

"Let's be honest here, my friends—"

"You have no friends," the Abbess reminded Ragna.

"—the Order of Righteous Valor can secure the crown for Queen Keeley, and this territory for all the sects."

"Are you mad?" Balla demanded. "Do you really think any of us would trust *you* to be in charge?"

"If that happened," Aubin admitted, "I would just climb up on the pyre right now."

"You just fear our structure."

"No, Ragna. We fear your insanity."

"But it's our order that can ensure this reign. Can *any* of you say the same? Anyone?"

Keeley gave her sister the smallest nod and Gemma held her hand out. Their mother yanked the battle axe off the back of one of the queen's soldiers standing guard in the hall. She tossed the weapon to Gemma, who tossed it to Keeley.

Keeley caught it easily, turned, and threw it. It slammed blade first into the stone floor right between Ragna's feet.

"Did . . . did you just throw an axe at me?" Ragna asked Keeley with a surprised smile.

Keeley took several steps across the table, her gaze locked on Ragna.

"I need you, War Monk, to find your vow of silence and to lock it into place. Or the next time I throw an axe at you . . . I won't miss."

"And my girl never misses unless she wants to." Gemma's mother dropped into her chair and put her feet up into her husband's lap. "Ain't that right, Gemma?"

"That's right, Mum."

"And that's why," the warlock said with great feeling, pointing at Keeley, "I pledged my loyalty to your sister."

Frowning, Gemma asked, "Because she never misses when she throws an axe?"

"What? No . . ." The warlock shook his hooded head, sighed deeply. "Forget it."

In order to keep Keeley from throwing any more axes across the room, Ragna left. So did Gemma's parents, but only because they wanted to eat their dinner alone in their room. Apparently, seeing their daughters threaten others brought out their amorous side.

With everything calmed down, even Gemma, Keeley could finally tell them what she actually wanted.

"What makes you think there's anything to find in the Old King's castle?" Balla asked.

"Ludolf," Keeley prompted the warlock.

"I've heard from a source very close to Queen Beatrix that she's ordered a lot of activity near a certain mountain range without the knowledge of King Marius."

"What kind of activity?" Aubin asked.

"I'm not sure. But she's been at it for nearly two years. And hiding it from Marius for all that time."

"What mountain range?" Caid wanted to know.

Ludolf shrugged. "Not sure."

"That's what I want you to find out," Keeley said.

"Why?" Gemma asked.

"What do you mean why?"

"I mean why? All we know is that she's doing something near the mountains and hiding it from her husband. So what?"

"Gemma, this is not some bored queen who might have taken one of the dark elves as a lover. This is Beatrix. If Beatrix is doing something that requires her to hide it from King Marius, there's a reason. And not a good one. I want to know what she's up to."

"Why? Our only goal at this moment should be to destroy her kingdom. Not worry about some little pissant thing she may or may not be doing to torment her husband."

"Do you really think that's all *Beatrix* would be doing? *Our* Beatrix? Do you really think she gives a bloody shit about her husband beyond the crown he's given her?"

Gemma closed her eyes, let out a breath.

"We need to know what she's up to. Especially if she's making the effort to hide it from Marius."

"Fine," Gemma said. "We go there. We find out what she's up to, and then what?"

"If it's something we can destroy, then we'll destroy it. If it's something that is not a big deal, then maybe I'll be able to *sleep at night*!" she finished on a healthy bellow.

Surprised, Gemma asked, "Why aren't you sleeping?"

"Just a guess, but maybe because her sister tried to kill her."

Gemma snarled across the table at Aubin but Keeley waved that concern away.

"That's not it."

"How can that not be it?" Léandre wanted to know.

"I don't think Beatrix considers me her problem anymore. Not really. I think in her mind I'm more Marius's problem. Now she has bigger concerns."

"Then why are you so worried about her?"

"You really don't know?" Keeley asked Gemma. "Because if she was willing to kill her own sister to get a crown, what would she be willing to do to anyone . . . *everyone* to keep it?"

Balla honestly didn't know what to make of this woman. Her sister was a typical war monk. Dedicated to her god and to battle. You could see it on her face. She couldn't wait to sink her sword into someone's spine. Queen Keeley, however . . .

Who knew what she wanted? She didn't seem to be driven by a lust for power. Those kinds of monarchs were always so obvious in their wants and needs, but Queen Keeley didn't strut around with a retinue of sycophants following behind her. She didn't snap at her servants or make ridiculous demands of her council.

Then what did this queen want? What was her purpose in doing all this? Revenge against her younger sister Beatrix? She'd heard the story. They all had. That Beatrix, in her quest for the crown, had attempted to kill Keeley. That she'd stabbed her or had her stabbed. The story changed depending on who told it.

It was clear that Brother Gemma definitely wanted Beatrix dead for what she'd done to her eldest sibling, so there must be some truth in the tale, but was it enough for all this?

Or maybe it was greed. But looking around at the limited comforts of what Brother Gemma continued to call a "castle," Balla wasn't exactly seeing it. This place was nice enough, but it wasn't as luxurious as where Beatrix was currently living. Maybe Queen Keeley hoped to one day move the remainder of her family into the Old King's castle. Balla had been there a few times decades ago, and it was quite a sight.

And yet that didn't feel right either.

"What do you think?" she finally asked Priska. Although her assistant didn't say much, the young novice watched everything. That's how one learned and advanced among the temple virgins. Balla had not chosen the girl to be by her side lightly.

"She loves animals."

When Priska didn't say anything else, Balla followed up with, "So?"

"It's how she makes all her decisions. She considers how her decision will affect animals and the people who care for animals. The farmers, the horse breeders."

"But her sister?"

Priska's eyes widened slightly. "The war monk?"

"Gods, no, Priska. Beatrix. What about Beatrix?"

"Oh. Well . . . she doesn't really care about anything except keeping her power. Keeping her crown."

"So, she's all about hate."

"That's not what I said."

"That's exactly what you said."

"That's the opposite of what I said. Cyrus hates all of us because we do not worship his god. But Beatrix feels no hate for anyone. She also feels no love for anyone. She simply doesn't care. She doesn't care about her family. About the animals. About people. She feels nothing for anyone. She is an empty husk that can only be filled with power over others. But Queen Keeley . . ."

They looked down the length of the large table at the bickering queen and monk.

"I'm not asking you for anything, *Brother* Gemma. You can stay here with the rest of your death cult—"

"It's not a death cult! Dammit, Katla, that's the last time I send you to tell my sister anything!"

"—and the rest of you lot can decide whether you want to help me or not on your own. We'll meet tomorrow morning and talk then."

"Keeley—"

"Until then—"

"Keeley!"

"—I'm done!"

The queen pushed her chair back but instead of storming off, she went under the table. The war monk was still attempting to speak to her sister but Queen Keeley was no longer answering, so she started banging on the top of the table with her fist, which got an "Owww! Stop doing that, mad cow!" A few seconds later, the queen crawled out from under the table carrying five wolf puppies.

Four of the puppies had eyes of flame like the rest of their pack, but one of them had plain brown eyes. She handed that one to Brother Gemma and said, "Take this little one. I think her mother is rejecting her because she's not like the others."

"I don't care," Brother Gemma replied, trying to give her back the puppy.

"You should. How would you feel if Mum rejected you? Unloved! That's how you'd feel."

"We have more important things to discuss than your demon puppies."

"Stop calling them that! And we are done discussing this."

"I'll go."

"What?"

"I'll go. I'll risk life and limb to find out if Beatrix is being naughty. Happy now?"

"Well—"

"But I'll only do it under one condition."

"Are you really that determined to kill your own sister?"

"In this case . . . ? Yes."

"Fine," Keeley said on a long sigh. "But only, and I mean *only* if you can, without a doubt, get out safely. If you can't . . . you walk away. You understand me, Gemma? This isn't the order of a queen. This is the order of your older sister. You walk away. Promise me."

"I promise."

A servant brought over a basket that seemed to be made for these particular wolf pups since it was not made of wood or anything flammable but steel. Queen Keeley took her time bending over the basket and tucking the five pups into the blankets inside. A good thing too, because she missed the horse that made its way into the main hall from the kitchens.

It wasn't surprising to see a horse wander into a castle. It was something that happened all the time in most lands. What was surprising was that at least half the horse was mostly dead. That's what Balla found so concerning. The centaurs immediately moved away from the beast as did the priests, monks, and assassins.

Brother Gemma immediately noticed the horse, her gaze widening in panic. But she quickly hid that panic when the queen looked at her.

"What's wrong with you?" the queen asked her sister.

"Nothing. Just thinking about how we're going to manage all this."

"It'll work out fine," the queen said, focusing again on the wolf pups.

Brother Gemma pointed at her younger sister Ainsley and then the horse.

Ainsley, wisely, shook her head.

Again, Brother Gemma silently pointed at the horselike thing, which had stopped to graze off the food scraps from the floor, and Ainsley again shook her head. But when the queen again looked up, the war monk immediately dropped her arms and smiled.

The queen's eyes narrowed. "Why are you smiling at me? What are you up to?"

"What? Nothing. You've become so paranoid. It's not very attractive."

"This coming from you? The most paranoid person I know." The war monk's head tilted to the side and the queen quickly amended, "Except, of course, for Uncle Archie."

"Thank you."

With great ease, the queen lifted the heavy steel basket from the table and took a step. But just as quickly she stopped and without turning around asked, "What the unholy fuck is that thing behind me?"

Brother Gemma shrugged. "What thing?"

"You lying cow . . ." Queen Keeley shook her head. "No. I'm not . . . we're not . . ." She continued to shake her head. "No, no, no. You know what I'm *not* going to do, my sister? I'm not going to base any judgment simply on what that thing looks like. It may look unholy and unnatural but I'm not going to *judge* it based on how it looks because it is still an animal. Or, at least it was. I'm making this decision because, unlike others who shall remain nameless, I am not shallow and hypocritical. *Am I, Quinn?*" she called out.

"You are not, my beautiful queen! And how I adore you for such an open-minded belief system!"

"Now if you'll excuse me, I'm going to take my bucket of beautiful—"

"Evil demon dogs from the very pits of hell?" Brother Gemma flatly asked.

The queen's eyes narrowed again at her sister. "Callous cow," she muttered before she carried her load of demon puppies up the stairs.

Once the queen had disappeared from the third-floor landing into one of the rooms, Brother Gemma rushed over to the beast and treated it as some favored thing.

"Told you she'd call you a hypocrite," the blond-maned centaur said to the war monk.

"I don't want to discuss it."

Father Aubin made his way to Balla's side, briefly glancing around before quietly asking her, "So what are you two going to do?"

Balla briefly glanced at Priska before replying, "Whatever Queen Keeley needs us to do."

CHAPTER 20

As the sheep was ripped from her hands, Gemma slammed the
stable doors closed, resting her back against them and doing
her best to ignore the desperate squealing coming from inside.

It finally stopped, but her relief was shattered by a simple "Are
you all right?" that nearly had her running off into the night until
she realized it was just Quinn.

"Thank Morthwyl, it's you," she gasped. "I thought Kriegszorn
had managed to"—she flicked her hands dramatically in front of
her—"materialize in front of me."

"And speak?"

"Possibly!"

Kriegszorn kicked the inside stable doors, sending Gemma flying into Quinn's body. He caught hold of her and pulled her away.

"She's not going to happily stay in there," Quinn guessed.

"I see that now, but I didn't want to put her in the main stables."

"Because she'll eat all the other horses?"

Gemma winced. "Probably. But Da reminded me we have this
single stable for our problem biters and figured she would do well
here, but now I'm not so sure."

"What's going on?" Keeley demanded, storming toward them.
"I can hear her all the way in the house."

Only Keeley would call Kriegszorn "her" right out of the gate.
Everyone else had been calling her "it" but no, not Keeley. Never
Keeley.

"She's unhappy," Gemma admitted. "And I'm not sure why."

"How could you live with Da for sixteen years and not understand animals? How is that even possible?"

"What's *that* supposed to mean?"

Quinn put his hands on the sisters' shoulders. "If you two start bickering . . . Kriegszorn will tear that stable down."

Gemma knew Quinn was right, but that didn't explain why her sister suddenly grabbed at her and began pulling her tunic.

"*What are you doing?*"

"Attempting to help you!"

"How? By assaulting me?"

"I need your shirt. The one under your chainmail."

"Why?"

"Just give it to me."

Gemma slapped her sister's hands away and pulled off her tunic, chainmail, and finally her dirty white cotton shirt. She handed it to her sister.

"It's a bit ripe," she admitted. "I've been wearing it for days and haven't had a chance to change."

"I dunked her in the river earlier, though." Quinn added. "That should help."

"That was just rude."

Keeley laughed and opened the stable doors.

"Keel—"

"I'll be fine. Just wait here."

She disappeared into the stable. Although her "Gods! What did she eat?" was a bit disconcerting.

"It was a sheep," Gemma replied.

"Poor sheep!"

Pulling the chainmail over her head, Gemma noticed for the first time that she needed a haircut. A random, nonsensical thought, considering everything that was going on at the moment. She forgot all about it a few seconds later when Keeley stepped out of the stable alive and well.

Gemma was grateful. She really didn't want to explain to her parents how she'd let her sister be eaten by her half-dead warhorse.

"There," Keeley said. "That should keep her quiet for the night."

"What did you do?" Gemma asked.

"Gave her your shirt. So she has your scent. That's all she wants. To know you're around."

Keeley rested her hands on her hips. "Can't you...I don't know...fix her somehow? At least so she has more...flesh? If nothing else, that way you could ride her into battle again. She's used to having a job and she'd be less terrifying to the children."

"What children?"

"All children."

Her sister had a point.

"Maybe those witches can help. That Adela seems nice."

Gemma felt a muscle in her cheek twitch. "Sure. The witches."

Keeley headed back to the castle. "Oh!" She kept moving but turned around and walked backward. "During the day, you can put her in the ring. We'll reinforce it a bit so she doesn't wander off and terrorize the townspeople. That way she's not trapped inside all day. She'll like that," she added with a smile.

Keeley gave a wave, turned back around, and continued toward the castle.

"Good gods in the heavens."

"What?" Quinn asked Gemma.

"Keeley *likes* Kriegszorn."

"Of *course* she likes Kriegszorn," Quinn insisted. "She's Keeley."

Quinn watched Gemma take one step toward the main hall but immediately stop. She closed her eyes and let out a sigh so deep and heartfelt, he knew he couldn't let her go to the castle. Because they were all in there. The priests, the assassins, the virgins, the witches. Arguing, complaining, eating. Just being annoying. She was sick of them and he didn't blame her. She'd gone from the horror of seeing her monastery burned to the ground while those she loved dearly rode off to their deaths to dealing with these pains in the ass. Useful pains in the ass but still...

"Come on," he said, grabbing her by the hood of her chainmail hauberk.

"Where?"

He didn't answer, just led her around the building until they reached one of the secret doors Archie had put in so the family could escape if need be.

He led her through several tunnels until they reached the kitchens.

"My uncle Archie came up with that?"

"He did."

"I thought only monks had such tunnels."

"Mary, my darling," Quinn said to the royal cook.

She laughed. "Don't even bother. Your food is over there. Enough for both of you. I had to send food up for the entire family. They didn't want to come down now that the religious convention is happening in the main hall. Not that I blame them. Your lot sure is a chatty bunch," she said to Gemma.

"I know. Sorry about that."

"Not your fault."

"No. But when you get a lot of us in a room without a vow of silence, this is what happens. A lot of philosophizing about what the gods want. What devotion means. What it doesn't. They'll be up all night. Do *not* give them the best wine. The cheap stuff will do."

"Do they drink?"

"I know that vicar does."

"No pie?" Quinn asked, looking at what Mary had provided them.

"You ask for pie?" Gemma questioned. Shocked. "There's a whole lamb there."

"I love her pie. She knows I love her pie. *I want my pie.*"

Mary moved across her kitchen and took a cloth off a tray, revealing six pies. Quinn threw his arms into the air.

"Yes!"

"Why do you baby him?" Gemma asked.

"Because she loves me."

"He does remind me of me boy."

"You do have other children, though, yes? Better children?"

Quinn glared. "That was just mean."

Mary brought out two wicker baskets and began loading the food with Quinn's and Gemma's help.

"My room or yours?" Gemma asked.

"Better. Come on."

Quinn picked up a basket and headed out, briefly stopping to kiss Mary on her forehead.

After they'd been walking for a while, Gemma asked, "Where are we going?"

"Don't be impatient."

"Not impatient. Exhausted."

"Then trust me."

"But you know I don't."

"That's just hurtful."

And not exactly true. There were few these days she trusted at her back as much as she trusted the centaur, which really surprised her. The first month she'd known him, she couldn't count how many times she'd wanted him dead. Now she could go weeks without even thinking about it.

He led her down a street with adorable houses that were some of the first built when Keeley took over. He opened the door of one and invited her inside. It took him a moment but once he had the pitfire going, Gemma blinked in surprise.

It was quite lovely. With a decent-sized bed under a window with closed curtains, a nice wood table, and the biggest in-ground bathtub she'd ever seen.

Gemma pointed. "What is that?"

"I paid the stonemason dwarves to make it for me. It connects to the river. I open this and fresh water flows in. And I open this and it drains into the garden outside. And under here"—they both crouched—"is the fire that heats the water."

"That's all wonderful and good but . . . why is it so big?"

Quinn grinned and shifted. That's when she saw that the tub was so big, he could get his giant horse's ass into it.

"You're ridiculous," she told him.

"I know. But you still want to try it out, don't you?"

"Well . . . it *is* heated."

The priests and others might be getting the cheap castle wine but Quinn had several bottles of the expensive stuff stowed away here in his little house. He wasn't much of a wine drinker, though,

246 • *G.A. Aiken*

usually preferring ale to wine. But the wine was a perfect choice for a night like this.

He thought that Gemma would insist on getting in the tub by herself but as she stripped off her chainmail, she asked, "Aren't you getting in?" Then quickly added, "Not with your horse ass, though."

Then he remembered that she'd lived for a decade in a monastery and on battlefields. Maybe she was simply used to being around naked men.

So they soaked in the hot water, drank wine, and ate the hard cheese Mary had packed with everything else.

"Maybe Keeley's right," Gemma mused.

"You have *never* said that before."

"I mean about healing Kriegszorn."

"Giving her her life back?"

"That I don't think I can do."

"That's too bad."

"But maybe give her more . . ."

"Skin?"

"Yeah. It'll take skills far superior to mine though, I'm afraid."

"Maybe the witches could help you like Keeley suggested."

Gemma immediately sneered. "I don't trust those witches."

"I don't trust Adela. Don't know anything about the other two."

"So it's not just me."

"No. She's up to something. And it's not because she suddenly wants to be helpful to your sister."

"Ten gold pieces says she'll be gone by morning after she takes what she wants."

"You don't seem too worried about her being a possible risk to your family."

Now she snickered. "Ragna is *looking* for an excuse to burn her the way she burned her grandmother. Adela wouldn't dare go near my family."

"If you lose Adela or all the witches," he asked, "will that make it more difficult for you to travel to the Old King's castle?"

"The witches have their uses, but we can make do with what we have."

"And, of course, I'm going with you."

She shrugged. "Okay."

Quinn immediately leaned away from her before asking, "You're not going to argue about that with me?"

"Argue about what?"

"About me going with you on this mission?"

"Why would I argue with you about that?"

"You argue about everything."

"I do not argue about everything! That is absolutely wrong!"

"At this moment, you are arguing about arguing."

"Well, I'm not arguing about this."

"Why? Are you plotting something?"

"Now you're just irritating me and it's starting to ruin my expensive wine."

Quinn ate more cheese. "And you're really going to go on this mission?"

"Keeley actually said I could kill Beatrix. Of *course* I'm going to go."

"She said only if you can get out alive. I'm holding you to that, because I know you. When it comes to Beatrix, you get all obsessive. And wasn't it just a few hours ago you were ready to join forces with the bitch?"

"No!" She ate a piece of cheese. "Okay, yes, I was. But this is my chance to find out what Beatrix is really up to, if anything. Besides, I didn't know Keeley wasn't sleeping."

"What does that have to do with anything?"

"You don't know my sister. Keeley can sleep through almost anything. One time she went to see a new batch of piglets in the barn and that's where we found her a few hours later. Sleeping with the piglets and their mother. It was adorable and disgusting in equal measure, but there she was. So if she's not sleeping, even with Caid right next to her . . . something is definitely wrong. And if it's Beatrix, now is the time to find out. Then I won't have any more doubts."

"Good."

"It is good. I also have a question and I finally feel drunk enough to ask."

Quinn sighed. "Of course you have a question. You're a Smythe. All of you have questions."

She moved around in the water until she was right in front of him.

"All right, here it is. The fact that you *thought* I was a virgin . . . is that why you didn't want to see me naked?"

"What the fuck are you talking about?"

"You went out of your way to lure Keeley into that naked river bath with the other centaurs but not me."

"Have you *seen* your sister? Have you seen the way that woman is built? I had to see her unencumbered with clothes," he admitted. "I had to. And I was not disappointed. Of course, I could have lured your mother instead, but I find your father fairly terrifying. He's extremely attached to her."

"And I'm not built like my sister at all, is that it?"

"No. You're more compact. Plus your scars are much more terrifying."

"Should I be insulted by that?"

"It's not an insult. Until recently, your sister's scars were all 'oops, I bumped into an anvil' or 'the horse bit me' or 'I dropped that sword I made against my chest.' All your scars, however, are 'Not only am I lucky to have survived, but I destroyed everything that was in my way and salted the ground my enemies walked upon.' I didn't necessarily want to know the backstories. Especially since the last few months you tended to get maudlin anytime the monastery thing came up."

"I did not."

"Oh, yes, you did. That's why we all thought you were drinking. In fact, I was shocked to discover that maudlin is not how you are all the time. But that when you were in the monastery, according to Brother Cries-a-Lot you were often the life of the party. So it's just since you've been home with Keeley that you've been like this. What makes you so sad, Brother Gemma? Is it Keeley's rise to power? Did you want to be queen?"

"That's it. I'm done."

Gemma threw back the rest of her wine and stood. No, she was not built like her sister, but he didn't mind. He was fascinated by Keeley the way he was fascinated by anything he'd never seen before. And Keeley was unique.

Watching Gemma, though . . . she was unique too. It was hard to see that when she was covered in chainmail and a religious tunic. But seeing her naked, she was just as muscular as her sister; just as powerful. Only in a smaller package. A smaller, deadlier package.

Quinn chuckled and Gemma glared at him over her shoulder. "What?"

"Just wondering which of you would win in a fight. You or Keeley?"

Instead of responding in anger, which was what Quinn actually expected, Gemma looked off thoughtfully and asked, "With or without weapons?"

"Without."

"Oh. Me."

"So confident."

"It's the first thing I was taught as a female novitiate. How to deal with bigger and stronger combatants before they can knock you out completely. If they knock you out before you have a chance to react, you're kind of screwed."

"That's why you're so paranoid."

She shrugged her own massively large shoulders. "Wouldn't you be?"

"Where's the wine?"

Busy drying off with linen, Quinn pointed at a table pushed against the wall. She'd just picked up the bottle when she heard what could only be Quinn shaking his horse body. He must have shifted so he could shake the water off his hide, something she normally wouldn't have minded except that now she was hit with a spray of water that got her wet all over again.

Not wanting to fight, she opened another bottle of wine and poured some into their chalices.

"Here," she said, handing his chalice to him before sliding onto the dining table.

She could have borrowed one of his shirts but instead she'd wrapped a long linen sheet around her body just as Quinn wrapped his around his waist.

Quinn dropped into the chair and put his feet up on the table, his legs resting near her ass. She moved the food between them so they could pick at it with their fingers, neither of them in the mood for sitting down properly and eating food like civilized people.

They ate in silence for a while, but when Quinn finally did speak, Gemma was more than ready for him.

"So—" he began, which was when she punched him in the throat, kicked him in the chest, and, as he was falling back in the chair, jumped over him so she could grab him from behind and throw him over the table.

By the time Gemma had sauntered around the table, feeling pretty good about herself, she found Quinn turning blue. A piece of boar had stuck in his throat when she'd punched him.

"Shit!" She ran around behind him and lifted Quinn's shoulders up. She put her fists on his stomach and brought them in until the meat exploded across the room.

"*What the fuck was that?*" he roared, proving he could breathe again.

"I thought you wanted to see how fast I could move."

Rubbing his hand against his throat, Quinn barked, "I know how fast you can move! I've fought side by side with you, crazy female!"

"I forgot about that."

"How? How do you forget about that?"

"I blame the wine."

"Let's make it clear then, shall we? I never question your battle skills. Just your sanity. And, when I'm feeling particularly saucy or incredibly bored . . . your standing within your family. That's it. So do *not* do that again. At least not to me."

Gemma scratched her nose to hide her smile.

"And stop smirking at me."

"I'm not smirking at you," she lied.

"Liar."

"Come on." She stood, held her hand out. "Let's have some more wine."

He grabbed her hand and she pulled him to his feet.

"You're really enjoying that wine," he noted. "I didn't think you were much of a wine drinker."

"I'm not, but this expensive stuff is really good."

They poured more wine into the chalices and sat on the table beside each other, legs hanging over the side.

"How's your throat?"

"I'm glad I'm a centaur." He rubbed his neck. "Some poor human would be choking on his own blood right now. And stop looking so proud about it."

"I didn't!"

"Liar!"

It was around the third bottle when it got ugly. Because that's when the dancing started.

"Now remember the steps I taught you," Quinn told her, cracking his neck. "Head up. Chest out. And don't forget, you must be regal, strategic, and elegant. Got it?"

Gemma gave him a thumbs-up and Quinn nodded. "Then let us begin."

And begin they did.

"First, trot. Now prance. Shoulder. Shoulder. Shoulder. Trot, trot, trot,"

"This is awkward."

"Only because you don't have four legs. If you had four legs, this would be *much* easier for you."

"I believe you."

"It would also be easier if you weren't chugging directly from the wine bottle."

"So are you."

"I am, but I also have four legs."

Gemma stopped trotting to insist, "Four legs doesn't make you better than me."

"They absolutely make me better than you. Centaurs are and always will be better than humans. Of course, we're also better than dwarves, elves, and minotaurs."

"I haven't met any minotaurs."

"You wouldn't want to. There's a mucous issue. On their snouts. It's disgusting. They're disgusting. Generally nice, though. Just disgusting."

"You're babbling."

"I'm drunk."

"Me too, which is surprising and unfortunate."

"Why is it unfortunate?"

"Before I was really drunk, I was going to suggest we go to bed and fuck."

Quinn pointed at his chest. "*I* was going to suggest we go to bed and fuck."

"See? But we're both so drunk now it would just be—"

"Tacky."

"Exactly."

"Besides, I don't want to do it when we're drunk." And Quinn couldn't believe how glad he was to hear her say that. Because he definitely didn't want that either.

"I see what you've got there," she went on, pointing at his back end. "I want to be fully awake and alert for that thing."

"You do understand that I'll be human when we finally . . . fuck? Right?"

"Gods, I hope so. Any other way would be just . . . too strange. For me, I mean."

"I understand that." He looked around. "Then what do we do now?"

"Uh, well, first . . ." She took the bottle of wine from his hand and put both bottles on a table off to the side. "Second, we go to bed."

"Together? I thought we weren't going to fuck."

"We can sleep in the same bed and not fuck. Can't we?"

"We're only wearing sheets of linen and I'm stunning. Can you keep control of yourself?"

"Get in the bed, centaur."

Laughing, Quinn crawled into the bed, dropping onto the pillow facedown. A few seconds later, Gemma stretched out next to him. A few seconds after that, she curled into him, burying her head against his side.

Quinn had just started to think about how warm and soft she was, considering she was the strongest, toughest woman he'd ever met, when he realized that she was completely naked.

Maybe having a little drunken sex wasn't that big a deal unless, of course, they both fell asleep before they could—

CHAPTER 21

Ainsley was heading out to do some early-morning hunting. With all these people in the castle, she figured Mary could use the extra meat.

She was nearing her big sister's room when Caid walked out, smiling and nodding as he exited. It was the smiling that threw Ainsley off. She wouldn't say that Caid never smiled. That wouldn't be accurate. But nearly never.

Caid closed the door to the bedroom he shared with Ainsley's sister, stepped away from it, then grabbed Ainsley by the shoulders and shoved her against the wall. She was so shocked that she didn't even think about grabbing her sword or dagger or simply punching him in the cock.

"What are you doing?" she demanded.

"Keep your voice down," he whispered desperately. He glanced at the bedroom door before leaning in closer and whispering, "One of her fucking puppies is gone."

Ainsley blinked. "What?"

"You heard me!" He was still whispering but if he hadn't been, she knew he'd be screaming. Hysterically. "We have to find it. She's completely unhinged about this."

"Oh, stop it."

"You don't believe me?"

Ainsley pursed her lips. "No."

He released her and stepped back. "See for yourself then."

"Fine." Ainsley walked to her sister's bedroom door and knocked.

"In."

Ainsley walked inside and found her sister tugging on her leather boots.

"Morning!" Ainsley greeted, smiling.

"Morning."

"I'm going out hunting for Mary. Want anything specific?"

"No," her sister replied. "Whatever will feed the hungry travelers will do. Or anything Mary wants to roast."

"Great." She paused a moment. "Everything all right?"

Keeley frowned a bit. "One of the puppies has disappeared. Can't find her anywhere." She glanced at the steel bucket sitting on the bed, filled with the remaining puppies. Ainsley was always surprised that those puppies stayed in the bucket. They were at the age that a bucket wouldn't keep them contained, but for Keeley, they stayed.

"Need some help?"

"No. I'll go look for her myself. But if you see her around, grab her, would you?" Keeley asked calmly.

"Sure. No problem."

"Thanks."

Ainsley gave a nod and walked out of the room, closing the door behind her and moving across the hall until she could lean against the wall, facing Caid.

The pair stared at each other a moment, and then Ainsley whispered, "*By the gods of all the universes, she's going to destroy us all!*"

"*I told you!*"

"What are we going to do?"

"We need help!" Caid insisted. "I'll round up the centaurs to look in the forest. You get Gemma to use those magickal travelers to do some spell or something. We find that fucking dog or we're all dead. Do you understand? Dead!"

The bedroom door opened and Keeley walked out with the steel bucket of puppies in her arms.

"Hey, you two."

"Heyyyyy," they both said, neither meaning to say it together like that.

"I'm going to take the pups down to Mum's room. She and Da can watch them until I find the missing one. I don't need another one going missing while I'm out looking, yeah?"

"Yeahhhhhh," they again said together, cringing when she frowned a bit. But, thankfully, she didn't question them, just headed to their parents' room.

When she turned her back, Ainsley and Caid began to slap at each other, only stopping when Keeley looked at them over her shoulder.

"You two sure everything is okay?"

"Sure."

"Yeah."

Keeley shrugged and moved on and Caid shoved Ainsley toward the stairs.

"Get moving," he whispered desperately. "Before we're all dead."

Ainsley charged down the hallway, to the stairs, past Isadora, who was feeding their youngest sibling, and down the stairs. She ran through the empty main hall and out the castle doors. It wasn't until she was standing in the merchant square that she realized she had no idea where she was going. She knew she was looking for Gemma. But she had no idea where Gemma was. She hadn't even checked her room or asked Isadora if she'd seen their sister.

Gods! What was wrong with her?

She knew. Ainsley knew what was wrong with her. Like Caid, she'd panicked. She'd just run off like a startled deer. Pathetic.

Ainsley had turned back toward the castle to start acting like a calm, reasonable person when she heard, "Ho, there, young princess!"

She immediately cringed, recognizing that voice instantly. It was hard not to.

"Good day to you, my lady," the truce vicar greeted her, bending at the waist.

"Yeah. Right. Must go."

She turned to flee but he caught her arm. "Is something amiss, my lady? Anything I can help you with?"

"Doubt it."

"Now, now. Don't be so sure. I can help in all sorts of ways."

Really? All she'd heard from anyone yesterday was what a loud pain in the ass the man was. Of course, Keeley seemed to like him, but Keeley liked almost everyone, and Ainsley felt sure it was because there was something bearlike about the vicar. Keeley did like bears.

"I appreciate the offer and all but—"

"Test me, child. The worst I can say is 'I don't know.' And then you can be on your way."

He was right. At the very least, maybe he'd seen Gemma this morning. She could be an early riser.

"Any chance you saw a puppy?"

"I've seen a lot of puppies. Your queen seems to have a warm spot for dogs of all kinds. She may want to hire someone to clean up all the excrement that comes along with the vile little beasts."

"I'll make sure to mention that to her," Ainsley said, already turning away again.

"Unless, of course, you mean a puppy with eyes of flame."

Ainsley froze, and slowly the truce vicar walked around her until he could gaze down into her face.

"If that's the puppy you mean, then I have seen such a thing this morning."

Ainsley took in a breath, let it out. "Now is not the time to toy with me, Vicar. Did you take it?"

"I would never touch such a beast, dear child. To do so would taint my soul. But the one who did was probably not concerned with such a thing."

"Who?"

"The witch. Adela. She had the puppy. I was able to follow her for a bit, but then I lost sight of it and her. I must admit, I did not feel good about her having it."

Ainsley gritted her teeth together to control her anger. Not at the vicar. She was glad they'd met. And she knew now that he'd purposely found her.

"Have you seen my sister? Gemma, I mean."

"Not since last night. She went off with that four-legged fellow. Quinn."

Ainsley instantly guessed where they were. "I'm going to get my sister. Could you keep looking for the witch?"

"Absolutely, my lady."

He gave another bow, but Ainsley didn't think she'd be rolling her eyes at him anymore.

"Thank you, Vicar."

"Wake up! Wake up! Wake up!"

Gemma had never thought about actually *killing* one of her siblings before except, of course, Beatrix, but to her Beatrix didn't count. But today . . . today she was considering killing one of her actual siblings.

"*Stop yelling!*"

"I'm not yelling. But you two need to wake up now!"

Gemma did her best to open her eyes and look at . . . gods, which one was it? It wasn't the baby. Too big. It wasn't one of the boys. Isad . . . no. No. Not her. Tits too big. Ainsley? It must be Ainsley yelling at her. Why was Ainsley yelling at her?

"What's happening?" Quinn demanded into his pillow. "Why is everyone yelling? Why won't you just kill me instead? Please, someone kill me," he begged, now putting the pillow over his head.

"See what you've done?" Gemma asked her sister. "You're making Quinn want to die. All because you won't stop screaming."

"I am not screaming and you need to get up. Both of you."

"Why? What's wrong?"

"One of the wolf puppies is missing."

Finally, Gemma lifted her head off the pillow to glare at her sister. She was so exhausted, all she could do was open one eye but she felt her glare was strong enough to get her point across even with just one eye.

"*That's* why you're being hysterical?" she demanded. "Because of one of those fucking dogs?"

"I'm not being hysterical and I think—"

"I don't care what you think. Get out! Now!"

"No, no," Quinn said, hauling himself up to a sitting position. He pulled the blanket over his groin to hide his massive cock from her sister's view, and Gemma appreciated that. Her sister was too young to see such a thing. It might overwhelm her. Gemma didn't want to scare her at such a tender age. "We should get up anyway. Keeley wanted to meet this morning to discuss next steps. We should be there to make sure Ragna doesn't attempt to shove one of her ideas down Keeley's throat." He thought a moment. "We should also make sure Keeley doesn't shove her fist down Ragna's throat. Speaking of which . . . did anyone ever manage to get that axe out of the floor?"

Gemma forced herself to sit up too as the centaur exited the house. She made her way over to a corner where he'd placed a chamber pot behind a lovely screen.

"How nice," she said. "So discreet."

She sat to relieve herself, giggling when Quinn leaned in through the window, his arms resting on the windowsill. The window was rather high, so it must be his horse body on the other side, which for some reason tickled Gemma to no end.

"I had a nice time last night," Quinn told her.

"I did too."

"Are you two flirting?" Ainsley demanded, moving aside the screen and glaring at them.

"Can we have some privacy?" Gemma barked. "We are peeing!"

"No! You do not seem to realize the urgency of the situation!"

"What urgency? That terrifying mother dog is probably starting to take her pups back to whichever hell she lives in."

"Except I met the truce vicar on my way over here and he told me he saw Adela with the pup."

Slowly, Gemma looked up at Quinn. They gazed at each other for a few seconds before jumping into action, ignoring the pain she knew they were both feeling in their heads.

"I'll get our weapons," he said, disappearing from the window.

They were both dressed and armed in less than five minutes. Before they ran out the door, though, Ainsley held up the wine bottles. "Is this what you were drinking last night?"

"Yes," Gemma answered, adjusting her sword belt. "Why?"

"You know this isn't the expensive stuff, right? Archie threw that out."

Gemma's head snapped up. "*What?*"

"This is the dwarf wine King Mundric gave to Keeley. Archie didn't want anyone stealing it. So he tossed out the expensive stuff some duke or whatever had sent over and replaced it with the dwarf wine." Ainsley looked at the number of bottles lying around, then at Gemma and Quinn. "You're both lucky you're still standing."

"We're both lucky we have all our bones!" Gemma snapped back. "Drink enough of that stuff, I heard it melts them."

"That's an old wives' tale," Quinn said, moving toward the front door, holding it open for the two women. "It just crumbles the bones. Like salt."

"How is that better?" Gemma asked.

"I didn't know we were going for better. I thought we were going for accuracy."

Quinn followed Gemma into the main hall, where their travel team was huddled in a group, whispering amongst themselves. Never a good sign. Even worse. No witches.

"Where is Adela?" she barked.

When all she got back were blank stares, "And the other witches?"

"We didn't know it was our responsibility to keep an eye on the witches."

Gemma stepped toward Father Aubin, one finger pointed, ready to start a good reaming, when Keeley came down the stairs.

"Morning, everyone," she called. When the others began to bow, she quickly waved all that off and instead asked, "Any of you see a missing puppy? Flamey eyes?" she added.

They all shook their heads and Keeley sighed.

"Well, let's meet later then. I have to find her. All of you eat and relax. Okay?" She patted Gemma's shoulder before disappearing deep into the castle.

Once she was gone, Gemma let out a long breath and dropped dramatically against the dining table.

"You didn't tell me she was hysterical," she accused Ainsley.

"Hysterical?" Quinn repeated. "Keeley?"

"You didn't see it?" she asked, shocked.

"That was hysterical to you?"

"You really didn't see it?"

"Uh . . ." He glanced at the others and merely got shrugs and expressions of confusion, which he had to admit did make him feel better. He was afraid he might be losing his mind.

Ainsley shook her head at Quinn. "It's like you're blind."

"Just forget it!" Gemma motioned to the others. "You lot come with me. I'll need your skills to help me track that puppy and the witches."

"You're serious?" Balla asked.

"I have never been more serious in my life. Now let's move!"

They went out the main hall front doors but Quinn immediately stopped and turned.

"Gemma?"

"What?"

He motioned to a spot against the castle wall where one of the other witches, Ima, stood wide-eyed, biting the fingernails of her left hand down to the quick.

Gemma swung around and moved quickly to stand in front of the witch.

"Where is she?"

"We didn't want this," Ima said. She'd never really spoken before. It was always Adela who'd spoken for them. Ima's voice was much lower than Quinn had expected. "She'd heard about the wolves long before we got here. But they didn't want anything to do with her. Nothing. I thought it was over. Until she saw the puppies and sensed the power contained in their bodies . . ."

Gemma stepped closer. "Where is she, Ima?"

Quinn understood the witch's struggle. Adela was her high priestess. She ruled their coven. By giving information to outsiders, she was not simply betraying Adela, she was betraying her entire coven. But this wasn't about the life of some hell beast. Gemma could not care less about the hell beast puppy or whether it lived or died. Her fear was how her sister would react to what she would definitely see as a betrayal. Of her and her queendom.

"If we're going to do something," Balla hissed, going up on her toes, "let's make it soon. Ragna's coming."

Ima lowered her hand and chewed on her lip. But after another moment's hesitation, she turned.

"This way," she said before quickly walking away, heading through the town.

They all followed her. But Ragna must have caught sight of them because she began to follow. Thankfully, it wasn't the first time most of these people had needed to lose Ragna in a crowd. Balla flicked her hand, sending Ragna tripping and sliding into a group of stonemason dwarves.

By the time they were all done yelling at her and accusing her of doing it to benefit the centaurs—an accusation they hurled at anyone who caused them the slightest problem—their group had disappeared into the nearby forest outside of town.

"By the hearts of peace," the Abbess gasped. "I know this place. The other sisters come here at dawn to pray."

"She's purposely defiling this area," Aubin growled.

"Then we stop her," Gemma replied, before quickly moving on.

Ima led the way until she cried out and suddenly ran forward, dropping down next to one of the other witches. Stretched out on the ground with blood pouring from her eyes, Wassa pointed.

Adela held the puppy between her hands, smiling at them.

Léandre charged forward but when he was about ten feet from her, he flew back as if he'd hit a wall or a tree head-on. Blood poured from his forehead and nose.

Balla threw lightning bolts but they simply bounced off and nearly struck Quinn, forcing him to drop to the ground.

The assassins unleashed poison into the ground. It moved across the earth like snakes, sliding under Adela's protective barrier. But she pressed her foot into the dirt and the grass around her froze, stopping the poison in place.

Gemma didn't bother to attack with her weapon, she simply walked up to where she assumed the barrier was.

"Give me that dog, Adela."

"Hand over all this power?" the witch asked. "You don't even want it. And your idiot sister doesn't even know what she has."

Gemma's hands twisted into fists at her sides. "Talk about my sister again."

"And you'll what . . . War Monk? What will you do? While I hold so much power in my hands?"

"It's a *dog*."

"See what I mean? So much power and it's wasted on all of you."

The Abbess circled around the barrier, sizing it up. Tapping at it with her battle staff.

Standing again, Quinn moved toward it, but the Abbess shook

her head. He felt he could get through any magickal protection created by the witch, but he'd let the others take the lead for now. Maybe it was wiser to make his move when it was absolutely necessary.

"Just give me the dog, witch."

Adela chuckled and held the dog up so she could stare into its fiery eyes. She began chanting and, within a few seconds, the puppy began to mewl and whine, twisting and turning in the witch's hands. Soon it began to scream. It was in pain and even though Gemma didn't care about the hell beasts, she did not like to see any animal—hell beast or not—tortured.

Gemma slammed her fists against the barrier, screaming, "Let it go, Adela! Let it go!"

Ima ran to the barrier, pressing her fingers against it and beginning her own chant. The gentle winter wind grew loud and wild, so strong the tops of the trees began to bend.

Startled, Gemma stepped back. Then she pulled her sword.

"*Go!*" Ima yelled over the screaming wind. "*Go now!*"

Gemma raised her weapon and began to charge toward Adela. Just as she reached the witch, about to strike, another blade was thrust into the witch from behind, tearing through Adela's chest and forcing Gemma back.

But she shot her hand out in time to catch the puppy as it was dropped by Adela.

Eyes wide, Adela looked over her shoulder. "You?"

The blade tore up higher until it reached the witch's throat. When it pulled out and the body dropped, it was the truce vicar who stood there.

He took a moment to wipe the blood off his curved blade, using the witch's gown.

"When we truce vicars need things to go a certain way," he said over the dying winds, "we don't let things like witches get in our way. Who has time for that?"

Ferdinand stepped over the body, briefly stopping to tuck his blade under his robes.

"Who has time to reason with the unreasonable?" he asked before throwing his arms wide and greeting Keeley with one of his happy grins and a "My queen! So good to see you on such a beautiful morning!"

His wide-open arms blocked the sight of the dead witch behind him, and the rest of them moved in to make sure Keeley saw nothing as she walked into view.

"Morning, Lord Ferdinand." She looked around as she moved. "Felt like a storm was coming, didn't it?"

"Our meeting is still happening, yes?"

"Yes, yes. I just need to find—Gemma! You found her!" Keeley immediately scooped the puppy out of her sister's arms, her smile so wide and happy that it nearly blinded them all.

"Hello, little one. I'm so glad to see you again." She leaned in and whispered, "I didn't know how I was going to tell your mother I'd lost you." Now she looked at Gemma. "She's her mother's favorite. So, excellent job."

Keeley turned around and headed back toward the castle. The truce vicar smiled at Gemma and followed the queen.

They began to relax but Keeley suddenly turned around and asked Gemma, "Is everything okay? You all look a little unwell."

"Yes, we're fine. Why?"

"Nothing. Just wanted to make sure." Rubbing the puppy against her chin, she headed off again.

When they were all sure the queen wasn't coming back, they turned toward what was left of the witch.

"What should we do with her body?" Balla asked.

"We can leave it for the wildlife," Tadesse suggested. "They'll eat her. She deserves no better."

Quinn shook his head. "Are we not going to discuss what we just witnessed—the peaceful truce vicar stabbing the witch? Because I feel that's something we should discuss. In detail."

Gemma frowned. "But he explained it. She was in his way."

"And we're just going to let him wander off with your sister?"

"Why would he stab *her*?"

Quinn was about to argue that point when he heard a growl. They *all* heard that growl. He could tell because they all stopped talking and began backing up.

None of them saw anything. Not even Quinn. But they could

feel it. Could sense it moving around them. Could hear it breathing. Eventually, Quinn could even feel the fur brushing against his legs, feel the tail curling around his knees.

When it finally settled behind the witch's body, it appeared.

And Gemma had not been exaggerating. It was huge. The mother of the demon wolf puppies stood over them all, even Quinn in his centaur form. Fangs oozing with blood and flames bursting not only from her eyes but from her nostrils as well. With each breath.

She looked over each of them and, for a brief, terrifying moment, Quinn thought they were all dead. All doomed to a lifetime in hell.

But they'd done the right thing, he quickly realized. They'd all fought to save the puppy and had returned it to Keeley, the one chosen to protect the puppies on this plane.

But the witch who had taken the mother's favorite? She would receive no kindness.

The she-wolf began to drag the witch's body off, and immediately the priests turned away from the sight. Until the screaming began.

Léandre turned around first, puzzled. "I thought she was dead."

"She is dead," Gemma said, walking away.

Quinn didn't understand at first. How could Gemma just walk away? But she understood all too well, didn't she? As a necromancer, she understood everything.

The screams weren't coming from the witch's body, but from her soul. The mother wolf was pulling the soul away from the body and, in desperation, the witch held on with all she was worth. Her soul actually left finger marks in the dirt where she dug them in, fighting not to be dragged off. It didn't help, though. She'd angered the mother wolf. She'd not only taken the mother wolf's favorite; she'd made the pup suffer. She'd hurt her. Quinn understood that the wolf had watched everything. She had waited to see what each of them would do. Would they help? Would they do nothing? She could have moved at any time to help her pup but she had wanted to see what she was dealing with first. That was cold and calculating but it told Quinn all he needed to know about the wolf demon. Why she still lived below in one of the hells while her mate lived with Keeley here among the humans.

The mother wolf dug her blood-covered fangs into the witch's soul and yanked, pulling it away from her body, and Quinn heard it tear away from its foundation. Heard the soul scream in absolute pain and suffering. A sound he prayed never to hear again.

The soul begged them all—*begged*—for them to help her. To pull her away from this thing that had her. But none of them felt she was worth it.

Once the mother wolf had the soul far enough away, she lifted her head and chomped, chewed, and swallowed until that soul disappeared down into her gullet. She gulped once. Swallowed again. Burped. Those flame eyes looked them over once more before she turned and walked off. The mother wolf's body grew fainter with each step she took until they could just hear her padding away into the forest . . . and then nothing.

They all stood there, staring straight ahead for several long minutes. None of them speaking. Unable to move.

Finally, it was Balla who broke the silence as she asked, "So does that she-wolf live here too?"

"No," Quinn quickly told her. Told them all. "Absolutely, no. Just no. She should be taking her pups and returning to her hell any day now."

"Okay. Good to know."

They all nodded and silently agreed never to speak about what they'd just seen. Because, honestly, why would they?

Ever?

CHAPTER 22

Ima helped Wassa to sit up, relieved her coven-sister was awake and alert. When she'd seen her lying there, just a few feet from Adela, Ima had thought for sure she was dead. That the bitch had killed her. She'd been so relieved to see her move and point in Adela's direction. Ima knew then she'd have to kill Adela or, at the very least, help these people kill her. If she didn't, Adela would put Ima and Wassa to death. As traitors. Even if they'd never betrayed her.

It was Adela who was the betrayer. While their coven-sisters were out there dying under the lash and sword of Cyrus's soldiers, she was thinking only of herself. She hadn't gone with the rest of the coven to the safety of foreign lands only because she wanted a chance at Queen Keeley's demon wolves. She could not care less about aligning herself with Keeley, Beatrix, or even Cyrus. She didn't care if every sect was destroyed. In her mind, if would be fine if they were, because all that would be left was Adela, her power, and the coven she would control.

When the vicar's blade tore through Adela's chest, Ima had the feeling he was one of the few who could have killed her body. The others were too tainted by war, by the blood of battle chaos. But not the vicar. He worked to stop war; to stop the chaos.

Now, however, the queen had the puppy again, Adela's soul had been dragged to hell, and Ima and Wassa were alone with those who had been known to happily burn witches.

As she brushed Wassa's hair from her face and checked the cuts and bruises on her cheek and neck, Ima saw chainmail boots standing in front of her. She looked up and found Brother Gemma of the Order of Righteous Valor standing over them. The rest of their travel companions were standing behind her.

Slowly, the war monk crouched in front of them. That hard face glared at them, looking her and Wassa over. Wassa's fingers dug into Ima's forearm.

They couldn't escape. All mystical doorways had been closed by the gods themselves to prevent Cyrus's minions from transporting themselves. So all they could do was fight with what power they had left.

"What do you know about horses?" the war monk asked.

"Uh . . ."

"And necromancy?"

"Well—"

"And raising creatures from the dead. But raising them alive. Not raising them to be undead. Do you know anything about that?"

Ima glanced at Wassa and then back at the war monk. "What?"

"You really fucked your horse up, didn't you?"

Gemma shoved the chuckling Quinn away before turning to the remaining witches.

"Can you help me or not?"

Ima watched Kriegszorn run in the training circle. "Is this really your focus right now?"

"I want to take her with me. I hate the thought of leaving her all alone here."

"Because you love her so much or you're afraid she'll eat your family?"

Gemma didn't bother turning around this time at the sound of laughter, merely reached out and slapped Quinn until he stepped away.

"Again, can you help or not? We're leaving in a few days."

"What exactly did you do to her when you raised her?" Wassa asked.

"I'm still not sure. I loved my Kriegszorn. If I'd had any other option, I never would have done that to her. But we needed a way out."

"What do you mean?" Ainsley asked. "That you never would have done that to her?"

"I would never raise a brother or a friend. And Kriegszorn was a friend."

"Why wouldn't you raise a friend?" Ainsley asked.

Gemma exchanged glances with the witches. She really didn't want to get into this with her younger sister.

Unfortunately, when they'd come to the stable to discuss the issue with the witches, the horse was already out in the training ring and she hadn't been alone.

"Answer your little sister," Ragna pushed.

"Maybe you should stay out of this."

"Someone answer me."

Ragna opened her mouth but Gemma would be damned before she'd let the master general tell her sister anything. So she quickly jumped in.

"The process of raising a body destroys the soul, Ainsley."

"Meaning you destroyed Kriegszorn's soul?"

"Some of it," Wassa muttered.

"Your immense guilt over doing that to her is probably what has caused such a . . ." Ima waved at the horse romping in the training circle. Half of her alive, half of her dead.

"Abomination?" Ainsley asked.

Ima shook her head. "I don't think we can fix that, War Monk."

Wassa turned her head to the side, studying Kriegszorn. "We might be able to mask it, though."

"You think?"

"Call her over," Wassa told Gemma.

Gemma clicked her tongue against her teeth and Kriegszorn immediately trotted to her, bringing her head over the fence so Gemma could pet her, which of course she did. Even missing half her face, how could Gemma not pet her? Even half-dead, she was still so gods-damn loyal!

Wassa gently placed her hands on Kriegszorn's side. The one

with actual flesh on it. She closed her eyes and, after a few seconds, she said to Ima, "I was right. This thing still has part of her soul."

"What does that even mean?" Gemma asked.

"We have no idea," Ima admitted. "But I am curious to find out."

"Give us a few hours," Wassa said. "We'll see what we can do."

Gemma walked away from the training ring. She wanted to change her clothes before Keeley's meeting.

"I'm going hunting," Ainsley said, swinging her bow off her shoulder. "Any requests?"

"Boar."

"I was thinking elk."

"Then why did you even ask me?" Gemma shot back at Ainsley.

Smirking, her sister ran off and Gemma rolled her eyes. She was in no mood for her younger sister's annoying . . .

"Is there a reason you're following me?" she asked Ragna.

"I wasn't following, just thought we were all heading back to the castle. Together. Like friends."

"Okay, what do you want?"

"What makes you think I want anything?"

"Friends? Seriously? Try again."

"Fine. I just wanted to remind you before this meeting where your loyalties lie."

"Oh . . . that's easy. Not with you."

Ragna forced a smile. "You think you're cute, don't you?"

"I'm adorable. My mother told me so."

"Just remember, your actions at this meeting today may affect the future of our order."

"Bullshit. My sister won't do anything to harm the brotherhood. She doesn't have a problem with the war monks. She just has a problem with you. She hates *you*. As long as you keep that in mind, everything should be fine."

With a grunt, Ragna stomped away and Gemma did an allover shake. Like a dog trying to shake off mud he'd accidentally rolled in. Maybe a mission with her brotherhood's most hated enemies wasn't a bad idea after all. It could be just what she needed.

Deep in her thoughts about Ragna, it took a few minutes for Gemma to realize they were nearly back at the castle and Quinn hadn't said a word. That wasn't like him. Especially after she had one of her confrontations with Ragna.

"You've been awfully quiet," she finally said to him.

"You destroy their souls," Quinn said flatly, surprising Gemma. Gemma stopped walking yet again. "What?"

"You destroy their souls. When you raise the dead."

"Oh. Well . . . yes. All magicks require sacrifice."

"Except you're not the one sacrificing. The poor dead bloke on the ground is."

"I didn't want to lose an eye or half a lung for my power. Necromancing seemed the easiest choice, and war monks have to pick something. I only use it on my enemies."

"And your horse."

"That's not fair. I didn't want to do it."

"But you did, knowing full well what you were doing to her."

Gemma gazed at Quinn. "You're really upset about this, aren't you?"

"You destroyed her soul."

"And if I could do it again—"

"But you already did it." He shook his head, looked off. "Just . . . no matter what happens, don't ever do that to me."

Startled, Gemma took a step back. "Excuse me?"

"I think I was very clear. Don't ever raise me. Don't destroy my soul. I have plans for my afterlife. They involve my grandfather and a lovely feast with the centaur gods. Can't do that if you destroy my soul because you had no choice."

Insulted, livid, and to be quite honest, just *hurt*, Gemma spun around and stomped off.

"Don't look at me like that!" the centaur yelled after her. "I don't think I'm being unreasonable with that request! Kriegszorn trusted you too! And that hand gesture is beneath you, Princess War Monk!"

Caid was standing on one of the ramparts, looking down toward the front of the castle. He eventually noticed his brother sitting on the rampart, with his back against one wall and his legs against the other; arms resting on his raised knees. At first, Caid was going to ignore him, but then he wondered if Quinn was up on the ramparts for the same reason as Caid was.

He went over to him and asked, "You feel it too, eh?"

"What?"

"I said you feel it too."

"Feel what?"

Caid frowned. "Why do you sound like me? Are you imitating me again? You know I hate when you do that."

When Quinn only gazed at him blankly, Caid actually began to worry about his brother. And he never worried about Quinn. Ever.

"All right, that's it. What's wrong with you?"

"Nothing. Just leave me alone."

Deciding he couldn't do that, Caid walked the ramparts until he saw his sister below. He put two fingers between his lips and whistled. A few minutes later, she was crouching beside Quinn.

"What did you do to him?" she demanded, glaring at Caid.

"I didn't do anything!"

"Are you sure? You can be mean."

"I go out of my way to ignore him."

"Caid didn't do anything," Quinn finally admitted.

"See?"

"Then what's wrong?"

"I found out Gemma destroys souls. When she raises the dead."

"Well," Laila said, shrugging. "She is a war monk."

"This is what you're sitting here looking so pathetic about?" Caid demanded. "I thought you had a real problem."

"When I found out . . . I didn't handle it well."

"What do you mean?"

"I might have overreacted."

"Gods," Caid guessed. "This isn't about you and Grandfather, is it? The plan you two have to dine with our gods? You know Grandfather's not dead yet."

"That's a very real plan, Caid!"

Laila rolled her eyes. "What did you say to her, Quinn?"

"I may have suggested I was disgusted by the whole thing and told her not to raise me from the dead for any of her unholy plans."

"Quinn!"

"I already said I overreacted!"

Laughing, Caid rested his arms on the rampart wall. "You're an ass."

"I just didn't realize she was destroying souls."

"All magicks require sacrifice."

"Yes, Laila. So everyone keeps bloody telling me."

"You should apologize."

"Why should *I* apologize? She never apologizes to me for anything."

"You apologize because you probably hurt her feelings, which isn't easy to do. A war monk is not someone with a lot of feelings to hurt. But you two are close—"

"We are not."

"—so I'm sure *your* saying something like that to her was far more hurtful to Gemma than if it came from anyone else."

"Oy," Caid called out. "You two. Come here."

His siblings stood next to him and he pointed, but he really didn't have to. They were so obvious. Two more blood warlocks, the only difference between them, the color of their robes. One all in blue. The other in yellow.

"Did Keeley say anything about more of them coming here?"

"I don't think she knew. She was too worried about those fucking dogs."

"Wolves."

"Shut *up*, Quinn."

"You get Keeley. I'll secure the main hall. Quinn, get Gemma. And when you see her . . . apologize."

"Even if I don't think I should—"

"Quinn!"

"Why is everyone snarling at me?"

"I'm shocked you actually asked that question," Caid said to his brother. "You know . . . with a straight face."

In a fresh set of clothes, Gemma opened her bedroom door to find Quinn standing there.

"What?" she asked, barely able to look at him.

"I'm sorry if I hurt your feelings by suggesting you're a soulless monster that's only happy when you're destroying the souls of others—"

"Wait . . . what?"

"—and two more blood warlocks showed up just now. Caid, Laila, and I just saw them from the ramparts."

Gemma grabbed her sword belt and bolted out the door, snarling over her shoulder at Quinn, "And I am *not* a soulless monster, you ridiculous horse's ass."

"You have to know that's not really an insult to me."

"Oh, shut *up*, Quinn!"

CHAPTER 23

By the time Gemma reached the last few steps leading into the main hall, nearly everyone who needed to be involved in what was coming was there. Including the two new additions, Ludolf's fellow blood warlocks. The three of them were deep in a private conversation in the corner, making everyone nervous.

Gemma was about to take those final steps into the hall but she stopped and faced Quinn one more time, so she could inform him in no uncertain terms through her gritted teeth, "You and I both know that was no sort of worthy apology!"

"Stop hitting me!"

She hadn't realized she'd started slapping his chest even before she'd begun yelling at him but once she did, she didn't really care. He deserved it.

"When you're ready to apologize like a proper . . ."

Quinn smirked. "You were going to say like a proper man, weren't you?"

"Centaur," she finished, "you know where I am."

"Destroying someone else's soul? *Owww!*"

She walked away, fighting the urge to shake out her now throbbing hand. She'd forgotten that punching him in the stomach could be just as painful as punching him in the face.

When Gemma reached Keeley's side, the warlocks finished their conversation and separated. The two newcomers moved to the large open doors. They faced Keeley and bowed in her direction. Keeley, being Keeley, waved in return. "It was nice meeting you!" she called out.

That caused the warlocks a moment of confusion. Probably trying to figure out if she was being sarcastic or plotting their deaths . . . or both. But, of course, Keeley wasn't. She meant that "It was nice meeting you," or she wouldn't have said it.

Once they were gone—moving a little faster than they'd come—Ludolf moved to the dining table and unrolled a large map across it.

"As all of you know," he began, "the original goal was a simple one. To track down Cyrus the Honored so he could be dealt with in any way Queen Keeley saw fit. We all thought this task would take some time. It hasn't. We know exactly where he is and it turns out that where Cyrus is, is a problem."

"What do you mean?" Caid asked.

Ludolf swiped his red-gloved hand across an area on the map that had the centaurs immediately looking at one another and then back at Keeley.

"Cyrus's legion has made camp here and Cyrus is definitely with them."

"What's the concern, other than it's right in our territory?"

"It's the location," Laila replied. "A lot of water comes from that region. Pours down into all the connected streams and rivers and lakes that travel as far down as—" She looked around. "Here. Into this valley."

"What about the Amichai Mountains? Your people?"

"He'd have to go *into* the mountains to get to our water supply. That would mean he'd have to deal with my people, the dwarves, the elves . . . all of us."

"But," Keeley guessed, "he can cut off *our* water supply from where he is."

"He can."

"And eventually destroy us from thirst alone."

"Yes."

Keeley nodded and stared at the map. Then, she announced, "All right." She looked around at everyone. "All of you know what to do. We move out in two hours."

Gemma looked around. Everyone in the room seemed to understand their role . . . except her.

She looked at Quinn. "Do you know what the plan is?"

"To follow you?"

Turning, Gemma realized that all those who'd traveled with her were standing around, waiting for her. Even the Abbess. Which meant . . .

"Gods-dammit!"

Gemma followed Keeley up to the room she shared with Caid.

"Are you planning to leave me here?" Gemma demanded, slamming the door behind her.

"No," Keeley said calmly, pulling out the leather armor that had been made for her two years ago by the centaurs; a hammer and anvil crest were burned onto the leather breastplate. "You're leaving for the Old King's castle." Keeley stopped dressing and faced her sister. "Aren't you?"

"You still want me to do that? Now?"

"Yes, now. What did you think?"

"That you'd want me to go with you to kill Cyrus since he's way more important in the big scheme of things."

"Nothing is more important than finding out what Beatrix is up to, Gemma. Nothing. And you're the only one I can trust to get it done. But remember what I told you. Killing Beatrix isn't your goal. Finding out what she's doing and stopping it is. Do you understand?"

"You're serious. You don't want me to go with you."

"I'd love for you to come with me."

"Good, then—"

"But I know what my instincts are telling me. What they're screaming at me. If we wait on this, it's a mistake."

"I . . . uh . . . was going to set off in a few days."

"Leave now. When we do. Tonight."

Gemma closed her eyes, cracked her neck. She silently reminded herself that Keeley was queen; that Keeley leads. And all Gemma had to do as a war monk, a princess, and even a younger sister was to follow Keeley's orders. No matter how ridiculous those orders might be!

"Fine. And who's going with you?"

"My army. The centaurs."

"And?" Gemma pushed.

"Ragna invited herself earlier in the day."

"And you didn't think I'd take that personally?"

"It was the only way the bitch would agree to leave your war monks here to protect the other sects."

"At least agree to let my battle-cohorts go with you. I want them watching your back."

"Do I have to talk to them?"

"After the death-cult discussion? No."

"That's fine then. But Keran stays behind to watch out for the family. If nothing else, she won't let Archie mercy-kill the children when Mum and Da's backs are turned."

"Good plan. I'll get everyone ready."

When Gemma reached the bedroom door, Keeley was suddenly there, wrapping her arms around her.

"What are you doing?" Gemma asked, unable to keep the wary tone out of her voice.

"Hugging you."

"Are you that sure I'm going to die?"

"No, but . . ."

"But? *There's a but?*"

Keeley swung Gemma around and grabbed her by the shoulders. "No matter what happens in that castle. No matter what Beatrix is up to or what she says to piss you the fuck off, I want you to get out of there alive. Do you understand me? Are you listening?"

"Yes, I'm listening. I'm just not sure what you're talking about."

"You always think you want to kill Beatrix. But nothing would bring her more joy in this world . . . than to kill you." Keeley rested her hand against Gemma's cheek. "Don't let her."

CHAPTER 24

Gemma took Dagger's reins from Samuel and told him again, "You're not coming."

"But—"

"Not this time. Not where I'm going." She smiled at him. "But thank you."

She led Dagger toward the stable doors, stopping when Ima and Wassa stepped in front of her.

"Well?" Ima asked.

"Well what?"

"Well—*oh, gods!*"

A seemingly normal-looking Kriegszorn rammed into Dagger, slamming him against the stable door with her front hooves and roaring at the poor horse.

"*Kriegszorn, no!*" Gemma bellowed.

Fangs out, ready to tear out Dagger's throat, the horse looked at Gemma over her shoulder.

"Let him go. Right now. Let him go."

She moved away from Dagger and dropped her front legs onto the ground.

"Samuel!"

Cautiously, Gemma's onetime squire eased up to them and took Dagger's reins back from Gemma. He clicked his tongue against his teeth and poor Dagger limped off.

Ima cleared her throat. "Uh . . . well, we did our best. As you can see, we managed to cover her dead side pretty well."

"How?"

"Used some of the skin from her other side. We noticed it restores dead flowers and grass around the ring so we thought it might work with her skin too. So far, so good. Um . . . it does not work on her attitude, however. As we all can see."

"She's just jealous," Gemma guessed. "She used to get that way sometimes when she was . . . normal. I'll ride her on this mission."

Wassa grimaced a bit. "Sure that's a good idea?"

"No, but you'll be coming with us. So if it's a mistake, you'll be there to experience it with me." She gave them a smile that she could tell neither liked, which she completely understood.

"Samuel!" she called out again. "Bring me my saddle. I want to see how it looks on Kriegszorn."

Keeley and her army rode out three hours before dawn. Gemma's team rode with them, each member discreetly splitting off from the main force when each person could do so without being noticed. They rode through a nearby forest until they could regroup behind a hill line without being seen.

As planned, Gemma's team was made up of the two priests, Balla and her assistant, the two remaining witches—who seemed grateful no one appeared to be holding Adela's actions against them—the divine assassins, the Abbess, and Quinn himself.

And, to the great annoyance of absolutely everyone . . . the truce vicar. He'd insisted.

"I will be of great benefit to you! I promise!"

No one truly believed him, but they decided not to argue the point. Besides, the vicar had earned a bit of respect as the one who'd put the blade into Adela's back.

The vicar managed to earn even more respect after their third day of hard riding, when all any of them wanted was some food and a good night's sleep. That evening they passed a city known for its great library. None of them had much interest in going into that library, great or not. But the vicar insisted they ride toward it. So they did.

When the library came into sight, Quinn was surprised that Cyrus hadn't already burned it down. It resembled a church. A church dedicated to books.

They rode past it, though, until they reached a very large house behind the library.

They dismounted from their horses and handed them off to the stable hands, then followed the vicar to the front door. He briefly spoke to a servant, and a few minutes later another man came to the door. As soon as the two men saw each other, they began hugging and speaking so loudly that Quinn knew immediately this was another vicar.

"Ferdinand, my good friend! I am so glad to see you!"

"And you, Gregorio! You look so well!"

"What are you doing here?"

"Any chance my friends and I can spend the night?"

"Of course! Of course! Come in! All of you!"

Without question or complaint, Vicar Gregorio invited them all inside his home.

"What an interesting group you have with you, my old friend. Divine assassins, war priests, a war monk, a nun, temple virgins, and even witches! The holy and the unholy all mixing together! You will make our fellow brethren proud when they hear about this."

"Oh, thank you, my friend!"

"Oy! Oy! Oy!" Gemma finally snapped, clapping her hands together. "I appreciate the meeting of the vicars. But I'm tired, hungry, and thirsty. So if you're not in the mood to help us out, I am more than happy to go to the pub we passed on the way here."

Vicar Gregorio smiled widely at Vicar Ferdinand. "War monks are the absolute *worst*, aren't they?" He crowed. "I forgot how much I love that!"

"I know. They really are! I've been with a whole army of them the past few days and they are miserable bastards. But how can you not love them for their miserable ways?"

"Well, come on, you lot," Gregorio said, motioning them deeper into the house. When he reached a set of stairs, they found a large staff patiently waiting for them. "My servants will be more than happy to help all of you. Even the rude and unholy ones!"

"By the gods," Gemma muttered to Quinn, "if I wasn't so hungry, I'd burn this fucking house down."

"See? Just like the vicar said," Quinn joked. "Rude."

* * *

After taking a hot bath and changing into a fresh set of plain white leggings and a white cotton shirt, Gemma was ready for some sleep but she still hadn't eaten. She dreaded the idea of sitting through dinner with her travel companions. She remembered the first night they'd set out together and how they'd almost come to blows. But she was so very hungry, she decided to just put up with the insults.

Gemma headed down the stairs where she was met by a servant who happily led her to the dining room. Why were the servants all so happy? she wondered. She didn't think she'd be happy as a servant. True, she was the servant of a god, but that was different. To be the servant of an actual human being . . . She'd do her job to the best of her ability to put food on the table and take care of her family, but she doubted that she'd do it with a smile.

They reached the dining room and Gemma paused outside when she heard laughter coming from her companions instead of the usual insults concerning unholiness, abominations, and whorishness.

Taking a step inside, Gemma was greeted with cheers that almost had her turning around and walking back out.

"Is everything okay?" she asked, sitting down in a chair next to Quinn.

"Excellent wine," Quinn said. "That they've all been enjoying."

Gemma studied the glass carafes of wine across the table. Her eyes narrowed a bit and she immediately covered her chalice when another servant offered her some.

"You should try some," Father Aubin urged. "It's the best I've had in a long while."

Remembering her night of dwarven wine excess, Gemma shook her head and said, "No, thank you, Father. And don't anyone forget that we ride early tomorrow. So don't get too . . ." She sighed and said to Quinn, "No one is listening to me, are they?"

"They are not."

Gemma glanced around the table. "Where are the vicars?"

"At the library."

"What?"

"That's what they said. Vicar Gregorio has the keys, so they packed up some food and off they went."

Gemma leaned back in her chair and watched as the servants continued to fill her companions' wineglasses. No food was on the table except loaves of warm bread. And the two vicars never seemed to return. And all the while her companions—except for Quinn, of course—seemed to get more and more unaware of their surroundings and out of control.

"Where's the kitchen?" she finally asked Quinn.

He lifted his head, sniffed the air, and pointed.

"I'll be back."

Quinn watched Gemma slip out of the dining room.

"You don't hide your feelings very well, centaur."

Balla sat at his right, a chalice of half-drunk wine in her hand and a rather adorable half-drunken smile on her face.

"Maybe you should have some bread."

"You wouldn't believe how many people who come to our temple want to consult about love. The fact that we're virgins . . . they don't care. They still want us to fix their shitty relationships for them."

Quinn let out a startled laugh. "*Balla.*"

"Don't get me wrong. It brings in a lot of gold, which we all appreciate. But the majority of those relationships are doomed. Still, I've seen enough to know . . ."

"What?"

"You two . . ." She giggled and sipped more wine.

"Us two what?"

"You're meant for each other."

"How do you figure?"

"Let's see. How do I put this?" She looked off a moment before hitting him with "Both of you are too annoying to be with anyone else." She quickly put her hand on his forearm. "But I mean that in the best way possible!"

"How could you seriously mean that in the best way possible?"

Before the priestess could reply, Quinn heard the front door open, then a hysterical scream from the kitchen. He was reaching for the dagger he had tucked into his boot when he saw that all his traveling companions were not as drunk as he'd first thought. Those with weapons already had them out, those who used magicks were already in their combat stances. The truce vicars rushed into the room, carrying multiple scrolls under their arms.

"What's happening?" Gregorio asked, his eyes wide and his face red from worry. "Is everyone all right?"

Gemma returned from the kitchen. She placed a large cooking knife down on the table and announced, "In case anyone was wondering . . . no one is poisoning the food. Or wine. If anyone sees any red flakes in the stew, it's simply red pepper." She caught sight of the vicars. "Oh. You two are back." She motioned to the scrolls. "And those are . . . ?"

"Ancient maps of the Old—"

"King's castle," she finished, wincing. "So, you didn't leave because of a double cross involving your vicar brother here?"

Ferdinand's mouth briefly fell open on a gasp. "Of course not!"

"Okay. I'm going to bed now. I'll see all of you in the morning." She reached across the table and grabbed several loaves of bread before quietly exiting the room.

When they all heard a door close on the floor above, all gazes turned to Quinn.

"Why are you all looking at me?" he asked.

Father Aubin snorted. "You know why."

Gemma didn't answer when she heard the knock on the door, but she wasn't surprised when Quinn came in anyway. She knew he would.

She didn't see him, though. She was under the blanket at the moment. Hiding from the horrifying reality of having threatened the kitchen staff with their own cutlery.

"I got you something to eat," he said. "But I spooned it into the bowls myself to make sure no one spit into it. Or anything else."

Gemma buried her face in her hands. "I can't believe I did that. What was I thinking?"

"You were exhausted and you're not used to seeing people who normally despise each other getting along."

"I've become my uncle Archie."

"No. You haven't." She felt the bed move as the centaur sat

down next to her and pulled the blanket off her head. "You don't have the engineering skills to be your uncle Archie."

"Thanks."

He brushed her hair off her face.

"I know. I need to cut it. It's too long."

"Anything else you'd like to point out that's wrong with you? Perhaps that freckle on your chin? Or the way you hold your shield?"

"What's wrong with the way I hold my shield?"

"Well, at least you continue to have strong confidence in your battle skills."

Gemma curled into a ball and fell onto her side. "I can't believe I attacked those poor people in their own kitchen. I'm so ashamed."

"Don't be. You were looking out for us. That's your job."

"They're probably all laughing at me."

"Yeah. Mostly."

Gemma threw up her hands. "Thank you! Thank you very much!"

"Do you know why?" he went on, ignoring her tone. "Because they can. You allow them to laugh and drink and eat in comfort and safety because you made sure they were safe. Because you made sure the servants are too terrified to poison their food or drink. These humans need people like you . . . and your uncle Archie." He thought a moment. "And my dad."

Quinn shook his head. "Forget that part. I can't think about that right now. So what I'm saying is don't feel bad. You were looking out for everyone. That's your job and you did it well. I'm just grateful it was you."

"What do you mean?"

"You found out everything was fine and you put the knife down and everything was over."

"As opposed to . . . ?"

"If it had been, for instance, Ragna."

"Ohhh." Gemma's entire face cringed and together they said, "Bloodbath."

Finally, Gemma laughed and Quinn joined her.

"See?" he said. "It could have been so much worse."

* * *

"Are you wearing leggings?" Gemma asked, finally noticing what was on the centaur's legs.

"I am. They didn't have a kilt and the servants took my clothes to clean them."

He stood up and stared down at his long legs. "How do you live in these? I feel trapped. I just want to tear them off and start kicking."

"It's not that bad."

"It is! My legs need to be free. Even these puny human ones."

"If you're that uncomfortable, take them off."

Quinn snorted, sounding more like a horse than he ever had before. "That wouldn't be fair to you."

"Why not?"

"Seeing me unencumbered? You wouldn't be able to resist."

"Resist what?"

"Me in all my magnificent human glory."

"By Morthwyl's mighty sword, just take them off and get over yourself."

"All right. But don't say I didn't warn you."

"I'll keep that in mind."

Feeling much better, Gemma moved to the far side of her bed, close to the end table where Quinn had placed her food tray. She picked up a bowl of stew and a spoon and had just scooped up a mouthful when she looked over to see Quinn standing there with his arms crossed over his chest, wearing only the white shirt he'd been given. The white shirt was long but his cock still extended past it. She nearly choked on the food she'd just swallowed at the sight of him.

"Told you."

She put her bowl back on the tray and wiped her mouth with a linen cloth.

With her throat clear, she finally got out, "Shut up."

"Should I put the leggings back on?"

"We're all adults."

"What does that mean?"

"That we're all adults . . . with needs."

Quinn smirked. "Sober needs?"

"Very sober, responsible needs."

"You might get attached," he warned.

"I am a war monk. I don't have to do anything I don't want to do. Except praise my god and kill on command."

Quinn slowly made his way across the room. "I don't know. We're surrounded by religious types. They may not like to hear us taking care of . . . our needs."

"Then we'll have to be very quiet."

"Sure you can be?"

"It'll be a challenge. But I love a challenge."

Quinn grinned, pulled off his shirt. "So do I."

Quinn scrambled across the bed. He didn't mean to. He meant to move with a little more care and deliberation but he realized too late he was beyond all that. He realized too late he'd been waiting for this for quite a while. Waiting to have Gemma in his arms.

By the time he reached her, she was already naked, having tossed her own clothes off. He was grateful. He didn't want to waste time taking her clothes off for her. He knew humans liked that sort of thing. But he just liked being naked. He liked the feeling of skin against skin. Just the feel of her scars against his was so intense, his cock got hard immediately.

Even better was Gemma's response to him. Her arms went around him right away and her lips sought his. It took him a second to realize this was their first kiss, but as soon their lips touched and mouths parted, it felt as if they'd been connected like this forever.

He pulled Gemma closer, hiking her up higher so she could wrap her legs around his waist. While she kept herself there, his hands were free to roam. Using his thumbs and forefingers to tease her nipples until she was gasping. Then sliding his hands down her body until he could ease his fingers inside her, finding her already hot and slippery, hips grinding, pushing.

She pulled out of their kiss so she could nip at his neck and ear; drag her fingers down his back.

Needing to be inside her, Quinn pushed her back a bit and pressed his cock against her. Then Quinn waited. He waited for her.

* * *

He'd stopped. Why had he stopped? Did he think she had time for him to stop? Was he playing games with her?

Not in the mood for any of that, Gemma locked her ankles behind Quinn's back and brought her hips forward hard.

They both gasped in shock, gazing into each other's wide eyes. Both panting. Both of them trying to control their sounds. They didn't want to alert the entire house to what they were doing. It was bad enough having the temple virgins still avoiding physical contact with her. If they actually heard her having sex . . . With a centaur, no less!

Gemma brushed that thought from her mind. She had more important things buried deep inside her at the moment. And if she was going to get through this with her sanity intact, she really had to focus.

She let out a breath to help relax her muscles and smoothed her hands against Quinn's shoulders. He leaned in and brushed his lips against her throat. That felt . . . so good. But then he moved his hands back to her breasts, again toying with them. Especially her nipples. Her nipples had never been especially sensitive but the way Quinn played with them . . .

Gemma's eyes crossed and she buried her hands in his hair.

To be honest, at this point, she really wasn't paying attention to what she was doing. She was just doing her best to keep quiet. So she pressed her mouth against his lower neck and dug her fingers deeper into his scalp. She was pretty sure it was the scalp thing that got to him. She should have left his hair alone, but she didn't.

Because the next thing she knew, she was flat on her back and he was buried hilt-deep inside her.

She didn't care, though. It felt so good. It had been quite a while since she'd had sex, much less a good solid fuck; she was more than ready for what Quinn was about to do. So instead of pulling her fingers from his scalp and putting her hands back on his shoulders in the soothing manner that seemed to calm him down, she just dug in deeper.

His mouth covered hers, his tongue sliding inside. Then he was fucking her. Gemma unlocked her ankles from around his waist and opened her legs wider. She pulled his head closer, returned his kiss harder. Their hips met, thrust for thrust. Each taking the other, harder and harder, showing no mercy until Gemma felt Quinn's hand slip between them and press against her, one finger moving around her clit until she began to shake and his entire body tensed on top of hers.

They groaned and gasped into each other's mouths, shuddering until they were drained completely and could do nothing more than collapse.

Quinn rolled away from Gemma so he didn't lie on top of her. He couldn't believe he was covered in sweat and was panting as if he'd just run a hard race.

Thankfully, he wasn't alone. Gemma was beside him, also panting and sweating; her legs splayed wide open. For a brief moment, he thought she'd fallen asleep. Until she asked, "Want some bread?"

"What?"

"Hungry? I'm starving." She closed her legs and sat up, stretching her arms over her head and yawning.

"After that you're . . . hungry?"

"Yes." She held out a loaf of bread to him. "You should eat too."

"Why?"

"Because when we're done eating, we're going to do it again. Probably a few times. It's been a while for me." She raised a brow at him. "You knew that, right?"

He took the bread from her. "Uh . . . no?"

"Well, it's called war monk stamina," she explained. "It exists."

"Oh. Great."

"Don't worry, centaur," she promised, leaning down to kiss him. "I'll make it worth every bit of sleep you lose."

CHAPTER 25

Setting up this meeting with the dwarves on their way to Cyrus's camp had been Keeley's idea. One Caid and Laila had not supported. But she knew she needed Mundric's help.

She'd sent a messenger ahead to ask Mundric to meet her at a halfway spot between their two kingdoms. An underground dwarven location since he was doing her a favor. From her talks with Mundric two years ago, she knew this cavern had its own massive forge.

She'd been planning to meet with the dwarves long before she'd thought she'd have to face off against Cyrus but the sudden change in her situation had pushed up the schedule, forcing her to send her army ahead while she headed to the mountain range.

Grinning as she caught sight of him, she opened her arms and hugged King Mundric. The king held still.

"What are you doing?" he asked.

"Hugging you."

"Dwarves don't hug."

"Well, I do." She pulled back, ignoring the stares she was getting from his retinue of soldiers and advisors. "I'm just so glad to see you!"

"You are?" he asked.

"You are?" Caid asked.

"Yes," she replied to everyone. "I like you."

"You do?" the king asked.

"You do?" Caid repeated.

"Both of you stop that!" Keeley snapped.

Mundric glanced behind her and gave a barely there nod to the centaurs. Although the races of the Amichai Mountains weren't remotely friendly to one another, they were loyal when it came to keeping their lands safe from humans. Keeley had the loyalty of the centaurs and the dwarves, and with their aid she hoped to keep out King Marius, but Beatrix had the elves. And so far, neither of the sisters had the loyalty of the barbarians. Then again, no one had the loyalty of the barbarians.

"I heard you've been working with the stonemason dwarves," Mundric said.

"I have. My uncle Archie knows them."

"A lot of them are my cousins."

"I'll try to be nicer to them then."

"You don't have to. I don't like my stonemason cousins."

Gripping his walking stick, Mundric asked, "So why are you here, human Queen? I thought you would only call on my army when you had to face off against King Marius. Is that happening?"

"No. I have a problem with his brother. Cyrus the Honored."

"The Religion Killer, you mean."

Keeley stopped walking. "You know about him?"

"Everyone knows about him."

"And yet you weren't planning to do anything about him?"

"Human religions aren't my concern." Mundric chuckled. "You look so disappointed in me."

"Because I am. You can't just ignore what's going on around you because it's happening to humans and you don't like humans. Isn't that a little simplistic?"

"I like simplistic. And no more speeches, human Queen. What do you want from me if it's not my army?"

Keeley pulled her hammer out from the holster secured to her back. She held it in front of him.

"A better hammer?" he asked.

"No!" She held her hammer to her chest. "I love my hammer. And it loves me."

"This just got so strange," she heard Caid mutter behind her.

"The question is, does she love you more than that hammer?" Laila asked.

Keeley swung her hammer around until she could point it at the two centaurs behind her. "Are you two done?"

"If we must be," Laila teased.

"Anyway," Keeley went on, bringing her hammer back around and holding it between her hands, "I need your help with my hammer. You see, Cyrus has stolen a lot of artifacts from the human religious sects he's destroyed. He and his wizards have apparently combined the artifacts to somehow create a protective barrier around himself that magicks cannot penetrate."

"Is that why you're the one who's going to kill him? Because there's nothing magickal about you?"

"Yes. Well," she added, "that and he sent assassins for me. That was just rude. Didn't even face me himself." She let out a breath to release her anger. "Anyway, I don't think I can have anything magickal on me when I face him. At least that's what the magickal ones around me have told me. So I need you to make this hammer more powerful without making it magickal. So it's magickal without being magickal. Understand?"

"Of course I understand."

"You understood that?" Caid questioned.

"There's only one here with the skill to help you." Mundric started walking. "Come along, Queen Keeley. You two wait here."

"Keeley," Caid called out.

"I'll be fine."

"You'd better be," her centaur warned.

Back in his kilt and chainmail, Quinn gulped his tea and ate his fried boar while the rest of the travel party stumbled into the dining room, glaring at the sun blasting through the tall windows and cursing the days they were born.

He'd warned them not to drink too much wine, but they hadn't listened, and now here they were. The only one who seemed unaffected was the Abbess and he'd watched her put quite a few glasses away last night before he'd left for Gemma's room. And yet she'd entered the dining room with her usual rosy cheeks, bright eyes, and soft steps as if nothing bothered her.

"Brightest day, all," she greeted, her hands tucked into her white robes.

"Is the yelling necessary, Your Holiness?" Balla barked.

"Are we sure those servants didn't poison the wine?" little Priska asked, her head cradled in both hands. "Because I think . . ." She moved her hands to her mouth, then bolted from the room.

"I have something to soothe the stomach," the Abbess proposed.

"I thought you'd want us to suffer," Ima said into the table since that's where her head rested at the moment.

"Perhaps on another day. But we have far to go and I must travel with all of you. I'd prefer not to spend all my time tiptoeing my horse around your vomit."

The Abbess stood. "I'll get my bag."

"Morning!" Gemma exclaimed as she swooped into the room, her grin wide. The servants, despite her misstep the evening before, had done a fine job of cleaning her white tunic and chainmail. She fairly sparkled. "How is everyone this fair morning?"

"You're in a much better mood," the Abbess noted.

"I *am* in a much better mood. How good of you to notice." She clapped her hands together and Quinn briefly feared everyone was going to attack her. "Now, we are on the road within the hour. Be ready. Where's the vicar?"

"I'm here, Brother Gemma!"

"Vicar!"

"Brother!"

Father Aubin slammed his fist on the table. "*If everyone does not stop yelling—*"

"You're the only one yelling, Father Aubin." Gemma motioned to the vicar. "I want to see that map of the Old King's castle."

She took one of the scrolls from the vicar's hands and, after moving the plates of food and chalices aside, she spread it out. They all leaned over the parchment, studying it closely.

"We don't know what changes your sister has made since she's moved in there," Quinn reminded Gemma as they studied the detailed maps.

"So when we get in, we find someone to help us out."

She rolled up the scroll and handed it back to the vicar. "Everyone get your things. We go. Now."

Quinn caught her arm but waited until everyone else left the room. When they were alone, he kissed her, then shoved a piece of toasted bread into her mouth before reminding her that "this isn't about killing Beatrix."

Gemma swallowed a large gulp of tea from Quinn's cup before asking, "Why do you and my sister keep saying that to me?"

"Oh, come on, Gemma. Why do you think?"

Keeley watched Queen Vulfegundis, master blacksmith of her guild, work on Keeley's hammer.

Every once in a while, Keeley would tear her eyes away from the beauty of watching a true master at her craft, simply to smile at Vulfegundis's husband, Mundric.

Using only metals the dwarves had mined themselves over the eons and a heat so powerful Keeley couldn't even stand as close as she wanted without worrying about losing skin, the dwarven queen added layers to Keeley's hammer again and again until, finally, she took it off to a table with several other dwarf women, where they spent another two hours on it.

Keeley couldn't see what they were doing but she patiently waited.

When Vulfegundis finally returned, she casually held the hammer in one hand. No fancy pillow held the weapon. No massive giant covered in jewels walked it toward Keeley while musicians played dramatic music. It was just the queen, walking along, occasionally swinging the hammer to ensure she still liked the weight.

"Yeah," she said when she was near. "This should do you quite nicely. At least until I have time to make you something decent. Not that there's anything wrong with this. I mean, for a human, you did a pretty okay job. Excellent for a human, really. Now all I did was . . . you all right, luv?"

Keeley couldn't hear her, though. She was too busy looking at her hammer. The hammer that now glowed like some fabled weapon held by a god. Her knees buckled and the king's guard caught her and helped her sit on a bench before she could hit the floor.

"You didn't feed her, Mundric?"

"We ate! I fed her while we waited and gave her drink too. I don't know what's wrong with her. I hope it isn't catching. You know how diseased these humans are. A sniffle and before you know it, they've spread a plague that wipes out half the earth!"

"I'm fine," Keeley said. "I'm fine. It's just . . ."

Keeley forced herself to raise her eyes to the dwarven royals.

"I've just never seen anything so beautiful, Queen Vulfe-gundis."

The queen looked down at the hammer. "You mean this?"

Keeley reached out to touch it but was afraid her hands were too dirty.

"Such exquisite workmanship. I can only dream of ever being this good."

"That's the truth," the king muttered. "Owwww! Watcha hit me for, female?"

Vulfegundis placed the hammer into Keeley's hands. "Take it. And give it a few practice swings."

She pulled Keeley to her feet. "I'll be right back."

The queen rushed off and Keeley closed her eyes and took several breaths. She did that so she wouldn't burst into tears. She knew the dwarves would be shocked and disgusted by such a display from a blacksmith. But the beauty of what she held . . . How could they not understand? Were they simply so used to having such beautiful things lying around? How spoiled they all were.

Determined to do what she would do with any weapon that had been modified, Keeley held the hammer in her hand. She held it at her side for a few moments, then she began to swing it a few times. Just as quickly she stopped, turning in astonishment to the king.

"How . . . how did she make it lighter? She didn't remove anything, but she made it lighter."

"Are you going to be all right? You look like ya might pass out. Don't pass out."

"I won't. I promise I won't." Keeley took control and again focused on the king. "Got anything I can hit?"

The king and his guards all moved back, leaving just one poor bloke standing there.

The dwarf's eyes grew wide and he shook his head. "That beast of a woman's not hitting me!"

The king rolled his eyes. "Not you, idiot! Move!"

The idiot scrambled out of the way, revealing a large block of stone that had come up directly from the ground where it still stood. It had to be thousands of years old, and since it had never been destroyed despite its proximity to all these busy dwarves, Keeley assumed that it couldn't be.

"Perfect," Keeley said.

She stood in front of the stone and loosened up her shoulders; took a few practice swings with her hammer. When she felt comfortable, she grabbed the weapon's handle with both hands, swung it back, delighting in how easy it was now that the hammer was just a bit lighter.

Grinning, Keeley swung the hammer forward just as she heard "wait!" in the distance, but it was too late. Her arm was already in motion and the distance was simply too short to pull back in time.

The hammer hit the stone and Keeley had to shut her eyes as it exploded into a thousand shards. Pieces of rock cut her face and neck, her bare arms and hands.

Keeley stumbled back and immediately began to shake the stone dust from her hair, terrified to open her eyes.

"What the fuck did you do to her hammer?" she heard Mundric yell.

"Not nearly as much as you think, ya dumb bastard!" Vulfegundis yelled back.

Hands grabbed Keeley and led her to another bench. Stone shards and dust were brushed away from her face and eyes so that she could finally see again.

"I am so sorry," she said when she could look at the king and queen.

"Not your fault, darlin' girl," Vulfegundis said. "It was this old fool."

"I didn't know you made my hammer so powerful."

Vulfegundis laughed. "That wasn't the hammer. That was you."

"But . . ."

"All I did was use our metals to make it lighter, so you don't have to put as much power behind your swings and so that human magicks can't destroy it. Oh! And it can absorb magicks. Can't really do anything with them, but it'll keep them off you during a fight." She shrugged. "But that was it."

Keeley pointed at the designs. "But these runes."

"Old dwarf runes. I think they look nice, and the sight will terrify your human mages. But that's about it. Didn't want to use anything truly magickal."

Now Keeley pointed at where the ancient rock had once stood. "Then how did I . . ."

"Since you were exerting less power to swing the hammer, you had more power to unleash on the stone, which me husband should have known."

"How was I supposed to know that?"

"Just look at her! That's ages of blacksmith breeding there! Och!" She dismissed the king with a wave. "Be careful with that hammer now," she warned Keeley. "Until you get used to it. Understand?"

Keeley nodded. Still in shock.

"And I wanted to give you this." She handed over chainmail, but it was not made of steel. "Don't worry. It's not magickal either. Should fit you well enough. Well, it might be tight in the shoulders, but it'll do you a bit better than that centaur shit you've currently got on."

"Be nice. They made this for me."

Vulfegundis snorted, but Keeley couldn't be too mad at the queen. Not after the hammer.

"How do I ever repay you for this?"

"Your firstborn," Vulfegundis replied. But when Keeley's eyes grew wide in panic, Vulfegundis laughed and said, "I'm only kidding. I wouldn't want that half-centaur baby. No one would."

"I've had such a lovely day—I'm going to go before you ruin it."

"Okay. Try not to get killed."

Knowing that was the best she would ever get out of the dwarves, Keeley simply nodded and returned to Caid and Laila with her new treasures.

Gemma didn't know why she bothered to hide her tunic under her cape. Several religious factions had come to King Marius's territory for protection, and they wore their robes and colors quite boldly. And she doubted she'd find her sister out here among the rabble. Beatrix barely associated with the people she'd grown up with all her life, including her own family. It was doubtful she'd care to meet the peasants lucky enough to be allowed near the castle where she slept.

But Gemma still kept the hood of her cape pulled low over her face just in case. No use taking risks this late in the game.

On the last two days of their ride here, they'd come up with a plan. Perhaps not the best plan but a plan nonetheless. It was better than nothing and it would do for now.

Gemma tugged on Quinn's sleeve. "Where's my sister?" she asked.

"Keeley?" he whispered back.

"No!" She couldn't believe he'd utter that name here. Now. Was he mad?

"Ainsley. I just realized we didn't really give her a task, and we should give her something to do."

Quinn didn't stop walking but his head dropped.

"What?"

"Ainsley's with your sister. Kee—"

She snapped her fingers to stop him from saying that name. "She is?"

"Yes. She asked you both which sister she should go with, and you both ignored her, so she decided where she should go herself."

"Oh." Gemma grimaced. "I guess we do forget her sometimes."

"All the time. You forget her *all* the time. I don't know why. She's a lovely girl with incredible bow skills. And if you're not careful, Ragna is going to take advantage of the way you ignore her."

"Would it be so bad if she joined the brotherhood?"

"Only you can answer that. But there's the brotherhood and there's Ragna's loyal monk-knights. I'm not sure you want her joining them."

He had a point.

"Speaking of which . . . what does that mean for us?" Quinn asked.

"What does what mean for us?"

"What does your precious membership in the brotherhood mean for us? Will we have to sneak around? Will you ever be able to show your adoration of me to others? Will you always have to pretend you loathe me even though it's not true?"

"I feel like this is one-sided, but we'll focus on that later. I won't say that relationships aren't complicated in the Order of Righteous Valor, because they can be, but not as complicated as they are in other orders. For instance, Joshua had a wife. She lived near the monastery and they loved each other and were loyal to each other until her death about a decade ago. Brother Thomassin, however, was much happier on his own. And that's how he stayed. Things were a little more complicated for Brother Bartholemew and Brother Brín because relationships were not allowed with fellow brothers. You know, because of the complications."

"Understandable. Who did they love?"

"Each other."

"Oh. Oh! Okay. Awww. So they died together in battle. That's nice."

"The brotherhood does not involve itself with who is doing what to whom as long as it doesn't disrupt the workings of the brotherhood."

"So, in other words, your love for me will never die."

Gemma started to say something but realized it wouldn't really make much of a difference and walked on instead.

Moving past two castle guards whose stumbling she ignored, knowing Quinn would catch them in his arms, she continued to follow the man they were protecting. Quinn kept the two guards walking until he could move them off to the side, sitting them under a tree so they looked as if they'd fallen asleep there and had not been poisoned at a distance by the divine assassins.

Gemma put her arm around the small man the castle guards had been shadowing and pressed her fingers against his throat.

"You're going to be calm and quiet," she told him as they kept walking while Quinn came up on the man's other side. "You're not going to cry out or call any attention to yourself. Do you understand me?"

"Yes."

"If you do what I tell you, I won't kill you. If you don't, you'll be begging me to kill you."

CHAPTER 26

Aubin and Léandre met the divine assassins outside the castle walls.

"They're in," Faraji said, referring to the war monk and the centaur.

"All right," Aubin replied. "We'll get inside from below. Keep the way clear for them and hopefully make sure they don't get caught. And you?"

"The war monk wants us to kill the queen," Tadesse said plainly.

Aubin rubbed his eye. "She is not letting that go."

"She sort of promised the other sister she wouldn't do it herself unless she had a clear shot."

"That doesn't mean you have to do it."

"No. But I did say I'd at least try."

"Remember we promised her sister we wouldn't get killed either."

"We'll keep it in mind. Good luck to you."

"You too."

The two once mortal enemies amiably separated.

Aubin and Léandre made their way around to the east side of the castle and another secret entrance, this one built into the ground. Aubin approached the guards at the entrance and kindly asked, "Excuse me, good sirs. I was wondering if you could show my brother priest and me where the religious sects are congregating."

"Yeah. Sure." One of the guards stepped forward to point out the way and Aubin cut his throat with his dagger.

When the second guard turned, pulling his sword, Léandre stabbed him in the back of the neck.

Together, they quickly opened the grate built into the ground, threw the dead bodies in, and scrambled down after them. They secured the grate once they were inside and pulled the bodies along for a bit so that they weren't the first thing anyone would see if someone happened to look inside.

Once they'd gone a few feet, they dropped the bodies and kept walking until they eventually arrived at a split in the tunnel.

"Which way should we go?" Léandre asked.

"Let our god tell us." Aubin threw his black steel spear into the air and waited until it fell. The point landed aiming to the left.

"Left."

Léandre nodded. "I love the simplicity of our religion. Don't you?"

"I do, old friend. I do."

Hurik walked beside the vicar. She didn't mind being stuck with Ferdinand. Not as much as the others would, anyway. Besides, it made sense that a nun and a truce vicar would be together. There were many more questions asked here about the religious refugees than in Queen Keeley's realm. The sight of her wandering around with witches or divine assassins would definitely raise alarms among the castle guards that roamed the streets questioning anyone they felt looked "out of place."

No. This wasn't like Queen Keeley's realm at all. Not that Keeley's territory didn't have its own sets of problems and concerns. For one thing, it was definitely a smaller principality. But that wasn't the only issue that bothered Hurik about this kingdom. There was something different in the air here. In the way the people looked. The energy of those around her.

Hurik had been here before when the Old King lived. He was like most who'd been born and raised knowing he would one day be king and then, when he was king, knew he would *always* be king. An arrogant fool of a man who believed everyone had been put in his path to be of use to him and nothing more.

Yet . . . nothing felt the same here. Nothing felt right.

"Stand back!" guards called out, pushing merchants and towns-people out of the way. "The queen comes!"

And she did come. A rather plain, small woman who would look more comfortable in a nun's habit than she did in the pink silk dress with gold trim that she currently wore. Her pale brown hair was piled high on her head and she had an entourage of royals following her, though Hurik had a feeling she had absolutely no interest in them beyond the fact that she was making them follow *her*. It was hard to believe that this woman was related in any way to Queen Keeley or Brother Gemma. She seemed so small and insignificant compared to them. Not in physical size—though there was truth to that—but in energy and vitality. The young sister that ran around with the tiny steel hammer seemed to be more interesting than this Beatrix, who focused on scrolls as she walked toward the castle.

The vicar began to raise his hand to catch the queen's attention. They were supposed to be a distraction to the queen while the war monk and centaur searched for information. But Hurik grabbed his arm, halting him.

"What?" Ferdinand asked. "What is it?"

Before she could answer the vicar, the queen's head snapped up and she was looking right at them with those eyes. Those eyes that didn't seem to have anything behind them. Yes, there was intelligence. Great intelligence. But no sympathy, no empathy.

Even worse, she continued staring at them. At the two of them specifically.

Hurik lowered her head and led the vicar into a crowd of merchants.

"What's wrong?" he demanded. "What did you see?"

"Nothing good," she told him.

Gemma led her captive to the secret door she'd spotted on the map and was happy to find it still there. Quinn eased it open and took a quick look around.

"It's clear," he said, pulling the man inside. Gemma followed, closing the door behind them.

Once inside, Gemma stood in front of the man and said, "I'm here for information and I've been told you're the one to see about it. They say you're very close to Queen Beatrix."

"You want me to lead you to her?"

"Well—"

"This is a test, isn't it?" he suddenly accused, bursting into tears. "Why is she doing this to me? Why is she testing me? I don't know how else to prove my loyalty. I don't know what else to do! *What does she want from me?*"

Gemma wasn't sure what was happening. Was this all just a performance? Was the man trying to catch her off guard, slice her with an unseen knife when she stepped in to comfort him? She didn't know. But there were so many tears! And his entire body was shaking.

She looked at Quinn but he just shrugged. This wasn't exactly going according to plan. A knife to the throat, a few threats. That's how it was supposed to go.

"I'm not testing you," Gemma told him. "I don't work for your queen. I'm really threatening you for information. I promise."

He'd buried his face in his hands and now lifted a bit so he could look up at her.

"You . . . you're not?" he asked.

"No. You are truly in danger from me."

"Really?"

"Yes. Really."

"Then kill me."

What was happening now?

"Pardon?"

He dropped to his knees. "Kill me. Now. Please. If you have any kindness in your heart at all. Kill me!"

"You know, when I said you would beg me to kill you . . . that was just a threat. You don't actually *have* to beg me to kill you. It's not required."

"But you could do it. You're a war monk. It'll be easy for you. Just do it!"

Gemma grabbed the man's arm and pulled him to his feet. "Get ahold of yourself! I'm not killing you. You haven't done anything to warrant such a thing."

"But a war monk kills for his god all the time."

"That's not the point. Calm down. Look, lad, I really just want information. If you can provide it, I'll be on my way. No need to kill you or test you. I get the information and I'm out of your life."

"What information?"

"I need to know what building project your queen is hiding from the king."

The man looked away. "You mean the tunnel."

"See? Already we're helping each other and without any bloodshed. Isn't that nice?" Gemma couldn't believe this. She was supposed to be threatening the man not soothing him or making him feel better about his life with Beatrix. "Now . . . what can you tell me about this tunnel she's having built?"

"Very little. She knows I fear her husband. Knows that if he asks me anything, I'll tell him because I'm terrified of him."

"Okay."

"I'm sorry."

"No, no. No need to apologize. Or cry. Please don't cry. Just breathe. Just breathe through it." Gemma briefly wondered if she should kill him out of mercy, but instead asked, "Does she keep all the information in her head or does she still hide things in plain sight?"

His eyes narrowed in distrust while he began to breathe heavily in fear. "How do you know she does that unless you're testing me?"

Gemma sighed. "Are we back here again?"

"Yes. Because how else would you know that unless she told you?"

"Because I am her sister."

"Prove it."

Gemma let out a long sigh. "Fine. She's got a scar behind her ear. That's where I once slammed her head into the dining table, but my sister Keeley caught me, and the next thing I knew, we were in a fistfight on the kitchen floor. Anyway, if anyone happened to ask Beatrix about the scar, her response was always to stare at that person until they became so frightened, they never asked about it again. Although the reason I slammed her head on that table . . . she knows what she did."

The man wiped his tears. "Yes. You are her sister."

304 • G.A. Aiken

"Yes. I am. Now that we know the truth of my words, what's your name?"

"Agathon."

"But you have an official title. At least that's what I was told."

"I am the Queen's Follower of Her Word. I used to be the Old King's but now I am the queen's. And you're right. She still hides things in plain sight."

"Do you think you can help me find out about that tunnel?"

"I'll do my best. Then will you kill me?"

"*Or*," Gemma said, putting her arm around his shoulders, "we will come up with another option that doesn't involve your untimely death."

Ima climbed to the top of the hill that looked down onto the Old King's castle. She rested her hands on her hips and tried to get her breath back.

"Is your whole body so weak?" Balla asked.

She wanted to make a rude reply to the temple virgin, but she was still trying to catch her breath, so Ima let it go. At least they weren't trapped inside the castle along with everyone else. She hadn't been in there herself, but she'd never heard anything good happening to the witches who ended up in that place.

She and Balla weren't merely waiting for everyone to come out. When the time was right, the witches and temple virgins had tasks and they were the only ones who could perform them. And if they hoped to be ready *then*, they would have to start their work now.

Wassa opened her ingredient bag and took out what they would need to begin. The temple virgins, not too far away, did the same. All four women would be using nature, but it was strange to be doing such work with a temple virgin so close. Unlike the war monks, the temple virgins had never attempted to burn her coven-sisters at the stake. Of course, Ima couldn't say that her sect had never used temple virgins as sacrifices back when they did that sort of thing more openly.

Yet here they were. Not exactly working together, but combining their powers to help other onetime enemies.

Ima had to stop for a moment.

"What's wrong?" Wassa asked.

"This is strange, isn't it? What we're doing?"

"Not as strange as that," Wassa replied, nodding toward the bottom of the hill, where they'd left all the horses.

Thankfully, the team's horses were just fine. All of them safe. But the war monk's half-dead horse had taken hold of a grazing elk by the neck and was swinging it around and slapping it against the ground like a dog playing with a dead cat it had found. It beat the poor elk against the ground until it stopped trying to fight and then the horse began to feed. Tearing flesh from the animal's neck and stomach, tearing out the ribs so it could devour the organs.

Ima, now sitting on the ground and preparing to create a power circle, nodded at Wassa. "No, no. You're right. That's definitely stranger."

Tadesse eased his way behind merchant stalls, doing his best to avoid the castle guards. He waited until they'd passed, then moved on until he caught up with Faraji. They slid into a group of religious travelers making their way into a section of the castle. He had no idea where this line led and wasn't too worried until he realized there was some kind of entrance process, which seemed strange. In Queen Keeley's queendom, the religious sects simply had to show up and she took them in. They didn't have to sign anything or give anyone their name or information.

The last thing two divine assassins wanted to do was put their names on any list. Unlike assassin guild members, divine assassins didn't become grand masters of disguise. They blended into their surroundings and hid their physical identities, but they didn't hide their religious affiliation.

That meant they had to get out of this line before they reached the front of it and caught the attention of the castle guards.

Tadesse touched the tips of his fingers to his silk robe and unleashed his magick. He felt it slither down his clothing and slip into the ground, separating out into several tendrils.

When he heard the first screamed "Snake!" he and Faraji stepped out of line and quickly moved away. They made their way around the castle walls and attempted to get to one of the hidden doorways they'd seen on the maps. But when they were only a few feet away, they were surrounded by castle guards and a guard captain, all aiming spears at them.

"Halt, monsters!" the captain ordered. "And raise those hands."

Tadesse gritted his teeth but did as ordered. The divine assassins were tethered to the ground. They needed their fingers and palms to touch inanimate objects. Dirt, wood, even steel. With a touch of his fingers, Tadesse could send his poisons or his "pets" to do his bidding. But with his hands in the air . . . he could do nothing but wait until they speared him and Faraji through like meat on a spit.

"Hold, good gentlemen!" Tadesse heard behind him, shocked how relieved he was to hear *that* particular voice.

The truce vicar and the Abbess came to the captain's side.

"What's happening?" the vicar demanded. "These men are with us!"

"They are divine assassins. We cannot allow them on royal lands to put our king and queen at risk."

"But they're our protectors." The vicar stepped in front of the spears aimed at Tadesse and Faraji.

"Assassins are protecting you? You expect us to believe that?"

"How do you think we made it this far, good lord? Without their help, we would have met our tragic ends on the sword tips of Cyrus's men."

"Sister?" The captain focused on the Abbess. "Is this true?"

Slowly, the Abbess lifted her head, dark eyes filled with such pain and fear that Tadesse wanted nothing more than to push all these men away and take her somewhere safe, where she could never be harmed again. By anyone. Which was, of course, ridiculous, because he'd seen this woman fight. He'd seen her strip the flesh off her victims as if she was skinning a chicken for dinner. She needed no one really.

"If it had not been for these men," the Abbess said in the softest voice humanly possible, "I would not be alive at this moment. They saved me from Cyrus's men. Those villains had me trapped in a valley many leagues from here and these honorable men not only rescued me, but gave me their protection all the way here. I never had to worry about my safety or my . . ." She gently cleared her throat.

"Purity," she whispered. "Something I can assure you I would have lost had Cyrus's soldiers had their way."

She covered her face, barely heard sobs coming from behind her hands, and turned toward the vicar.

"Good sirs," the vicar said, "you cannot take these honorable men away from us. Not now, when we rely on them so much."

The captain swung his finger and the soldiers brought their spears up so they weren't pointing directly at Tadesse and Faraji, but the men didn't move away.

"Stay here. I'll be back," he ordered.

Once the captain was gone, the vicar patted Tadesse and Faraji, calmly telling them to put their arms down, even as the soldiers immediately grew tense again.

"It's all right, lads," the vicar soothed. "Everything will be all right."

The captain returned and motioned toward them. "Come on then."

"Come where?" the vicar asked.

"Queen Beatrix would like to meet with you, Vicar." He smiled. "And all your . . . friends."

Uh-oh.

Quinn and Gemma searched through Her Majesty's room but found nothing. They'd also searched the king's study, his privy chamber, her privy chamber, the queen's study. Thankfully the rooms had been close by and they'd been able to avoid most of the castle guards. Not easy. They were as numerous as the rats in the walls. Keeley's castle didn't have any rats . . . Quinn was sure that was due to the demon wolves.

For the first time ever . . . he loved those demon wolves. Because he hated rats.

"What about the library?" Quinn asked, which got him nothing but matching looks of disdain from Gemma and the Follower of Her Word.

"What?"

"That's a little obvious, isn't it?" Gemma asked.

"I thought obvious was the point."

"Not *that* obvious."

"Her husband has the library searched thrice weekly," the Follower—er . . . uh . . . Agathon—informed them.

"There is not a lot of trust between them, is there?" Quinn noticed. What a sad marriage. It seemed the pair went out of their way to spend as little time together as they could manage. There were even rooms, apparently, just for the king's women. Women who had been handpicked by the queen, according to Agathon. Women she allowed him to use for his "sexual needs but who knew their place."

Quinn couldn't imagine living like that.

After all these years and despite all the bickering, his parents still slept together and still found things to laugh about. Mostly others' misfortune, but they still laughed. What they didn't do was search each other's things like Marius and Beatrix.

"Does Marius search himself or just have servants do it all?" Gemma asked.

"Well, since King Marius cannot . . ."

Gemma stopped searching and turned to Agathon. "Cannot . . . what?"

The Follower cleared his throat. "Read."

She sneered. "My sister must be making full use of that."

"She is, I'm afraid. But he uses his mother to assist him."

Gemma began to pace. "Where else can we look? Some place obvious but not too obvious."

"And where her husband doesn't obsessively look," Quinn said, sitting on the bed.

Gemma jerked to a stop, her arms swinging wildly. Her reaction was so exaggerated that both males leaned away from her.

"Agathon, is Marius like his father?"

"In what way?"

"Does he have a lot of bastard children?"

"Um . . . yes. From the years before he was married to Queen Beatrix. I think he's afraid to have any now."

"Are they here? In the castle?"

"They're still the children of the king, so yes. They're taught by pacifist monks along with the other children."

"What other children?"

"Queen Beatrix has brought other royal children here and keeps them in the castle to ensure the . . . uh . . . loyalty of their parents."

"She's holding them hostage?" Quinn asked.

"She doesn't put it that way."

"Where's the classroom?" Gemma asked.

"It's a room in the monks' tower." Agathon's eyes grew wide and, for the first time, he began to smile. "Oh. I see."

"Because I'm guessing King Marius never sees his bastard children. Just as his father never saw *his* bastard children even though they all lived in the same castle."

"Can we get to the tower from here?" Quinn asked.

"Yes, but the monks, they might be a problem."

Gemma smiled, which did not put Quinn at ease.

"I'll deal with the pacifist monks."

Quinn couldn't help but ask, "You're not going to *kill* the monks . . . are you?"

Gemma turned to him. "Why would you even ask me that?"

With a grimace, Quinn admitted, "That's not really an answer."

She walked away from him.

"*Still* not an answer."

Ferdinand knew that the Abbess and the assassins were uncomfortable. He didn't blame them. But he wasn't yet ready to rule out the possibility of negotiating a peace with Queen Beatrix. Maybe they could avoid a war between these two strong queens. Maybe dividing the lands between the two was a new way to approach the situation, a new way to deal with a changing way of life. He knew the sisters had a lot of bad blood between them, but bad blood could be dealt with. He just needed to find out what he was dealing with on both sides.

He'd already looked into the eyes of Queen Keeley. She was stubborn, clear-eyed, extremely naïve, and only average when it came to the knowledge of the ancients—at least concerning subjects not having to do with the blacksmithing arts. The thing he appreciated most about Queen Keeley was her good heart. She cared about others. It wasn't a necessity for a ruler, but it didn't hurt.

Now he just needed to assess Queen Beatrix, and without all the hatred the war monk spit out anytime her younger sister's name was mentioned.

All four of them were led into the Old King's castle. Midday meal was currently underway. Long dining tables were arranged around three sides of the room, with the king and queen at the very head.

Four servants brought up four chairs and placed them across the table from the king and queen. Ferdinand, Hurik, and the two assassins were led to the chairs. The guards pushed the two assassins onto theirs but simply directed him and the nun to their seats. It seemed rude that no food or drink was offered to their little group, but that could have been a simple oversight. He wouldn't hold that against anyone at this point.

Ferdinand studied the room. The lower-level royals had no interest in them at all. They continued eating and talking amongst themselves. The king also had no interest in their presence. He was busy speaking to a very pretty and very young woman next to him, who seemed flattered by his attention. If the queen was bothered by this, she didn't show it. And the longer Ferdinand watched, the more certain he was that, no, the queen wasn't bothered at all by the king's lack of attention to her and his obsessive interest in this young woman.

The queen herself wasn't completely alone. She had a mystic sitting next to her. A mystic that Ferdinand immediately recognized. His name was Ivan. His hair was very long now but it still didn't look as if he washed it as often as he should. He wore only black and ate with his hands. He was not affiliated with any sect, because none would have him. Ferdinand didn't know which god or gods Ivan worshipped because Ivan never mentioned any.

And yet here he sat, next to a queen.

When their eyes locked, Ivan nodded at him and Ferdinand nodded back, but that was all the acknowledgment he was going to give him. His patience with others could only be stretched so far.

"So you all traveled together," the queen finally said. She wasn't much for preamble, was she? No welcome, no offers of food or drink, and not even a perfunctory smile.

"We did, Your Majesty," Ferdinand replied. "If not for these good men, we would not have survived."

"And you're a truce vicar, yes?"

"I am. Here to smooth the way for all involved. So if there's anything I can do for you, Queen Beatrix, please just let me know. I would love to assist you in any way to avoid tensions between yours and any other realm."

"Even Prince Cyrus?"

"That would be difficult . . . since he keeps killing rather than listening to reason."

She gave what might be considered a chuckle and glanced at Ivan, the pair sharing a moment. "Excellent point, Vicar."

"Of course, your assistance with fighting Prince Cyrus would be greatly appreciated," he noted.

She lifted her gaze to Ferdinand's and, in that moment, it was as if an icy wind had slammed into his back. He couldn't explain it. He was not sure he wanted to. It was just something he felt.

"We have been doing our best," the queen said. Ferdinand noticed that she kept her sentences short. Probably to hide her peasant accent. An accent her sisters didn't bother to disguise. "Sending out protection units."

"But an army to go toe-to-toe with him . . . ?"

"We're doing our best."

A soldier entered the room and walked over to the queen. Leaning down, he whispered in her ear. Her jaw tightened and she said, "Then find him. *Now.*"

Certain she must have noticed that her personal assistant was missing, Ferdinand kept himself facing forward and his expression artfully blank.

"So Ivan," he said, smiling at the mystic, "what brings you here to our lovely queen's side?"

Gesturing with both grease-covered hands to the air around them, he vaguely replied, "All things. For instance"—he dropped his arms to the table and stared at Ferdinand—"I am simply *fascinated* by this little friendship you four seem to have. Not too long ago your sects were all such enemies."

"War makes strange bedfellows, does it not, old friend?"

Ivan gazed at Ferdinand for a long moment. "If you say so . . . old friend."

* * *

With the children off for the midday meal with their parents—the only time they got with their mothers and fathers, and all under the watchful eyes of castle guards—the monks could not only get some time to eat but some quiet time to themselves as well. Blissful, wonderful quiet.

How they all missed it.

Most pacifist monk orders only dealt with children sent to them as orphans who would, one day, become pacifist monks themselves. That meant they were taught the ways of the order from the beginning, especially the practice of quiet meditation and worship of the suns god. But to secure their own safety in the Old King's castle, away from Prince Cyrus and his mad armies, these monks had been forced to agree to teach the royal children. Not the ways of their order, but simple things like language, math, history. On a good day, the children were loud and demanding. And, as royals, they could only be reprimanded but so much. It was daunting to say the least.

Yet none of the brothers could complain. At least they were alive. Many of their comrades were dead, their souls lost when Cyrus's soldiers tortured and killed them before burning down their monasteries, eon-long symbols of safety and healing.

They'd heard the nuns had not been doing well either in this political climate. Who would attack defenseless women?

The door to the schoolroom opened and the queen's Follower of Her Word rushed in with a . . . Oh, by the good blessings of the suns!

The brothers looked at each other in panic and their leader quickly motioned them out, into the safety of the upstairs cells.

The war monk swept into the classroom. She'd brought some kind of barbaric pet with her. It wore a kilt and had unruly hair. Weren't war monks bad enough? But now they dragged Amichais around with them like pet dogs as well?

She had her arms behind her back, her fur cape sweeping the floor at her feet. She glared at everything in the room as if she was *looking* for something out of order.

"Yes, Agathon?" he asked.

"Sorry to interrupt, Brother. This—"

"Yes. I know what she is. What do you want here?" he asked the war monk directly.

"Are you questioning me?" she demanded.

"Well, if you want my help—"

"Show me your papers."

"What papers?"

"All your papers. *Now.*"

He had no idea what this woman was asking for, but he knew better than to challenge a war monk. He'd been a pacifist monk since he was a child and he remembered the day he'd watched the Abbot's head roll down the stairs after he'd questioned a war monk's demands. It could have happened yesterday, the memory was so clear.

Not wanting to relive that day yet again, he led them up the stairs to the small private library where the brothers worked on translations and hand-published prayer books.

Agathon, the war monk, and the Amichai searched the room carefully but, to his surprise, they never once ripped anything apart, which he'd truly expected. He'd thought he and his brothers would be cleaning up after the monk and her dog for days. Yet they were very careful—almost . . . respectful?—of their work until the war monk suddenly gasped and said, "I think I've found it!"

The three huddled together and looked over some scrolls he did not recognize, their gazes scanning each one, their expressions growing more somber with every passing moment.

The brothers who were in the room watched the intruders with horror, but they wouldn't leave these strangers alone among their important work. So they stood by and waited for the real ugliness to set in.

Agathon turned back to the table where the war monk had found the scrolls.

"Look. I think I found a—"

The door swung open and the castle guards stood there.

"Lord Agathon, are you . . ."

He knew, as soon as he saw the expressions on the guards' faces change from relief at finding the queen's Follower of Her Word to shock at the presence of the others, that something was terribly wrong.

"Get out!" he yelled at his brothers. "Get out now!"

That's when the war monk grabbed Agathon from behind and put a knife to his throat. Confusing, since the Follower seemed to be helping the two outsiders.

"Oh, uh . . . help," Agathon suddenly announced. "Yes. Help me! I'm in, uh . . . great danger!"

With the blade against Agathon's throat and the Amichai brandishing his spear, the three went out a side door, slamming it behind them and securing something against it. The guards ran after them, hurling themselves against the wood until it splintered and broke so they could keep up the chase.

A few minutes later, the rest of his brothers returned.

"Are you all right?" one of them asked.

"I am."

"Do you know what they took?"

"No. Because we didn't see anything," he told them. "They were simply . . . trying to escape."

"They were?"

He blew out a breath. "They were, Brothers. They absolutely were, and that's exactly what we will tell anyone who asks us *anything*."

Gemma bolted down a back staircase, pulling poor Agathon behind her. Quinn took the lead, spearing any guards that got in their way.

"Should we be killing them?" Quinn asked, after he'd killed a few more.

"Yes." Now that they had what they needed, she wanted Beatrix to believe they'd come here to kill her. Not to steal information. She didn't want her sister to follow her to where they were going. At least not yet.

"Where would my sister normally be now, Agathon?"

"Main hall most likely."

"We're *looking* for her now?" Quinn asked, turning and shifting to centaur, simply so he could use his hind legs to kick several soldiers in the chest and out of their way.

"You knew the plan would change, Quinn, if we got to this point. Or were you not listening again?"

"Should I actually answer that?" he asked, taking his human form again.

They continued through halls, down more backstairs, and through a tunnel until they pushed open a door and practically tumbled into the main hall. All activity stopped and all attention turned on them.

Beatrix's head tilted to the side as she stared at the doorway. When she spotted Agathon, her expression didn't change. But then her gaze locked with Gemma's, and across the hall the sisters stared at each other.

Gemma's sister had matured. She looked a little older. More royal. Colder. This was definitely where Beatrix belonged.

The guards moved to swarm them, and Gemma pulled Agathon close and again put the knife to his throat.

"Hold!" Beatrix commanded, halting everyone in the room.

Leaning back in her chair, Beatrix said, "You didn't really think this was going to work, did you?"

"You know I had to try," Gemma replied.

"Cyrus is out there burning down convents and monasteries and you're worried about *me*? Keeley must be so disappointed in you. Trying to kill your own sister."

"She'll get over it."

"She doesn't know you're here? The out-of-control princess. How not like you."

"What are we waiting for?" Marius demanded. "Kill them."

"She has Agathon."

"You can get a new Follower anywhere. *I'll* get you one. Guards! On my orders—"

"No, no," the queen interrupted, the back of her hand gently touching the king's shoulder. "I want to see *her* do it."

"What?" the king asked.

Beatrix gestured to Gemma. "You heard my husband, Gemma. He can get me a new Follower. I don't need Agathon. So you do it. You slit his throat." She motioned to the guards. "Step away. All of you move back. Now go on, Brother Gemma. Do it."

Gemma let out a sigh. "But you already know I can't."

Beatrix glanced at her guards and said dismissively, "*Now* you can kill them all."

The ink-black snakes, poison dripping from their fangs, appeared before her so fast, Beatrix didn't have time to move. But the long-haired man next to her cut off their heads so quickly Gemma wasn't even sure what weapon he used. He pushed Beatrix back into the guards who stood behind the king and queen and put himself protectively in front of her.

Quinn shifted to centaur and used his hind legs to batter the guards behind him, his spear tearing open the ones in front. Gemma buried her knife into the man closest to her and yanked out her sword to gut a guard that came within range.

She shoved Agathon over to Quinn. "Get on!" she ordered.

"What?"

"Get on!" She didn't wait for Agathon to understand; she simply shoved him onto Quinn's back. She would not leave him behind to face Beatrix's wrath.

She turned and saw the Abbess was tearing a guard's chest open with her split spear. The truce vicar was battering his way through the panicked royals using mostly his brawn. And the assassins were slaughtering the guards any way they could to protect the Abbess and get her outside with the vicar.

"Protect him, Quinn!" Gemma yelled before she charged across the main hall toward her sister.

She grabbed a shield and used it to block spears and swords, while using her own sword to cut a swath through the castle guards.

Her sister watched her, a small group of guards surrounding her and that man with the long hair. The king had already fought his way outside, probably to summon more guards or even his hardened soldiers, meaning Gemma was running out of time.

She slashed at a throat and jumped onto the table where her sister had been sitting. The long-haired man raised his hands and began to chant. Gemma flicked her hand and sent him reeling across the room. She flicked her hand the other way and the guards surrounding her sister flew, leaving Beatrix standing there alone.

Beatrix didn't even flinch, which somehow made this easier for Gemma.

She secured her sword and was charging across the table when she sensed something behind her. Gemma turned and raised her shield at the same time, blocking the soldier's sword just before it could meet with her head.

She fought back as Marius's soldiers advanced on her, then jumped off the table and landed on the ground. But when she glanced over her shoulder, her sister was gone.

More blows came, the shield providing cover until it was finally torn from her hand. She still had her sword, but she had a wall at her back and about twenty soldiers in front—

A black spear was thrust up from the ground, ramming into a soldier's groin. She hadn't seen the grate until it was pushed away and the two war priests emerged from the tunnel underneath. They rammed their spears into the closest enemies and pushed back, allowing Gemma to place her hands on several bodies. She chanted and unleashed her god's power. The dead soldiers jerked back to life and Gemma moved to a few more bodies, raised them too. She then picked up her sword, motioned to the priests and the Abbess, and together they ran for the front doors.

The soldiers outside tried to stop them but they were tackled by their dead cohorts, who chewed their flesh and ripped them open.

Soldiers on horseback charged after them through the streets, ignoring the commoners going about their daily lives. They ran those people down simply because they'd been ordered to stop Gemma and the others.

Thankfully, powerful streaks of lightning rammed into the riders, knocking them off their horses, and damaging parts of buildings so that rubble fell on them.

Gemma and her team reached the town gates but more riders were already closing in. That's when the ground began to shake, spooking their horses. The horses went up on their hind legs, tossing off their riders or, even worse, landing *on* their riders.

Then there were screams and the people began to run. A swirling mass of air and dust drew near and Gemma only had time to yell, "Hold on!" before their entire group was lifted up and carried away, then unceremoniously dropped near their mounts.

Coughing and spitting out the dirt and debris that filled his mouth, Quinn was just grateful to feel ground beneath his ass. Because it was official . . . he did *not* like to fly.

"Sorry about that!" he heard Balla call out. "Never have managed to get that spinning air spell quite right."

He was the first to get to his hooves. He made sure Agathon had survived and then checked on all the others. To his surprise, they'd all made it out alive.

Even . . .

"*You idiot!*" he yelled at Gemma.

She didn't even bother to pretend she didn't know what he was talking about.

"Beatrix was *right there*. I had to try."

"Horseshit! You knew when you attacked that even if you killed her, you wouldn't make it out alive. You knew! But you went anyway. If it hadn't been for the priests, you'd be dead right now."

"You're welcome," Aubin said, walking by them.

"She was right there!" Gemma argued. "All smug. How could I just walk away?"

Quinn simply glared down at her. It was all he could do, really. He knew no words would penetrate that thick Smythe skull of hers.

"He wants to hit you," Balla told her.

"Of course he wants to hit her," Ima chimed in. "*I'd* want to hit her."

"But he's too good a centaur to do such a thing. To knock some sense into you."

"Sadly for you," Wassa added, "not everyone else can say that."

Quinn never expected it to be Kriegszorn to kick Gemma in the face with her back hoof and send the monk head over ass down the hill they'd just been dumped on. But she was very loyal to her rider, and if anything had happened to Gemma after everything the half-dead horse had done to get back to her side . . . well, it wasn't exactly shocking that she'd been the one to make the point.

The truce vicar clapped his hands together and joyfully said, "All right, let's get all our things packed up and be on our way! I'm assuming we know where we're going—is that right, dear sir?"

"It's Agathon. My name is Agathon."

"Yes. Agathon. It's lovely that you've joined us. Why don't I introduce you to everyone?"

"No," everyone else said together.

"No one has time for that," Balla complained.

"Fine. We'll do it on the way."

"*Do* we know where we're going?" Quinn asked Agathon as he watched Gemma pick herself up off the ground below and start back up the hill.

"I think we do."

"What did you lot find anyway?" the Abbess asked.

Quinn let out a breath. "If what I saw was accurate, nothing good."

Gemma ran up onto the hill. "Run!" she said as she charged by. "Everybody go! Run!"

"What?"

"She knows." Gemma mounted Kriegszorn. "She knows where we're going. She's sent out a battalion for us."

"You sure she's just not pissed you tried to kill her?"

"I saw her face when I was charging at her, Quinn. She doesn't care that I tried to kill her. What she doesn't want is me destroying what she's built, which means we need to find it and destroy it. Now."

Quinn grabbed Agathon's hand and hauled him onto his back again. "Hold on tight and be ready to give directions."

With the Follower secure on his back, Quinn took off seconds before the first arrow shot past him.

CHAPTER 27

Ainsley kept low and moved carefully through the bushes. She could see that Cyrus's wizards had created at least five totems and each totem had several artifacts melded to it. They were spaced around Cyrus's camp, and from what she was guessing, each of them would have to be destroyed before anything truly magickal could get near Cyrus. That meant only Keeley, Ainsley, and Keeley's human troops would be able to attack him.

That would not be easy. Cyrus had more soldiers than Keeley did. Ainsley wished now that they had brought the war monks with them. She understood why they hadn't, but Keeley could certainly use their skills even if the war monks couldn't get near Cyrus.

Maybe if they could . . .

Ainsley froze, attempting to blend into the world around her. But it was too late for any of her hunting tricks now. Because someone was standing right next to her.

A hand reached down and grabbed her by the back of the neck lifting her off her feet. She dangled there, like a fool, unable to reach her bow, while he ripped her quiver off her belt, tossing it aside.

She expected the man holding her to say something but he spoke no words. He simply carried her back to his camp and to Cyrus.

The arrows kept coming and so did the battalion.

Gemma was right. These soldiers weren't trying to protect their queen. They were trying to stop the outsiders from escaping. And the harder their team rode, the harder the battalion came after them.

"They're not going to stop!" Aubin called out.

"They're part of Her Majesty's guard!" Agathon yelled over the pounding hooves. "Her hand-chosen men! They're loyal only to her!"

"Fuck!" Gemma roared, pulling on the reins of her horse and turning the beast around.

"What are you doing?"

"Go ahead, Quinn. You know what to do!"

"Gemma!"

"Go!"

The Abbess turned her horse and Ima did the same. They followed Gemma while Quinn, ignoring what he wanted to do, kept going forward.

"Queen Keeley!"

Keeley came out of her tent and looked in the direction Ragna was pointing. One of Cyrus's soldiers held her younger sister by the neck from the top of an extremely tall trebuchet.

"What the fuck?" She looked around at the others. "What the fuck is Ainsley doing over there?"

"She was scouting the area," Laila explained.

"Why the fuck was she doing that?"

Laila faced her. "You *told* her to."

"I did?"

"Yes. You looked right at her and said, 'Ainsley, go scout the area. See if we can find a way into Cyrus's territory.' "

Keeley gritted her teeth, scrunched up her face, and finally growled, "*Shit! Shit, shit, shit!*"

She really did have to start paying more attention to her sister.

"What do you want to do?" Laila asked.

"Ragna."

Smirking, the war monk held out her hand and her squire placed her long bow in her palm. She nocked her arrow and aimed.

"Keeley, don't do this," Laila practically begged. "This isn't Ainsley's fault."

"I know that. Don't you think I know that? Ragna, fire."

Ragna released the arrow and it flew out of their camp, across the valley, over Cyrus's camp, and into the throat of the man holding Ainsley. He took a step back, a step forward, and then, before he died and his body fell, he lost his grip on Ainsley and she dropped from that great height.

They briefly lost sight of her as she disappeared among the trees. But Keeley wasn't surprised when she climbed back to the top of the trebuchet a minute or two later and gestured at her with two fingers.

"*You heinous bitch!*" Ainsley screamed at her, the distance insignificant when she was this angry.

Keeley laughed until she realized that Laila was gawking at her.

"What?" she asked the female centaur. "She used to fall from treetops all the time when she was little, but she taught herself to catch a branch on the way down. Then she'd climb back up."

"There is something really wrong with all you Smythes."

"*Keeley!*" Caid bellowed, galloping toward her. "Cyrus's troops are attacking our rear flank!"

"Laila, send in your troops to protect our flank and push back Cyrus's men."

"Centaurs! With me!"

"Generals! Follow me!" Keeley reached one hand behind her back and pulled out her hammer. "And on my orders, *charge!*"

Gemma rode Kriegszorn straight into the battalion sent out to stop her. She knew her sister was attempting to keep her from discovering something specific. Not just that she was building some tunnel. She could only hide the tunnel for so long. It was something else. Something Gemma hadn't had a chance to read about in all those scrolls.

If making sure Keeley found out about what Beatrix was up to meant sacrificing herself, Gemma was more than ready to do it.

She pushed Kriegszorn hard, and the horse seemed more than happy to be pushed. As she neared the men, Gemma took her feet out of the stirrups, and brought one leg over the saddle. She grabbed the pommel with one hand. When the riders were just a few feet away, Gemma let go of the pommel and curled into a ball so she rolled with the fall.

When she finished rolling, she came out of it in a crouch, yanked her gladius from its sheath, and swung her sword into the horse legs going by, cutting the animals' tendons so their big bodies went down fast and very hard. As their riders hit the ground with them, she stabbed them in the spine or chest, whichever was available.

A horse reared up behind her and Gemma turned, ready to strike, but Kriegszorn rammed her body into the animal, taking it and its rider to the ground.

The Abbess used her battle staff to break backs and necks, occasionally splitting it into two pieces so she could bury the spear tips into faces, thighs, and groins.

Ima didn't have time for chants and spells; instead, she used a long dagger in each hand to stab and cut any soldier that got too close to her.

A soldier came at Gemma from behind, slamming her face-first onto the ground. She still held her sword but a foot slammed down on her hand, pinning it to the ground, and another soldier came at her with a spear.

She began to spit out the spell that would knock over one of the men, which might give her a chance to fight back. But then she heard Ima scream, and suddenly flames were exploding all around Gemma. They didn't cover her, but were close enough that they were burning her sword arm. She could feel the skin on her forearm bubbling. The men that had surrounded her were screaming as their bodies burned.

When it stopped and Gemma could move again, she rolled onto her back and quickly realized she was looking up at Kriegszorn.

Her horse leaned down and licked her burned arm. She hoped the move would heal the wound. It did not. If anything, it seemed to make it worse.

Gemma screamed out and Kriegszorn backed away from her.

"It's all right," Gemma soothed, reaching up to pet her. "It's all right."

One of the soldiers shoved a spear into Kriegszorn's side. Gemma screamed again, but this time in horror as her horse stumbled to the side and fell over.

"No! Kriegszorn!"

Gemma crawled to her side, pressed her head against her horse's snout. "My sweet girl. Not again."

"Gemma," she heard Hurik call. "Gemma, please. Move back."

"No. I won't leave her again."

"Gemma, you don't understand. Move back."

"No!"

Gemma's fingers twitched and she realized she no longer felt horse's hair under her fingers but bone.

She lifted her head. The remaining soldiers still surrounded her but none had attacked. Although this would be the perfect time to do so. What were they waiting for then?

Gemma looked down at Kriegszorn. Her hide was mostly gone, leaving bone and flesh . . . and rage.

So much rage.

Now Gemma moved away and her horse slowly got to her feet. A moment later she was gone.

They all looked around but no one seemed to see Kriegszorn until Hurik pointed behind the soldiers.

Although it would be more accurate to say she pointed behind . . . and up.

Kriegszorn's roar shook the ground they stood on. The flame that came from her nostrils set the nearby trees and bushes on fire. And she'd grown so tall. Bigger than any centaur. Too big to ride. She went up on her hind legs and Hurik grabbed Gemma's burned arm, ignoring her scream of blinding pain, and yanked her toward her own horse, Scandal. They ran and mounted him, setting off at a gallop, with Ima and her horse close behind.

Gemma looked over her shoulder to see Kriegszorn's front legs come down hard, landing on some of the soldiers that didn't move out of her way fast enough and instantly crushing them under her hooves. She picked others up in her giant maw and gulped them down in one or two bites.

The last thing Gemma *felt* without even looking back was fire sweeping through the forest behind them.

"Did you do that?" Gemma had to ask Ima as they rode on.

And the look the witch gave her. It almost made Gemma ashamed.

"*Are you joking?*" the witch demanded in a voice so high, birds took off from the trees and nearby wolves howled although it was the middle of the day.

For hours Keeley attempted to get past Cyrus's army to reach the man himself. She needed him dead. Not simply because he was such a bastard—although he was—but because without him, his fanatics would have no true leader. She needed to stop him here and now, but she couldn't get close to him.

Even worse, Ragna, the centaurs, and anyone else with even a sliver of magick about them were unable to cross some invisible barrier that protected him. All because of those damn totems.

She needed to destroy them so the others could wipe out Cyrus's protective soldiers and she could take on Cyrus directly. But the power emanating from the totems made them impossible to approach, even for Keeley, who found herself dizzy and confused when she got too close. Even Ainsley's well-aimed arrows couldn't touch the stupid things. Her aim was true but each time she shot an arrow, it skittered off to the side, frustrating poor Ainsley, who still hadn't forgiven Keeley for letting her fall from that trebuchet.

Screaming that she was an abomination, one of Cyrus's soldiers ran toward Keeley. She swung her hammer and knocked him several feet forward. Even with his chest caved in, he was still moving, and Keeley didn't want to leave him there suffering. She walked up to him and swung her hammer overhead. But he managed to roll over and her hammer hit the ground instead of his head.

That's when she saw a tree several feet away shake, the snow on its branches and limbs fall to the ground.

Keeley immediately forgot about the soldier at her feet and she jogged over to the edge of the hill near where she was currently fighting. She looked out over everything. Cyrus's military camp. The totems. Where the battles were taking place. Everything.

Then she studied the mountainside that Cyrus had at his back and looked down at her hammer.

"What?" Caid asked, coming up beside her. While his sister

continued to protect their flank from the onslaught of Cyrus's men, he'd insisted on remaining near her side.

"I need you to pull back our troops."

"What? Why?" She whistled for the gray mare that she still rode into battle. She kept thinking the horse would leave her, but so far, she hadn't. Although she had found herself another wild herd to run with near the castle and had given birth to another foal. But when Keeley put on her chainmail and weapons, there the gray mare was, waiting for her by the stables, snapping at poor Samuel or any of the stable hands when they got too close to her with Keeley's saddle.

The gray mare galloped to her side and Keeley mounted her.

"Just do it, Caid. Pull them back. Now!"

"What's happening?" Laila asked when Caid started to pull back their troops. She'd just gotten their portion of the battle under control but that could easily change.

"I have no idea, but be ready to move."

Her party had settled behind some big boulders when Gemma and the others rode up. Quinn had her in a hug before she could say a word. And to his surprise, she didn't complain. She simply hugged him back. Hard.

When they pulled away from each other, she winced as his arm brushed hers, and he caught her sword arm and carefully pulled up the sleeve of her hauberk. He expected to see a wound from an edge weapon but it was a bad burn. That's when it occurred to him that Gemma had ridden up on the back of Scandal with the Abbess.

"Where's Kriegszorn?"

Gemma opened her mouth to speak but Ima suddenly pulled her away and asked Balla, "Are you good at healing burns, virgin?"

"You think you'd be better at that sort of wound, *whore*."

"Could someone just give me something for the pain? I feel the need to start crying."

"We found something," Aubin said, returning with Tadesse. "About a half a mile that way."

As there were no fresh herbs for a poultice, it was decided that treating Gemma's wound would have to wait.

Instead, their group snuck down to the location found by the priest and the assassin. It didn't take long. The tunnel began at the mouth of a mountainside opening. King Marius's soldiers were guarding the area.

But that was not why Gemma had to walk away. Why she nearly ran away.

Quinn followed, finding her behind a large, ancient tree. She was bent over at the waist, her hands on her knees, struggling to breathe. She'd already vomited, and tears spilled from her eyes. They had nothing to do with the pain from her burned arm, though. This was worse.

"How could she?" Gemma kept repeating. "How could she? How could she?"

Quinn crouched next to her, stroking her back and resting his head against hers.

"I wish I had an answer for you," Hurik said, coming around the tree. She had her hands tucked into her white robes, which had been splattered with blood from the battle she'd just fought. "I wish I could tell you it's because your sister is pure evil, a soulless devil who was placed with your family without your parents' knowledge. That you weren't related to her by blood. But you'd know that wouldn't be the truth. You know that there are no easy answers in this world. You know that your sister is simply and sadly very human."

"But she's using slaves," Gemma choked out. "She's using slaves and they're all children. They're all children. They're all children!"

Gemma stood tall, her entire body vibrating with rage. "*She's using children as slaves!*"

"Whose children are those?" Wassa asked.

Agathon began to obsessively rub his forehead. "She convinced King Marius to strike several barbarian tribes. She told him they were endangering some nearby villages. She insisted those troops that are loyal to her were part of the legion the king sent out. They must have taken the children after or even during the battles. And because they're children, she could put the costs of feeding them under expenses for war orphans. King Marius would never know."

"Do we know where this tunnel goes?"

Gemma pushed away from everyone and pulled out her sword. "I don't care where it goes."

Quinn quickly grabbed her, pulling her back against his chest.

"Before you do something very brave and very stupid, remember there are children *in* that tunnel. You start killing the soldiers, the first thing they are going to do . . ."

"We need to get the children out of there," Balla said. "But how?"

"I know my mistress," Agathon warned. "I'm sure the soldiers have been told that if anyone is about to find out anything, they are to eliminate the children first."

"What if you call on your gods?" Hurik suggested.

"All doorways are closed," Ima reminded them. "They don't want Cyrus or his fanatics traveling through them to attack our people."

More calm now, Gemma pulled away from Quinn. "She's been working on this tunnel for two years. Do you think there's a way out on the other end?"

"I saw something about that in the messages to the queen."

Agathon pulled out the scrolls he'd handed off to Aubin, who'd put them in his travel bag. He began to shuffle through them quickly.

"Yes. Here. From the captain in charge about three months ago. He's telling her that they've reached their destination. The tunnel is big enough for the children and one man to get through. But not yet for the armies."

"Gods-dammit!" Gemma snarled, her hands curling into fists. "She's doing all this to launch a bloody attack."

"On who?"

"The crazed queen of whatever whatever. The one that lives in a land filled with dragons." Gemma briefly closed her eyes and blew out a breath. "I can't think about that right now. Okay, so the children can get out on the far side."

"But we don't know how long that trek is. The children might have to run for days."

"Without food or water."

"You know what?" Quinn realized. "All we need to do is get the soldiers *out*."

"What do you mean?"

"We get them out, slaughter them. Then rescue the children and take them to safety in Keeley's territory. We all know she'll happily take care of them until we find out if the barbarians will want them back. They can be a little...strange about that kind of thing."

"We don't know how many troops are in there," Léandre pointed out.

"So we go back home to get more troops and leave these children to be slaves for another day? Another hour? Another second?"

"I'm guessing from your tone, War Monk, that any response I may give would be the wrong one."

"Let's draw the soldiers out and slaughter them all," Hurik said.

"And how do we do that?"

She snorted. "Easy."

Keeley quickly dismounted from the gray mare and sent her back with the other troops.

She had to move fast. Cyrus's archers were already raining arrows down on her. She was just lucky that she was far enough out of range not to get hit. But when they moved closer...

She wasn't even sure her idea would work, but she still had to try before her army was completely exhausted.

Keeley took in a deep breath, lifted her hammer, swung it up and around and then *into* the mountainside.

She took a step back, thinking about trying again and wondering if she was only wasting her time when she realized someone was screaming at her. Keeley turned toward the yelling and she saw that *everyone* was screaming at her. All her troops, the centaurs, even Ragna. They were all screaming at her to run. Run now.

"*Fuck!*" she got out before she started running. Running for her life. Running as she'd never run before.

Even as she heard part of the mountain coming down behind her, she ran. She saw Caid galloping toward her. He circled around her and when he was alongside her, she leaped onto his back and wrapped her arms around his chest.

She looked back and saw part of the mountain sliding down, taking out half of Cyrus's camp in the process as well as two of his totems. He was still partly protected, but she'd opened up an area where the centaurs could get in. She just had to wait until the mountain stopped coming down. . . .

Caid slowed from a gallop to a trot, then stopped completely. He turned and they both saw that everything had finally finished moving, the damage devastating.

That's when Caid asked, "What exactly did those dwarves do to your hammer?"

He loved his queen. She paid him well and was very straightforward. But he couldn't say that he enjoyed his job. Making sure chained children moved rocks out of the way was simply boring. At least most of them weren't too young. The older ones were fairly strong and could be made to move the rocks and dirt faster than the younger ones. But the older they got, the more difficult they became. They tried to get away a lot more often than the little ones and were full of backtalk.

He could think of a thousand things he'd rather do than stand around all day doing this job. But he knew when his year here was finished, the queen would come through for him just as she'd come through for the ones who'd gone before him. Put in a year, she'd promised, and keep your mouth shut, and not only did you get your regular pay, but also a big bonus and a promotion. Bastards that should have stayed privates for decades were already corporals and some even sergeants, all because of Queen Beatrix.

So, yeah, this was not his favorite job. In fact, this would go down as his most hated job. But who cared if it got him his dream in three more months?

"Come on, you," he shouted at some kid. He'd learned long ago not to bother with anyone's name. That was just a quick way to get attached and you didn't want to get attached. That only brought trouble. So "you" and "boy" or "girl" were good enough. Especially for these people. Barbarians. They were barely human as it was.

He heard something and looked around. It was like a crack.

"What?" a fellow soldier asked.

"Did you hear that?"

"Hear what?"

"A weird—"

The two men stared at each other. Now they'd both heard it.

He looked up at the rock ceiling, wondering how sturdy those wooden beam supports were when he heard another loud "crack" and saw a line zigzag through the tunnel.

"*Run!*" he screamed, taking off.

"What about the—"

"Fuck 'em!" he yelled back at his cohorts. "Just run!"

He ran around the slave labor his queen had stolen, shaking off their groping hands, ignoring their screams for help, their pleas for him to unlock their chains, and headed straight for the light of the tunnel exit. He could hear his fellow soldiers right behind him.

"Come on, lads!" he urged them. "Come—"

The bitch opened him up from throat to hip with one slash. Her expression so angry, he thought it could have killed him all on its own. She slashed him again, though, for good measure, and as he dropped, one of his fellow soldiers tripped over his legs and got his head cut off before he even managed to hit the ground.

Keeley rode the gray mare to the third totem, now vastly weakened by the loss of the other two, and with a swing of her hammer, destroyed it. As soon as she did, centaurs swarmed the area, attacking Cyrus's soldiers. She charged on, going after the fourth totem. This time, she and the mare simply rode by, and she swung at the totem, crushing it on impact.

The fifth one was in her sights, but soldiers and wizards surrounded it. She dismounted the gray mare and sent her off.

With the hammer tight in her hand, she approached. Soldiers charged, but she swung her hammer, sending one flying off. She swung the other way and crushed another soldier's leg. When he went down, she bashed in his head.

A wizard stepped forward, raised his hands, and unleashed lightning. She lifted her hammer but it was a poor shield, and the lightning struck her in the chest. But other than stumbling back a few steps . . . Keeley felt nothing. She looked down at the armor Queen Vulfegundis had given her. It wasn't magickal but maybe it absorbed other magicks, keeping her safe from their effects.

Grinning, she continued forward, knocking soldiers and wizards out of her way with a joyous glee she hadn't felt since she'd last been in her old forge. Especially when all the wizards' magickal attacks were simply absorbed by her armor or her weapon.

She bashed in a wizard's entire back and kicked his broken body out of the way, leaving her alone with the totem.

Keeley had just raised her hammer above her head when a voice asked, "Do you really think this will change anything?"

She glanced over her shoulder and saw what she could only guess was Cyrus the Honored standing behind her in his full armor with a sword in his hand.

"I don't know," she told him. "Let's find out."

She brought the hammer down and crushed the last totem into the ground.

With a swipe of her hand, Balla released all the children from their chains.

Unfortunately, there were many more soldiers inside the tunnel than they'd thought. Soldiers willing to fight to the end for their queen. Unwilling to run, even when they believed the stone walls were crumbling around them.

Which meant they had to find a way to get the children who were further back in the tunnel out past them. Because the soldiers seemed determined to keep them inside.

At least Balla knew that she'd unlocked *all* the children in this very long tunnel. Right now, all she could really do was focus on the ones next to her and—Balla gasped, her gaze moving to Priska and Ima, wondering if they'd felt it, too. Felt that shift in universal magicks. Felt the unlocking of mystical doorways that had been closed for so long. Looking at their faces, Balla knew they had. They had all felt the change. And they knew what it meant. Knew what freedom it had just rewarded them with.

"Where do we send them?" Priska asked.

"The other end of the tunnel?"

"Are you sure? I thought we were going to leave it up to Keeley. Where they go."

"The children's villages were destroyed," Hurik replied, fighting two soldiers with her battle staff. "If we leave them in this area and we don't make it out alive, there's a risk they could end up right back under Beatrix's thumb. We can't take that chance. But at the other end . . . they can at least run. Do it, Balla."

The nun was right.

Balla looked at Priska and the witches. With a nod, they all called on their gods, and finally did what they hadn't been able to do in weeks. They opened doorways that allowed them to safely send the children to whatever was on the other end of Beatrix's tunnel.

"Now what?" Ima asked, shoving her dagger into the throat of a soldier.

Balla smiled. The safety of the children had been the only thing holding them back. . . .

Balla opened another doorway and moved everyone out of the tunnel, including herself.

Shocked to be outside and away from obvious danger, Gemma spun on her. "What the hells are you doing?"

"What I need to do."

Balla then flung all the soldiers, including those outside of the tunnel, or those at either end, into the very middle of it. This way, they wouldn't have a chance to escape.

Then she said, "Ima."

Giggling a little, the witch crouched to the ground and dug her hands into the dirt. She began to chant and the earth shook beneath her fingers. In seconds it began to split apart, opening up as the chasm raced down toward the tunnel. When it hit, the entire earth opened beneath it and the tunnel broke in the middle and disappeared inside.

Balla thought maybe she could hear the soldiers screaming but that could have been her imagination. She really didn't know. Or care.

When Ima finished, Balla called up the winds and let the power of them fill in the hole with dirt and rocks until everything was completely covered.

"Huh," the vicar said. "That was efficient."

"The gods opened the doorways, I gather?" Gemma noted.

"They did."

"Why?"

Balla and Ima both shrugged and Balla admitted, "We have no—aaaaaaaah!" she ended on a scream, jerking several feet away. When she'd calmed down, she jerked her thumb over her shoulder. "Your horse is back, Gemma."

"Oh." Gemma forced a smile. "Great."

"Something you want to tell us about Kriegszorn, Gemma?" Quinn asked.

"No. Look at her over there with all her skin and whatnot. She's just a normal-sized, half-dead animal. What's not to love nor ask questions about?"

Keeley faced Cyrus. He wasn't near enough for her to hit him with her hammer. And he was well surrounded by his soldiers.

"Your army is still losing, peasant Queen," Cyrus laughed. "Even with your half-horse abominations."

"If you're so confident, Prince Cyrus, fight me."

"I'm not my brother, foolish woman. You can't goad me into a fight by challenging my manliness. Not when my army can simply wipe out yours and then . . . wipe you out. You see, I have nothing to prove. I have my god on my side. What do you have, heretic?"

A flash of bright light distracted Keeley from the conversation. And when she looked out over the valley, she saw that there was an army of war monks. But it wasn't Ragna's war monks. It was another order. And another. And then another. Plus several orders of war priest armies. And an army of battle witches. An army of temple virgins. A small unit of divine assassins easing out from the nearby trees.

Then it got strange. She heard the sound of a lot of chains and . . . snarling. For a moment she thought her wolves had come too, but it wasn't her wolves. It was a large army of women on horseback. They were barely dressed considering it was wintertime. And covered in thick tattoos. Their horses were even more interesting, though, with bright red eyes . . . and fangs. Sitting beside their horses were something like dogs . . . maybe. Whatever they were, they were snarling and snapping and ready for a fight.

Keeley didn't understand what was happening. She didn't understand how or why all these sects had appeared here now.

Then she saw a gleeful Ragna hanging midway from a trebuchet with one hand, screaming toward Cyrus.

"Do you see, Prince Cyrus?" she called to him. "Your protection is gone! Destroyed by Queen Keeley! Now our gods have opened the doorways and unleashed their mightiest warriors to wreak their revenge. There is no escape for you now! Our gods will have your soul, foolish Prince! And they will have it for eternity!"

Slowly, Keeley faced a now sick-looking Cyrus.

"I guess I have what every god really needs," Keeley said to the fallen prince. "Blacksmithing skills."

Behind her, Keeley heard Ragna bellow out, "My fellow brothers and sisters, destroy Cyrus's sycophants! Kill his followers! Leave none of them alive to ever speak his name! Or the name of his god! It is now that our gods call upon us to take our vengeance in the names of all those we have lost! Let none of our enemies live! *Kill everyone!*"

With that last call, the battle started, but Keeley didn't bother to turn around.

She slapped the head of her hammer into her left hand. "Come on, Cyrus the Honored. Just you and me."

"Kill her!" he ordered his men. "Kill her."

Keeley sighed, not really in the mood to fight a whole bunch of men just to get to that one idiot she absolutely had to kill, but if she had to, she had to.

She raised her hammer but before she even had a chance to swing, something blew past her, and the soldiers charging her disintegrated into ash before they were even close enough to strike.

Stunned, Keeley looked over her shoulder, expecting to see one of the religious groups using their magicks, but they were all too busy destroying Cyrus's other soldiers. Even Ragna wasn't paying attention to Keeley at the moment.

Hearing screams, Keeley looked back and saw that Cyrus was being dragged off the field of battle.

Well . . . that wasn't quite accurate. His *soul* was. His body was still there, on its knees, staring at her. His soul, however, was being dragged away by a god.

The god stopped, turned toward her. "Keeley Smythe." He smiled at her. It was stunning. No one should be that beautiful. Or that giant. Especially with that many scars and open wounds. He must be a war god.

"I am Morthwyl. I and my brother war gods are grateful to you for your help." He lifted Cyrus's soul, shook it a bit. "Stop screaming! It won't help you!" He chuckled.

"This one," he said to Keeley, "and his god have been quite a problem. Killing our followers, without permission. That's not acceptable. But now my brothers and sisters . . . we can have some fun. But we couldn't have without your help. So thank you."

"You're welcome?"

"The body is yours to do with as you will. It's still alive . . . so enjoy!"

He took a few more steps, then abruptly stopped, looked over his shoulder and down at her, adding, "By the way, nice work on your hammer. I mean *before* the dwarves got to it. Don't get me wrong, they did a nice job too. We all know that's their thing. And I can tell you from personal experience that Soiffart, their god, is a cocky fuck. But seriously, the work you did on it before they ever touched it . . . ? Nice. Just thought you'd want to know."

With that, the god went on his way, yelling out, "Hey, boys! I've got something for us to play with!"

Then he was gone, disappearing from her sight.

Keeley didn't know how long she stood there, staring blindly into nothing. Cyrus the Honored sobbed at her feet, screaming about his missing soul.

Long enough, it seemed, for Ragna to show up, demanding to know if Keeley was going to finish off Cyrus or not.

"What?" Keeley asked the war monk.

"Are you going to kill him or not? Or do you want me to do it?"

"I don't care." Keeley hugged her hammer tight against her chest.

"What's wrong with you?"

"He said 'nice work.' About my hammer. He said it. He *meant* it."

"Who meant it?" She looked down at the sobbing prince. "Cyrus?"

"No. The god."

Ragna gave a small laugh. "You're talking to gods now? Who compliment your hammers? We need to get you home, I think."

"It really happened."

"Sure it did."

"He was beautiful. Giant."

"Uh-huh."

"Blond hair. Green eyes. Talked about his war god brothers."

"Of course he did. And I'm sure he loved your work, Your Majesty."

"He even mentioned the dwarves and called their god, Soiffart, a cocky fuck."

Ragna's eye began to twitch. "What . . . what did you say?"

"He said Soiffart was a cocky fuck, which I think I will not mention to the dwarves. I'm sure that would only insult them."

Ragna gawked at Keeley a long moment before asking, "Wait . . . you . . . you . . . *you* spoke to Morthwyl? You really did speak to him?"

Keeley frowned. "*Now* you believe me. Two seconds ago you didn't believe a word I said and thought I was insane."

"I've read every text about Morthwyl since I joined the monastery, and there are tales of wars between Morthwyl and Soiffart because he called Soiffart a cocky fuck. But you couldn't know that. Can you even read?"

"I can read. I learned."

"And Morthwyl spoke to you? *You?*"

"Why do you say it like that for? I am a—"

"Queen?"

"No. Blacksmith."

Keeley walked a few feet away and that's when she screamed out, "*And he said nice work!*"

Needless to say, Keeley was *not* surprised to hear Cyrus's head being cut off by a growling war monk a few seconds after that.

Donan put the baby in his crib and picked his toddler daughter off the floor.

"You lot!" he barked at his older boys. "Stop doing whatever you're doing that your mother is going to yell at you about and get back to work outside."

"I'm reading," his eldest son complained.

Donan grabbed the book from his son's hands and threw it across the room.

"Read later."

"Fine!"

His son stormed out but he came right back in, his eyes wide.

"What now?" Donan demanded.

The boy just pointed. His eldest wasn't thrown off easily. He couldn't be with so many siblings and a big farm to help manage. He had dreams too. Of being a librarian, which seemed a sad dream to Donan, but if that's what the boy wanted, he wouldn't stand in his way, but still . . . The look on his face.

Donan walked outside and froze. Now his eyes went wide. His wife always said that his eldest looked just like him, so the pair probably looked like matching tapestries at the moment, wide-eyed and pale. Both of them shocked into confused silence.

"What's going on out here?" he heard his wife ask. She pushed past her husband and son and gasped.

"Where did they come from?"

There were so many. All of them children. Undernourished and desperate. Frightened and alone.

His wife did what she always did when faced with the unexplainable. She took care of it.

"Tommy lad, get as many blankets as you can find and then go to Lady Sheela's house and tell her we'll be bringing some guests over. Tell her I won't care about her complaints!"

She turned to their eldest. "Listen. I need you to take Bessie and ride to—"

"*No*," Donan quickly cut in. "We can't send him there."

"We have no choice. We can't handle this on our own. Look at them. It's not about how many. It's about what's been done to them. She's the only one who can handle this."

His wife was right, of course. Not that he'd admit that out loud.

"Go, Son," his wife said, pushing her son toward their stable. "Go straight to Garbhán Isle and demand to see Queen Annwyl herself. Tell her exactly what's happened here."

CHAPTER 28

When word of Cyrus's death spread, all those needy religious sects were gone in a blink. Some simply walked out the gate. Others just vanished. Only those who'd belonged in the area in the first place were still behind the castle gates. It didn't matter, though. They'd been unneeded. Unnecessary. And had only taken up space.

As always, there were more important things to worry about than those who did nothing but pray and sacrifice their lives to air.

The door to the privy chamber slammed open and the king stormed in.

"Did you really think I wouldn't find out?"

Beatrix snorted. "It only took you two years."

He came across the room toward her but the captain of her guard stepped between them and the king reared back in stunned rage.

"Have you lost your mind?"

The captain said nothing but he didn't let Marius near her either.

"You need to understand something, dear husband," Beatrix said, stamping her seal in hot wax. "You are king of this territory and, of course, that will never change. But everything else *is* changing. And I fear you are just not ready to keep up with that."

"What does that mean?"

"It means"—she looked up from her scrolls and papers—"stay out of my way. You and I will get along a lot better if you do."

"There is no way you can seriously think I would—"

"Ivan, please show the king out. I have a meeting in a few minutes and I need to get ready. We can talk more later tonight. About his new duties and what I expect of him."

"Of course, Your Majesty."

Ivan stood and walked past Beatrix. He gestured toward the door. "Your Majesty, this way, please."

Marius looked back and forth between them, but he wasn't quite sure what to do. He never was when he was faced with others' confidence. But he knew Beatrix well enough to know that she never made a move without securing her situation.

He started toward the door, Ivan behind him. When he reached it, he stopped and asked, "Where's my mother?"

"On a long trip. To see some distant family. I was concerned for her safety. What with my sisters making such a bold move in that attack." Beatrix looked directly at her husband. "I knew you wouldn't want her to be in danger. You do love her so."

Marius left, Ivan went back to his seat behind her, and the captain continued to monitor her security.

"Any word on my tunnel?" Beatrix asked Ivan.

"We found some remains of the soldiers that went after your sister. All dead. Nothing yet on the tunnel, though."

Beatrix nodded, continued writing. "And the other tunnels?"

"No evidence your sister found out about those."

"Good. I need a new assistant, Ivan."

"I will find you one, Mistress. Much more loyal."

Beatrix put down her quill and said, "Can I admit something to you, Ivan?"

"Of course you can."

"I usually don't waste my time on anger and resentment. There's so much to do, you understand."

"Of course, my lady. You are very busy."

"Exactly. But I have to say, when it comes to my sister Gemma . . . I hate that fucking bitch."

Gemma rode through the gates and let out a sigh. She was glad to be home. They reached the castle and found Ainsley standing outside, holding their parents' youngest.

"What's going on?"

"He's teething again. I was hoping walking him around would help."

"I'm not talking about the baby. I'm talking about the state of our sister's queendom."

"Oh. Sorry."

Gemma frowned. "What happened to your neck? Why is it all bruised and swollen?"

"I don't want to talk about it."

"Where's Keeley?"

"Daydreaming on the ramparts again."

"Give me the baby."

"Why?"

"I need Keeley to stay calm when I talk to her."

"Things went that badly?"

"Just give me the baby." Once she was holding her youngest sibling, she stepped close to her sister and said in a low voice, "Look, I need you to find someone to take care of Kriegszorn. Someone we can trust."

"But not care if they go missing?"

"That is *not* what I meant. Just find somebody."

"Okay. Anything else, Lady-In-Charge?"

"As a matter of fact, Princess Demands-A-Lot, yes." Gemma motioned to her team. "Make sure they get rooms, food, anything they need. Understand?"

"Does that include whores?"

"Why do you test me?"

"It's my nature and you never say please. But I'll take care of them."

Gemma leaned in again and added, "Be extra gentle with Agathon there. The new one. He's sensitive and easily startled. He's been through hell with Beatrix, so . . ."

"Got it."

Gemma tracked Keeley down to the ramparts just as Ainsley had said. She was gazing out over her queendom but Gemma couldn't tell from her expression whether she was happy or sad. Or simply pensive.

"Keeley?"

Keeley looked away from the world outside her gates and focused on Gemma. The smile that bloomed on her face made Gemma feel surprisingly happy.

"You're back! And alive!"

Keeley smothered Gemma and the baby in a hug.

"I'm so glad you survived!"

"Same to you."

Keeley stepped back and Gemma shoved the baby into her arms.

"Why did you give me the baby?"

"We need to talk."

"Who died? It wasn't you. Gods, was it Quinn? Please tell me it wasn't Quinn."

"It wasn't Quinn. He's gone off to find his siblings."

"They're running with the herd and then bathing in the river." Keeley gasped and whispered, "Did you kill her? Did you kill Beatrix?"

"No! I didn't." She shrugged. "I did try. Very hard. Very, very hard."

"*Gemma.*"

"I said I didn't kill her, so let's move on. But you were right, Keeley. About her. She was doing something very bad."

"What was she building? How bad was it? Was it a giant tower? A giant evil tower?"

"What she was building was only part of the bad."

Keeley studied Gemma. "What are you talking about?"

Gemma moved close to her sister and gently stroked the baby's head. "She was using slave labor to build her tunnel, Gemma. Child slaves that she had taken from the barbarians her armies killed."

Keeley shook her head and moved a few feet from Gemma. She finally sat down, her back against the wall, the baby tucked against her chest.

Gemma sat next to her.

Keeley didn't bother denying what Gemma had told her because she knew Gemma would never lie to her about something like that. Not now, not ever.

So they just sat there like that. Neither speaking. Gemma put her head on Keeley's shoulder and Keeley just stroked the baby's back.

They did speak once, though. But only once.

When Keeley finally said, "We can never tell Daddy."

And Gemma replied, "I know."

"This is going to kill Keeley," Laila said as she moved out of the river to stand beside Caid, her tail flicking back and forth.

"She's strong enough to handle it," Caid said. "But I think we've finally found the one thing she can never forgive her sister for."

"Where was this tunnel going?"

"We're not quite sure," Quinn said, finger-combing his wet hair off his face with his hands. "Although we've all got some solid guesses."

"Guesses? You didn't ask?"

"There was some anger there, when the soldiers began running out of the tunnel. And once those mystical doorways opened . . . the witches and virgins simply went to work. So no, Sister, we did not ask."

"You know what we may have to worry about, though?" Caid suggested. "A test attack on us from Marius. We should be ready for that."

"A test attack?"

"Yeah. He may send some troops here, hoping that we lost so many men in our clash with Cyrus, we'll be too weak to fight back."

"You're right." Laila motioned Cadell and Farlan over with a wave. "We'll get everyone ready for that just in case."

"Even if they do, the war monks are fresh and ready," Quinn reminded them. "They stayed behind to protect the territory and can handle a fresh battle."

"Speaking of which," Laila asked, "did you lose anyone?"

"Nope. We all came back safe and sound. Just some wounds. But nothing missing. Gemma got a bad burn, though. But again, the witches and virgins are working on that. Oh, and before you hear it from anyone else . . . Gemma's madly in love with me."

His onetime battle unit gazed at him for a very long time until Laila rubbed his arm and said, "Awwww, my dear brother, don't you worry. We'll find you someone."

"You don't believe me?"

Laila scrunched up her nose as if she'd smelled something strange but didn't want to admit it. "Gemma? Really?"

"Yes. We've been together. It was glorious."

Caid just laughed. "You and *Brother* Gemma, the war monk? You're such a bad liar."

"I know I am. That's why I don't lie. I'm annoyingly honest. I'm telling you, she adores me."

Now Laila patted his cheek. "We love you so much."

"I don't," Caid muttered.

"And we'll find you a lovely mare who adores you for *you.*"

"Or adores you because she thinks you have power and wealth because of our queen mother," Caid added. "That's just as good . . . right?"

Gemma handed the baby off to her mother and hugged her tight.

"Glad my baby girl is home."

"Me too. Everything been all right?"

"Now that my girls are back safe."

Their mother no longer considered Beatrix part of her girls. Not anymore.

"Excuse me, Brother Gemma?" Gemma faced the pacifist monk she'd met all those weeks ago. "Sorry to bother you."

"No bother, Brother. What can I do for you?"

"Some of the sects—"

"Want to leave now that Cyrus is dead?"

The monk seemed to withdraw a bit, glancing down at the ground. "No. Actually. Does the queen want them to go?"

"Oh, gods, no. No, no, no. I just assumed many would *want* to return to their monasteries and convents now that Cyrus is dead and most of his army destroyed. I wasn't trying to rush them out. I know my sister would never ask them to leave."

"Some of them have nowhere to go. Their sanctuaries have been destroyed and new buildings will take time to rebuild. Others just need time to . . . feel safe again."

"They can stay as long as they need to."

"Are you sure Queen Keeley would be—"

"Oy! Keeley!" Gemma called out.

"What?" her sister called back from across the main hall.

"Mind if the religious sects stick around for a bit? You know, until they feel comfortable?"

"Of course! Long as they want. Let them know, Brother, would you?"

"Absolutely, Your Majesty."

"See?" Gemma said, glancing at the pint of ale someone shoved into her hand. "Told you she wouldn't mind. I think she likes having all of you here. She finds it very comforting. Very soothing. All these different religious representatives being able to live in the same place and not only get along, but thrive. It makes Keeley feel good to be part of that."

Gemma grabbed the monk's arm and yanked him out of the way just as the Abbess hit the ground where he stood, her hand covering her mouth, blood dripping from behind her fingers.

Her mouth open, Gemma gawked at Ragna, who stood behind the Abbess.

"Did you just punch a *nun* in the face?" she asked her fellow war monk.

"She deserved it."

"*She's a nun!*"

A throat cleared and Gemma heard Katla say, "Sorry to interrupt, but we have some fellow brothers here from other orders who wanted to meet with our *current* grand master."

Although they were from different orders, Gemma immediately recognized the other war monks who'd survived the attempted purge by Cyrus. But the way they were glowering at Ragna while Aubin and Ferdinand helped Hurik off the floor, there was no way they'd be willing to have a civil conversation with her now. Or possibly ever.

"Get them settled with our brothers, would you, Katla?"

"I'll take care of it."

"What are you staring at, Brother Damian?" Ragna challenged. "I think we all remember how you defiled that temple virgin!"

Gemma dragged Ragna a few feet away and demanded, "What the fuck is wrong with you?"

"Nothing," Ragna barked back. "Absolutely nothing is wrong with me."

Gemma watched Ragna storm out of the castle. She went to Hurik's side where Aubin was carefully wiping her split lip and the vicar was pressing snow from outside onto her swollen jaw.

"What did you say to her?" Gemma asked.

"Nothing I hadn't said before."

"*Hurik.*"

"I simply asked if her god had spoken to her lately."

"What's so funny?" Gemma asked when Aubin and Balla snorted a laugh and then quickly turned away.

"Oh. You haven't heard the story, have you?"

"What story?"

Hurik waved at Keeley across the room. "Queen Keeley, dear? Could you come here a moment."

Keeley rushed over. "Are you all right? I saw Ragna hit you. Do you want me to hit her back for you? I don't mind hitting her."

"It's all right, dear. I'm fine. But you haven't told your sister the newest story about your hammer."

"Oh, right!"

Keeley reached back and pulled her hammer out of her holster and held it in front of Gemma between her two hands.

"Look at the work the dwarves did on my hammer before I faced down Cyrus—"

"Not that, dear. The other story."

Keeley briefly frowned. "Oh! Yeah." Keeley suddenly grinned. The kind of grin she used to get when she was a little girl. "A god said 'nice work' about my hammer. Not this hammer. But this hammer before the dwarves worked on it. Nice work. A god said that."

"That's impressive."

"Tell her which god, Keeley."

"Oh. Yeah. The one you like. Um . . . I keep forgetting his name."

And Gemma felt all the blood drain from her face.

"A . . . a war god told you this?"

"Yeah. More-something."

"*Morthwyl?* You spoke to Morthwyl?"

"Yes! And he said nice work! About *my* hammer! But, you

know, that could be why Ragna's a little bitchy these days. She did not take it well when she realized she'd missed him."

"Missed him?"

"Yeah. He'd already dragged off Cyrus's soul. I guess I should have been nicer about it, but he'd just complimented my work and I couldn't hide my excitement."

"And why should you?" Hurik asked. "If you're excited, you should show it. Don't you ever be ashamed of that."

"Awww. Thank you, Sister."

"You're more than welcome."

"Oh, look." Keeley pointed. "Centaurs are here. Farlan wanted to see the changes the dwarves made to my new hammer after I told him it was lighter."

Gemma waited until her sister had gone before facing the only ones she knew would understand: her team of sworn enemies.

"There's a part of me," she told them, "that is appalled and disgusted that my heretic sister is the one who now has spoken to *two* gods in the last two years, while I have spoken to none. See?" she said, pointing. "There she is playing with her demon puppy friends. And yet . . . the fact that it bothers Brother Ragna so much has given me more joy than possibly anything else in my entire monastic life. And I honestly do not know how to manage those inconsistent feelings."

"That is a tough one, Gemma." Aubin patted her shoulder. "But we all think you should allow yourself to enjoy this time. You have definitely earned it."

"Besides," Hurik said, "after seeing Ragna punch a defenseless nun in the face, you can now put someone in charge of your order who is fair-minded and willing to learn. Not a psychotic nutbag that everyone hates."

"Is that why you did this?" she asked the nun.

"Mostly. And because it brought great warmth to my heart."

"That's all well and good, Abbess. But who, exactly, am I going to find to be the grand master of our order?"

Hurik and the others stared at Gemma for several long moments until Hurik said, "Sooo, you're not really a quick-witted girl, I see."

* * *

Quinn saw Agathon standing outside the main hall, attempting not to have a panic attack. He was trying his best, but Quinn could see the struggle.

"How are you holding up?" he asked.

"The queen is inside, but I was afraid to say anything to her. I was afraid she'd find out who I was and decide to have me killed. I didn't realize I still wanted to live."

"Living's good."

"Now that I'm away from Beatrix, it seems like a new option."

"Maybe you should hold off on meeting the queen tonight."

"Can I do that?"

"Of course you can."

"Won't she be insulted?"

"She won't care."

"Because she already hates me?"

"She doesn't know you, so she won't care."

"I don't know. I don't know what to do."

Keeley and Caid walked out of the main hall.

"Quinn! I'm so glad you came back alive and well." She kissed him and gave him a hug. "And not a word to my father about what you found inside the tunnel. Understand?" she whispered against his ear.

"Not a word."

"Big feast tonight. Mary made pie for you."

"Of course she did. She loves me."

"Like Gemma does?" Caid mocked.

Keeley blinked. "Gemma loves you?"

"He thinks so."

"Quinn never lies. He's annoyingly honest. If he says my sister loves him, she loves him. Although why anyone would want to be with a monk . . ." She grimaced and kissed Quinn again. "We'll be back in time for dinner."

"Oh, Keeley, this is Agathon. We rescued him from Beatrix."

"From Beatrix? Poor Agathon. Well . . . welcome. Let me know if you need anything."

The pair walked off and Quinn winked at a stunned Agathon. "Told you."

"Her sister is Beatrix?"

"Hard to believe, isn't it?"

"The shoulders alone ..."

Chuckling, Quinn went inside and discovered Gemma sitting on the dining table nursing a pint of ale.

He sat next to her, their feet dangling. "My brother and sister do not believe you're madly in love with me."

"My sister has now spoken to *two* gods, including the one I worship. I haven't even spoken to one."

"That doesn't seem fair."

"I know!" She sipped her ale. "And your brother's a muttering know-it-all."

"He *is* a know-it-all!"

Gemma handed him the ale and he took a sip, passed it back to her.

"There's a push for me to become grand master of my order."

"Really? I thought it would be Ragna."

"It probably was going to be. But then she punched a nun. In front of other war monks."

"Which nun?" Quinn asked.

"Hurik."

"Okay. I was worried it was, like, a nun-nun. Not Hurik, who can actually take it."

"No. It was Hurik. And she actually goaded Ragna."

"Of course she did."

"Because she wants me to be the grand master."

"Then be the grand master."

Gemma shook her head. "I don't know if I'm ready for that. I haven't even been general of an army yet."

"Yes, you have. You are, at this moment, general of a legion in your sister's army."

"I forgot about that."

"Because you were too drunk?"

"Shut up."

Quinn laughed, then added, "If you really hate it, you can always resign later."

"Good point. The reality is the next few months and, possibly, years are going to be tough for everybody. We just need to get through them. I still need to be here for Keeley, though. She can*not* lose against Beatrix."

"No, she cannot. None of us can."

"Oh, and my father can never know—"

"I know."

"Gemma," Katla called out from the doorway. "Brother Damian wants to see someone in charge. Now."

"Why?"

"To talk about Ragna."

"Dammit." She let out a breath and then, without even looking, chastised their travel companions, "All of you stop staring at me right this second! I haven't made up my mind and stop pushing me!"

"Oy, Gemma!"

"Katla, I'm coming."

"Not that. I'm sending you something." Katla handed a scroll to a servant who rushed it across the room to Gemma.

Holding it up, Gemma asked, "What is this?"

But Katla was already gone. She looked down at the seal and Quinn heard her breath catch.

"The scroll from Joshua. The one Katla tried to give me earlier."

With shaking hands, Gemma opened the sealed scroll, read its contents, and immediately began laughing.

She held the scroll against her chest; shining, tear-filled eyes looking at Quinn.

"What does it say?"

Clearing her throat, she asked, "What do *you* think it might say?"

Quinn shrugged. "Uh . . . love you always? You were the daughter I always wanted? You can find my gold fortune in the mountains behind the monastery. Here's the map?"

Gemma turned the scroll toward him but he read what was written out loud. "Take the bloody job, spoiled child."

Wiping tears from her cheeks and laughing, she said, "Fucking Joshua."

"I would have liked him, wouldn't I?" he asked.

"You would have. And he would have adored you."

She tucked the precious scroll into the bag attached to her sword belt and wiped any remaining tears off her face and from her eyes.

With that, she jumped off the table and started to walk away, but she came back and cupped Quinn's face in her hands. They gazed at each other a long moment before she went up on her toes and he leaned down a bit. They kissed and Quinn realized he'd attached himself to a true challenge. Their lives would never be easy. Thankfully, he had never been one for an easy life.

"I won't be long," she said against his mouth.

He watched her disappear out the door and didn't realize he was being watched until he reached for another pint sitting on a tray near his leg. That's when he saw his sister a few feet away with her mouth hanging open.

Quinn smirked, sipped his ale, and said, "Told you."

EPILOGUE

Keeley walked toward the training ring with Gemma and Ainsley, and already Ainsley was complaining.

"Why are we up this early?" she asked again. "The suns aren't even up yet."

"You wanted to be trained to fight."

"Training can't happen at a decent hour?"

"If she's going to act like this . . ." Gemma began but her voice trailed off and Keeley immediately saw why. It was the woman standing in the middle of the empty training ring.

She was turning in a slow circle, appearing quite confused.

"Excuse me?" Keeley called out as she and her sisters moved to the ring. "Are you all right? Do you need some help?"

The woman slowly faced her and Gemma defensively stepped in front of Keeley while Keeley pushed Ainsley behind her. Their reactions weren't surprising considering the two swords strapped to the woman's back and all the scars on her bare arms, neck, and face.

"What do you want?" Gemma asked the woman.

"I'm looking for the queen of these lands," she said. "The one who has slaves. The one who has child . . . *slaves*."

Keeley opened her mouth to tell the woman she was *not* that queen when something giant landed hard behind her, shaking not just the ground beneath her feet but the ground for miles. Then it happened again. And again. And again. And again. The buildings around them shook each time. The horses in the stables panicked, kicking at their stalls, some breaking loose and running.

Soldiers ran out of their barracks and froze. Many pissed themselves. Others immediately ran back inside, screaming.

Dragons. In different colors. Different sizes. But all in armor and armed. With wings and horns and fangs. Ready for war.

The dragons continued landing until they completely encircled the four women.

"Invaders!" one of her men called from the watch towers. "Invaders!"

All Keeley could think was, "Little late," until she realized he wasn't talking about the dragons.

"Marius's men! Invade—*gods in heaven!*" Seeing the dragons for the first time, the alarm-raiser panicked and ran from the dragon poking its snout into the tower. Unfortunately, there was nowhere really to run except out of the tower and to his death. So that was tragic.

The side gates were battered open and Marius's riders charged in.

The woman said to no one in particular, "Deal with them."

And a silver dragon lowered its head, turned its long neck toward the invaders, and unleashed a line of flame that engulfed Marius's small army, wiping them out in seconds.

When the dragon was done, settling back into its original position, Keeley noticed she heard nothing but silence. No birds. No screaming. Not even the wind. Just silence.

The woman walked closer and Keeley realized for the first time that she was gazing into the eyes of a madwoman.

Gemma put her hand on her sheathed sword. If the woman saw her, she didn't show it. She just abruptly stopped.

"I want the bitch queen who has child slaves," the woman practically whispered, "and I want her *NOWWWWW!*" which she ended on a hysterical bellow.

Even though Keeley wasn't the "bitch queen" with child slaves, she really didn't know how to respond to that kind of insanity. But she didn't have to. Because the dragons did.

"Uh-oh," a gold one said. "Annwyl's gone 'round the bend. Again."

"I thought we were going to play nice with these"—the silver one glanced around, appearing vaguely disgusted—"people."

"Annwyl," a black dragon calmly stated, "you promised. You promised you were going to be calm and rational. Does this seem calm and rational to you? Does it?"

The madwoman spun around and faced the black dragon. He towered over her the way Keeley's castle towered over her. And yet, she stomped across the training ring to that giant black dragon and screamed, "*I am sick of being calm and rational! They're using children as slaves! What are we waiting for? Kill all of them!*"

"Anyone else enjoy," one dragon muttered to another behind Keeley, "how Annwyl acts like she's *ever* been calm and rational?" The two dragons began to chuckle.

"I know. Like this is all out of the ordinary somehow."

That comment brought out snorts and more stifled laughter from the surrounding dragons.

Keeley leaned toward Gemma and whispered against her ear the only thing she could think to tell her sister in this very dire moment, "By Soiffart's mighty hammer, we are *so* fucked."

Did you know that G.A. Aiken also writes as Shelly Laurenston?
Don't miss her Honey Badger Chronicles, available now!

HOT AND BADGERED

It's not every day that a beautiful naked woman falls out of the sky
and lands face-first on grizzly shifter Berg Dunn's hotel balcony.
Definitely they don't usually hop up and demand his best gun.
Berg gives the lady a grizzly-sized T-shirt and his cell phone, too,
just on style points. And then she's gone, taking his XXXL heart
with her. By the time he figures out she's a honey badger shifter,
it's too late.

Honey badgers are survivors. Brutal, vicious, ill-tempered
survivors. Or maybe Charlie Taylor-MacKilligan is just pissed that
her useless father is trying to get them all killed again, and won't
even tell her how. Protecting her little sisters has always been her
job, and she's not about to let some pesky giant grizzly protection
specialist with a network of every shifter in Manhattan get in her
way. Wait. He's trying to help? Why would he want to do that?
He's cute enough that she just might let him tag along—that is, if
he can keep up . . .

What had she been thinking? Using the "Ride of the Valkyries" as a ringtone? Because that shit waking a person up at six in the morning was just cruel. Really cruel.

And, as always, she'd done it to herself. Forgoing her anxiety meds so she could get drunk with a couple of cute Italian guys that she dumped as soon as the first one's head hit the table.

Charlie Taylor-MacKilligan slapped her hand against the bedside table next to the bed, blindly searching for her damn phone. When she touched it, she was relieved. She had no plan to actually get out of bed anytime soon. Not as hungover as she currently was. But she really wanted that damn ringtone to stop.

Somehow, without even lifting her head from the pillow she had her face buried in, or opening her eyes, Charlie managed to touch the right thing on her phone screen so that she actually answered it.

"What?" she growled.

"Get out," was the reply. "Get out now."

Hangover forgotten, Charlie was halfway across the room when they kicked the door open. She turned and ran toward the sliding glass doors she'd left open the night before. She'd just made it to the balcony outside when something hot rammed into her shoulder, tearing past flesh and muscle and burrowing into bone. The power of it sent her flipping headfirst over the railing.

"What do you think?" the jackal shifter asked.

Sitting in a club chair in his Milan, Italy, hotel suite, Berg Dunn gazed at the man holding up a black jacket.

"What do I think about what?" Berg asked.

"The jacket. For my show tonight."

Berg shrugged. "I don't know."

"You must have an opinion."

"I don't. I happily have no opinion on what a grown man who is not me should wear."

The jackal sighed. "You're useless."

"I have one job. Keeping your crazed fans from tracking you down and stripping the flesh from your bones. That's it. That's all I'm supposed to do. I, at no time, said that I would ever help you with your fashion sense."

Rolling his eyes, the jackal laid the jacket on the bed and then stared at it. Like he expected it to tell him something. To actually speak to him.

Berg wanted to complain about this ridiculous job, but how could he when it was the best one he'd had in years? Following a very rich, very polite jackal around so that he could play piano for screaming fans in foreign countries was the coolest gig ever.

First class everything. Jets. Food. Women. Not that Berg took advantage of the women thing too often. He knew most were just trying to use him to get to Cooper Jean-Louis Parker. Coop was the one out there every night, banging away at those Steinway pianos, doing things with his fingers that even Berg found fascinating, and wooing all those lovely females with his handsome jackal looks.

Berg was just the guy to get through so they could get to the musical genius. And, unlike some of his friends, being used by beautiful women wasn't one of his favorite things.

It was a tolerable thing, but not his favorite.

"I can't decide," the jackal finally admitted.

"I know how hard it is to pick between one black jacket and *another* black jacket. Which will your black turtleneck go with?"

"It's not just *another* black jacket, peasant. It's the difference between pure black and charcoal black."

"We have a train to catch," Berg reminded Coop. "So could you speed this—"

Both shifters jumped, their gazes locked on the balcony outside the room, visible through doors open to let the fresh morning air in.

Another crazed female fan trying to make her way into Coop's room? Some of these women, all of them full-humans, were willing to try any type of craziness for just a *chance* at ending up in the "maestro's" bed.

With a sigh, Berg pushed himself out of the chair and headed across the large room toward the sliding glass doors. It looked like he'd have to break another poor woman's heart.

But he stopped when he saw her. A brown-skinned woman, completely naked. Which, in and of itself, was not unusual. The women who tried to sneak into Coop's room—no matter the country they might be in—were often naked.

What stopped Berg in his tracks was that *this* woman had blood coming from her shoulder. The blood from a gun wound.

Berg motioned Coop back. "Get in the bathroom," he ordered.

"Oh, come on. I want to see what's—"

"I don't care what you want. Get in the—"

The men stopped arguing when they saw him. A man in black military tactical wear, armed with a rifle, handgun, and several blades. He zipped down a line and landed on the railing of their balcony.

Berg placed his hand on the gun holstered at his side and stepped in front of Coop.

"Get in the bathroom, Coop," he ordered, his voice low.

"We have to help her."

"Do what I tell you and I will."

The man in black dropped onto the balcony and grabbed the unconscious woman by her arm, rolling her limp body over.

"Now, Coop. Go."

Berg moved forward with his weapon drawn from its holster. The man pulled his sidearm and pressed the barrel against the woman's head.

Berg aimed his .45 and barked, "Hey!"

The man looked up, bringing his gun with him. Gazes locked, fingers resting on triggers. Each man sizing the other up. And that was when the woman moved. Fast. So fast, Berg knew she wasn't completely human, which immediately changed everything.

The woman grabbed her attacker's gun hand by the wrist and held it to the side so he couldn't finish the job on her. She used her free hand to pummel the man's face repeatedly.

Blood poured down his lips from his shattered nose; his eyes now dazed.

Still holding the man's wrist, she got to her feet.

She was tall. Maybe five-ten or five-eleven. With broad, powerful shoulders and arms and especially legs. Like a much-too-tall gymnast.

She gripped her attacker by the throat with one hand and, without much effort, lifted him up and over the balcony railing. She released him then and unleashed the biggest claws Berg had ever seen from her right hand.

Turning away from the attacker, she swiped at the zip line that held him aloft, and Berg cringed a little at the man's desperate screams as he fell to the ground below.

That's when she saw Berg. Her claws—coming from surprisingly small hands—were still unleashed. Her gaze narrowed on him and her shoulders hunched just a bit. She was readying herself for an attack. To kill the man who could out her as a shifter, he guessed. Not having had time to process that he was one, too. Plus, he had a gun, which wouldn't help his cause any.

"It's okay," Berg said quickly, re-holstering his weapon. "It's okay. I'm not going to hurt you."

"Yeah," Coop said from behind him. "We just want to help."

Berg let out a frustrated breath. "I thought I told you to get into the bathroom."

"I wanted to see what's going on."

Coop moved to Berg's side. "We're shifters, too," he said, using that goddamn charming smile. Like this was the time for any of that!

But this woman rolled her eyes in silent exasperation and came fully into the room. She walked right by Berg and Coop and to the bedroom door.

"Wait," Berg called out. When she turned to face him, one brow raised in question, he reminded her, "You're naked."

He went to his already packed travel bag and pulled out a black T-shirt.

"Here," he said, handing it to her.

She pulled the shirt on and he saw that he'd given her one of his favorite band shirts from a Fishbone concert he'd seen years ago with his parents and siblings.

"Your shoulder," Berg prompted, deciding not to obsess over the shirt. Especially when she looked so cute in it.

She shook her head at his prompt and again started toward the door. But a crash from the suite living room had Berg grabbing the woman's arm with one hand and shoving Coop across the bedroom and into the bathroom with the other.

Berg faced the intruder, pulling the woman in behind his body.

Two gunshots hit Berg in the lower chest—the man had pulled the trigger without actually seeing all of Berg, but expecting a more normal-sized human.

Which meant a few things to Berg. That he was dealing with a full-human. An expertly trained full-human. An ex-soldier probably.

An ex-soldier with a kill order.

Because if he'd been trying to kidnap the woman, he would have made damn sure he knew who or what was on the other end before he pulled that trigger. But he didn't know. He didn't check because he didn't care. Everyone in the room had to die.

And knowing that—*understanding* that—did nothing but piss Berg off.

Who just ran around trying to kill a naked, unarmed woman? his analytical side wanted to know.

The grizzly part of him, though, didn't care about any of that. All it knew was that it had been shot. And shooting a grizzly but not killing it immediately . . . always an exceptionally bad move.

The snarl snaked out of Berg's throat and the muscles between his shoulders grew into a healthy grizzly hump. He barely managed to keep from shifting completely, but his grizzly bear rage exploded and his roar rattled the windows. The bathroom door behind him slammed shut, the jackal having the sense to *now* go into hiding.

The intruder quickly backed up, knowing something wasn't right, but not fully understanding, which was why he didn't run.

He should have run.

With a step, Berg was right in front of him, grabbing the gun from his hand and spinning the man around so that he had him by the throat. He did this because two more men in tactical gear were coming into the suite through the front door they'd taken down moments before.

Using the man's weapon, Berg shot each man twice in the chest. They both had on body armor so he wasn't worried he'd killed them.

With both attackers down, Berg refocused on the man he held captive. He spun him around, because he wanted to ask him a few questions about what the hell was going on. He was calmer now. He could be rational.

But when the man again faced him, Berg felt a little twinge in his side. He slowly looked down . . . and found a combat blade sticking out.

First he'd been shot. Now stabbed.

His grizzly rage soared once again and, as the intruder— quickly recognizing his error—attempted to fight his way out of Berg's grasp, desperately begging for his life, Berg grabbed each side of his attacker's face and squeezed with both hands . . . until the man's head popped like a zit.

It was the blood and bone hitting him in the face that snapped Berg back into the moment, and he gazed down at his brain- covered hands.

"Oh, shit," he muttered. "Shit, shit, shit."

The other intruders, ignoring the pain from the shots, scrambled up and out of the suite. As far away from Berg as they could get.

Someone touched his arm and he half-turned to see the woman. She raised her hands and rewarded him with a soft smile.

That's when he calmed down. "Shit," he said again, holding out his hands to her.

She stepped close, held his wrists, studied the blade still stick- ing out of his side. She then examined the wounds in his chest. Un- like the intruders, he hadn't been wearing body armor. The bullets had hit him, had entered his body, but he was grizzly. Even as a human, you had to bring bigger weapons if you wanted to take down one of his kind with one or two shots.

Berg knew, just watching her, that she was going to help him.

She was going to try. But she was in more danger than he was, and she needed to get out of here.

"Go," he told her and she frowned. "Seriously. Go."

He pulled away from her, went to his travel bag, paused to wipe the blood off his hands on a nearby towel, and took out a .45 Ruger, handing it to her. "Take this."

Her eyes narrowed again as she stared up at him.

"I get the feeling you need it more than me," he pushed. "Just go."

She took the weapon, dropped the magazine, cleared the gun with one hand before shoving the loaded mag back in and putting a round in the chamber.

Yeah. The woman knew how to handle his .45. Maybe better than he did.

Connect with U s

Visit us online at
KensingtonBooks.com
to read more from your favorite authors, see books
by series, view reading group guides, and more.

for sneak peeks, chances to win books and prize packs,
and to share your thoughts with other readers.

facebook.com/kensingtonpublishing
twitter.com/kensingtonbooks

Tell us what you think!

To share your thoughts, submit a review,
or sign up for our eNewsletters, please visit:
KensingtonBooks.com/TellUs.